A NOT~~O~~

ROUGH

rough

AND

READY

ready

Harper,

Are You Ready?

Hau

HAYLEY FAIMAN

Rough & Ready
Copyright © 2017 by Hayley Faiman

Editor - Rosalyn Martin, The Green Pen
Cover: Cassy Roop, Pink Ink Designs
Formatting: Champagne Formats

ISBN-13: 978-1542497190
ISBN-10: 1542497191

Miracles come in moments. Be ready and willing.
—Wayne Dyer

prologue

Cleo

I hear his boots hit the foyer, and I know he's home. My heart starts beating rapidly in my chest, my belly begins to flutter, and my lips part into a huge smile. I jump up off of our bed, a bed we shared for only a week before he was shipped off to foreign lands to fight for my freedom. I don't bother looking in the mirror to check my appearance. I know that only one person has a key to this house—and it's *him*.

I am so very proud to be married to him. He's good, and clean, and *perfect*. We're young, of course; I'm only eighteen and he's twenty, but what we have is beautiful. I knew, the moment my eyes met his stormy blue ones, that there would be no other man for me, *ever*.

I bound down the stairs and almost falter on the last two steps when I see him standing there in the foyer.

1

My eyes sweep his body, looking for any type of injuries. We've endured a long eight months apart since he's been gone. He's thinner, so much thinner, his face perfectly chiseled—almost gaunt. He's standing there in his uniform, looking commanding—beautiful, even. Tall and thin, but handsome and all mine. It seems like he's been gone from Texas and from my sight, for years.

When my eyes met his, I gasp.

They aren't the warm, boyish blue ones that I had fallen in love with; they are cold and harsh. *Dead.*

I blink.

I run to him anyway, shaking off the shock at seeing the obvious coldness to his eyes, and jump into his arms. I feel his face in my neck, hear his nose inhale my scent, and I sigh at the beautifulness of the whole thing.

His arms wrap around my body as my legs lift up and around his waist, my own arms around his neck. I pepper his face with kisses. I didn't expect him home yet. He wasn't due back until tomorrow. I even have an outfit all picked out. Tonight, I was prepping. I'm only wearing one of his workout shirts that says *AIR FORCE* across the front and a pair of panties.

"Baby, you're home," I breathe, smiling wide.

He stares at me blankly.

"I am," he agrees, his voice ragged.

Instantly, I decide he is just emotional and trying to hide it. Probably jet lagged, too.

"I didn't expect you," I state. His eyes immediately sharpen and turn ice cold.

"Who in the fuck were you expecting?" he barks harshly as he drops me. Luckily, my knees don't buckle, and I don't fall on my ass.

"Nobody. I was going to pick you up tomorrow morning. How did you get home?" I ask quietly.

"Got a ride," he shrugs, leaving me alone in the foyer as he walks toward the kitchen.

I stand there for a moment, completely shocked by his attitude, by his quick anger, and then I follow behind him. He's never been angry with me before. I've seen him get pissed with other people, with his friends, but never, ever with me.

"Fuck, I'm starved," he announces as he opens the fridge and starts rifling through it.

It's as if he hasn't been gone for eight long months; like he's just had a long day at work, and now he is home for the evening. I don't know what to say or what to do. He's acting so strangely.

Granted, I don't know him that well. We only dated for a few months before we were married, and then he was gone. But I don't think this is normal. I didn't expect *this* at all.

"You didn't get me any fuckin' beer?" he barks, making me jump again.

I just stand in the kitchen, unable to speak, move, or even *breathe*.

"I-I-I," I don't get anything else out because I start to cry.

I turn to run back to the bedroom, tears streaming down my face. I can't buy him beer. He knows that. *He* can't even buy beer. I didn't know he expected me to have it. I didn't know what he expected of me. I feel so stupid and scared, and so very foolish.

Every single phone call and e-mail he sent had been sweet, *kind* even—never once had he talked to me this way. I don't know what to do, and I have a sinking feeling that becoming his wife was a grave mistake.

I feel an iron band clamp around my bicep, and it stops my body from fleeing. Then I am hauled backward into a hard chest. I feel his nose at my ear before he whispers, his breath warm on my skin, his voice soft but ragged, and it sends shivers up and down my spine.

"Christ, Cleo, I'm sorry. I'm bein' an ass, and I ain't even been home ten minutes. Fuck the beer. Let's go upstairs. Eight months without your sweet pussy was long enough."

I press my thighs and my lips together as I nod. Eight months has been a *long* time, especially for a girl who was a virgin on her wedding night; a girl who only had sex with her husband for *one week* before he was deployed.

"You still my shy girl?" he asks.

One of his hands slips down the front of my belly and under the hem of his shirt before diving into my panties. I whimper at the feel of his large, warm hand on my mound. His finger slides through the folds of my most intimate place. I wrap my hand around his tanned, muscular forearm, trying to brace myself.

"Yeah, that's right. *Fuck,* still my shy, sweet, innocent wife, aren't you?" his voice is soft, but there's an edge I don't quite understand.

Two seconds later, it doesn't matter, because one of his fingers slides deep inside of me. I gasp and arch my back.

It feels good.

He feels good.

I missed this.

Every piece of it.

Paxton quickly pushes my panties down my thighs and pulls my shirt off, spinning me around to face him. His eyes look up and down my body, but it's as if he's looking straight through me. I feel like I could be anybody. Who I am doesn't matter because he isn't *seeing* me.

His lips crash down on mine, and his warm, wet tongue slips deep inside me. I taste him, and he tastes like sunshine. He is warm and masculine, and I melt into his body. I hear one of his hands rustling his clothing, and then the sound of his pants dropping onto the tile flooring fills the air.

My body is whirled around again, and his hand is on my back, pushing my chest and cheek against the cold kitchen countertop. Before I can say a word, I feel his boot kick at my ankle, spreading my feet farther apart. One of his big hands is at my waist as he forcefully pushes himself inside of me.

It burns.

I'm not ready.

My body isn't ready.

I haven't been touched in eight months, except when the need was too much and I touched myself, which I wasn't even very good at. It usually just left me even more frustrated.

"Pax, that hurts," I cry out in pain.

He isn't listening to me. He is pulling out and thrusting deep, over and over again. I can't help the tears that spring from my eyes as he fists his hand in my hair and pushes into my body. Then he stills, groans, and I feel him fill me with his release.

We haven't talked about birth control *at all*. He used condoms before he left. I had no reason to be on anything while he was gone, and I'm still not. He could have just gotten me pregnant, and I would have this memory, *forever*, as the way I conceived a child.

"That was good, babe. Thanks."

He slaps my ass and pulls out of me.

I don't move. I can't.

I see my shirt hit the counter next to my head. Finally, I stand up, against the protest of the screaming pained area between my legs, and I pull the shirt over my head. I look at the face of my handsome husband, and my whole body shudders. He is blank. Blank face, blank eyes—freaking blank.

What happened to him over there?

What did this to him?

Eight months ago, he treated me like glass, like something so precious he couldn't believe that he had me all to himself. Now, I don't know what he's treating me like, but I don't like it—not at all. I also don't understand any of it. I don't understand the sudden change, and it scares me.

"I'm gonna go out drinking with the guys. I'll get some food while I'm out. Don't wait up," he says, his face impassive.

"Paxton," I whisper, feeling his release slide down my thigh as my tears slide down my cheeks. I'm lost in a sea of confusion and pain, both emotional and physical, as I search his cold eyes.

"Don't nag me, all right? You got fucked. What else do you want?"

I shake my head. I didn't want what he just gave me—not today, and not ever.

"I never asked for that, Pax. You hurt me," I whisper.

Something flickers through his eyes before they become a blank mask again.

"Wasn't good for you? You don't like it? Maybe you should fucking leave then," he growls as he walks away, grabbing his bag before he leaves, slamming the front door behind him.

I don't know what just happened. I feel totally clueless,

6

shocked, hurt, and upset.

I make my way to the bathroom and clean up, noticing the blood mixed with semen and crying a little bit more. I shower and slide into bed, forgetting the pedicure I had been giving myself; forgetting everything happy and good that I had planned for Paxton tomorrow.

I need a friend, but I can't call anyone. There are people in the support group I could reach out to, but they are all spouses of Paxton's coworkers. I can't tell them what he just did to me. Besides, I'm embarrassed.

I have nobody. Nobody but him.

I cry myself to sleep after taking a handful of ibuprofen, and hope, for the first time since I met him, that he won't come home.

Several hours later, I'm awakened by a noise.

I look at my clock. It's four in the morning. There's a loud crash, and I bite my bottom lip before I hear his curse. My husband is home, apparently. I don't know where he's been all night, but after his ill treatment of me earlier, I don't really care.

I sit up and make my way downstairs to see him trying to walk up the staircase. He keeps stumbling backward. For every step he takes up, he stumbles down two more.

He is trashed.

I choke back the stupid tears that begin to form. I walk right up to him and tip my head back, wrap my arm around his waist, and proceed to help my drunk, asshole husband up the stairs. I should leave him down here to his own devices, but I'm afraid he'll fall and really hurt himself.

"Cleo, you're so fuckin' hot," he groans as I push his heavy ass through the bedroom door. I snort at his words.

"How did I get so goddamned lucky? Huh, baby?" I roll my eyes.

He sure didn't seem like he felt lucky to have me earlier. I strip him down to his boxer briefs and push him into bed. Then I pull the comforter over him and slide in next to him, getting on my side—giving him my back.

"Cleo, baby," he whispers.

I feel his fingers trailing up and down my arm. It's sweet, and I don't like how just the simple act warms my heart. I want to hate him.

"You're drunk. Go to sleep, Paxton," I sigh. He groans and wraps his big hand around my waist, pulling my back toward his front.

"I missed you, baby," he whispers as he nuzzles the back of my neck.

It is then that I allow myself to cry again. *This* is the Paxton that I know. He was always soft spoken toward me, sweet, loving, and caring. That man that showed up and hurt me? I don't know him, and I don't like him, not one bit.

He doesn't push for more. In fact, his breathing evens out and I know when he is asleep before his arm on my waist becomes so heavy it pushes me a bit further into the mattress.

The next morning, male snoring wakes me up too freaking early. I have a hot arm wrapped around my waist still, and a warm body practically on top of me. I nudge Paxton a few times before he groans and flops onto his back.

"Fuck, what time is it?" he asks as I grab my cell phone and look at the time.

"Ten," I grumble.

It isn't as early as I had anticipated, but yesterday had been long and horrible, so I slept later than I normally would.

We lie in silence, no longer touching and not even looking at each other. The ceiling is now suddenly fascinating to me.

"Cleo," he whispers. I feel his hand slide up the inside of my leg, and my entire body freezes.

When his fingers brush over my sensitive center, I whimper and flinch with pain. His hand stops, and I feel his eyes on me, so I turn to look at him. His silver blue eyes are no longer cold but hold a bit of the warmth I remember.

"I hurt you that badly?" he whispers in horror.

I nod, unable to speak.

"Fuck, I-I'm sorry," he murmurs.

It is the most beautiful thing he has said to me since walking through that front door—which in itself is pathetic as hell.

"Why?" It is all I can choke out, but luckily he understands me. I know this because he gets this far away look on his face.

"One of the guy's wives left him while we were there. Had an affair. One guy's fiancée left him because she couldn't handle the distance. Four other guys' long term girlfriends left them for the same reasons. We don't really know each other, and *fuck*, I would die if you left me for some other guy," he admits.

"So you wanted to push me away?" I guess.

We stay silent for a few more moments, and I reflect on what he's just told me.

"I *should* leave you," I mutter.

It's true. I should leave him. The way he treated me last night, and then the way he came home drunk—I should be gone in the wind.

Yet, there is something holding me back from that; maybe

9

it's the fact that we aren't just dating, we are married; maybe it's because I'm an idiot; maybe it's because I have nobody else in the world but him.

"I understand," he whispers, sounding pained.

"But I don't think I can," I admit.

Paxton lets out a heavy breath before I feel him roll on top of me. His blue eyes meet mine and hide nothing. He looks so scared, nervous, regretful, sad, and relieved all at the same time.

"I'll make it up to you, baby. Fuck, I'm a fuckin' bastard," he mutters.

I snort. No shit, he's a bastard. That's an understatement. Paxton's lips lightly brush over mine, soft and gentle, before they slide down to my neck and collarbone.

"I want to apologize to my girl," he murmurs against my skin.

I'll let him apologize any way he wants to, when his lips are softly caressing me this way.

"I'm going to put my mouth and tongue on you, baby. Can you handle that, or will it hurt too much?" he asks as his lips kissed down the front of my shirt, making his way toward my breast.

His lips pull my nipple in his mouth through the material, and I can't hold back my groan. I arch my back in response, loving the way he feels against me.

"I think I can handle it," I whisper as his hands pull my panties down my legs.

I feel his fingers caress my thighs as he lightly spreads them open and settles his body between them. Slowly, his lips travel down my stomach, and I feel his nose nuzzle my belly button before he kisses my mound and then my clit.

"Paxton," I gasp, my fingernails raking through his short, cropped, dark hair.

He slowly slides his tongue over my core and apologizes with his mouth until I come all over him. My first real orgasm since he left me, eight months ago. It is bliss. But it is also bittersweet all at the same time.

I haven't forgiven him, and I will never forget the way he used my body. I'm ready to move on, though. I know that it has something to do with what he's seen or done while he was gone, and not a true representation of the man he is.

Hurdles happened in life, and this is just that. Gram taught me that. She taught me that people do stupid things, but they can feel regret and sorrow for them, so we must always look past the stupid things and into the heart of the person.

I fall asleep, thinking this is a new beginning. I can move on from yesterday, if this is the man I have for the future.

When I wake up later that afternoon, he's gone.

Every trace of him is just—*gone*.

Even his cell phone number is disconnected.

The only thing he left was a note.

I will only continue to hurt you baby. I can't do that.

I love you too much.

Be Happy.

Paxton

That selfish bastard.

I cry until I can't cry anymore. I stay holed up in our townhouse for four weeks, until rent is due and I can't pay it.

He never once tries to contact me in those four weeks.

So I have no other choice. I leave.

chapter one

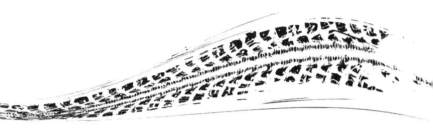

ELEVEN YEARS LATER

Torch

I look out at the grounds of my new clubhouse in Cali. It's dark, but not as dark as it is in Idaho. It's a different environment altogether here. There's a party happening inside, but I'm not interested in the bullshit tonight. Pussy and booze aren't on the forefront of my mind. I have one thing and one thing only on my mind—*Cleo*.

In fact, Cleo dominates my thoughts on a regular basis. For the past eleven years, she's been in my mind. She's my biggest regret in life.

Shit's going down with *The Cartel*, and her safety has been at the top of my mind, lately. Fury, my old Prez in Idaho, thinks I need closure with her, or some shit. Honestly, I just need to know that she's safe, and that my foul shit doesn't leak onto her—*again.*

As soon as this war bullshit is handled, I'll be on my way, and she can be on hers. I'm never going to live peacefully, not with the demons that swirl around inside of me, but she can. I aim to keep her not only breathing, but doing so safely.

"You got your shit locked down tight, brother," Texas says as he walks up behind me.

I nod, unsure of what he wants me to say. I don't talk about myself to anyone—ever. If he's coming to me for information on my personal life, he'll be disappointed as hell. Even if I was a man who shared his burdens, it wouldn't be to a stranger; it would be to one of my closest brothers, Fury or Sniper, not to this guy.

"I'm ex-military. Medic, actually. Served two tours in Afgan and two in Iraq. You need to unload any of that shit you got inside of you, I'm here. You wanna unload it to a shrink, I got a good one. You wanna unload a few rounds into some targets, love doin' that shit, so I'm down," he murmurs as he sits down next to me, taking a cigarette from his pocket and lighting it.

"That obvious I served?" I chuckle, trying to brush off his offers.

"Your haircut don't lie. It's not regulation, but it still don't touch your collar, if you were wearin' one. Plus, I see those demons that haunt your eyes every day I look in the fuckin' mirror," he grunts.

"Not into sharing my feelings, but thanks," I say.

"Not asking you to talk about your feelings. Those demons aren't simply feelings, Torch. They're living, breathing things. If you're not careful, they will grow inside of you and kill the remainder of the man you once were."

"That man died when I was twenty years old. The demons can't kill him. He's been gone over a fuckin' decade," I growl as I stand up.

"Brother, he ain't gone. Not completely. You don't wrestle with those demons, fight them back, then yeah, he'll be fuckin' toast—but he's still around. Buried deep, but he's there."

"How you figure?" I snort.

"Cause you got a whole club in Idaho that loves you, thinks of you as blood and not just because you wear that cut. You got their women frettin' and textin' and worried about you—buggin' the shit out of MadDog. But then again, you got MadDog, too, don't you?" He doesn't say anything else.

Instead, he stands before he snubs out his smoke, turns, and walks away. I don't watch, listening as the door closes behind him. I continue to look out at the darkness ahead of me. It's fuckin' pitch-black, and I inhale the cool air around me.

I never thought I'd be livin' in California, not ever, but Cleo's here. It's her home state, and I knew I'd find her here. It wasn't hard. Found her using fucking *Facebook*. I shake my head, thinking about her profile and her profile picture. It's a picture of the side of her face. She's smiling, that much I can see, and it's windy, her mass of red hair flying around.

Her account is private, smart girl, and I'm half tempted to get someone to hack into her shit so that I can look at her pictures, mainly so I can see if there is a man in her life. I shouldn't give a shit if she's got a man. I've nailed so much pussy since leaving her that I would be ashamed if she knew the exact number. Still, she's technically my wife, and I can't help my curiosity.

I pull up her address, using my phone. It's in Sacramento,

three hours away from me. I can't do a drive by tonight, but I need to see her. Being in the same state as Cleo, being just a couple hours away from her is making me antsy. The last time I was this close to her was when I was stationed in Texas and we were living together.

When I left her I went back to my base and requested barrack housing, explaining that we'd separated. It killed me to know she was so close, yet I wasn't in a good place to be near her. I didn't breathe easy until she left and moved back to her home state.

I have to know what I'm walking into in offering my protection—no, *demanding* it. She'll accept, too, my shy girl. I'm sure she's exactly the girl she was when I married her all those years ago. I can't see that part of her changing. There's no way she's changed; not like I have. She lived a hard life before I even met her, and it didn't make her coldhearted or uncaring. In fact, she was always the exact opposite.

"Texas said that you needed company?" a sweet voice calls out from behind me.

I tip my head to the side, craning my neck around slightly to look at who is walking up to me. It's a pretty young thing, dark hair and eyes. She's a whore, wearing nothing but some scraps of material to cover her tits and pussy. She's probably freezing her ass off out here, but she won't complain, not to me—not to a brother of the Notorious Devils.

"Not tonight, honey," I murmur.

"Okay," she nods and turns to walk away.

I watch her pert ass cheeks as she goes, thinking that I probably should have taken her up on her offer. However, I'm not feeling stable right now; the last time I fucked someone when I felt this way, I hurt her a fuck've a lot.

Swore I wouldn't do that shit again—*ever*.

Cleo

I wake with a start. Closing my eyes, I listen for a noise. There isn't anything, until I hear my neighbor's door slam, and then they start screaming at each other. I turn my head to the side and groan. It's seven in the morning, which means my neighbors just got off of working the night shift. They're drunk and arguing, which will lead to them being drunk and fucking. It's a cycle I'm used to, and I don't want to be around.

Hurrying to the shower, I bathe and then dress in record time. I don't have to be to work today, but I do have a brunch date, and I better get a move on it or I'm going to be late. I hurry to my crappy, maroon sedan. Well, it's not so much maroon anymore as it is a lovely, oxidized, *former* maroon color.

I drive through the city, annoyed at the traffic and wishing I would have never moved back here. I should have stayed in Texas, but there were way too many memories there. Texas holds both good and bad memories. In the end, even the good ones felt tainted, so I left. I came back to the only other place that I've called home, Sacramento.

I park the car, shaking off the cloud of memories from the past, sliding out of the driver's side seat. I then hurry into the little café, where I know my date is waiting for me.

"I'm sorry," I say in a rush as I walk over to him and press my lips to his cheek.

"You're late," he scolds with disapproval before his face completely changes and he gives me a wide smile. "But I could give a shit. You're here, I'm here, and we have antipasto coming," Lisandro announces with a flourish of his hand.

I hide my smile, knowing that Lisandro likes to use fancy words, antipasto being one of them, which is just what he calls appetizers.

"Lis, seriously it's so good to see you," I whisper, dashing the tear from my eye.

"You need to come and work for me. That attorney you work for is an asshat. Come sell *diamonds*," he says, purring the word diamonds as he usually does.

Lisandro is my best friend in the whole world. I've known him since the day I moved back to Sacramento. We met at this exact café. I was a pathetic mess, a crying pathetic mess, and he walked right over to me, sat his flamboyant ass down in the seat across from mine, and we've been friends ever since.

Three years ago, he fell in love with Theo. When he did, his lover moved him out to Redding, California. Theo is a pharmacist. He took a position in Redding, grabbed onto Lisandro, and they've never looked back, except an occasional visit to me and Lisandro's grandmother. They live two hours away. Redding isn't the smallest town in the state, but it's not the biggest, either. Lisandro became bored as hell, quickly, so he opened a jewelry store.

"He's an asshat, but working there pays the bills. Honestly, it's fine," I sigh.

"He used you, Cleo. He fucked you and then pretended it never happened. Now you're like this *nothing* to him, and that's exactly how he treats you," Lis growls.

"I was young and stupid. It's my fault, too," I whisper.

"You were twenty, still fresh from your failed marriage, and he knew it. He knew how to get into your pretty pink panties, so he did it. He's twice your age, Cleo," Lis points out, though I already know the story. I was there.

Just the mention of my failed marriage still sends pain slicing through me as if it happened only yesterday.

"I've been there ten years. I can't just walk away," I sigh, trying not to think about Paxton. Though, now that he's been mentioned, my thoughts will probably drift back to him all day long. *Great.*

"You can; and with his clientele, you should," he states.

It's true. My boss' clientele is pretty scary. He's a criminal defense attorney, and while, *usually*, his clients are criminals of the white collar variety, that's not always the case. Still, even the white collar criminals scare me.

To be honest, it doesn't take much to frighten me. I'm a complete and total wimp. I don't know how I've lived alone almost my entire adult life, not when I'm pretty much terrified of my own freaking shadow.

"It's not that simple," I grumble as a waiter brings over our antipasto. Today, Lis has ordered brie covered in a sweet fruit spread with crackers. Sinfully delicious.

"It is. You walk in, give two week's notice, and hopefully he lets you go on the spot. You pack your meager belongings, or just your clothes, and you come to my house where I have a guest suite with your name on it. You live there for as long as you wish, or until you can't handle the way I scream when Theo makes me come. Its completely up to you," he shrugs as he spreads brie on his cracker and then pops it into his mouth.

I can't hold back my giggle at his words. First off, he doesn't have a guest suite. It's a small bedroom and nothing else; the bathroom is down the hall. Secondly, his screams would probably drive me out on *night one.*

"Lis," I sigh. He shakes his head before pinning me with a serious stare.

"I'm not fucking around, Clee. That guy is an asshole, his clients are fucking terrifying, and you live too far away from me. I have the ability to help you, and I want to. Think about it," he urges. I gulp as I nod.

"Okay, yeah," I agree.

"I swear, you're worse than a toddler," he chuckles.

"Whatever."

"Have you been out on any dates?" he asks, changing the subject to another matter that I do not wish to discuss.

"Lis," I warn.

"It's been a decade," he points out.

"It's not as if I'm sitting around waiting for him to come home. I doubt he even knows where I live. I know that I don't know where he is. It's just…"

"He's your Theo," he whispers.

"I tried with other men," I murmur.

"You tried with your asshole boss, that doesn't count," he grunts.

"I tried with Brad, too. You remember him, don't you?"

"He was a pussy. That was you being safe, knowing it wasn't going to amount to anything," he points out as he smothers another cracker. I've lost my appetite completely with this topic of conversation.

"He was nice," I defend.

"He was a pussy, and you know it. Don't try to kid yourself," he mutters.

Luckily, Lisandro doesn't mention anything else. Changing the topic to his store, he talks about the new inventory and shows me pictures of the beautiful pieces he's picked to carry. When our brunch date is over, we decide to go on a walk and do some shopping. Lis loves to shop, and I just love to be with my best friend.

"You know I didn't bring up all that shit to be a jerk, right? I do it because I love you, and I want you to be happy," he whispers later that afternoon, leaning against his car.

It's late, and he's going to head back to Redding—back to Theo and his life there. I already feel the loss of my friend, the only person in my life that knows absolutely everything about me—the good, the bad, and the really ugly.

"I know," I sigh, biting my bottom lip as I look down at my shoes.

"You deserve to be happy, blissfully happy. I'm your best friend, and yet, I've never seen you that way," he continues.

I nod, closing my eyes tightly before he slips his fingers beneath my chin and lifts my head up. Slowly, I open my eyes and look into his dark brown ones, his *concerned* dark brown ones. He cups the side of my face and brushes his thumb across the apple of my cheek before he rests his forehead against mine.

"You are the most beautiful woman I know. Inside and out, Clee. You deserve so much happiness in your life. I want you to explode with it, sweetheart. You're breathing, but you're not living. I fucking hate that for you. Come to Redding, make a new start," he whispers.

"I tried that when I came back to Sacramento," I admit.

"No, you didn't. You came back to a place that was familiar so you could lick your wounds. It's time, sweetie pie. You have to move past him and move on. He's not coming back to you; and honestly, I don't think he should. He's a piece of shit." I stiffen at his words, feeling defensive, but refusing to speak out. "He is. He did something unspeakable to you, and then he left you high and dry. He's not worthy of you."

"We were young," I whisper on a tremble.

"But you aren't young anymore. What's his excuse now?"

I shake my head, refusing to speak, knowing that if I do, I'll cry. Lisandro shakes his head as well, but it has nothing to do with wanting to cry and everything to do with the torch I obviously still hold for my husband, Paxton Hill.

"Talk to you soon, sweetie pie. Stay safe and think about coming to Redding," he whispers, releasing his hold on my cheek and bending down to brush his lips against my forehead.

I nod and give him a shaky smile as he sits down in his car. I have no intention of moving, though I don't know why. I really have nothing for me here in Sacramento, except exactly what Lis said—familiarity. My parents are gone; any friends I had as a child have all moved on with their lives; and my boss is a dickhead.

Smiling I hurry to my shitty car and head home, not wishing to be out past dark. I'm a scardy cat, and a homebody all wrapped into one.

Once I'm locked inside of my apartment, I decide to draw a warm bath, pour a glass of wine—which will also be my dinner—and then go to bed. My plans are perfect for this Sunday evening. My plans are also *pathetic*, but I have no desire to do anything else.

chapter two

Torch

Climbing on my bike, I have one mission today, and one only. I'm going to check on Cleo Hill, my wife. Fuck, it's been so long since I've seen her; but with the threats of *The Cartel* and the unknown of their reach, I have to protect her. I don't know why I feel the urge to do so right now. It wasn't as if I protected her during our short time together. I was the one that hurt her.

Fuck.

Just thinking back to that time makes me feel like a piece of goddamn shit. That's exactly what I was, and what I am. The only excuse I have for myself is—*war*. War is so fucking complicated. The shit I saw, the shit I did, and the shit that happened around me was too much for my twenty-year-old brain to process.

Instead of coming home and leaning on Cleo for support, I sabotaged our relationship—or I tried to. When she didn't completely give up, and I knew deep in my bones that she never would, I left her. I removed myself from the situation at hand, a situation where I knew that I would do nothing but continue to hurt her.

The three-hour ride to her place gives me time to think. I haven't found very much information about her, just her address and her workplace. I want to know more, but I don't deserve to. I don't know that I can handle knowing she's got a man, either; something that has been bothering me lately.

The past ten years, I've tried to deny myself the thought of her—drinking and fucking bitches until I'm so far gone, I can't pull up her memory even if I tried. But it never really works. The second I'm sober, the minute I close my eyes and there's no booze flowing through my system, all I see is her.

When I pull up to her apartment building, I grind my jaw at the sight before me. She lives in a fucking shithole. There is a group of men drinking at the bottom of the staircase, and their eyes are on me. Well, probably more on my bike than me, hoping I'll park it and walk away from it so they can fuck with it.

Not to-fucking-day.

It's late afternoon, six in the evening, and I hope she will be arriving home any minute. I know her job is administrative, and she should get off around five. I have nothing better to do, so I wait for her. I don't have to wait long.

A few minutes later, a shitty, oxidized maroon sedan pulls into a parking spot, and my jaw drops when a sexy as fuck redhead exits. She's wearing a tight skirt that skims just above her knees, and a suit jacket that shows off her small waist. Her dark red hair is longer than I remember it being, and her ass fuller—but fuck me, she looks better, even from afar, than she did at eighteen.

I watch as she walks past the pieces of shit at the bottom of the stairs. They all have eyes for her, watching her, and then every single one of them adjusts their dicks as they try to look up her skirt while she climbs the stairs. She doesn't notice them; or if she does, she doesn't acknowledge them. This is normal for her—normal everyday life—and I fucking *hate* it.

Cleo shoves her key into her door and slips inside, hopefully locking it up behind her. I stay planted in my spot, my eyes drifting from the pieces of shit at the bottom of the stairs to her door for at least an hour. I want to approach her, but I don't know how.

If she were any other bitch, I wouldn't hesitate—but I hurt her, and I abandoned her, and I don't know how to broach that. I'll have to. I owe her explanations, but those are something that I've never given another human being on earth.

The men at the stairs eventually disburse, so I take the opportunity to start my engine and move around to a different spot, trying to find a place where I can hide my bike so it doesn't get jacked. This neighborhood is fucking shit, and I cannot believe that my Cleo actually lives here; and as far as I know, she does that *alone.*

I climb the stairs and walk down the shitty open hallway. I place my hand on the railing and give it a slight shake. My eyes narrow when I realize it's unstable. With only just a little more pressure, I could break it; which means if someone were to lean over it, they'd fall down an entire story into some dead bushes. I scowl at the railing even harder at the thought before I turn around and knock on Cleo's door.

I don't even have to strain to hear her moving around inside of her apartment, which proves that the insulation is fucking nonexistent and that she can probably hear every single thing her neighbors do on either side of her, and vice versa. The thought causes my scowl to deepen even more.

Cleo's foot falls bring her to the door, and I know when she sees me because she gasps. But she doesn't open the door. I look right at her peephole, she can see my face, and I've not changed so much that she doesn't recognize me.

Sure, my eyes hold a darkness in them that wasn't there before, but I'm still clean shaven; my hair's not cropped, but it's still short; and although I've put on some bulk muscle, that hasn't changed my looks one bit.

"Open the door, Cleo," I demand, my voice low.

"What are you doing here?" she asks, not opening the door.

"I'll tell you when you open the door, babe," I murmur.

I hear her suck in a breath, and then the door slowly opens. When it does, I'm met with the most magnificent woman I have ever laid eyes on.

Cleo, at the age of thirty, puts the Cleo of eighteen to fucking shame. My eyes scan her face, taking in her red freckles, spattered all over her nose and cheeks and down to her chest. At the sight of her lush, full tits, I bite my bottom lip, wanting nothing more than to yank her flimsy tank down and look at her naked flesh, knowing those freckles cover them as well. Her waist is small, but her hips flair out. Looking at her from a distance did not do her justice. Up close, her body is phenomenal.

I press my hand to her belly and push her inside, following and slamming the door behind me. Her chest heaves as

25

her soft brown eyes widen at my move. I watch as her nostrils flare slightly with her heavy breathing, and she opens her mouth to speak, but then clamps it shut before her eyes narrow on me. Her gaze goes from surprise to anger in an instant.

Anger I've fucking earned.

Cleo

With narrowed, angry eyes, I look at him. Paxton Hill, my husband. He's back. From where, I don't know, but it's been over ten years—more like eleven—and he's suddenly standing in front of me. Why? I have no clue, but I aim to find out.

I'm not only angry at him because of the way he left me all those years ago, but I'm angry because he looks even sexier than he did back then. And back when I married him, he was the sexiest man I had ever seen in my entire life.

Paxton's bigger than he was at twenty. His body is ripped with muscles, and his shirt is stretched to capacity trying to contain them. He's wearing a leather vest, holey jeans, and big black boots. *Damn.* If I thought he looked hot in his dress blues, and boy did I think he looked hot as sin in those, he's beyond that in what he's wearing right now.

"What are you doing here?" I ask again, trying to keep my voice from trembling.

Though I'm not scared to be in his presence, something I don't understand, I'm trembling for a completely different reason. I feel as though my body is on fire as his light stormy blue eyes scan my body.

Damnit to hell, he's still absolutely beautiful. I'd kind of hoped he'd gotten fat and gross over the years.

"You live in a shithole," he announces.

It's as though he's doused cold water on me—*thankfully,* I might add.

"I'm glad you came here after a decade to inform me of something I'm already aware of. Thanks, you can leave now," I snap.

I watch as his face transforms and his lips tip into a grin. *Christ,* and here I go again, my body getting hot at the sight.

"Shit ain't safe for you, Cleo. It fuckin' kills me, but it's my fault it ain't," he rumbles.

I blink once and then look back into his blue eyes, wondering what on earth he's talking about. Before I can ask, he continues on with his speech.

"Not in the Air Force anymore, baby. But the work I do, the men I associate with, it's not always the good and clean kind. Some guys, they're trying to get the drop on us, and one way they're doin' that is coming after women and children."

I look at him, confusion surely written all over my face. I honestly have no clue what he's talking about.

"I'm a *Devil,* babe," he says, pointing to a patch on his vest, as though I'm supposed to understand what he's talking about. "Fuck me. Still my innocent girl, aren't you?"

"I'm thirty, Paxton, so no, I'm not exactly the same *innocent* girl I once was," I spit out. "But I don't know what a Devil is, so you'll have to forgive my ignorance on that."

I watch as he lowers his head slightly and tips it to the side to look into my eyes. He scans my face, then locks in on my gaze again as he clenches his jaw. His nostrils flare and he dips his face a little closer to mine.

"Don't talk about not being innocent, Cleo, because when

you do, it puts images in my head that I don't need to fuckin' think about," he snaps.

"Like what, Paxton?" I ask smartly.

"Like you fuckin' some other dick, that's what," he barks. My eyes widen as I snap my lips shut. "Yeah, what I fuckin' thought."

"You cannot seriously even pretend to act crazy about that. I'm not confirming or denying, but it's been eleven years," I say, dipping my voice slightly and pinning him with my stare.

"Doesn't matter. Could be a hundred years, and I never want to think about another man's dick in a pussy that was exclusively mine, which still belongs to me—at least in marriage," he says. I feel my hackles rise at his words.

"Get the fuck out," I whisper.

"You don't get it, babe. You're in danger," he says.

"I don't give a single shit. Get out of my house," I say a little louder.

"Cleo…"

"*Get the hell out*," I scream. "You don't get to talk to me that way and stay in my home. Get out or I'm calling the police," I announce.

His eyes widen and he takes a step toward me, but I take two away from him. If he touches me, I'll scream bloody murder. While nobody would probably give a shit in this complex, it could hopefully garner a little attention.

I watch as he shakes his head and reaches into his pocket, pulling something out. He sets, what looks like a slip of paper, on my table and then lifts his eyes to look back up at me.

"You feel even slightly scared, anybody out of the ordinary approaches you for anything, or anybody follows you around, you call me. That's my cell. I'm a few hours away, but I'll come to you, night or day," he says. I nod as I cross my arms over my chest and watch him.

Paxton turns around and wraps his hand around the door handle, twisting his head to look at me one last time. The defeat I see in his gaze almost sends me into his arms— but not quite.

"We got the rest of our lives to figure us out, my shy girl. I'm here to protect you, but lookin' at you, don't think this is me givin' up right now," he whispers.

Then he's out the door, the sound of his boots fading away in the hall. I hurry and lock the door behind him before I turn around and press my back to it, sliding down until my ass hits the floor.

"Holy shit, what just happened?" I ask the empty room. "Oh, my god."

I sit in stunned silence for at least thirty minutes before I stand up and rush to my phone, knowing without a doubt that the only person that can make me snap out of my shock is Lisandro. I decide not to tell him about the whole protection thing, instead I just tell him about Paxton showing up out of the freaking blue.

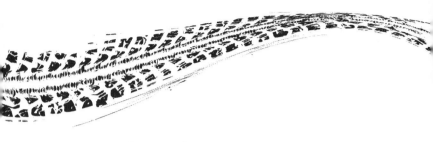

chapter three

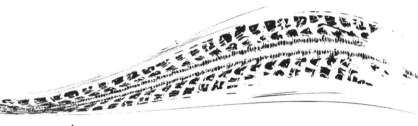

Torch

Walking away from Cleo again is harder than I thought it would be. She's still fuckin' gorgeous. She's also angry. The way her anger flashed toward me, maybe she has changed. If she has, then it's all my doing, and fuck, that means I fucking broke her. Granted, we didn't spend a whole lotta time together when we were married; but even with the way I hurt her, I've never seen her so angry or hurt.

"Fuck," I curse as I climb on my bike.

I start the engine and turn my motorcycle around, slinging gravel everywhere before I speed off and head toward the clubhouse. I'm pissed. Pissed at my fucking self and the fact that I stayed away for eleven years.

Fucking hell.

I want her again. All of her. I want to fix what I broke,

and yeah, my dick wants back inside of her—but my heart, it's pulling me toward her in a way that's familiar. I know that there's more to us. There's a need to be with her. A need I've ignored. A need I drank and fucked away for far too many goddamn years.

I spend three hours inside my own head as I race back to Shasta. I need to blow off some steam. I need to drink, and smoke, and fuck. I don't want to know what that says about me. Right now, I could give a fuck. I want her, but she's not available, so as fucked up as it is, I need to find someone in which to lose myself.

I slide off my bike and make my way toward the clubhouse. The place has been a fuckin' mess since MadDog, the president, was shot. Then his Old Lady, Mary-Anne, left him. I know Mary-Anne, known her since she was a kid livin' in Idaho. We went to high school together. She was just some tall lanky thing back then, all knees and elbows, but she grew into a beautiful woman, and prez loves her.

He's just bein' a fuckin' dick right now. Hard thing to do, swallow that pride that threatens to choke you, and that's exactly what he needs to do. Though, ain't I just some kind of special hypocrite? It's easy to dish out advice, but I don't take my own, or anybody else's.

I walk into the clubhouse and see my prez, a bottle in his hand, which he shouldn't have. He was shot, almost died, and it was only three weeks ago. The old fucker is strong—I'll give him that much. I walk over to him and sit down at his table.

"It's been three weeks," I announce.

"You fix your shit here, yet?" he asks with a grunt.

"Workin' on it," I grunt back. Fuck, we sound like god-damn animals, the two of us. "You stood up to her brother,

31

your brother; you claimed her, you knocked her up, and then you let her walk away. Not the kinda man I thought you were, Prez. That's the kinda shit we pull when we're still punk ass kids, not men," I state before I stand up and walk away.

He needs a goddamn wake up call. Otherwise, he'll be like me, wasting ten fuckin' years for no goddamn reason other than being a broken pussy.

No good man like MadDog needs to do that shit. He's got a good woman, a woman that fought for him and will always stand next to him. No, prez doesn't need to be like me and let that kind of woman walk away from him without a fight, or worse—push her so fucking far away that there's nothing left between you but pain and regret.

"C'mon, babe," I say, lifting my chin to the pretty dark haired whore who approached me a few days ago.

She stands without another word, wrapping her hand around mine as I tug her toward my room. I don't say a word to her. I don't give a fuck if she's even got a brain between her ears. She's here with me for one reason and one reason only— the holes her body can provide me so that I can lose myself for a while. So that the pain I feel from my meeting with Cleo can vanish for a little while.

Once we're in my room, I lock the door and watch as she quickly strips off the tiny shorts and bikini top she's wearing. My eyes sweep down her body, and I grin as I take in her nakedness. She's a skinny little thing, but her tits are perky and her legs long and lean. I'm thankful nothing of her body reminds me of the lush, curvy Cleo that I left a few hours ago.

"Lay down, legs spread, don't move," I instruct.

Her head jerks in a nod, and I watch as she does exactly as I've ordered. I grab a condom out of my back pocket and unzip my pants, shoving them and my boxer briefs down my hips before I slide the condom on. I spit in my palm, rubbing it on the head of my hard cock as I look at her pussy spread open for me.

"Got a pretty little pussy, honey. Anyone ever told you that?" I ask as I let my pants falls to the floor. I step out of them before I divest myself of my cut and t-shirt.

"No," she whispers.

Dragging my fingers along the inside of her thigh before gliding them through her center, I bite my bottom lip and slide two fingers inside of her. I pump in and out of her cunt as she throws back her head with a moan, her pussy growing wetter with each thrust. I'm a dick, and I'm going to fuck her and kick her out in a few minutes, but I'm not into dry fucking. I'll get her nice and wet first.

"Well, you do. It's wet, too. You like the way I touch you?" I ask as I wrap my other hand around my cock.

"Feels good," she groans, arching her back.

"Remember, no moving, no matter how good it feels. I want you still while I fuck you," I grumble as I pull my fingers out of her soaked cunt.

I coat my dick with her wetness and then slowly sink inside of her, watching her thighs tremble as she fights to keep them spread wide open and frozen still. Once I'm fully seated inside of her, I slide my palm between her tits and wrap it around the front of her throat as I ease in and out of her center.

"Torch," she gasps when I thrust harder with each pump of my hips.

"Quiet," I bark.

I squeeze her throat as I focus on my dick, the way it

disappears inside of her body. She's tighter than I expected, and I'm glad for it. I need a release, and she's going to give it to me. Her legs shake, trembling as I continue to fuck her, harder and harder with each drive from my hips.

It's got to be difficult as shit to stay still while I continue to fill her over and over again, but she's a trooper. I decide immediately that if she makes it until I come, I'll reward her—something I typically don't do with whores.

"Stay still, honey," I murmur as I squeeze her throat a little harder.

I feel her pussy flutter around me, and it spurs me on. I fuck her harder and faster than I intended, until I plant myself deep inside of her and I come, spilling into the tip of the condom and squeezing her throat a little harder than I should. I feel her body tighten, but she doesn't move, and I release my hold on her throat as I pull out of her cunt.

"Did you come?" I ask, knowing full well that the answer is no, even if she was close.

"No," she admits truthfully.

"Do you want to?" I ask, arching a brow as I look down into her eyes.

"Please," she whispers.

I grin and sink to my knees, wrapping my hands around the inside of her thighs and burying my face in her pussy. I don't eat bitches out very often, but she deserves it. She did exactly what I told her to—no lip and no complaints.

"You can move, honey," I whisper, lifting my head before I dive back down.

She moves, and it doesn't take her long before she's coming undone against my mouth. I remove myself from her and walk over to the trashcan to dispense of my condom, tying a knot in it before I dump it in the can.

I reach for a bottle of tequila and bring it to my lips, taking a pull before I turn to the little boneless brunette on my bed. My original plan of kicking her out is immediately thwarted, mainly because I'm not done with her. She was so good and followed directions so nicely.

"Let's rest a bit, yeah?"

She sits up, resting on her elbows, and turns her head to look back at me, her eyes bright and her lips curving into a grin. That right there, that spells trouble, and it's why I don't keep them in my bed after I fuck them.

They get *hopeful*.

I ignore the longing eyes and crawl into bed, allowing her to curl up next to me. I'll fuck her from behind next time, then kick her boney little ass out. I don't need her getting comfortable.

Cleo

"Cleo, I have a client coming in at nine-thirty. I need you to greet him first, then buzz me when he's here," my boss practically shouts into the phone.

I roll my eyes. I've been working here for years, and it's not as if I don't know how to greet clients. If I didn't know how by now, I would think that he'd fire me.

"Yes, sir," I mutter into the intercom before I turn back to my computer.

I'm trying so hard to stay focused on my work and not on Paxton and his surprise visit. I spent the majority of last night freaking out over the phone with Lisandro. It was so bad that

Theo volunteered to come and get me. I forced myself to calm down enough so that he wouldn't, and then once I was off of the phone, I worked myself right back up again.

I don't know what kind of danger Paxton insinuated that I could be in, and I don't care; seeing him is dangerous enough. I wanted to run to him, to hold him and kiss him, and it pissed me off. Then he acted like a dick, which was nice because it fizzled out any feelings I had for him. Unfortunately, that only lasted a few minutes, and then I was right back to wanting him again. He needs to stay away. For my own sanity, he needs to just go.

"I'm here to see Mr. Voight," a man says, interrupting my thoughts.

I look up and see a rather dashing man, in his late fifties, standing right in front of my desk.

"Oh, I'm terribly sorry. Are you Mr. Garcia?" I ask as I smile up at him.

"Yes, miss, I am."

I stand and hold out my hand, introducing myself and offering him a refreshment, which he kindly obliges to. Once I'm in the breakroom, making Mr. Garcia's coffee, I call my boss and let him know that his client has arrived and is waiting for him.

"Good," he grunts before he hangs up the phone.

I deliver Mr. Garcia's coffee to him, and he smiles kindly at me. I don't know why he's here to see my boss, but I can't imagine that this sweet, older gentleman has done a darn thing wrong. He asks me how long I've worked here and if I'm from California.

I find myself opening up to him in the few moments we have alone to chat. I tell him that I grew up here but moved

36

away after my parents died; that I lived with my Gram in Texas until I was eighteen, and then moved back here after she, too, passed. He gazes at me with gentle eyes and comments with condolences for such great losses in my young age.

"Mr. Garcia, I'm sorry to have kept you waiting. I do hope my secretary was courteous," my boss says in a booming voice. I fight against grinding my teeth and rolling my eyes simultaneously.

"Take care, girl," Mr. Garcia says as he walks past me and wraps his fingers around my shoulder.

I spend the rest of the morning working. Luckily, I have so much to do that I don't think of Paxton even once. Two hours after his arrival, Mr. Garcia leaves, without so much as a glance in my direction, which I find odd.

"Take your lunch early, Cleo," my boss shouts from inside of his office.

"Would you like me to pick up anything for you on my way back, sir?" I ask.

"If I did, I would have told you," he rumbles. I nod before turning and walking away.

My boss is a total prick, but he's good at his job, and the pay is decent for a girl with zero education living in the city. Lisandro is right, though. He treats me like shit, and he used me. I should quit and go up to Redding, start fresh. Maybe in doing that, I can throw Paxton off and he won't be able to find me again so easily.

Though, maybe I want to see him fight for me a little, even if I don't want him. I think that I deserve a little more than him warning me about some kind of danger. I think I deserve a real conversation, and an apology.

Then I want a divorce.

I need to be free of him to completely move on with my life.

"How are you doing today?" Lis asks as his greeting.

"I'm fine," I lie.

"You lie," he hisses. It causes me to giggle.

"I'll be okay."

"Oh, I know you will, but you still lie. I want you to be more than just okay," he says. It makes me break out in a huge smile.

I love that he wants that for me. He's my best friend in the whole world, and he wants me to be happy, really happy, just as I've always wanted for him.

"I will be," I say with a nod as I continue to walk toward the café that I frequent for a quick lunch. "I have to go. I only have thirty minutes for lunch."

Lisandro grumbles that my boss is an asshole before he lets me go. I order a half a sandwich and a side salad before I make my way to an empty table outside and sit down to wait for my food. It's a gorgeous fall day, and I'm going to soak up the rays before it becomes too cold and gloomy to do so.

I go over my conversation with Paxton, how he told me to watch out for anyone following me. I don't know why that portion of the conversation slips to the forefront of my mind, but I find myself scanning the street for anything suspicious.

There is a fancy black sedan sitting across the street, the windows blacked out, but not necessarily suspicious in any way. There's a delivery van set up in front of this little bakery that I sometimes go to, but the workers are loading up sweet treats, so that's not out of the ordinary.

Then my food arrives, so I push Paxton's warnings to the back of my mind. He's crazy. I don't know what his game is, why he's suddenly back in my life, like he's always known where to find me, but I want him gone again.

The pain he brings just by showing up, just by looking at me, is more than I can handle. It's ridiculous, actually—completely ridiculous that I allow him to affect me in such a way.

Once I'm finished eating, I let out a sigh and make my way back to work. The rest of the day is long and tedious, but at least my boss has left and the quiet of my office and the amount of work I have helps me to relax and not think about him or Paxton. That is, until I go home.

chapter four

Torch

I pull up to Cleo's shitty apartment building. It's evening again, same douchebags hanging at the bottom of her stairs as before, and her car is not in the parking lot. It's growing dark, and I wonder just where in the fuck she is.

Pulling my bike around to the hiding place I stowed it last time, I make my way up the stairs and then to her front door. It takes me about thirty seconds to jimmy her lock and walk inside of her apartment.

"Fucking hell," I curse as I lock the door behind me.

Her locks are shit, the door is as thin as the walls, and since I can hear her neighbors fuckin', that means they're pretty goddamn thin. She lives in a complete fucking shithole. *The Cartel* could come in here, completely undetected, in seconds. She wouldn't even know what the fuck happened.

I sit down on her sofa and face the door, waiting for her. I wonder if I'll feel the same way about her, seeing her again—if the initial shock will have worn off, or if she'll still be the most magnificent thing I've laid eyes on. Maybe it was just a fluke. Just a shock at seeing her after so many years?

Less than five minutes later, the door opens, she flips the light switch, and I know that it wasn't a fluke. She's absolutely, hands down, the prettiest thing that's ever filled my vision. Eighteen or thirty years old, still a goddamn knock out.

"Your locks are shit," I murmur, watching as she snaps her head up. She lets out a scream that lasts about two seconds, until she realizes just who I am.

"What the hell are you doing in my apartment? Trying to give me a heart attack?" she asks, crossing her arms just below her plentiful tits.

"Your locks are shit, the door is shit, and your neighbors are shit," I announce.

"Yeah, tell me something I don't know," she snorts.

"You can't stay here, Clee."

"Pretty sure it's not your call where I live," she says, like a smart ass. I want nothing more than to shove my dick between those smart lips—show her how I tolerate smart ass women.

"I'm not fucking with you, Cleo. This shit that I'm dealing with is not a fucking joke. I'm about five minutes from carrying you outta here, putting you on the back of my bike, and taking you to my place to keep you safe," I grind out.

"So you'd kidnap me. And how is that safer than some unknown *thing* that probably isn't even going to affect me?" she asks, arching a brow.

I stand up and walk toward her, wrapping one hand

41

around the side of her neck and the other at her waist, tugging her against my chest before I dip my chin slightly to look into her pretty, light brown eyes. Goddamn, she smells so fucking good. I can't even fight my cock from going completely hard. Her smell, her softness pressed against me, it's impossible.

"If I gotta kidnap your smartass mouth to keep you safe, I will. These fucks will do a lot worse than kidnap you, Clee. They'll take you, keep you, fuck you, and sell you. That something you want to leave to chance?" I ask, squeezing the side of her neck gently. I watch as her eyes widen, surprise marring her features.

"What on earth are you involved in, Pax?" she whispers. It's like a goddamn punch to my gut.

Pax.

I haven't been called that in years—eleven years—not since the day I left her.

"Not me bein' involved with them, sweetheart. They want control over my club, and they're willing to try to take that in ways that are… unsavory," I murmur, my thumb tracing her big, full lips.

"Pax, baby," she whispers.

Fuck, my cock goes rock hard as her eyes search mine. I lean down slightly and press my lips to hers. Inhaling her sweet scent, feeling her warm lips against mine as I press my hand against her back a little harder, bringing her even closer to me.

"Not lettin' a fuckin' thing touch you, Cleo," I murmur after I pull my lips away from hers slightly.

We stay silent for a beat, and then her body stiffens. That's when I know that she's putting her defenses back up. I don't blame her a bit, but having her sweetness in my arms again, *fuck* it was better than I remembered. She takes a step back, and I let her, allowing my hands to fall away from her.

"You need to go," she grinds out.

"I'm not fuckin' with you, Cleo. This shit is dangerous, and I'm worried they'll come after you," I inform her. She's not listening. I can tell by the pissed off look in her eyes.

"I've been just fine for eleven years. I'll be fine for eleven more without you," she says, lifting her chin slightly as she delivers her blow. A blow I wholeheartedly deserve.

"Know you're pissed, sweetheart, and you have every fuckin' right—but you have to put that shit to the side and listen to what I'm telling you. This is no fuckin' joke," I practically plead to her.

"If I have any problems, I'll call Lisandro," she says.

My eyes narrow as I ask, "Who the fuck is Lisandro?"

"None of your business," she says, adding a little grin.

"Cleo," I snap.

"Seriously, none of your business, Paxton. I'll keep an eye out, like you said. I'll watch out for suspicious things, and I'll call Lisandro if I need help," she retorts, a little too brightly.

"We ain't done talking," I say, pointing at her.

"No, I do want to talk, but we can do that when I have divorce papers drawn up that you can sign."

I feel my stomach drop and my eyes widen slightly at her words. Divorce papers. I hadn't thought about that.

Divorce.

The word is ugly, though it's not as if I hadn't thought of it over the past decade. I have. However, right now, it doesn't feel right. There's something here between us, and no way in fuck am I going to walk away just yet. Once *The Cartel* is handled, then maybe it's something we can discuss; but for some reason, it definitely doesn't feel right.

"No divorce, Cleo," I growl. Her eyes widen.

"Paxton, you can't be serious. Why not?" she practically screeches, her voice hitching up higher.

"'Cause," I shrug, taking another step toward her.

Cleo backs up with each step I take until her back hits the wall. I cage her in, one hand wrapped around the side of her small waist, the other at the side of her head, my fingers buried in her soft as fuck red hair. She breathes heavily, and I can't help the smile that tips my lips. I know it's me, my proximity to her, that makes her that way.

Cleo

He's so close to me, I can smell him. He doesn't smell like he did all those years ago. I can still remember how he smelled like dirt, spice, and just him. Now, there are hints of oil and leather mixed with his scent, and I wouldn't have ever thought it was possible, but he smells *better* than he ever has.

I'm trying to stay still, caged in his arms as I tell myself to breathe, his eyes stormy blue and looking right at mine. Dammit, he's still so gorgeous that he renders me speechless and stupid. Nothing has changed. I'm still this *shy* girl when I'm near him. He's always owned me and had control over me, just with one look.

"You need to leave," I whisper.

"Sweetheart, my innocent girl," he rasps. It makes my knees shake.

Sweetheart. I'd almost forgotten the way he would whisper that to me, when he was deep inside of me—the week I had him, that is. I should have cherished it more, knowing he was going to take it all away in a heartbeat. I should have committed it to memory better, instead of the haziness I'm stuck with now.

"I'm not," I whisper.

"Yeah, baby, you are. My Clee, so shy, so innocent, my sweetheart," he mutters pressing his hard length against my stomach.

"I'm thirty years old, Paxton," I say lamely.

"Yeah, baby, I know how old you are. Doesn't make you less innocent; less shy," he chuckles. I grind my teeth together in annoyance. "You can't deny it, so don't even try."

Paxton's lips touch mine again and for whatever asinine reason, I don't push him away. Rather, I stupidly open for him. When his tongue touches my lips, then swipes inside of my mouth, I can't stop myself from grabbing his t-shirt with my fingers and holding onto him with a moan.

He tastes better than he smells, and he's so good at this, kissing, making me feel absolutely beautiful in his arms. I'd forgotten it all. I thought I'd remembered how he felt. I was wrong. Nothing prepared me for the wave of emotions the second his tongue slid inside of my mouth.

Pulling away from me slightly, he rests his forehead against mine, and we both breathe heavily, our chests rising and falling a few times before he speaks, his voice soft and gentle.

"Sweetheart, I missed you," he whispers.

I close my eyes for a moment, trying to keep my tears at bay. These words, I've wanted them, I've wished for them, and I've prayed for them. They're here now, mine for the taking, but they aren't as sweet as I'd hoped they'd be. Instead, they're marred by the years of pain between us. It's been too long. Eleven years too long.

"Leave, now," I urge softly.

"You don't mean that, baby," he says, his voice still gentle.

"I do. You need to leave, now," I state a little firmer. He takes a step back from me, and I force myself to release my hold on his shirt. His eyes scan my face and he nods.

"Not gonna be gone for long, Clee; and I ain't far. You feel uncomfortable at all, call me. You want to talk to me, call me. You need me for whatever reason, *call me*," his last words end on an urging type tone, but I can do nothing but nod.

I step aside from the door and watch him walk away from me. I lock the door and then I bring my fingertips up to my lips and touch them. They're slightly swollen from his kiss, and I can't tear my eyes away from the door.

Paxton Hill is going to obliterate me.

I can't let that happen, not again.

True, I'm not the sweet eighteen-year-old I once was, the overly trusting innocent child. But that doesn't mean that I've changed all that much.

I'm still, as he pegged me, very innocent in a lot of ways. I haven't been in a lot of relationships. I have one best friend, and Paxton was the great love of my life.

I haven't lived a lot, nor have I loved a lot. He knows how to talk to me, how to play me, and I refuse to allow that this time. Unfortunately, I don't know how to stop it. Deep down, I want it, and I want him.

I still want my husband.

chapter five

Cleo

I pull my car into the same parking spot that I always park in—every day for the last ten years. I'm not big on change, obviously, and the same goes for my general habits. It's Tuesday, and it's seven-thirty in the morning. I arrive at the office at seven-thirty so that I have adequate time to prepare for the arrival of my boss, Stephenson Voight.

Although, I was only allowed to call him Stephenson while he was fucking me. The next day, it was back to *Mr.* Voight, and has been for years. It doesn't bother me, though. I'd rather be detached from him. It makes my colossal mistake of allowing him inside of me to burn a little less.

When I arrive upstairs at my desk, I let out a surprised squeak when I see Mr. Garcia sitting in my chair.

"C-Can I help you, Mr. Garcia?" I ask, furrowing my

brow in confusion.

"You're a very pretty girl, Cleo. Voight has enlightened me that you're also a very single girl," he rumbles. "That's not the case exactly though, is it?" he asks.

Alarm bells ring in my head. Is this what Paxton was talking about? I start to panic, my breathing coming faster and faster.

"Don't be scared. I actually wanted to know if you were single because I found you quite alluring, but I looked into you, and you're married," he grunts, narrowing his eye at me.

"My husband and I are estranged," I whisper, trying my hardest to calm down.

"Then it would do me great honor if you would accompany me to dinner Friday evening," he says with a flourish of his hand.

Honestly, I want to tell him no. Aside from the fact that he's old enough to be my father, he scares the heck out of me. He's meeting with a criminal defense attorney, which means he's possibly done something very bad. I don't need that.

I've got Paxton, who is obviously not hanging around at churches and helping nuns cross the street to get to mass on time. The last thing I need is another trouble making man in my midst.

"Sure, that sounds just lovely," I say, hoping he'll scurry on out of here so that I can call Lisandro and panic like the scardy cat that I am.

"I'll pick you up around eight," he murmurs. With a wink, he walks away from me.

I reach for my phone but then decide to sit down after he's left.

"This is all a big coincidence. It's not as if he's the first client that's ever asked me out. I can't believe I let Pax get to me, and that I said yes to Mr. Garcia. This is all so silly," I whisper to myself.

Mr. Voight walks in five minutes later, and I'm so busy throughout the day, even working through my lunch, that I don't even think about calling Lisandro. I definitely don't think about calling Paxton. It's all just a silly coincidence, I decide.

Yeah.

That's it.

A complete and total coincidence.

The parking lot is absolutely empty, save for my shitty maroon car, when it's time for me to leave the office. I'm usually not this late, but there were some important court documents that had to be prepared tonight so that first thing in the morning Mr. Voight could send them out to be filed.

Now it's late, really late, and I'm all alone in a deserted parking lot, in an area that is sparsely populated in the evenings. I fumble with my key, trying to hurry and get it into my lock, pissed off at myself for not having a car with automatic entry. Once the door is unlocked, I yank it open and slide inside of the driver's seat, locking myself inside with a long exhale.

Starting my engine, I switch on my headlights and gasp. An expensive, black sedan is parked directly across the lot from me. The windows are too dark to see if there's a shadow, indicating that there's someone inside. Nevertheless, I get a foreboding feeling, as though I'm being watched. It sends a chill up my spine.

I decide to drive home. I should go somewhere else, in case this person is following me, but I don't. Though, I keep my one eye on my rearview mirror and another on the road. It doesn't appear as though the sedan is following me, but now I'm more than a little freaked out.

Now, I'm flat out scared.

Once I'm home, I turn on all of my lights, after locking myself inside, and I try to breathe. It's time to call Lisandro.

"Did that fucker show up again?" he growls into the phone.

"Not tonight," I whisper.

"Clee, what's happened?" he asks, his voice dipping a little lower in obvious concern.

I take a deep breath and then I tell him everything. I tell him about *The Cartel*, Paxton's warnings and then seeing that car, more than once.

"It's all a coincidence, right?" I ask on a whisper.

"Theo and I will be there as soon as we can, pack a small bag, leave everything else in your place," he says. I can hear rustling around.

"You're overreacting," I cry out.

"Nope. Paxton said some shit, and maybe it was just that—*shit*. But sweetie pie, he also mentioned a scary as shit group, and that they could know who you are; and for whatever crazy reasons, could try to get to him *through* you. Now, I'm not having that shit. I'm not going to let that crazy as hell group take you away from me. Not when I haven't meddled in your life nearly enough to get you to be blissfully happy."

"Lis, it's fine. I'm fine. I don't even know what I believe from Pax," I say, shaking my head.

"Don't care if it's all bullshit, I'm not willing to take that chance," he cries. A second later, Theo is on the line.

"He's a Devil. That's what you told Andro?" Theo asks, his voice deep.

"Yeah, that's what he told me, and that's what a patch on his vest said," I confirm.

"That's a motorcycle gang, Clee. *Notorious Devils.* They're famous, and they're dangerous as shit. He says *The Cartel* could be after you to get to him, then they probably are. We're comin' to get you."

My phone goes dead, and I look down to see that he's hung up on me. I glance around my crappy little apartment with wide eyes. Then I close them, wondering who on earth I'm married to.

Granted, I haven't seen him in years; but when I married Paxton Hill, he was an active duty enlisted member of the Air Force. I didn't know his exact job in the military, he never talked about it, but I didn't think it had anything to do with motorcycle gangs.

Biting my bottom lip, I realize, not for the first time, that I didn't know Paxton at all. He told me that he wasn't close to his family and that was why he left Idaho and joined the military, but I don't know *why* he wasn't close to them.

He knows everything about my childhood—about how my parents died; how they weren't really caring loving people, but they provided for me—then one day, they were just gone. House fire. Dad passed out drunk, and his cigarette fell onto the shag carpeting. Luckily, I'd been at school, so I survived. I went to live with Gram in Texas immediately after.

But I don't know anything about my husband. I never did. He didn't share a thing about his past or about his life. I would ask him, and he'd shrug off my questions and then change the subject.

I didn't push him. I never pushed him. He was sweet and loving toward me, and I was enamored by him. I soaked up the attention he flourished onto me. I'd never had that before.

Then I agreed to marry him, giving him my virginity and thinking that finally, *finally*, I was going to have some grand adventure. That I was living a real-life fairy tale of sorts, the strong military man and his devoted wife waiting for him.

That is, until he burst my bubble, hurt me, and then crushed me as he walked out of the door and never even bothered to look back.

There's a knock on my door , and I look through the peephole to see both Lisandro and Theo standing on the other side. I unlock it and yank it open before throwing myself into their waiting arms. They envelop me in their embrace, and I take in a deep breath.

"I was freaked out, and then I decided it was silly, and then I freaked out again," I admit as they shuffle me inside of my apartment.

"You got your stuff?" Theo asks.

"Not yet," I admit.

"Leave your purse and everything here. We'll figure out that shit later. For now, it needs to look like you vanished. *The Cartel*, they're dangerous. I can't believe you didn't tell me this shit before. Whatever your ex has going on with them, the last thing you need to be is a pawn," Theo rumbles.

"Paxton was warning me. He seemed concerned, but I didn't think it was anything, not really," I say lamely.

"That's because you don't know what he's into, what this group is into. Now knowing a little, how are you feeling?"

"Terrified," I whisper.

"Got her shit?" Theo asks above my head. I hadn't even realized that Lisandro was gone. Turning around, I see he's walking out of my bedroom.

"A few things. We'll go shopping. You need to update your pathetic existence of a wardrobe anyway, sweetie pie," he grins, but I can see that it's shaky, his lips trembling. He's scared for me, too.

"My husband is an asshole," I whisper, looking between my two friends.

"That's not any news, but I do have to give him credit for at least trying to warn you," Theo says.

"Whatever," I snort.

Theo grabs my phone out of my hand and tosses it into my purse on the counter before wrapping his fingers around mine and tugging me to my front door.

I don't think about the rent, what'll happen to all my stuff when I don't pay it, or anything. All I can think about is that my life has just been turned completely upside down. Once again, it's Paxton's fault.

Asshole.

Torch

I watch the skinny brunette ride me, her small tits bouncing as she fucks my cock. My mind should be on the way she's working me, and she fuckin' *is*, too. She's giving me a beautiful show, but my thoughts are lost in all that is Cleo and her safety. She's being stubborn, and it surprises the shit out of me. Granted, I don't know the woman she's become, but I knew the girl that she was pretty fuckin' well. Stubborn was not a characteristic she carried.

"Torch—oh, fuck, you feel so good," she moans above me.

Wish I could return the compliment, but truth be told, she feels adequate, at best. She'll do, but she isn't doing what I wanted her to, which was take my mind off of Cleo.

I reach over to the night stand and grab my bottle of tequila, bringing it to my lips before I take a long pull. She doesn't even realize I'm not into this. My cock is hard because a warm pussy is enveloping it, but that's friction and nothing else.

"I'm gonna—."

I watch with nothing more than curiosity as she completely shatters around me. Her pussy pulses and she throws back her head as she lets out a squeak. I reach over to her boney ass and slap it hard, causing her to jerk and look down at me.

"Keep going," I order.

Her eyes wide, she whispers, "But I came and I'm—."

"I give a fuck that you came? Ride me until I come, bitch," I grunt, taking another swig of liquor.

She doesn't argue with me. I watch as she musters up her strength and starts to ride me, grinding down hard through the obvious discomfort. Maybe it was mean to tell her I didn't give a fuck, but that's not me trying to be mean, that's me being honest.

"Torch," she says, her voice trembling.

I take one last swig, setting my bottle to the side before I sit up and I maneuver her so that she's on her back and I'm hovering above her. She reaches up and wraps her small hands on my shoulders.

"Want me to be still again?" she asks, biting her bottom lip. I thrust in and out of her wet cunt a few times before I lean down to whisper in her ear.

"Only way I'm gonna come is if I fuck your ass. You want that, I'll take it; you don't, then you need to send Serina in," I say, suggesting she brings in another whore. She gasps and wrenches her head back.

"I've never…" I pull out and look down at her, leaning back on my knees.

"Well, either I pop that cherry or you go and get Serina," I grunt.

I watch as she sits up and then crawls over to me, her hands skimming up my thighs, my stomach and chest. She presses her small tits against my chest and her lips brush my cheek.

"Any other way you want it, Torch, I'm yours," she whispers as one of her hands wraps around my condom wrapped dick.

"Only way I want to fuck right now is in someone's ass. Don't give a fuck whose ass it is, honey," I murmur.

"Don't you like me?" she asks.

"I don't know you," I state. "Now you got about thirty seconds to either bend over or run out to Serina before I kick your ass out and get her myself."

"If you wanted me, only me, I'd give that to you, baby," she says with wide, pleading eyes.

I can't help myself. I try not to, but I burst out laughing. She blanches and scrambles off of the bed. I reach out and wrap my hand around her bicep, holding her loosely and giving her a slight shake.

"Hate to break it to you, honey. If I wanted to take your ass right now, if I demanded it, I'd take it. There's not a goddamn thing you could do about it. I could keep you for only me if I wanted that, too, but I don't."

Her eyes fill with tears and I let out a sigh as I release my hold of her arm. This is why I don't like to let them stay in my bed. This is the exact reason I kick them out after I fuck them. *Attachments.* I don't want her attached, and she's gone and done that. Now she's got her feelings hurt, and I'm the bastard.

"Go get Serina, yeah?" I urge softly.

She nods as she grabs her scraps of fabric and runs off. A few minutes later, my door opens and Serina is standing in the entrance, her naked flesh on display.

"You made her cry," she frowns as she closes the door behind her.

I know Serina. She was at my old club in Idaho. She fucked up and they did a whore trade with a girl who fucked up here. She's a good clubwhore; been around a while and knows her place, for the most part.

"Yeah," I grunt, pulling out a bottle of lube from my cheap nightstand.

"When are you gonna learn, you can't give those pretty blue eyes to the young ones. They'll fall every time," she purrs.

"Yeah, like you fell for Dirty, huh?" I ask on a chuckle. She had it bad for my brother, Dirty Johnny, caused problems with his Old Lady. That's how her ass ended up right here.

"Hard lesson to learn, Torch," she says with a flinch.

"Shut up and give me that little asshole, Serina. I'm ready

56

to fill it up."

"Yeah," she moans as she positions her body for me to take.

Sinking inside of her ass doesn't do what I thought it would. It doesn't take away the thoughts of Cleo that invade my mind. She's infiltrates my head the entire time. When I finally come, it's lackluster, and I feel like the biggest asshole on the planet. I fall back against the headboard and reach for my bottle, sucking the liquid back and hoping it will make thoughts of her go away, at least for the night.

"You can't drink and fuck her away, Torch."

"Get out," I grunt.

I close my eyes and Cleo appears. Then, in an instant, she's gone, and I'm back in hell, sinking my knife into the soft sandy dirt, hitting metal. A bomb. Then it happens, thirty feet in front of me—an explosion. I look up just in time to see my best friend flying through the air.

My eyes open as my heart starts pounding.

It takes me a good minute to realize that I'm not there. I'm on U.S. soil. In a clubhouse, my clubhouse, not the desert.

Fuck.

When will they stop?

chapter six

Torch

I can't shake her. Since my nightmares started, they haven't stopped. I haven't slept in three weeks, and I know that there is only one way to at least make them subside, if only for a while.

I need to make sure Cleo is okay. Her safety is the only thing I can control right now, and I'm tired of fucking around with her. She's either coming with me tonight, or I'm going to be her goddamn shadow, and that means sleeping in her place, right next to her warm, curvy body.

With a semi-plan in place, I pull into the parking lot of her apartment and frown. It's only four in the afternoon. Her car shouldn't be here, yet it is. I make my way upstairs and knock on her door. I don't have to strain my hearing too much, but I do anyway. I hear absolutely nothing. I decide to break into her apartment, my gut telling me something is very wrong here.

The sight that greets me makes my stomach drop. Sure, everything is in its place, but with one scan, I can see that it isn't. Her purse is on the counter, her phone tossed on top of it. I close the door and call out her name, but silence is the only thing that greets me.

I jog into her bedroom and see that her bed is unmade, clothes strewn on the floor; and a glance at her closet proves that all of her clothes are still hanging in their designated spots. I walk back into the kitchen, taking her phone and noticing that its dead. I plug it in and power it on, when I see, that she's got a dozen missed calls. They're all from the same number.

I don't bother listening to the half a dozen messages. Instead, I call back the number.

"Voight," a voice growls into the phone.

"You been trying to reach Cleo Hill?" I ask through gritted teeth.

"Where is she?" he barks.

"Who is this?"

"This is Stephenson Voight, her boss. If you get ahold of her, tell her she's fired," he snaps before he ends the call.

My brows knit in confusion. She's not at work, her shit's here—her money and her car.

She's gone.

Fuck. Fuck. Fuck. *Fuck*.

She's gone.

I don't know how long she's been gone. I haven't been back to check on her in weeks. I needed to try and get my shit straight, try and give her time to get hers straight, too. She hasn't called me, so I wasn't overly worried. Now I know why she hasn't called. She's fucking gone.

I slam her front door closed and race down to my bike. It's going to take me three hours to get back to the clubhouse. Maybe if I go fast enough, I can make it in two.

I focus on the highway and then the mountain roads ahead of me, pulling into the clubhouse two and a half hours later. I look around and realize that MadDog isn't here. Pulling out my phone, I scroll to his name.

"What's up, brother," he grumbles.

"My wife's gone missing," I announce.

"You're what?" he asks in surprise. I don't blame him. Nobody knows I'm married, not even my brothers in Idaho.

"I'm going to need some more information, brother," he says, his voice a low growl.

I tell him that I'll be by his place in ten, and he agrees before ending the call. He's just arrived back from Idaho with his woman, Mary-Anne, in tow. They've worked their shit out and I'm pleased as fuck for them, but my mind is on nothing but Cleo as I climb on my bike, revving the engine before I roll over to my prez's house to tell him about my wife.

Fuck.

Cleo

My eyes flutter open and I roll over. Looking around in mild panic, it takes me a moment to realize exactly where I am. Though I've been here for three weeks, it's still all new to me. The circumstances surrounding the reason why I'm in my friends' home still frighten me. It could have all been a coincidence, but something deep inside tells me that it absolutely wasn't.

My door slowly opens and I turn to find Lisandro making his way toward me, two coffees in his hand. I quickly sit up, reaching out for a cup, and he smiles as he climbs onto the bed and settles down beside me.

"You look better," he murmurs.

"Theo gone?" I ask.

"You know he is. Now, are you going to be okay at the shop alone today?"

I've been working for cash at Lisandro's jewelry store since I arrived here in Redding. Well, since he and Theo marched me here, refusing to take no for an answer. Though, I can't complain much.

I absolutely love working for Lisandro. Not only do we get to take lunches together, even if it's only in the back room sometimes, but he's actually a great boss. He's knowledgeable about the product, patient with teaching me everything I need to know so that I can properly inform the customer, and he's my best friend. I love him.

"Gina will be there, right?" I ask as I take a sip from my drink.

"She will, but you know how I worry," he murmurs.

"Go and visit with Granny B. Don't worry about me," I whisper with a smile, encouraging him to visit with his grandmother back in SacTown.

"You know she'd slap that smile off of your face if she knew you called her that, don't you?" he asks, arching a brow.

Bellatrix, or Granny B as I call her, is Lisandro's very well-to-do grandmother. All of her good friends call her Trixie, which means that Lisandro calls her Trixie, because she refuses to be called anything else. I've taken to calling her Granny B behind her back solely, of course, because, as Lisandro said, she'd slap the look off my face if she knew I called her that.

She's a very sweet woman, if not eccentric and exciting all rolled into one teenie tiny, four-foot-eleven package of dynamite. She's had five husbands, each one wealthier than the last, and none staying for too long—mostly because when they annoy her too badly, she divorces them. Lisandro visits her the first weekend of every month. This is his weekend, and I'll be damned if he's missing it for me. He loves the old coot.

"Give Granny B hugs from me, okay?"

"You know she only accepts cheek kisses," he murmurs. It makes me giggle.

"Well, give her those from me, and throw in a *dah-ling* or two."

"Theo will have his phone with him, glued to his hand, all day long. You can take my car, just make sure to pick him up on your way home from the shop after you close," he instructs as he hands me his car keys.

"You're taking Theo's to town?"

"Theo has a Beemer, and Granny B say's it's much more comfortable than the *American made trash* I drive," he says, rolling his eyes.

"I love your *Jeep Cherokee*. I'll gladly drive it around," I grin.

Lis eyes me, all joking escaping his face, and he looks so serious. I gulp down a drink of the hot coffee in my hands and wait for him to speak, knowing that when he does, he's going to be completely honest—and possibly downright scary with me.

It doesn't happen often, but when he decides he needs to lay something on me, he really lays it on, and with a tone that assures me he means every single well thought out word.

"You need to make peace with your past. That means Paxton. It's obvious, from the conversations you've had with him recently, that there are still some things between you unsaid, untouched, and unshared. You'll never be able to move on, to be happy, or even just to be content until you do. I know Theo said his group was dangerous, and I'm sure it is, so maybe this is a good time for that divorce and to sever ties with him completely. It's not as if you've been truly married. Not really," he says.

I know he's right, and this isn't the first time he's said these same words, almost verbatim. The time has come, and even though I know it's going to hurt, hasn't the pain always been there anyway? Anytime I've thought of him, it's felt like the wound has been shred wide open. It's never quite healed. After eleven years, it still feels as fresh as it did on day one of his leaving me.

"When you get back, maybe we can meet him together? I don't want to go alone. Every time I'm alone with him, we argue and he kisses me and I let him. Then I want more," I say quietly.

"I got your back, sweetie pie," he whispers as he slides his arm around my shoulders to comfort me.

"Why does he still affect me the way that he does?" I ask, not really looking for a direct answer.

"Because you're a woman who, when she falls, she falls deep. You're a woman who sees the good in everybody. You're so fucking loyal and sweet, it's almost sickening," he grins.

"Thank you for being…everything," I whisper.

Lis doesn't say anything else. He leans down, presses his lips to my head, and then walks away. I have a feeling he's crying but doesn't want me to see him, and that's just fine. As soon as the door closes behind him, tears fill my own eyes.

The shop is slow this afternoon, so I decide to send Gina off to lunch, fairly confident that nobody will even chance a walk inside. We've not had one customer all day long as it is. I choose to take the quiet down time to clean the glass cases. The tops are smudged from fingerprints, and it seems like I'm the only one who is anal enough to clean them several times a day.

I'm just finishing up my first case when the bell above the door rings. I look up and my eyes widen. There's a hulking man with a full beard, leather vest, worn jeans, and black boots walking inside, thick black glasses on his face hiding his eyes.

"How may I help you?" I ask, my eyes staying glued to the man's vest. It looks exactly like Paxton's, patches and all.

I try to calm my breathing, clenching my fists and attempting not to freak out and run.

"Here for a wedding ring. Whatever she wants," he murmurs gently. I jerk slightly to look at the woman at his side.

She's about my age, making her at least *half* his age. She's also tall and very slender, with long dark hair and shocking blue eyes. She's absolutely beautiful, and I feel like a troll just standing in front of her.

I shake myself out of my creepy staring long enough to ask her what she has in mind. She says that she wants something simple, nothing too fancy, and I lead her over toward the engagement rings. If we have something close to what she likes, I can always have a ring made or ordered to her taste.

I pull out a very small stone solitaire ring to show her first. It's definitely not fancy, and it's the smallest diamond we have in stock.

"There's no budget," the gruff man announces.

I jump, having forgotten that he was even standing in front of me. I don't know how—he's the most intimidating man I've ever seen.

"Oh, that one. Can I please see that one?" the woman asks, pointing to one of our most expensive vintage inspired pieces. The clarity is the best we carry, and it's designer—completely outstanding.

"Put it on," he grumbles. I hand it to her to try on. The man nods and then orders me to ring it up.

"Sir, this ring is forty-five thousand dollars," I whisper as my brows knit together.

I know that I shouldn't judge the amount of money people have based on their clothing, or anything at all. I try really hard not to judge people in general, but this is almost fifty-thousand dollars. It's definitely not peanuts.

"Ring. It. *Up*," he growls as he leans forward over the counter.

I jump again and take the ring from the woman, hurrying to the cash register to ring up the purchase. My hands are shaking with each button I push, and I really wish that Gina were back already. I scurry to the couple and hand him a piece of paper with his total, including tax. I watch as he glances at it and then hands me his credit card. My eyes widen as I take it from him. A credit card. He's going to pay with a credit card. I can't even fathom having a credit line for that much money.

65

"I'm sorry, but you look really familiar. Can you tell me your name? I'm better with names than faces," the girl says sweetly.

I try to hurry and run *Maxfield Duhart's* credit card, telling her that I don't think we've ever met. I would never forget a girl as pretty as her, not ever. She should be on a fashion runway modeling—she's *that* tall, thin, and stunning.

"I'm Mary-Anne," she offers with a kind smile.

"Cleo, my name is Cleo," I whisper, glancing at Maxfield; or, more importantly, the patch on his vest that reads *Notorious Devils*.

I smile and finish ringing them up. I give the receipt for him to sign, and then hand them the little, light pink bag with leopard print tissue paper; Lisandro's signature design and color scheme. I do all of this with a shaky smile.

Maxfield takes it from me, but his eyebrows are furrowed, and he's staring at me with a look that I can't quite describe. I really, really, wish he would just—*go.*

The two of them walk out of the store, and I place my hands on the clean counter and let out a breath. I don't know who he was, and I don't care, but he has to be part of Paxton's group, or gang, or whatever it is, making him dangerous, according to Theo.

Where the hell is Gina? I wonder again, really wishing she would get her skinny ass back here.

Torch

I throw back another shot, everybody sensing my mood and

giving me a wide berth—thank fuck. I don't want to talk to anyone, and I sure as shit don't want to fuck. I want to sit right where I'm at and drown myself, wading in self pity because she's gone. My Cleo is fucking gone. I know it's all my fault, too. Nobody to blame but me. I ruined her when she was just eighteen years old, and I never fucking stopped. Only now, she's probably living a hell she never dreamed possible.

"Prez," I slur into my phone after I pick it up from dancing across the table.

"I found her," he announces. I blink before I ask a question I never thought I would have to about my sweet girl.

"Dead?"

"At work. Didn't you check her job?"

"*What*?" I cry. "Of course, I checked her job. She's a receptionist at an attorney's office in Sacramento," I explain.

MadDog proceeds to explain that she's workin' at a jewelry store, here—which is Redding, because there ain't shit in Shasta. Then he describes her, and I know, just from the few words, it's her. My Cleo. My fucking wife.

"Don't let her out of your sight. I'll be there in five," I say, ignoring the fact that it takes an hour to get to Redding from the clubhouse.

"You'll have Camo drive you," he orders. I growl and open my mouth to reply. "West'll drive you and that's a fuckin' order," he says, beating me to it.

"Fine," I snap as I end the call and walk over to West.

"You're takin' me to town," I demand.

"I am?"

"Prez's orders. I need to get to where he is. A jewelry store."

Camo nods as he stands, and then I watch as he takes out

his phone. I walk behind him, adrenaline pumping through my system, so much of it that I no longer feel the effects of the alcohol I've been consuming. No, now I feel wired as fuck.

This shit with Cleo, it ends now.

I'm going to protect her, and she doesn't get a say in how I do that anymore. I don't know how she ended up practically in my backyard, or why she left the way she did—leaving all her shit back in SacTown—but I aim to get to the bottom of the whole goddamn story. *Today*.

"Who're we gonna go see?" Camo asks once we're half-way to our destination.

"My wife," I grunt. The truck swerves slightly before he rights it and continues driving.

"I didn't know you had an Old Lady."

"Married her twelve years ago. Haven't seen her in eleven, until I moved here," I admit. Just saying the words out loud makes me feel like the giant piece of shit that I am.

"What happened?" he asks before he clears his throat, mumbling, "never mind."

"Was a fuckin' stupid ass twenty-year-old back from war. Wasn't right in the head. That's what happened, more or less," I shrug.

I omit the part where I was fucked up before I even joined the Air Force and the war. It just added to my fuzzy head. Then there's Cleo, best thing that happened to me, and I sabotaged it because I was a pussy. Still am, probably, if I think hard enough about it.

"We're almost there. Your shit locked down?" Camo asks.

"Not even close," I admit.

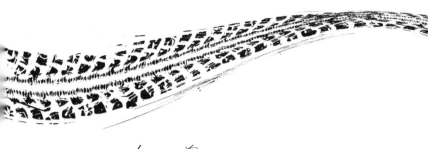

chapter seven

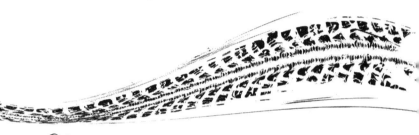

Cleo

I'm a jittery, nervous wreck. I'm tempted to call Theo more than once, but I decide against it, especially after Gina walks through the door. She looks all dazed with a small smile playing on her lips.

"What were you out doing for so long?" I snap, regretting it immediately.

"Uh, I had lunch with this guy I've been seeing," she whispers, her eyes wide.

"I'm sorry. I shouldn't have yelled," I murmur, looking down at my feet.

A customer walks in and we both drop our conversation, unable to pick it back up; between breaks and customers meandering in, we don't get to really talk again. Gina takes off at the end of her shift, leaving me to work for another thirty minutes by myself.

I try to keep busy by cleaning the glass, and I'm so thankful when my alarm rings, alerting me that it's time to close up shop. It takes me another thirty minutes to do all of my closing duties, and then I let out a sigh of relief as I set the alarm, walk out, and lock the front door behind me.

With my head down, I walk toward Lisandro's black *Jeep Cherokee*, stumbling when my eyes catch a figure leaning against it. I lift my head the rest of the way and gasp at the sight in front of me.

Paxton.

"How'd you find me?" I whisper, my feet frozen to their spot.

"Why were you hiding from me?" he counters, unmoving.

"My friend talked to me. He told me that your group is dangerous."

"He?" he asks with a growl.

"Yeah, *he*. What on earth are you into, Pax?" I ask, tipping my head to the side.

"This his ride? You stayin' with him? He keeping you hidden?" he asks, ignoring my question.

"Answer me," I say, snapping for the second time today.

Paxton doesn't answer. He closes the distance between us with two short strides and then wraps one hand around my waist, the other around the side of my neck—something he likes to do when he's trying to keep me still, I've noticed.

"Club's not a bunch of choir boys, sweetheart. Told you that already. What I wanna know is why the fuck you ran off the way you did? Why you been hiding? And why in the *fuck* didn't you *call* me?"

"It doesn't matter. I'm gone, and I'm safe now. You don't

have to worry about me anymore. I can continue to work under the table and nobody will even realize I've left; except my landlord, who will just throw all my stuff away and then rent out my fully furnished apartment to someone new," I explain.

Paxton jerks his head back as though I've physically assaulted him with my words. He then dips his chin, lowering his face to mine so that he's only a hair's breadth away from my face.

"It matters. I asked because it fuckin' matters to me, Cleo. Tell me," he demands.

"Just go, Pax. I'll call you when I have divorce papers drawn up. You can sign them and then you can be done," I sigh.

Paxton picks me up slightly and carries me toward the Jeep, pushing my back up against the door as he presses his hips against my stomach and lowers his face again to just in front of mine.

"No divorce, sweetheart. Fuck that. You're my wife, and we're gonna fix this shit. I wanna know why in the hell you ran off the way you did?" he demands.

"There's nothing to fix, Paxton. Don't be crazy," I grind out, pressing my hands against his chest and pushing him. He's rock solid and doesn't move even a millimeter.

"There's plenty of shit to fix; but good news, Clee, you're comin' back with me, and we'll have all the time in the world to fix 'em," he says with a grin.

He's crazy. Certifiable. That's the only explanation I can come up with for his demands.

"I have to go. I have to pick up Theo," I say instead of calling him out on his craziness.

"Who the fuck is Theo?" he barks in my face.

"None of your business," I snap back.

His grip on my waist and the side of my neck tighten as he growls like an animal, his chest rumbling. Having him pressed up against me—tits to hips—I can *feel* the sound.

"Think about the words you choose, Clee. Who the fuck is Theo?" he asks again.

"A friend, okay?" I shout.

"Not okay," he counters.

"He's gay, Paxton, and I've been staying with him and his lover—who is my best friend, Lisandro," I exhale.

"Why'd you run and not call me?" he asks, his voice softening a touch. I suck in a breath when he lowers his face. His nose skims my jawline and travels until his lips are at my ear. "Tell me, baby. Why didn't you call me?" he whispers, sending chills throughout my body.

Then I feel his hand slide up from my waist to just below my chest, his thumb gently grazing the side of my breast, slow and soft—so good.

"I'd been asked out by an older guy, a client of my bosses. He intimidated me, frightened me a little, and caught me off guard. He had a Spanish last name. Then a black sedan was following me around. I freaked out, called Lisandro, and told him everything. He and Theo came that night and made me pack a small bag but told me to abandon everything else. They said your club was dangerous, and being mixed up with *The Cartel*—I didn't need that. They wanted me to lay low for a while. I was going to call you and get the divorce started when I wasn't a target anymore," I say, spilling everything.

"Got friends that care about you, mm?" he whispers gently, pressing his lips to the spot just behind my earlobe.

"Lis and I have been friends since I moved back to Cali,"

I admit as my eyes roll in the back of my head.

"I'm not letting you out of my sight until I know those fucks are not going to come after you. I'm going to find out about this guy who asked you out, too. I'll keep you safe, baby, but you have to trust me to do that," he murmurs.

"You haven't cared, ever. Why should I trust you now?" I ask.

Paxton takes a step back, releasing me and leaving me surprised and cold. Then he narrows his eyes at me before he speaks. I expect his speech to be bitter, to feel the bite of his harsh words that I know are on the tip of his tongue, but he smiles and stormy eyes look so sad that it causes me to inhale a sharp breath.

"I made a lot of mistakes, Cleo. I can admit that; and one day, you'll understand why I did what I did; and maybe you might even be able to forgive me," he murmurs. "But I thought I lost you, sweetheart. I thought you were fuckin' dead. I can't lose you."

"You pushed me away," I whisper.

"No more, Cleo. I'm not pushing you away from me again—swear to fuck."

Torch

I watch the silent battle happening, her eyes giving every thought away. Then she lifts her dazzling green gaze to meet mine, shifting her focus away from my throat. I'm practically holding my breath, waiting like a fucking pussy for her to speak to me. But I can't push her. Not yet.

I want her to make the right decision. If she doesn't, I'll do it for her; but it would be better all-around if she came willingly.

"I don't want Theo and Lis to be in danger," she whispers. I grind my teeth together, pissed that she's so concerned over these men and their safety, but not her own. "Can I continue to work here?"

"This place is over an hour away from where I live," I state.

"I can't leave Lis," she murmurs.

"You don't have a choice, babe," I grunt.

Cleo's eyes narrow, and I watch as she places her hand on her hip. The move makes me grin, and I wait with anticipation for her to bring out this new attitude of hers. She never had a mouth on her before, and I have to admit, it's cute as fuck.

"Are you going to kidnap me, then?" she asks, arching a brow in question.

"Absolutely," I shrug. Her eyes widen slightly, and she shakes her head.

"I like working for Lis, and I'm good at it. I've never liked my job before, Pax. Please?" she pleads, changing tactics.

"Clee," I sigh, placing my hands on my hips and looking up to the sky.

"Don't take me away from my only friends. You want to keep me safe? Okay, fine. But don't take me away from the only people who love me," she says, placing her cool hand on my forearm.

I think about her words for a second. The only people who love her? How can these two men be the only people who love her? Cleo is the sweetest woman I have ever known. I *still* love her. I couldn't stop if I tried.

"Sweetheart," I rumble, cupping her cheek with my palm.

"Please, Pax. What you want from me, I'll give it, but don't take me away from them," she whispers.

I close my eyes for a second and then open them, focusing on her green ones. She looks pained, stressed, and on the verge of tears. I trace her bottom lip with my thumb and nod once.

"You come with me, in my bed and under my protection. You can still work here, but you'll have a man at your back at all times," I murmur.

"A man at my back?" she asks, furrowing her brow in cute confusion.

"Yeah, sweetheart. A man for protection. Me or one of my brothers will always be with you. I don't know what's going to happen with *The Cartel*, who or when they'll strike, but I'm not leaving you swinging in the fuckin' wind like a giant goddamn target, either."

"Okay, Pax," she murmurs sweetly. I can't help myself, I lower my chin and press my lips to hers.

"Let's go, sweetheart," I urge.

"This isn't my car, and I need to pick up Theo from the pharmacy," she explains.

"Camo is right over there; he'll follow us," I say, pointing to the truck that's parked across the lot.

"You're taking me *now*?" she asks with wide eyes.

"Uh, yeah. Not letting your friends talk you out of coming back with me, and I sure as fuck ain't leaving here without you. When I say that I'm protecting you, Clee, it means *I'm* fuckin' protecting you."

She trembles beneath my fingertips, her body visibly shaking, but I can't control my anger. She isn't fucking getting it. This shit, it's not a goddamn game. *The Cartel* is not a fuckin' joke, and the shit they would do to her, it would ruin her. My sweet wife would never recover.

"Give me your keys. Camo will follow," I inform her.

Holding out my hand, I wait for her to slip the keys into my palm while I call Camo and let him know to stay on my tail. I'm not as drunk as I was a couple hours ago, so I feel confident enough to drive to wherever Cleo needs to go.

I open the passenger side for her and watch as she hesitantly slides inside. I jog around to the driver's side and start the engine, then she gives me directions on which pharmacy to pick up her friend. I'm still not quite sure about their dynamic, but because these guys have dicks, I don't like it. I don't give a fuck if she says they're gay. They have cocks, and she's been livin' with them. That shit stops now.

I pull the Jeep into the parking lot and watch as the door to the pharmacy opens. A tall man walks our way. He's got brown hair, and he's muscular—not the geeky looking nerd that I had anticipated. He eyes me through the windshield, and I watch his jaw harden as it clenches.

Opening my door, I get out of the car, leaving Cleo inside, not bothering to say anything to her. I make my way toward the guy that looks like he could give me a good run for my money in a fight. I'd still win, but he'd give me a workout.

"So, you found her," he grunts.

"Thought she was dead, the way you left her place."

"Good, that's the way it was supposed to look," he shrugs.

"Should punch you for that. My wife. You made me believe my wife was fuckin' kidnapped or dead," I grind out.

"The wife you haven't given much of a shit about in over a decade? Forgive me if I don't give a flying fuck how you felt,"

76

he barks, delivering his blow.

"I'm here now," I grunt.

"Why is that, Paxton?" he asks, crossing his arms over his chest.

"Doesn't matter. I don't have to explain shit to you. I'm taking her with me, and I'm going to protect her. That's all you need to know," I state, widening my legs and tipping my head down a notch. I have about two inches on this guy.

"Doesn't work like that, partner," he rumbles.

"She's agreed, and she's comin'. It definitely does work like that, *partner*," I hiss.

"Cleo?" he calls out. His eyes stay glued to mine.

"I don't want anything to happen to you and Lis. I'm going with Paxton, but I'm still going to work at the store," she calls out.

"You don't have to go with him, Clee. Nothing's going to happen to us or you. I'll make sure of that," he calls out. I can't hold back my snort. His eyes narrow on mine and his jaw ticks, but he doesn't say a word.

"I'll be okay, Theo. I promise," she says gently.

"You call me and I'm there, do you understand? I don't give a fuck about *Billy-Badass* here. I only care about you," he growls.

Cleo slips in front of me and wraps her arms around his middle, hugging him and whispering something to him. I can't hear her as blood rushes through my ears at the sight of her touching another man. I clench my fists and try to calm down. Thankfully, two seconds before I pummel the fuck out of this dude, she takes a step away from him.

"I have to pick up a few things from Theo and Lis', then we can go," she says, tipping her head back to look at me.

I wrap my hand around her waist and give it a squeeze before dipping my chin down to look into her eyes.

"Yeah, all right, sweetheart," I murmur.

She looks tired, stressed, and on the verge of turning into a sobbing mess. I don't do crying bitches. In fact, the last time I held a woman when she cried, it was her. Cleo unloaded her life story on me when we were dating, the defining moment when I knew I needed to make her mine, and she cried. I held her and comforted her, back when I had a fucking heart.

chapter eight

Cleo

I never thought that I would ever, and I mean *ever*, be sandwiched between two big ass, albeit hot as shit, bikers. Yet, here I am, sitting directly between them, in a single cab pickup truck, on my way to what Paxton called his *clubhouse*.

"You sure you don't wanna take her somewhere else?" the man Paxton calls *Camo* asks.

"Nope. Got a room and a bed there—kitchen, tequila and protection," Paxton rumbles.

I glance up at him to see that he's staring straight ahead of me and at the window.

"She ain't in the life, brother," he informs.

"She's also sitting right here," I snap, looking up to the handsome, young, bearded man.

"Sorry, babe," he chuckles, grinning down at me before

he turns back to the road.

The rest of the ride is silent. It does nothing to calm my nerves about going to this mysterious clubhouse of Paxton's. I have zero clue what to expect, just that Theo warned that the group was dangerous.

When I was packing my small bag to leave, he gave me a long hug and whispered to call if anything happened, if I needed him at all, and he'd come get me. He told me to watch out for myself and try to stay out of sight in general. He did nothing but make me even more nervous.

The pickup pulls up to a gate, and without touching a button or rolling his window down, it opens and Camo continues to drive straight through, parking the pickup.

My eyes widen when I take in the big, plain, solid stone building. It looks like nothing. It's all brick with a metal roof. To the left is a huge metal building that looks like a warehouse, storage, or shop area—I'm not quite sure what it is, but it's big.

"C'mon, babe. I have a killer fuckin' headache," Paxton grunts.

I didn't even realize he'd opened the door. He's now standing outside, holding his hand out for me. I was taking in my surroundings and not paying attention at all. He's got my bag dangling from his fingers, and his light blue eyes are looking at me with nothing but impatience in them.

I slide out of the pickup as quickly as I can and step onto the gravel and dirt as I wait for him to close the door behind me. His hand presses against my lower back, and I fight the smile that's threatening to form on my lips from his gentle touch.

We walk inside of the building, and my smile dies. It's

only around seven in the evening, but there is loud music playing, men drinking or playing pool, and smoke fills the air. Even still, that isn't what kills my smile. It's the women. They're either naked or practically naked. Some are walking around, a couple perched on men's laps, and one is on her knees in front of a man lounging in a chair. My eyes widen and my feet refuse to move.

"C'mon, Cleo," Paxton practically growls, pressing his hand a little harder to my back and propelling me forward.

This.

This is his *clubhouse*?

This is where he expects me to *live*?

Where *he* lives?

The further into the room we walk, the sicker I feel. My stomach is tied up in knots, and I can feel the bile rising in my throat.

The women—holy shit, the women. This is where my husband has been for the past decade? No wonder he hasn't given a shit about me, where I am or what I'm doing. He's had his pick of skinny, young women every night of the week.

Why would he want me?

Paxton pushes me into a room, and I glance around. It's a plain room, with a dresser, a bed, a nightstand and a closet. It's nothing special at all, but it's decently clean, which was more than I expected from the activities happening in the main room.

"I'm going to call Theo. This isn't going to work," I announce as I turn around to face him.

Paxton flips the lock closed and lifts his eyes to look at me.

"Why's that?" he asks, arching a brow.

"I can't live here, Pax. I didn't know this is the way it was going to be. Protection or not, I'll just take my chances with Lisandro and Theo," I try to explain.

"Can't let you do that, sweetheart," he murmurs gently. His tone is actually very sweet.

"You can't really expect me to live here," I whisper.

"Get some sleep. You work tomorrow?" he asks, ignoring my question.

"No, I don't."

"Good. Lock up behind me. I have a key," he barks before he turns, walks out of the room, and slams the door behind him.

"*What the hell?*" I whisper as I lock the door.

I try not to think about where I am, what's happening just a few feet away from me, or the fact that Paxton just left me to go to where all the action is. Instead, I change into my soft, cotton, bubblegum pink sleep shorts and tank before I crawl between his sheets. I close my eyes and cringe, trying not to think about the last time these sheets were laundered or what has been done on them.

Rolling to my back, I look up at the ceiling and am unable to stop the tears from rolling down the corners of my eyes to my temples, and then the pillow beneath my head.

This is my life.

Paxton has had a hold on me since the day I met him at eighteen years old. He's had a hold that I fear will never subside. He left me for over a decade, and I never moved on. I tried, in my own way, but I never let go of the hope that he would come back to me. Then he came back, he brought a mess of danger when he did, and here I am, completely dependent on him, once again.

I hate it, and I hate myself for allowing it. I didn't fight him, not really, and he knows I won't. Like the fool that I am, I still love him. I probably always will.

He's my weakness, my Achilles' heel—the one person that I always forgive; that I always let walk all over me; and that I always seek out.

He was the one person, aside from my Gram, who showed me affection, and who took care of me when not even my parents did. He held me when I cried and told him about my childhood; he held me when I cried about my Gram passing. He's always felt, right, good, and comforting in times when I hadn't ever felt that way before.

I roll over to my side and close my eyes, hoping and praying that eventually my exhaustion will take over and I'll fall asleep in this strange place, in this strange bed, and all alone.

Torch

I shouldn't leave Cleo alone in my room, but I do. I can't be with her right now. The look in her eyes when she realized where I live, and undoubtedly what and who I've been doing the past eleven years, was too fucking much for me to take. I decide to get some green and some tequila to relax.

"Got any green?" I ask Soar as soon as I walk into the bar.

"Always for you, brother," he chuckles as he pulls out a bag and hands it to me.

"Pre-rolled, nice," I comment.

"Know you don't want to waste your time when you're feelin' the urge to smoke," he grins.

"For someone who acts like he's not paying attention, you do, don't you?" I ask him.

Soar always appears to be high as a kite. I don't doubt that he usually is, I just think that he's way more aware of his surroundings than he lets on. Most of his incapacitated state is nothing but a pure act.

"Brother, I've been getting drunk and high since before puberty. It's when I'm sober that I got problems," he chuckles as he reaches for the little brunette I sent crying from my room a couple weeks ago.

She looks at me from beneath her lashes and gives me a small smile then presses her small tits against Soar and whispers something in his ear.

"You down for that?" he asks with wide eyes. She grins with a nod.

"Honey here wants us both to fuck her; she wants to know if you're down with that, brother?" Soar asks with a chuckle.

I blink at his words. *Huh*, her name is actually *Honey*—that has never happened to me before.

"Not tonight, Honey," I murmur, touching her nose with the tip of my finger.

"C'mon, Honey. It's just you and me tonight, babe," Soar says as he slides her off of his lap to stand up.

I look at her. *Honey*. Fuck, I didn't even know her name, and I don't give a shit, either. Not even now. I do find it interesting that I called her by her name. That's probably another reason why she started attaching her fuckin' self to me.

She walks up to me and wraps her hand around my bicep as she stands on her toes and leans into me.

"We're cool, right?" she asks on a whisper, her bottom lip pushed out into a pout.

"Yeah, Honey. It's all good," I murmur.

"Miss you and your cock. Anytime you want me, Torch, I'm ready for all you want," she grins before she turns around and walks up to Soar's side.

I watch as they leave, her bare ass moving with each step she takes. I take a joint out of the bag Soar gave me and I put it to my lips, lighting it as I continue to watch Honey walk away from me. Her big eyes, the way she looked so hopeful, and the way she offered to share her body and her ass with me spells trouble. It's the reason I typically don't keep girls around me for too long. *Fuck.*

Making my way toward the bar, I decide to order a few beers instead of the tequila I had originally planned on for the evening. I have Cleo locked up in my room. I don't want to get completely plastered. If I do, I'll probably try to fuck her. Knowing her, even if she doesn't want it, she'll probably let me.

"Wife, huh?" Texas asks as he sidles up next to me.

"Yeah, wife," I murmur, taking a pull from my beer.

"She's a pretty little thing, Torch."

"Fuckin' beautiful," I admit, thinking about her lush, curvy body, her dark red hair, and her stunning, warm, green eyes.

"She's up there alone, and you're down here, though," he observes as I take a hit.

"Yup."

"So she's your wife, but is she your Old Lady?" he asks, arching a brow in question.

"Nope."

"Not giving me more on this, are ya?" he asks with a chuckle.

"With *The Cartel* shit going down, I'm just trying to keep her safe, that's all."

"Liar," he laughs as he stands up and walks away from me.

I would call him out, fight with him for calling me a liar, but he's not wrong. I *am* a liar. When I thought she was gone, stolen or murdered, all I could think about was how I was married to this gorgeous woman, and all of the time I lost running from her, from us, all because of my own fucked up issues. None of it, not a single part of me leavin' her, was her fault; and yet, I never told her that.

I need to make it right, and maybe have her again, if she'd let me back in.

I wouldn't deserve her if she even gave me half a chance.

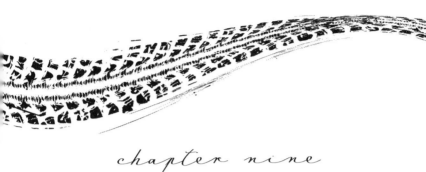

chapter nine

Cleo

A warm body presses against mine, and an equally as warm hand wraps around my breast from the outside of my shirt. Then I feel a hard length press between the cheeks of my ass, along with a deep moan, as fingers grip my breast a bit tighter.

My entire body freezes, and I try to wiggle out of the grasp, but the arm around me tightens even more as soft lips graze my neck.

"You're so fuckin' soft and sweet, Cleo," Paxton whispers against my skin. I relax, only slightly, now that I know it's him.

"Pax," I breathe as his hand squeezes my breast and then travels down my stomach to the waistband of my shorts.

I inhale sharply when his fingers dip below the band and

caress my lower abdomen. With each sweep of his fingers, he dips lower and lower, until he reaches the top of my panties.

"Missed you, sweetheart," he whispers, pressing his mouth against my shoulder and sweeping his tongue out to touch my skin.

My entire body shakes beneath his touch, and my back arches when his finger grazes my clit. It's been so long since I've been touched, and even longer since I felt the only touch I've wanted—*his.*

"We shouldn't be doing this," I sigh as I lift my arm and wrap it around the back of his neck, my fingers diving into his short hair.

"That's where you're wrong, Clee. This is exactly what we should be doing," he murmurs as his fingers slide through my center before two fill me.

I gasp, my body jerking with his movement, and I feel his chest rumble against my back as he starts to pump in and out of my pussy. I feel a light sheen of sweat cover my body as my hips involuntarily meet his thrusting fingers.

Paxton's palm presses against my clit, and I can't stop myself from grinding against it, feeling him all around and inside of me, years of dreams coming to reality.

I pinch my eyes closed tightly as my body starts to shake, and I know that I'm close—so close to my climax that if he stops, I'm going to scream and cry simultaneously.

"Come, sweetheart. *Fuck, baby,* come all over my hand," Paxton whispers against my ear, and I do.

I completely shatter in his hold. My entire body freezing as I let out a squeak and then a long moan. I sag against him. He continues to pump his fingers in and out of me a few more times before he removes himself from beneath my pajamas.

A wave of guilt, disgrace, and remorse washes over me the instant my breathing becomes normal and I'm back to myself. How could I let this happen? After everything he's done to me, and after the life he's obviously been living, I'm allowing him to touch me. What is wrong with me?

"Not askin' you to ride my dick yet, Cleo. You don't have to freak out," Paxton hisses. I feel the bed dip behind me as he climbs off.

I roll over and place my hands under my cheek, watching him from behind. He's wearing only black boxer briefs, but, shit, his back is so wide, and he has muscles there that I've only seen in pictures. He also has a tattoo that covers his entire back. It matches the back of his vest, and I wonder if every single member of his gang has it as well.

"We shouldn't have done that," I whisper.

"Why?" he asks, turning to face me as he pulls up a pair of jeans over his hips. "We're married, Clee, or did you forget that? I sure as fuck didn't. I told you that shit between us was going to change. Mean that, babe."

"And this change you've decided to make, this is all because you thought I was kidnapped or dead or whatever?"

"Well, can't say I didn't want back in there the second I watched you walk up your stairs the first night I went to your house, sweetheart. You're absolutely the prettiest fuckin' thing I've ever seen, at eighteen and at thirty," he says, as if it's supposed to make the fact that he only wanted me when he thought he lost me all okay.

He never wanted me when he could have had me, only when he thought he couldn't. My heart aches with the truth; at the fact that I'm not enough for him. Obviously, I never have been. Then, out of the blue, I'm supposed to just accept whatever he decides to give me, because he's had a change of heart for this moment. What happens in six months when I'm an old-hat?

"How many women have you been with since you left me?" I ask.

Paxton's jaw clenches and his whole body stills at my question.

"Don't matter. Not anymore." He shrugs, but his face is still hard, his eyes narrowed to slits and focused on me.

"I'm your wife, right?" I ask. "I think it's safe to say that you've been with more than I would ever care to know. So why would you want to settle down now? Just because you want what you can't have? No way. That doesn't work for me, Paxton. You had me. You had all of me once, and you threw me away. I don't want to go through that again," I whisper.

"Not planning on throwing you away anytime soon, sweetheart. You *are* my wife, and I'm willing to shovel some shit, because I bought that, baby. But you gotta meet me halfway," he murmurs, looking down at me, unmoving from where he's been standing at the side of the bed.

"Why'd you leave me? Why'd you walk away the way you did, knowing that I had nobody but you? I was completely alone, Pax, and you just left. Forget what you did to me before you did that—why did you leave?" I practically beg as tears fill my eyes.

"It doesn't matter; just know that I had to," he grunts.

"It matters, Pax. To me, it matters," I whisper.

"I was messed up, Cleo. I wasn't right in the head, and I was so not right that I knew I would only hurt you, over and over again. And you, you're so fuckin' good and sweet, you would have just taken it, over and over. You proved that

90

shit when you were willing to forget the way I hurt you so quickly."

"You walked away from me with no explanation because I *loved* you?" I ask in surprise.

"Doesn't matter now. It's over. Now we move on," he murmurs as he sinks his knee into the bed and crawls toward me.

"It matters to me, Paxton. You abandoned me for eleven years. I loved you more than anything in this world, and you just walked away from me. I was young, and I was so lost, and you didn't give a shit. I can't trust anything you tell me, not a single word," I whisper.

"I'll fix it, Cleo. Swear, baby I'll fix it all," he states as his hand lifts to cup my cheek.

"You can't just fix it, not by telling me to just forget it and move on. That's not how it works," I say, my lips trembling as tears stream down my cheeks.

"Tell me, then. Tell me how to fix this," he mutters.

"I don't know, but it's not by just pretending it never happened. It happened. You left me and you didn't care where I was, if I had money or food or a place to live. You didn't care about me at all. You joined this group, and you had these people to lean on while you drank, and did drugs, and had sex with whoever those girls downstairs are. Not once did I cross your mind, in eleven years, not once—did I?"

"Not once, Cleo," he admits with a shake of his head. "But millions of times. Every minute of every fuckin' day, I thought about you. I don't sleep because my mind is filled with visions of you, and nightmares from the desert, both of you fucking haunt me."

"Why didn't you look for me, then? If you were so consumed with me, why wait so many years?" I ask on a sob.

"Was fucked up in the head, baby. By the time I got my shit straightened out enough that I could contact you, it'd been years. Honest to fuck, thought you'd moved on, and I didn't want to disrupt your new life," he explains.

"I need time to think," I whisper, moving my head to the side and out of his hold.

"Sweetheart," he murmurs.

I press my lips together and look at the sheets, the place where he was lying next to me just a few minutes ago. I breathe in and out of my nose, trying to keep from crying more. I know that he was probably very messed up. He went to war, he saw horrific things, but I can't let that be a viable excuse and just accept his abandonment for over a freaking decade. Not just a few weeks, or months, or even years.

He was gone from me for *eleven* years.

He *didn't* know if I was happy. He didn't know *anything*.

And I don't think that he really cared, not really. Sure, it probably kept him up at night—the never knowing—but it didn't bother him enough to ever find me, not until he thought that I was in real danger.

I don't know where we go from here, but I do know that we don't start over from scratch; that I don't just forget everything that he did, and the way he did it. I can't pretend none of the past happened, especially the way it did.

Torch

I slide off of the bed and look at her. My Cleo, my wife. She's ignoring me, refusing to look at me, and pressing her lips together, probably to keep from crying. I halfway want her to scream at me, and the other half wants her to just forgive me and agree to start over, as if the past eleven years had never happened.

I don't know her, anyway—the woman she is—and she doesn't know the man I've become. No matter what, we're going to have to learn a whole hell of a lot about each other as it is.

"Shower's across the hall. They're shared here. There's a full kitchen, and when you're ready, you can come in there. If there's any food, you can eat that, or I can take you out for breakfast," I inform her. She jerks her head in a slight nod.

I walk away from her again. I always seem to be walking away from her. I make my way to the kitchen and see Honey leaning against the counter, a coffee mug in her hand.

"Hey, Torch," she whispers, lifting her eyes and giving me a smile. I jerk my chin as my greeting and walk over to the pot to pour my own coffee.

"Soar said that girl you brought in was your wife," she murmurs, biting her bottom lip.

"She is," I grunt as I take a sip of coffee, glancing at her over the rim.

Honey looks unsure—shy. If I didn't know the kind of woman she was, I might believe her act. She's pretending to be what she thinks I want. Cleo came in at my side, her sexy little skirt and her cardigan covering her arms, her fantastic tits highlighted by her tight undershirt, but not overly so. Then there's Clee's sexy as fuck hair—natural, thick curls, and the most gorgeous deep red I've ever seen. No woman on earth holds a candle to Cleo.

"I—she's really pretty," she whispers.

"Know that, Honey. One of the reason's I married her," I murmur gently.

"I—I promise I won't tell her anything about us," she offers with a furrowed brow.

"Know you won't, 'cause whore's aren't allowed to speak to Old Ladies, so it won't be a problem, now will it?" I ask, arching a brow.

"'Course not," she whispers before she sets her cup down and scurries out of the kitchen.

"You married me for my looks, and you were with that girl. By the stars in her eyes, not too long ago," Cleo's voice says harshly, filling the room.

I turn around to face her and expect to see her angry gaze focused on me, but instead I see nothing but pain etched into her features.

"Cleo," I whisper.

I close the distance between us and wrap my hand around hers, tugging her into my chest before I slide my other hand around her waist to keep her close to me.

"Then you brought me here to shove it in my face?" she asks, pain now filling her voice as well.

"Of course, I didn't do that, sweetheart," I murmur.

"I want to go back to Lis and Theo. They love me and they'll watch out for me. I don't want to be here," she whispers as tears start to fall from her eyes.

"Can't let that happen, baby."

"Why? You obviously don't care about me. Just let me go," she urges.

"Clee, baby, I care. Trust me, I care," I say, my own voice sounding husky with emotion.

"Fuck you," she hisses. My head rears back as though she's

physically hit me. "Fuck you. Fuck you. *Fuck you.*" She yells as her little fists beat on my chest.

I let her. Christ, do I let her. This is nothing compared to what I deserve from her. Tears continue to fall down her cheeks, her body wracks with sobs, and she physically wears herself out. I pull her into me and just hold her as she continues to cry. Goddamn it, I fucked her up more than I thought I had—more than I imagined I could. My selfishness, my need to shield her from myself, fucked with her.

"There have been two men since you, Paxton. One used me, and the other I was in a relationship with. He loved me, but you were always there. I couldn't love anyone because of you," she whispers. I hold her a little tighter.

Fuck, I feel rage that she's been with anybody else. Once, I was the only man who knew her body.

That feeling quickly fades. I hadn't thought she'd been celibate. Eleven years is a long fuckin' time. Now, I feel sadness and guilt. I'd decided that she'd moved on with her life but she hadn't, not even a little, and a man took advantage of her because of it.

"Who used you, Clee?" I ask as my fingers comb through her hair.

"Doesn't matter," she sniffles.

"It matters, sweetheart. It matters to me. Any man that hurts my sweet, innocent, shy wife fuckin' matters."

"Even you?" she asks, tipping her head back. I bury my fingers in her hair and hold onto the soft strands as I look into her warm, green eyes.

"Yeah, baby, even me," I whisper tipping my lips into a grin.

"It was my boss, Stephenson Voight, when I first started

working for him," she shrugs.

"He'll pay for that," I grunt.

"No, it's been years Paxton. I just want to forget it ever happened; forget that I was ever so naïve."

"Yeah, what else you gonna try and forget about in your past?" I ask, narrowing my eyes.

"Him I can forget. It was once and I was hurting and it meant nothing. I could never forget even a moment I had with you. You were *everything*," she whispers, making me feel like an even bigger asshole, something I didn't think was possible at this point.

Fuck. I've fucking hurt her in a way where I don't know if I can fix it. But dammit, I'm gonna try.

"C'mon, sweetheart. Let's get some food in you," I murmur.

"Paxton," she sighs.

"We ain't fixing our problems in a couple conversations. You have to eat, and I'm starved. We'll go, get some food at this good little diner, and maybe talk a little more, maybe just about nothing much at all. But we need food and fresh air, no matter what way you look at it."

"Okay," she nods, giving me a slight smile. It feels like a huge victory.

chapter ten

Cleo

I look down at the giant egg white omelet, hash browns, fruit salad and toast that the waitress just set down in front of me. It could feed about five men, and there's no way in hell I can eat even a quarter of it by myself.

"Looks good; but egg whites, babe?" Paxton asks as his lips curl in disgust.

"Can't fit into my clothes if I eat the real stuff, Pax," I explain. He shakes his head but looks down at his plate and doesn't say a word. "What?" I ask.

"Nothin'," he snorts.

"No, tell me, what?"

I cut some of my omelet and stab it with my fork before I slide it between my lips. I almost moan, it's so good, the swiss cheese and ham perfectly melted together.

"Hate it when bitches talk about their weight. That's all. Like *you* need to watch your figure? You look better now than you did twelve years ago," he mutters. I look up at him, widening my eyes.

"First off, I don't want to think about how many *bitches* have complained to you about their weight. Secondly, I know for a fact I couldn't fit past my calves into my jeans from twelve years ago. So, yeah, I have to watch my weight. Aside from all of that, I like to be healthy, or healthy-*ish*."

"You think I'm only talking about bitches I fuck? Babe, been around Old Ladies and heard them complain, heard them talk about working out and diets and all kinds of shit. Put that shit about me being with whores out of your mind, because I'm not gonna shove that shit in your face. I'm an asshole, but even *I'm* not that big of an asshole. You looked fuckin' great back then, Clee, and that's because you looked like an eighteen-year-old girl. I was into eighteen-year-old girls when I was twenty. But would make me a perv if I was into eighteen-year-old girls now that I'm thirty-two. I like tits, ass, thighs, hips, and long red hair. Lucky for me, you got it all, and all of it I fuckin' like."

With my fork suspended in the air, I stare at him, slack jawed. I stare at him while my brain processes everything he's just said to me. The only thing I can think about is how he likes everything I've got; and while I should be focusing on other pieces of that speech, the self-conscious girl inside of me is beaming and excited.

Lucky for me, you got it all, and all of it I fuckin' like.

"Paxton," I whisper.

"Not fuckin' with you, sweetheart. Fucked up bad back then, and I'll tell you about everything I've been through one day, and maybe you can find it in your heart to forgive me for bein' so fuckin' young and so fuckin' dumb," he mutters, his eyes looking straight into mine, never wavering.

Maybe I only want to see the truth in them, but I see it, and I want to know what demons hide behind his gaze. They look like quite a burden. I wanted so badly to be his partner, to share in his burdens and his joys, but he shut me out and abandoned me before I even had the chance.

"You swear you'll tell me this time?" I ask, biting the corner of my lip.

"Swear to fuck," he murmurs.

"I'm not making any promises on the future or anything, but I want to know."

"Fair enough," he whispers with a nod before he cuts a piece of his chicken fried steak and eats it.

I turn back to my food as well, but I'm only able to take a couple more bites, my appetite lost as I start remembering the past.

"Clee," Paxton calls. His voice takes me away from my thoughts, and I am forced to look up at him. "Think we can move on from the past, and when we do, swear to Christ, you'll be happy with me."

"That's a lot to promise a girl, Pax," I murmur.

"Not a kid anymore, babe. Ready to get this shit done and over with, and I'm ready to move the fuck on," he announces.

"What does moving on look like, then?" I ask, narrowing my eyes slightly, my breakfast now forgotten.

"Looks like me and you—you on the back of my bike, bein' my Old Lady and poppin' out those coupla kids you always wanted," he grunts.

"You're crazy," I whisper.

"Watch what you say. You ain't seen my brand of crazy yet, Clee," he rumbles.

"Seriously, you're fucking insane if you think that's what's going to happen between us. Aside from the fact that I only understand about three-quarters of what you just said, how do you know I still want kids? And who the hell says that I'm going to be anywhere near your motorcycle or okay with you being my children's father?" I rant.

"I'm your husband, so I'm pretty fuckin' certain it'll be my kids in your belly," he barks, his voice rising in the diner.

"We will never work, Paxton—not for a freaking minute. There's too much hurt between us. I'm glad you like the way I look, but you don't *know* me anymore, and I never knew *you*."

"The first time I went overseas, when I came back to you, I know I said some shit about my buddies' girls leaving them, and they did; but that's not what I was so fucked up about, Cleo. It was only a portion of my problem. I watched my best friend over there get blown to fuckin' pieces, baby. Other guys died, too, but he was my best friend. We went through basic together, went through school together—we were brothers, babe, and he fucking blew up into a million pieces right in front of me. They sent him home in goddamn pieces, Cleo."

Tears stream down my face at his words, at the obvious pain he still feels just speaking about his friend. I imagine his nightmares are even more painful. I reach across the table and place my hands over his wrist giving him a squeeze.

"You could have told me all of that back then. I was prepared for it, Pax. I'd taken classes and gone to meetings on how to help you acclimate back to your life here at home," I whisper.

"Love that you were prepared, Cleo; love that you thought

you were, at least. But, honest to fuck, sweetheart, you could not prepare yourself for the shit I was dealing with. Then I went back less than a year later and it happened all over again. I got out after eight years, halfway to retirement, and I'd been to that desert hell four times. I couldn't do it again. I was lost—an alcoholic addicted to pain killers and sleeping pills. I wouldn't have just hurt you, Cleo. I would have destroyed you."

"I would have stayed right by your side, and you don't know that because you wouldn't let me try to be there for you," I whisper as more tears fill my vision.

"Trust me. Fuckin' hell, baby, *trust* me when I tell you that me leaving was the best thing for you back in the day," he announces as he stands up.

I watch as he throws some money on the table and then holds out his palm for me. I slip mine inside as we walk out of the little diner and toward his vehicle. It's like a pickup, as in it has a bed, but it's low, like a car, and it's old, seventies old. It seems like he's fixed it up, because it isn't falling apart and the paint is dark blue and shiny new, nothing like my oxidized maroon car.

"What kind of car is this?" I ask, turning around to face him. I watch as his face softens and he smiles down at me.

"It's a nineteen-seventy-three *Ford Ranchero*," he murmurs.

"It's like a truck, but it's not," I point out. His smile widens.

"Was my daddy's. Found it in an old barn on some property he owned and left to me after he died," he shrugs.

I look at him, opening my mouth to say something, but he's right there in front of me. His hands cup my cheeks as he lowers his head, and his lips brush mine, quieting me as his

101

tongue fills my mouth. I accept his kiss, my body warming and going hot as he continues to devour my mouth. I slide my hands around his sides, beneath his vest, and fist the fabric of his t-shirt at his lower back.

We move, he walks forward, forcing me to back up until my ass hits the door to his car. He presses his hips against my belly, his length pressing into me.

My entire body shivers, and I know he's felt it when he groans into my mouth. Then he slowly pulls away from me so that we can breathe, and his forehead rests against my own, his nose touching mine and his breath fanning my face.

"This is who we are, sweetheart. End of the day, this is what's important," he mutters.

"What? Because we enjoy kissing each other?" I ask breathily.

"No, baby. I could kiss a million women, could even like it a fuck've a lot, but not one of them would feel the way it does when I kiss those pretty lips of yours."

"I want to know you, Paxton. I want to know about your childhood, your past, and the last eleven years. I want it all from you," I admit, giving myself whiplash.

I want him and to know about him, but it feels like it's all going just as fast as it did when I was eighteen. That scares the shit out of me at the same time.

He releases me and takes a step back, his eyes focused on mine. He doesn't, or can't, hide the pain that slices through his features before he arranges himself so that it's hidden again.

"You're the only one that *does* know me, Clee. You'll learn more as time goes, but what you know is more than anybody else in my life," he says.

"If you really want there to be an us, I have to be able to

trust you, Paxton. In order to trust you, I need you to be open and honest with me. I'm not the starry-eyed girl I was, willing to jump into anything head first. I have to know that I won't be abandoned again," I whisper, my eyes connecting with his.

"No guarantees in life, sweetheart. This could go south, for you or for me. You could abandon me, too, you know."

"I could, but we both know that I'm not that kind of person," I say, watching as he flinches with my well delivered blow.

"When do you work again?" he asks, changing the subject.

"Tomorrow. I have to be there at ten," I state.

"Let's go," he grunts, walking over to the passenger side. Opening the car door, he waits for me to slide inside.

I let him have his silence and allow the conversation we were having to come to an abrupt end. He probably had no idea the adult version of me wasn't going to be exactly like the girl I was. I've been hurt, and he's the main person who hurt me.

I've had years to think about those hurts, and it's going to take more than a few empty promises to be anything other than two people who are married but estranged.

Torch

I glance at her, sitting next to me as I drive us back to the clubhouse. *Fuck.* I fucked her up. She's still naïve, innocent, and shy, but there's a piece of her spirit that's been broken; her trust in anyone, too. I did that, just me, and I hate myself a little more for it.

I don't know how to fix it, though, and I'm sure as fuck not going to be an open book for her. She doesn't need to know about my entire childhood, about the horrors I've seen in the military, or a damn thing I've done or could do for my club. I don't want to erase that little bit of innocence she so obviously still has inside of her. I love that part of her. I always have.

"Got some shit to do today. Stay in my room," I say as I pull up to the clubhouse gate.

"You're leaving me alone?" she asks with wide eyes.

"Yeah, but you'll be safe in there. Just stay away from everyone."

"Why?" she breathes. Goddamn, it's so fuckin' sexy.

I throw the *Ranchero* in park and turn to face her.

"You don't have a brand, babe, which means someone could think you're fair game. I'm still new here, and though I know all the brothers, I don't know all of them *real* well—not like my brothers in Idaho. That bein' said, I don't know who would take it upon themselves to take you and not give much of a shit if you say no. You're not claimed, so it's a possibility," I explain.

"Are you telling me that someone in there might *rape* me? And what's a brand?" she asks. I start to get annoyed, forgetting that she's never been a part of this life.

"You aren't branded with a tattoo of my name, which means you're not claimed and you're fair game," I explain.

"So, you're actually saying that unless I have your name *permanently tattooed* onto my body, your *brothers* think that they can rape me?" she says, sneering.

"That's the life, babe," I shrug.

"I'm not comfortable being here without you, Paxton. Can't you just take me with you?" she asks, biting her plump bottom lip.

"Sorry, sweetheart, can't take you," I say. I *am* sorry. She looks fuckin' terrified.

"Paxton," she whispers with a trembling lip.

"I'll lock you in my room," I shrug.

I step out of the front seat and walk over to her side, helping her out. She looks up at me with teary eyes, and though they pull at my heartstrings, I'm going on club business and she can't come, even if I wanted her to.

Plus, this is something she's going to have to get used to—my life, my club, and my brothers. I don't think anyone here would hurt her, but the fact is that I don't know all of them that well.

I take her to my room, telling her that I'll be back in a bit before locking her inside. I can't look at the way her lips tremble, the way her eyes are scared and wide. I have shit to do, and I need to get going on it. On my way out of the clubhouse, I run into Camo.

"Hey, brother, Cleo's locked up in my room. Here's my key. She need anything, can you handle her?" I ask.

"Sure, I'll be around for a while."

"She isn't branded," I murmur.

"Got an Old Lady," he grunts.

"Know that, trust you, that's why I'm talking to you. I haven't claimed her, and I don't know all the brothers well enough to know if she'll be safe…"

"I got you, brother. I'll take care of her," he offers.

"She get's hurt…" I trail off.

"No problem. I got sisters and a woman. Not into allowing

105

women to get hurt on my watch," he grins.

"Thanks, brother."

I leave Cleo in Camo's care and hope that she'll be all right while I'm gone. I hope it isn't too long, but it's club business, and it could very well take the rest of the evening.

chapter eleven

Cleo

Istare at the closed door, wondering not for the first time, what in the actual hell I'm doing here. I feel like this is some alternate universe, and nothing makes sense. Not a single damn thing. Brandings, tattoos, brothers, rape, and whores, it's all a completely different language to me.

I knew after seeing Paxton for the first time in years, dressed in faded jeans and leather, that he was different, but I didn't expect him to be *this* different. It just further reiterates the fact that I don't *know* him.

There's a knock on the bedroom door, and I jump, afraid to walk over to it. Then it slowly opens. I suck in a breath when I see the man who drove Paxton and me here from Redding standing in the doorway. He's tall, with a full beard, and shaggy hair. He's young, but no less good looking as he takes me in, then grins, showing off his straight white teeth.

"Torch said he warned you, but it's all good. I got an Old Lady, she'll be here in a few. Thought maybe you'd like a drink and to relax a bit," he offers with a shrug.

"Umm."

"Won't hurt you, Cleo. Won't let anybody else hurt you, either," he says gently.

"Who's Torch?" I ask with confusion.

"Your man," he murmurs, lifting a brow.

"You mean Paxton?"

"If that's his name, then yeah. Gotta tell ya, babe, I only know him as Torch," he states. "It's his road name."

"I don't understand any of this," I whisper.

"Come down to the bar, have a drink, and the women will explain," he says.

"What women?" I ask, scrunching my nose.

"Figured you had no fuckin' clue about the life, so I called my Old Lady and had her gather up some of the others. They can tell you about it," he offers.

I tentatively take a step toward him and he slides to the side to let me walk through door. Together, we walk to the bar, and he tells the man behind it to grab me whatever I want. I look around at the shelves and see a bunch of tequila and whiskey, so I decide to ask for a beer, thinking they won't have a white riesling wine like I'm used to when I drink with Lisandro and Theo.

Taking the bottle of beer from the man behind the bar top, I follow Camo, over to an empty table.

I suck in a breath when a mountain of a man walks up beside us and sits down across from me. Camo doesn't leave me, and I'm grateful. Maxfield, from the jewelry store, stares at me. He's intimidating. He's big, and the way he's watching me makes me feel as though he can see through me.

"Don't know much about Torch, but not sure you do either, do you?" he mutters, lifting a brow as he leans back in his chair.

"I thought I knew him, once," I admit, looking down at my beer bottle as I tug at the corner of the label.

"You probably know more than anybody," he murmurs.

"I don't know anything about his life, about this world he lives in," I say with a wave of my hand.

"Only thing I can do is tell you about the life of the club, not his personal life. Don't know much about the shit he's been through, but I can tell you about the club life," Maxfield offers.

"What does Torch mean?" I ask, taking a swig of the cold beer.

"Torch is his road name, what we all call him. We don't use our first names here. We're all given a road name, and some of them have deeper meanings than others. I'm the president, and I'm called Prez or MadDog. Torch was an EOD in the Air Force, so when we need to blow shit up, he's the guy we call," he explains and I gasp.

"EOD? Blow shit up?" I mutter in surprise.

"Explosive Ordinance Disposal. You didn't know what he did in the military?" Maxfield, or MadDog as he's called, asks, his brows drawn together in confusion.

"He never told me what he did, just that he was in the Air Force," I explain. "So, that's what he meant when he said he watched his friends being blown up," I mutter to myself.

"I'm sure he *has* seen that," MadDog rumbles.

"I don't know anything about him, not a single thing," I

mutter, looking down at the table.

"Good news is you're married, and you got time to learn," MadDog booms causing me to jump slightly.

I press my lips together, refusing to talk about my *marriage*, or whatever the hell it's called. I lift my eyes to see MadDog staring at me, studying me, and then he stands and leaves without saying a word.

"Did I make him mad?" I ask, turning my head slightly to watch him walk away.

I try really hard not to admire his ass encased perfectly in his jeans. He's old enough to be my dad, and very engaged to a stunning woman, but he's *built*.

"Prez? Nah, not at all, babe," Camo shrugs.

A few moments later, a pretty blonde, a brunette in her forties, and a petite redhead make their way over and sit down while smiling widely at me. They don't say anything. They just stare, and I squirm under their scrutiny.

"This is Ivy, my woman, and some other Old Ladies. It's my cue to jet. I'll be at the bar if you need me," Camo announces as he stands and walks away from us.

"So, you're Torch's Old Lady?" the brunette in her forties asks with an arched brow.

"I'm technically his wife, if that's what you're asking," I say as my eyes shift from one woman to the next.

"West told me that you don't know anything about this life?" the young blonde murmurs. "I'm Ivy, by the way," she smiles.

"Oh, I'm Cleo," I say. "No, I don't know anything at all," I admit.

"But you're married to Torch?" the petite redhead mutters. "I'm Teeny, Mammoth's Old Lady."

I blink in surprise, thinking about this tiny little thing with a man named *Mammoth*.

"Uhh, yeah, Torch and I have been married for twelve years, technically speaking," I say.

"I'm Colleen, and I've been around this club my whole life, married my Old Man, Texas, when I was sixteen. You want to support your man, be his partner and not someone he just comes home to every now and then, you stick with us and we'll help you," she offers with a kind smile.

"Honestly, I don't know what Paxton and I are," I say, sucking down some more beer.

"Do you want him?" Colleen asks, her intelligent gaze honed in on me.

"I always have, but that doesn't mean that he's good for me, or me for him," I admit. I swear, my heart aches at the admission, the admission that this really could be what's in store for us, nothing but an ending.

"The fact that you even said that, that you think that, it proves to me you have the makings of an Old Lady," Colleen announces.

"He told me a little about brandings, and that the other men could force themselves on me if I don't have one. That doesn't sound like something I could really be part of," I whisper.

"Oh, god," Teeny says, rolling her eyes. "That shit only happens at big parties, and it doesn't really go down like that. Most of these guys are gentle giants and wouldn't hurt a woman in this building, especially one who is on the arm of one of their brothers, branded or not," she says. "Granted, I'm sure he's still unsure of all the men, since he just moved here a couple months ago from his original club," she explains.

"I don't understand why he's even part of this club," I sigh.

"We can only help you with the club stuff," Teeny explains. I nod.

"Whores, what's that?" I blurt out.

All three women cough and cringe at the same time.

"Umm, well, they're these girls," Ivy says, flicking her wrist to the women on the other side of the room.

"Their purpose being?" I ask, lifting a brow. I'm not stupid, and I think I have it figured out, but I want to know for certain.

"They live here, for free, and pay rent with their bodies. They're available to any man wearing a *Notorious Devils* patch, no matter what club they come in from," Teeny explains in her soft, small, voice.

"So they really are just that, whores?" I ask with wide eyes.

"Yeah," Ivy says, nodding.

"You take care of your man, you give him what he needs, and he won't go looking elsewhere," Colleen announces. My face blanches.

"I think I'm going to be sick," I mutter.

"It's part of the life, sweetie, you have to understand that," Colleen coos.

"My husband has been out fucking whores for over a decade. I knew he'd been with women, I'm not stupid, but *whores*? And he wants something with me? Of course, because when he's had what he wants from me he, can just trot on down here and fuck whoever he wants," I ramble, my eyes shifting from one woman to the other. Then I wrench my head around and look at the girl I know, without a doubt, that he was with not very long ago—a *whore*.

"Cleo," Ivy says, reaching out to take my arm. I quickly stand and let my chair topple to the floor.

"No, no I can't be okay with any of this," I whisper, horrified as I start to back away from them, visions of whores and Paxton running rampant through my head.

"Cleo, you need to calm down," Colleen says as she reaches out for me.

I can't take anymore *lessons* on how to live this life. This isn't something I want—ever. It's rude, I know that it is, but I turn and leave the three women who have been nothing but nice to me, and I run back to Paxton's room. I have nowhere to go, but I know that I can lock myself inside and the only person who can come in is Camo, but I doubt that he will.

Slamming the door behind me, I flip the lock and press my back to it, sinking to the floor and drawing my knees up, my eyes filling with tears as I think about the sad state of affairs my life has become in the matter of just a few weeks.

I miss Lisandro and Theo. I miss my boring, predictable life. I miss not knowing where my husband was, and more importantly, I miss not knowing what or *who* he was doing.

Torch

My phone buzzes in my pocket, *a-fuckin-gain*, but I ignore it—I'm working. Tonight, I'm overseeing the loading up of the guns and dope that will be driven to Denver in just a few days. Thank fuck it's not my turn to drive that long ass fuckin' drive. Not only do I not feel like it, I still have Cleo to deal with. I'm on the next rotation, so by then, shit between us should be all good.

The buzzing starts again and I angrily pull it out of my pocket, punching the green button on the screen to accept the call.

"What?" I bark.

"She totally freaked the fuck out, brother," Camo mutters on the other end of the line.

"About what?" I ask.

"Old Ladies were talkin' to her, I thought it might help. Thought she'd want to get to know them, have a couple beers, hang out. She freaked out, and she's locked herself in your room. I haven't bothered her, but I don't know, man, she looked rattled," he explains.

No telling what those women told her; shit she probably didn't want to hear. Knowing our conversation earlier, it probably has to do with whores. I haven't fully explained that to her, hoping she'd just let it go.

"I got a coupla hours here still. She'll have to wait," I grunt, feeling like an ass the second the words spill from my lips.

"Right. I'll keep an eye out if she ventures out again, but I doubt she will," Camo mutters before he ends the call.

I close my eyes for a second and shake my head. *Fuck.* I thought I had her closer to working on this shit. Closer to understanding me, my life, and what our future could be.

Watching the shit being taken off of the freight ship and put into the waiting truck, I let my mind wander, I let myself think. Maybe we're just way too different? Maybe I should just let her go.

Goddammit.

"You good?" Soar asks.

"Nope," I admit.

"Need to talk about it?" he asks, his usually jovial demeanor gone.

"Don't have a pussy, so no, I'm good."

"Don't have to have a pussy to talk about shit, especially with a brother," he murmurs.

"Wanna talk about why you're high all the time and you fuck everybody but your hot as shit wife?"

"Nope," he grinds out.

"Didn't fuckin' think so."

It takes another hour to finish loading the truck, and Soar and I drive back to the clubhouse in silence, the whole four hours. By the time we pull into the parking lot and back the truck into the warehouse, it's after four in the morning.

I climb out of the truck and stomp into the quiet clubhouse, making my way to my room. It only takes a second for my eyes to adjust and land on the curled-up ball in the bed. She has to work today, but I don't give a fuck right now. We're hashing this shit out.

I slam the door closed and flip the light on. I watch as her body jerks awake, and she sits up with her wild red hair and big green eyes, her chest heaving with her startled breathing. I stomp toward her and ignore her gasp, along with her trembling body.

Wrapping my hand around the back of her neck, I grip her hair in my fingers and wrench her head back, lowering my face to hover above hers, and I press my lips to her soft ones, taking her in a hard, bruising kiss.

chapter twelve

Cleo

His lips. Dammit, they own me, every part of me. When I gasp, his tongue slides inside of my mouth and owns me all over again. I should pull away, kick his ass out, but I can't. I don't know that I could ever truly walk away from him. I think my body wouldn't allow it. I hate myself for it, too. I was ready to run, then one kiss and I'm rendered *his* all over again.

"Shit stops now, Clee," he whispers against my lips.

I lift my hands and try to push him away, but he doesn't budge, except to press his knee into the mattress and climb onto the bed and over the top of me. He leans down, forcing me onto my back as he stares at me, just millimeters from my face. I can feel his breath fanning my skin with each exhale.

"Paxton, or should I call you *Torch*?" I ask, lifting a brow.

"You'll call me Pax. I'm your Pax when my dicks inside of you, sweetheart," he murmurs as his nose slides alongside mine.

"That's not going to happen," I say weakly.

"Yeah, baby, in about fifteen seconds," he whispers before his lips touch mine again. *Again*, I melt.

My entire body trembles as his warm palm slides beneath my sleep tank and gently wraps around my breast. His fingers find my nipple and lightly tug on the tight bud, which forces a moan to escape from my mouth as I wrench my head back.

"Pax," I breathe.

My top is roughly hauled off of me, and my shorts pulled off seconds later. I open my eyes to see Paxton on his knees dropping his shirt to the floor and unbuckling his jeans in front of me. My eyes widen when he pulls them down over his hips, along with his boxer briefs, and wraps his big hand around his hard length.

"Spread your legs, sweetheart," he whispers.

I shake my head. It's been so long, and I've always been so shy in bed, never one to just show off that part of my body. My legs tremble as his free hand slides up the inside of my thigh. Wrapping his strong fingers around me, he presses my thighs open. My eyes widen as he lowers down in front of me, his mouth at my center Then his eyes flick up to meet mine.

"When I tell you to spread your long legs so that I can see your exquisite pussy, I expect you to, sweetheart," he murmurs, his warm breath touching my center.

"Paxton," I say as my face heats. I know I'm blushing.

"Love that you're thirty fuckin' years old and you still blush," he rumbles before his tongue snakes out and he licks my entire entrance.

My hands fly to his hair, feeling the soft strands with my fingers, something he didn't have all those years ago, when he was in the military and wore his hair in a traditional high and tight. I grip the strands as he nuzzles my clit before sucking it between his lips, his teeth grazing me.

"Holy shit," I cry out, lifting my head slightly as my mouth falls open.

One of Paxton's hands slides up my waist and cups my breast, his fingers toying with my nipple while the other moves to where his mouth is. Two fingers fill me as his mouth moves to focus on my clit.

"Oh, god," I moan as I roll my hips to accept his fingers inside of me, my eyes rolling in the back of my head.

I'm so close, on the verge of my climax as his tongue flicks and he sucks my clit over and over again, his rhythm feeling delicious but not enough to send me over the edge. My thighs start to shake as I climb closer toward my release, and I let out a cry as he completely releases me, his fingers taken from my center, along with his mouth.

"Ready for me, baby?" he asks as he lines his cock up with my center.

I can feel the head pressing against my entrance, and I'm so ready for him, I don't think I've *ever* been more ready in my entire life. I want it now; I want *him* now. I shouldn't, I know I shouldn't—but right now, I don't care. Those stormy blue eyes are looking at me, and I see my Pax in them. The man-boy I had twelve years ago, he's still there.

He slowly sinks inside of me, hooking his arm beneath my knee as he does, spreading me wider for him with each centimeter that fills me. My teeth bite down on my bottom lip as I try to relax and allow him inside of me.

"Fuck, you feel good, sweetheart," he whispers when he's inside of me completely. His free hand slides beneath my head, and his fingers twist in my hair.

"Pax," I whimper. I need him to move, or do something, *anything*.

"I don't fuck as sweet as I used to, baby. You gotta tell me if I hurt you, okay?" he murmurs against my ear.

"Okay," I whisper.

Paxton's hand beneath my knee presses that leg against the mattress, and I am surprised that it doesn't hurt, as I'm not extremely flexible. Then he rears back, pulling almost completely out of me before he slams into my core with a moan.

"Goddamn," he grunts as his fingers tighten in my hair. "Look at me."

My eyes open and I look directly into his light blue ones. His dark hair has fallen slightly, and I suck in a breath at the serious look that's etched across his face.

"I was a fucking fool—for years, a fucking idiot," he announces before he repeats his move, slamming back inside of me a bit harder with each thrust of his hips.

I lift my arm and wrap my hand around the side of his neck as he continues to drive into me, deep and hard. My entire body moves with each down stroke, but it feels so much better than I'd ever imagined.

My fingers tighten at his neck, and I grip onto him, holding him as my body climbs higher and higher with each drive forward of his hips.

"Gonna come for me, sweetheart?" he asks.

I bite my bottom lip and nod, unable to find the words to speak. He grins as the hand holding onto my leg slides down my thigh before his thumb presses against my clit, circling me. A loud moan escapes me, and I gasp, my whole body locking up with my release.

"*Fuck*," he curses, moving his hand from my clit to join his other hand fisting my hair.

Then, with wild abandon, he fucks me hard and fast. There's no rhythm to his movements, and I don't care. Each stroke feels like I'm in heaven. He suddenly stills above me and lets out a long deep groan before shoving his face in my neck.

Paxton's lips softly kiss my neck, licking and gently nibbling my skin as he lazily slides in and out of me, causing me to moan in delight.

I wrap my hand around his shoulders and hold onto him, unsure of what to do, unbelieving that this has even happened—especially after I cried myself to sleep.

"We should talk," I whisper.

"You on the pill, sweetheart?" he whispers in my neck.

I freeze at his question before I jerk in his hold, but he acts as though he doesn't even notice, still lazily moving his hips, filling me with his semi-erect cock.

"Yeah, I am," I say through gritted teeth.

"Good. Nothin' else to talk about then. This, it proves there's something between us that needs to be fed," he announces. He lifts his head and gingerly releases my hair before holding himself up on his elbows so he doesn't squish me.

"There's plenty to talk about."

"You don't want to be part of this life I got here, Clee? That's cool. You don't have to come to shit, except a couple family parties a year. Some brother's Old Ladies are like that," he shrugs as he pulls out of me and rolls to his back. I watch as he removes the rest of his clothes, his boots and jeans. He then gathers me in his arms and pulls me halfway on top of him, his legs tangling with mine.

"What do you mean by that?" I ask, lifting my head.

"Some of the Old Ladies don't come here unless it's a family party. Don't know why, maybe they don't like the scene? Maybe they don't like the whores, the sex, or the booze; or maybe their men don't want them here. Fuck if I know their personal shit. You wanna be that way? Then it's cool," he announces.

"We're going to revisit this, after we talk about whores, and after you tell me the last time you were tested for STIs and if I need to get a test done myself, since you just took me unprotected," I say bitchily.

"Not used to this attitude from you. Though, would like it a hell of a lot more if you weren't here thinkin' I'd even take a slight chance at hurting you like that, Cleo," he spits. "Get tested every year. Never fuck bitches, whores or otherwise, without protection."

"Me?" I ask, raising a brow.

"You're my fuckin' *wife*. I'm thirty-two years old, babe, and I ain't using a fucking condom with my *goddamn wife*," he growls.

"Paxton, I'm not comfortable with all of this. I don't think I can just turn a blind eye, not to the women," I say.

"What is it you think this will be between us, exactly?" he asks, gripping my hair tightly and tugging my neck back for me to look at him.

"I don't know. This group of yours, this life, I don't know anything about it. But I've seen those women, and I know

121

that they're *available* to you, *for* you. I can only imagine that you've enjoyed that perk of your new life and quite often. And what exactly do you do for money? And how did I not know that your job in the Air Force had to do with explosives and that you're called Torch? I don't understand any of it; and what I'm coming to learn, I don't like very much," I say as my chest heaves. My breathing becomes erratic as I completely and totally freak out in a panic.

"You need to relax, sweetheart," he murmurs. His fingers start to sift through my hair in an attempt to calm me.

"I can't," I admit, clenching my jaw.

"What I can tell you is that you don't need to worry about how I make money, just know that I make it and I make more than enough to take care of you. I've fucked women in the past. I haven't been a saint, sweetheart. And I didn't tell you about my job in the Air Force because I didn't want you to worry. It was dangerous—really fuckin' dangerous," he murmurs calmly.

"I'm thinking your job now is the same, since you're mixed up with *The Cartel*."

"I'm not mixed up with them, babe. Personally, I can't stand the fuckers, and all the shit they're threatening or attempting to do is fucked. We don't mess with women and children; not like they do. It's why I was worried about you. They're unpredictable," he explains. I bite the inside of my cheek, trying to understand him, but knowing that I don't and probably never will.

"I don't know you," I blurt out.

"What?"

"I don't know you. I don't know anything about you. I loved you so much, but did I really? Because how could I if

122

I didn't even know your job, anything about your childhood, or even how you liked your coffee?" I ramble.

For whatever reason, I can't seem to stop talking to him. Maybe it's because he's right here and he's calm and willing to talk *back* with me, instead of getting pissed off and walking away. I don't know; but if he's going to be open, then I want it all—as much of it as I can get.

"Whatever you want to know, Cleo, we have time now," he murmurs.

"Do we? How much?" I ask, looking into his light blue eyes. They're relaxed and sated from earlier.

"Our whole lives, sweetheart," he mutters as his nose runs alongside mine.

"How long before you go to those women without telling me? Or will you just always go to them," I ask as tears fill my eyes.

"Fucking hell, woman," he grunts as he pushes me off of him and then slides out of bed.

"It's a valid concern," I point out as I pull the sheet up to cover my naked body.

"Is your self-esteem that fucking low that you think I'm going to run right over to them? Is it so low that you can't see the way I look at you? So low that you can't understand why I would want to build a life with you again, pick up where I stupidly left off? *Christ*, Cleo. You aren't eighteen any-more. You're a fucking thirty-year-old woman. If I wanted a self-conscious eighteen-year-old, I could have one. Fuck, I could have ten. Figure out what the fuck you want, and do it fast," he growls as he grabs his jeans and then storms out of the door, slamming it behind him.

I stare at the closed door, cursing myself for not standing

up to him and for just spreading my legs for him, as if he has any kind of access to my body. Just because we're technically married by the state of Texas, doesn't mean that we have to have sex.

I pinch my eyes closed tightly and shake my head. I need to get away from him. He makes all of my good reasoning completely fade away, and I listen to my stupid body and my heart instead of my head. I end up hurt at every single damn turn.

Torch

Slamming the bedroom door behind me, I pull on my jeans, then make my way to the bar. I don't give a fuck that it's only six in the morning, I'm drinking, and I'm doing it all god-damn day.

Walking behind the bar, I search for my favorite bottle of tequila and frown when I see that it's the last one left. Snatching it up, I walk over to the order sheet that's hanging on the side of the bar and see that it's not even on the list.

Figuring there must be some more cases in the back, I decide to go over to one of the sofas against the wall and open the bottle. I don't bother with a shot glass, choosing to drink straight from the neck, since my plan is to drink the whole fuckin' thing.

I don't know how much time passes, but eventually, the bar starts filling up—brothers going in and out to start their day, get to work, check up on shit and whatnot. Then I see whores stumbling around in half-hazy sleep and the same clothes, or lack thereof, from the night before, including makeup and ratty assed hair.

"You need some company, today?" Honey asks as she slides up next to me, planting her bony ass right beside mine.

I glance down at her and notice that she looks fresh. She's showered and changed, and her young face is free of makeup. She's prettier without all that shit on her face, but she doesn't hold a candle to Cleo. I open my mouth to tell her to scoot when something catches my eye.

It's Cleo, frozen in the middle of the room, her eyes focused in on me and Honey. I'm still shirtless, my pants only zipped up, not buttoned, and she's nestled in close to my side. It looks damning as hell, but I'm so fucking drunk, I can't seem to find it in me to explain. Besides, she already wants me to be this big asshole who fucks everything that breathes, who doesn't give a shit about her, so I might as well just let her think whatever the hell she wants to.

"I need to get to work today," she says after she closes the distance between us, her eyes zeroed in on mine and never wavering.

"Good luck with that," I shrug, taking another swig from my bottle.

"Paxton, I have no car. Are you going to give me your keys?" she asks, raising a brow.

"Fuck no. You can ask someone for a ride," I say, sounding like a fucking dick.

"You need a ride to Redding?" Soar asks, walking up behind her.

"I do," she murmurs as she looks back at him.

"Sure, babe, I'll give you one," he grins. I don't like what he's insinuating, but I'll be damned if I make a big scene. She's completely pissed me off.

Cleo looks at me one last time, her eyes pleading for something I can't quite read, and then she shakes her head once as she turns and starts to walk away from me. I watch her sweet ass sway in her tight skirt, and then red fills my vision when Soar's hand presses against her lower back, right above that sweet ass of hers. He turns his head slightly to look at me and grins before he continues on outside of the clubhouse.

"Oh, good, the wet blanket is gone for the day. I do not know how a man like you ended up tied down to a bitch like that," Honey says with a sigh.

"Go," I boom.

"What?"

"Get the fuck away from me before I remove you myself—and trust me, you wouldn't like the way I would do that," I growl.

Honey stands and scurries away from me in mild panic, but all I can think about is the fact that Soar is touching my woman, taking her an hour away from me to work, and I'm way too fucked up to attempt to go after them.

Goddammit.

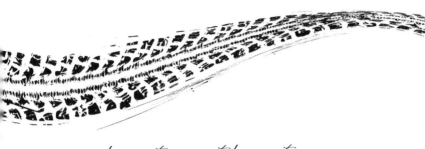

chapter thirteen

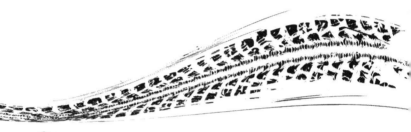

Cleo

"What kind of car is this?" I ask the man who introduced himself as Soar just a few moments ago.

"*1967 Shelby GT500e Super Snake*," he grins as he presses his foot on the gas and sends us flying in his gorgeous white muscle car.

"Holy shit," I breathe as he soars down the road. I wonder if this is how he got his name, because this car practically floats.

"Got it at an auction, day I turned twenty-one," he shrugs.

"Why then?" I ask, arching a brow.

"That's when I got the rights to my inheritance," he smirks with a wink.

I don't ask him anymore. Though he's smiling, it doesn't seem like he wants to talk about it. The ride is silent for a bit, but then Soar starts to talk.

"Pushing him and trying to force him into someone he isn't, that won't get you very far."

"I don't know him well enough to try and make him someone he isn't," I whisper, looking out of the window.

"Thinking you know enough, Cleo. Maybe you forcing him to open up, maybe that's pushing him to be someone he isn't. I don't know Torch well, but I know he doesn't talk about *anything* that's rolling around in his head," he says, his wrist resting on the top of his steering wheel; his fingers dangling in that way that only men can do. That move alone amps up his sexiness.

"I don't think this life, the women and everything, I don't think I could do it," I murmur.

"Whatever you decide, you need to talk about what your relationship will look like. What you don't want to do is promise yourself to him, and he do the same to you, and then turn into a complete stranger right before his eyes. All that'll get you is a lot of hurt and sleepless nights," he says. He's not looking at me. He's staring straight ahead, and looks as though he's lost in his own thoughts.

"Need to talk about it?" I ask as he pulls the car into the jewelry store parking lot.

"Nope. It's all good, baby. Though, you get tired of dealing with Torch's angry ass, you come on over my way. Think we'd have a good fuckin' time. Never tried a redhead before," he grins. My eyes widen in surprise. "Get to work, Cleo, before I decide that Torch is no longer a factor."

I throw the door open and scramble out of the car, practically falling on my ass. All the while, Soar chuckles behind me.

"Hey, babe," he calls out as I take my first step away from the car. I turn to face him, my hand on the door ready to close it behind me. "What time you get off tonight?"

"I'm staying here in town," I whisper.

"He is not going to be cool with that," Soar murmurs.

"I don't really care what he's cool with today," I state.

"Fire. *Fuck, baby*, get going," he rumbles.

I close the door and practically sprint into the building. Lisandro is standing behind the counter as soon as I walk inside of the store. His eyes widen and he stares at me for a moment before he drops what he's doing and runs over to me, wrapping his strong, warm arms around me and holding me tightly.

"I almost chopped Theo's dick off for letting you go with him. I had no way to contact you, sweetie pie," he whispers, his voice thick.

"I'm here, and I'm not going back," I murmur.

Lis moves his hands to my shoulders and straightens his arms. Taking a step back, he looks down at me. I lower my eyes under his intense perusal of my face, and then his fingers tighten on my shoulders.

"You had sex with him. What did he do to you?" he practically growls.

"Nothing, it's fine. I'm just not going back," I state.

"It's not fine," he shrieks dropping his hands from my arms.

"We had sex. It was better than I ever remembered, but I'm not doing it again—ever," I say as I turn from him and walk behind the counter to stow my purse.

"What do you mean, you aren't doing it again? If it was better than anything else, you definitely *need* to knock on that door again," he says.

"Lis," I sigh as I stand and straighten my skirt. "His club has *whores*—whores specifically for them to *use*. It's their job to screw the members," I say, scrunching my nose. "And he was drunk before I left to come to work sitting right next to one."

"Clee," Lisandro says. His voice is full of pity for me, something I'm used to from him. It doesn't make me hate it any less.

"It's fine. Seriously, it is. I'm going to finally get the divorce paperwork handled that I keep avoiding, now that I know where he is; and then I'm moving on with my life. I have the closure I needed. He's a dick, and I never really knew him. All of this, it was good for me," I babble.

"Sure it was, sweetie pie," he murmurs.

"Seriously, it was great. I'm going to be just fine," I say, giving him my fakest, shakiest, wide smile.

"All right, now tell me about this huge sale you had over the weekend," he says, trying to change the subject.

My fake smile falls and tears fill my eyes.

"What?" he asks, sounding horrified.

"It was his president and his beautiful fiancée," I blubber as I bury my face in my hands and let my tears fall.

"Good lord, those people are everywhere," he snaps. I wonder why he's mad at me, but then I turn around and see the man I was just referencing walking up to the doors.

"That's him, the president," I whisper.

"Damn, he's hot—but *Jesus, Mary, and Joseph,* can't they just leave you alone for a hot damn minute?" he asks. I can't help the giggle that escapes.

"Sorry to bother you at work, Cleo, but I was wondering

130

if I could have a chat?" Maxfield asks. I turn to face him, watching as his eyes search my face. A look of concern crosses his features.

"Sure," I shrug.

"Wanna talk outside?" he asks as his eyes flit from me to Lis.

"No, Lisandro knows everything," I inform. Maxfield lets out a breath before he speaks.

"Know you left the clubhouse to come here. Soar didn't answer his phone, probably because that car of his is so fuckin' loud you can't even hear yourself think. Anyway, shit is goin' down soon in New York with *The Cartel*. Don't know if that'll affect us here, but we have to stay sharp and aware. You're supposed to have a brother on you at all times. Torch didn't set that up for today; don't know why, but I've called a prospect to hang around the building. You need anything, you just ask him. Don't want you leaving without him. He'll give you a lift back to the club when you're done with your shift," he explains.

"Torch didn't set it up being he's drinking tequila and probably fucking one of those whores you have down there. He's not worried about me, so why are you? And don't worry about a ride back. I'm not *going* back," I say, smarting off, though Maxfield hasn't done a thing to earn my crappy attitude.

"Protecting you, babe—not for any other reason than you're still Torch's wife, which makes you a member of the family and deserving of our protection. You don't want to go back, that's cool, but the prospects will just do a shift change and they'll hang outside of your house, wherever you're stayin'," he explains gently, side-stepping the whore part of my response.

"Okay, thank you," I whisper shakily.

He takes a step toward me and wraps his big hand around the side of my neck. I look up at him, and he gives me a squeeze before he grins, his blue eyes staring down at me. He's so handsome, I can understand how he totally landed a younger woman.

"You get yourself sorted, then you get him sorted. He switched clubs, came from his home in Idaho to watch after you. Regardless of how that's playing out right now, how stupid he's bein', or how stubborn the both of you are bein', know that he changed his entire life to protect you, and that's something pretty fuckin' amazing," he murmurs.

"Oh," I say, unable to speak another word, my lips frozen in an O shape.

"Now, I gotta go. My woman and I are gettin' married this weekend. You feel like you want to come to a party, meet all the women and see the real families that make up the club? Not just the whores and drunken parties, but a real family party, you're more than welcome to come on down," he smiles before he releases his hand from my neck, turns and walks out of the front door.

"How old do you think he is?" Lisandro whispers.

"I think he's close to sixty," I announce.

"Hot damn, he's got a great fucking ass. Theo better look that good when he's older," Lis sighs.

"Lisandro," I say, completely exasperated.

"So, take the *protection*," Lis rolls his eyes, "but don't spread those thighs unless he grovels. Although I would feel better if you just came home to us," he says. I can feel his eyes boring into me from beside me.

"Yeah, I'm not spreading anything," I mumble, looking down at my feet. "I just don't want to put you guys in danger."

"I understand, but you know we'd protect you. As long as you're going with him, I think there could be some spreading, especially if he's as good as you say he is."

"He is," I admit.

"You deserve some good orgasms," he nods. "Just don't give him your heart. I have a feeling he'd completely crush it all over again."

"Yeah," I sigh. I don't tell him that there's no use. Paxton's had my heart, and I don't think I'll ever get it back.

The rest of the day is pretty calm, and nothing too crazy happens. The protection Maxfield sent shows up thirty minutes after he leaves, and I see him a few times, walking past the front of the store. He never comes inside, and he doesn't bother me at all, which I appreciate.

"Ready to head home?" Lis asks once we count our cash drawers and go through the shutdown procedure for the day.

"Yeah," I sigh as I grab my purse from beneath the counter.

Once we're outside and Lisandro is locking up, I notice the prospect across the street. I give him a small wave and he just lifts his chin as he straddles his bike, his eyes zeroed in on us.

"They're all so pretty. Nothing like I imagined," Lis sighs as we walk toward his black *Jeep*.

"Yeah, well, I've seen more than I want to of some of them," I say, giving an over exaggerated shiver.

"Don't tease me, bitch," he scolds, making me laugh.

It doesn't take us long to drive to Lis and Theo's house, and I'm grateful to be there. Though I don't have anything to wear to bed or to work tomorrow, since the only things I have are the clothes on my back and some casual clothes that I'd left, nothing appropriate to wear to the shop. At this point, I'm so emotionally exhausted I don't even care.

"Well, this is a surprise," Theo says as we walk through the door, the motorcycle that followed us idling in front of the house.

"She's back," Lis says with a flourish. "For now."

"For always," I state. He grins with a shake of his head.

"What?"

"He had a taste of you. He liked what he had back then, and if I'm to guess, he likes it even more now. He won't just let this go," Lisandro mutters.

"He liked it so much he was drunk and cuddled up next to another woman almost immediately after?"

"You've explained that fight and, sweetie pie, nowhere in it did he say he didn't want you. If you think he won't be knocking down our door as soon as he sobers up, you're living in a dreamland," Lisandro says, crossing his arms over his chest and staring at me.

"Is my self-esteem that low, Lis?" I ask after we've had dinner. We've since cleaned up, and I'm settling into bed for the evening.

"Clee," he sighs, refusing to look at me.

"Lisandro."

"Yes, *fuck*. Emotionally, relationship wise at least, you're stunted. I understand it, I really do. Your parents were shit, then they died; your Gram loved you, but then she died; and then Paxton did what he did and abandoned you. You've got issues, Clee. He just wants you to be fixed overnight because he's a guy and he doesn't get why you aren't more confident. You're absolutely gorgeous. Is he what you want, though? Or is it just sex?"

I stare at my best friend in shock. The way he's let his words flow makes me realize that he's thought of this before, he's just never said it to me. This isn't a new concept to him, and I don't know if I'm glad he's never told me or pissed off because he hasn't.

"I don't know," I admit.

"I want you to be happy, if he's what you want, then I want you to have him. If he's just sex, then have that and move on—but take what you want, sweetie pie. You deserve whatever makes you happy, whatever that looks like," he mutters, "Now, get some sleep."

"I'm nothing special," I whisper.

"That's where you're *dead* fucking wrong," he states as he stands. "You're gorgeous. You have a body most women would kill for, and it's effortless, which even pisses *me* off. Then there's your demeanor. You're sweet, and it's not an act—you just are a sweet person. The only thing you lack is confidence. Maybe that's something Paxton can pull out of you; or if you're really done with him, maybe it's a gift for the next man who finds his way into your sweet heart," he says. Without another word, he leaves me alone in my room.

I stare at the closed door, then I lay down and stare at the ceiling. I let Lisandro's words, along with Paxton's from earlier today, roll around in my head. It's true. I have zero self-esteem.

I don't see this woman he's described in the mirror when I look at myself. I see *me*—redheaded Cleo. Nobody special or even extremely pretty. I'm average, in all ways, including body shape.

I don't think I'm dog ugly or anything, but I don't feel extra-spectacular, either. I let out a breath and roll to my side to stare at the wall. At this rate, with the way my head is spinning, I'm never going to get to sleep.

Torch

After I go to bed, sleep, and sober up a bit, I decide to head downstairs. It's early in the evening but I'm not drinking anymore today. I could use some food and water, though. Showered and dressed in clean clothes, I run my hand through my damp hair as I walk into the kitchen.

Soar is standing with his ass leaning against the counter as I walk into the room. I see red just looking at his smug ass face, but I refuse to say anything to him. I choose to walk over to the fridge to grab a water, instead.

"She's not coming back," he announces. My head shoots up from inside the open fridge.

"The fuck's that supposed to mean?" I bark.

"Cleo, she's not coming back. She's staying in Redding with her friends," he shrugs.

"No, she's not," I grind out.

"Yeah, she fuckin' is," MadDog says as he walks into the room. I slam the fridge closed and turn to look at him, surprised that he even knows any of this shit. "You let her go to work, an hour away, with zero protection. You didn't even fucking *drive* her because you were drunk off your ass hanging around some whore. Soar called me, and I drove all the way there to talk to her. I set up prospects to keep an eye on her, twenty-four seven, using resources I don't really have to cover *your* woman."

I slept all day long while this was going on. When Cleo should be on her way back here to me, she's at her friends. Fuck. I don't have anything to say, mainly because he's right. I let her walk out of the clubhouse without a second thought, except that I was pissed she went off with Soar. I let my personal shit with her outweigh the whole reason I even had her here—for protection.

"You need to get your shit in order, brother. I allowed you to come here because you said you needed to be near her. You aren't showing me you give much of a shit. She's your wife on paper, but do you really give a fuck what happens to her? I'll keep protecting her because she has your last name and she seems like a sweet girl, but you gotta get your head outta your ass," he barks before he turns and walks away, leaving me alone with Soar.

Stepping back, I let my head hit the wall behind me and close my eyes. Goddammit, I'm a fuck up. I thought I was finally ready for more, for Cleo, and to slay the demons inside of me instead of drowning them in booze and pussy.

"She has fire, your little redheaded beauty. Better grab ahold of her and hold on tight before someone else see's that fire and wants a piece of her," Soar warns.

I lift my head, my eyes connecting with his and narrowing. I know exactly what he's saying because I made the same kind of threats to Sniper when he was being an ass to his wife Brentlee. Except, I was in a position to have an Old Lady; Soar is not.

"Is that a threat?" I ask

"More of an observation," he shrugs before he walks away.

"You make any more *observations* like that and, brother or not, we're goin' fisticuffs out in the parking lot," I growl.

"Better get your shit handled then, *brother*," he states.

"Fuck," I shout.

chapter fourteen

Torch

The weather is shit today. Winter is quickly approaching. I can't get on my bike, so I jog toward my *Rachero* and shove my key in the ignition, pissed off at myself because it's so late in the evening. I slept all fucking day, and now Cleo's had hours to think. Obviously, she doesn't want to come back. *Who could fucking blame her?*

I was a dick.

I said some shit that wasn't nice. It was true, but it wasn't nice. She frustrates the absolute fucking shit out of me. Cleo has always been soft and sweet, willing to do whatever it takes to make someone happy. She doesn't know just how much light radiates off of her, how much fucking purity and happiness just oozes from her. Her vulnerability does things to me, I yearn to protect her, to watch over her. In a different world,

I might not ever want to hurt her, but it seems like that's all I do.

Now that she's a woman? It's frustrating that she has no fucking confidence. It's even more frustrating because I know that I'm the major cause of that shit. She should be able to hold her head up high, knowing that she's definitely *not* average, because she isn't. But she's had a shit life, and most of that is because of me. I shouldn't be surprised that after the way I've treated her, she doesn't see all that beauty in herself.

Patience has never been something I've had in abundance. It seems as though I'll have to dig as deep as I can to practice what little patience I have with her.

I see the prospect hanging around the front of the house as soon as I pull up. He lifts his chin and I signal to him that he can leave. With a nod, he turns and walks over to his bike, promptly starting it and taking off. It's late, later than I realized, so I hope I don't piss off her little *friends* as I ring the bell.

"Wondered when you'd show up," a man announces as he opens the door. I realize that it must be her best friend, Lisandro.

"She here?" I ask lamely.

"Of course she is, but she's asleep," he says, standing right in front of the door.

I'm about two seconds from bowling his fucking ass over when Theo steps up behind him and narrows his eyes on me. Good god, these men truly love her. If she didn't love them back, I'd grab the gun from my side holster and shoot them because they're in my fucking way.

"I'm here to get her," I say, trying not to growl.

"Then what? She comes back to me tomorrow in tears? I

don't think so," the man in front says.

"What's your name again?" I ask, knowing the answer before he even speaks.

"Lisandro," he says with a shake of his head, lifting his chin slightly.

"Well, Lisandro, I don't plan on her ever comin' back to you, tears or otherwise. She's my wife and she'll be with me," I announce.

"You're telling me that you're suddenly ready to be a husband?" he asks, arching his brow.

"Not your business," I grunt.

"Cleo is my business. I've been friends with her since the beginning. I saw the broken girl she was all those years ago—how she's lived an empty life, always waiting for you to make an appearance; waiting for you to suddenly realize how wrong you'd been; wondering what she ever did to make you abandon her. So, yeah, it's absolutely *my fucking business,*" he shouts, his face turning red with anger. I watch as Theo wraps his hand around Lisandro's shoulder and gives him a comforting squeeze.

"I was no good to her all those years. Fuck, I'm no good to her now. But I can't walk away from her," I admit.

"We let you walk in this house, what does the future look like?" Theo asks, his voice deep and almost booming.

"I can't predict the future," I shrug.

"*Try.*"

I lift my eyes and allow them to go from Theo to Lisandro and back again before I let out a curse under my breath. Opening up, about *anything*, is not my thing. I keep everything that's happened in my life buried deep.

If it were up to me, I'd tell nobody about my past, my

childhood, my time in the military—none of it. But these men, they love my Cleo, and I understand that they only want what's best for her. So I give them what they want.

The unfiltered truth.

"Been fucked up for a long time. PTSD. I saw some shit in the desert, and instead of getting the help I should have, instead of leaning on my wife, I pushed her away. I'm on and off meds, but nothing takes the nightmares away. Nothing makes me the man I was when I met her. Thinking she could be in danger forced me to seek her out. I'd imagined her life was probably pretty good, all these years. I hoped she'd found a good man to love her. Seeing her, seeing how beautiful she is but how obviously lonely she is, and the fact that she's not moved on," I lift my hand and place it behind my neck as I shake my head. "Want her back, and I'll work for it—but goddamn it, she is not making this shit easy."

"The other women?" Lisandro asks.

Lifting my eyes, I look up to him. He's got unshed tears filling his eyes, and I know that I'm almost in—almost back to where I not only want to be, but need to be, back with Cleo.

"Right now, the only woman I'm concerned with is Cleo," I murmur.

"But what does tomorrow look like?"

"Not sure. But whatever happens between me and Cleo is exactly that—between me and Cleo," I say, starting to lose my cool.

"Let him in, Lis. If Cleo wants him in her life, we're her friends and we're here to support her," Theo murmurs.

"You hurt her, and I don't care how big and hot you are, I'll cut you," Lis announces as he takes a step to the side.

"First door on the right," Theo calls out as I walk past

them and start down the hallway of their single-story ranch home.

I open the first door on the right and gently close it behind me, thankful that it has a lock on it. The moon shines in, and I see Cleo's sleeping form in the center of the bed. I strip my clothes completely off, boxers and all, before I pull back the bedding and climb in behind her. Once I'm next to her warmth, I wrap my arms around her.

My lips skim the back of her neck and shoulder as I lift my hand and wrap it around her full breast. Fuck, *her tits*, they're one of my favorite parts of her body. All her curves are pretty fantastic, but *goddamn,* her tits are phenomenal. I pinch her nipple gently, and she moans as she presses her ass against my hardening dick.

"Sweetheart," I whisper against her ear before I suck the lobe into my mouth.

I know the second she wakes because her body stiffens in my hold. I don't release her, not when I have her in my arms, so warm and so alone.

"Why are you here?" she asks.

"Don't want to make a habit out of sleeping without my wife."

Cleo

It takes my mind a minute for his words to fully register.

Don't want to make a habit out of sleeping without my wife.

"You didn't have a problem with that when you were cuddled up with that girl earlier," I snap, trying to roll over in his arms.

"Nothing happened," he murmurs as his fingers continue to play with my nipple, tugging and pinching me.

"What?" I whisper, unable to stop myself from further arching my breast into his hand, loving the way he makes me feel.

"Honey, nothing happened with her. No other woman exists when I have you, Cleo," he whispers. I love his words, but I'm not sure if I trust them.

"Paxton," I sigh.

"I won't lie to you, Cleo. I'll be brutally honest with you. Anytime you need the truth from me, you fuckin' got it. I didn't touch her, and I sure as hell didn't fuck her," he growls.

His hand leaves my breast and travels down beneath my panties to touch my center. I'm only wearing one of Theo's old t-shirts and a pair of panties. I shake slightly when his finger slides through my wet center. His touch, it feels spectacular every single time.

"Brutally honest?" I breathe as my hips shift and his finger fills me.

"Yeah, sweetheart. I'll try not to be a big fuckin' dick, but baby, I'll always tell you the truth," he murmurs as he starts to pump in and out of me.

"What about the past?" I ask on a moan when he curls his finger inside of my core.

"Not gonna lie, there's shit I want to shield you from. I want to keep it all from you, sweetheart. But I'm willing to try and tell you what you want to know. The only things I can't tell you are club business, and that's for your safety as well as mine," he mutters.

I suck in a breath as he pulls his hand out from between my legs and rolls me onto my back. He crawls over me as he wrenches down my panties. I feel the fabric scrape my legs, and I wonder how on earth my skin became so sensitive all of a sudden. Then the head of his cock presses against me, and his eyes, though I can only see them illuminated by the moonlight, I swear, they glimmer.

"Pax," I whisper.

"You want it all from me, Cleo? You fuckin' got it, but you gotta take the good shit with the really fuckin' horrible shit," he breathes as he slowly sinks inside of me. I'm rendered completely speechless as he fills my body, stretching me in a way that nobody else ever could.

"I've always been prepared for you, all of you, Paxton. I've always been willing to take what you'd give me," I shamelessly admit.

I watch as something works behind his eyes. Then it's gone, and he's fully seated inside of me. His nose comes down and runs alongside mine before his lips travel to my ear.

"Some of that shit you gotta take from me will be in bed, sweetheart," he whispers as he pulls out and then slams back inside of me with a moan.

I widen my legs and lift them to press against his rib-cage, enjoying how he feels at this angle. He lifts his head and looks at me, taking in the slight smile and my face, relaxed and turned on all at the same time. He does this to me. He makes me feel so good that I can't help but smile and enjoy what he gives me.

Without a word, I feel his hand wrap around the front of my throat as he gently squeezes. His hips continue to move, his cock filling me over and over again. I lift my hands and wrap them around his biceps, holding on to him.

"Relax your body, Clee," he murmurs. "Be real still for

me, sweetheart."

I look up at him and nod, forcing my body to relax and freeze for him. He continues to fill me, stretch me, and choke me. His eyes are focused on mine, never wavering as he slides up to his knees for more leverage, his thrusting hips, pounding harder with each down stroke.

My thighs start to shake as I climb closer toward my release, and I start to panic, knowing that he's asked me to stay still. I press my lips together and breathe when I can through my nose. He tips his head down and then looks back at me as he squeezes his fingers around my throat a tad harder with a grin.

"Come all over me, Cleo," he whispers.

I can't hold back, not even a little bit, as my entire body starts to shake. I do come all over him, my pussy squeezing and my legs shaking uncontrollably.

My eyes roll in the back of my head as I let out a gargled moan. Paxton doesn't stop thrusting; in fact, he fucks me harder, releasing my throat only to move his hand to the back of my hair and fist it, holding me tightly.

"Take my cock, sweetheart," he whispers as he lowers down and presses his chest against me, his lips against my ear as he drives inside of me repeatedly. "Widen your legs and take me."

I don't know how he can keep going, and I'm so sensitive, I feel like crying. Nonetheless, I widen my legs and accept him inside of me, every bruising hard thrust he gives me. His lips skim my sweat soaked neck, sending goosebumps over my body, along with a shiver, which makes his fingers tighten in my hair.

"Your pussy only takes what I give it, what I allow," he

whispers. I shiver again as I wrap my arms around his back.

"Pax," I gasp as he grinds his pelvis against my sensitive clit.

"We're gonna be okay, sweetheart," he promises.

I feel his muscles shake beneath my fingertips, and I wonder if he's going to come, but he doesn't. He growls and wrenches his body up and away from mine. I gasp when his thumb presses against my clit as he continues to fuck me, unstopping and unwavering in strength.

"Pax," I sob quietly.

"Take it," he grunts.

I sink my teeth into my bottom lip as he brings me to the brink of my orgasm, and when I feel like I'm going to cry from the sensitivity, when it all feels like it's too much, I come.

My eyes widen, and I lift my head in surprise, looking right into Paxton's face. He grins as he moves his hands to wrap around my waist, and he holds my shaking body still as he thrusts inside of me a few more times before I hear him groan as he fills me with his release.

"This is what we have, and we'll work on the rest," he murmurs.

He slips from between my legs and lies down on top of me, his arm braced next to my head to take his weight, while his other hand moves from the back of my hair to trace my sweaty face.

"We can't base a relationship solely on sex, let alone a marriage," I whisper.

"Know that, sweetheart. I also know that without you, I don't breathe," he murmurs.

I look at him, unsure of his meaning. It seems like he's been *breathing* just fine for the past eleven years, but I don't verbalize my thoughts. He may have been breathing just fine, but I wasn't, not even a little bit.

"I wasn't ready for you when I had you. I did something so fucking stupid when I walked away from you, and I regretted it every second of every single day. I didn't know how to fix it. I thought I'd lost you forever and that there was no way to get you back," he explains.

"So, you didn't even try? You didn't even check?"

"I was in such a bad place for so fuckin' long that I was completely useless—a useless excuse of a man. By the time I was in a place to find you again, it'd been so fucking long that it was easier to pretend you were happier without me in your life."

"About what you said, about me, earlier today," I start. He shuts me up by pressing his lips to mine in a hard, closed mouth kiss.

"Don't," he murmurs.

"I do have low self-esteem; but honestly, Paxton, I'm not anything special," I continue, looking into his stormy blue eyes. "I'm nowhere near as handsome or as sexy as you are. I'm average, on a good day. Every other day, I'm just Cleo."

"Then I got some fuckin' work to do with you, sweetheart," he says, shaking his head. "But first, we sleep, then I'm gonna wake you up with my mouth between your sexy thighs, tasting that sweet as fuck pussy. Then I'm taking you back with me," he rasps as his lips press against mine and his tongue fills my mouth. I sigh when his hand gently tugs up the shirt I'm still wearing and he breaks the kiss to pull it over my head. "Never wear another man's shirt, ever again."

"It's Theo's," I explain. He shakes his head once.

"Don't give a fuck if it's the Pope's, you don't wear another man's tee, ever. I'm your husband. You don't have *my* tee to wear, you can sleep naked until I get to you," he murmurs.

"Paxton," I sigh.

His lips kiss down my jaw, to my neck, and then along my collarbone. Then he continues down to my breast and sucks one of my nipples into his mouth, sucking for only a moment before his tongue gently laps at me. My hands automatically dive into his hair, gripping his soft strands tighter with each sweep of his tongue against my hardened bud.

"These tits. Fuck, baby, love them," he murmurs against my skin.

"Pax," I gasp as he moves to my other breast.

"You'd look pretty with piercings," he rumbles, releasing my nipple and looking up at me.

"Like rings?" I say, scrunching my nose.

"Fuck, no," he grunts as one of his hands comes up and cups my breast, his thumb sweeping over my wet nipple as he watches it grow even harder. "Pretty little bars with diamonds on the ends. I'd buy you the real deal, sweetheart."

"Pierced?" I whisper.

"Real diamonds, too, sweetheart," he murmurs.

"You think it would look good?" I ask as I bite my bottom lip.

"Baby, everything about you looks fucking spectacular just as is. But, yeah, they'd look fuckin' hot."

"Can I think about it?" I ask, cupping his cheek with my palm.

"Whatever you want, Clee," he mumbles, turning to press his lips against my palm. "Let's sleep now."

I watch as he moves down my body a bit and presses his cheek against my stomach, his chest nestled between my thighs—my still wet thighs.

"Pax," I say, shaking his shoulder.

"Mmm."

"What are you doing down there?"

"Gonna sleep with my woman's pussy pressed against me. Then when I wake up, all I have to do is move down a few inches to taste that sweet cunt," he explains. My eyes widen.

"*Paxton*!"

"Get some sleep, sweetheart."

chapter fifteen

Cleo

Paxton woke me up just as he promised he would, with his face between my thighs. My inhibitions somehow took a backseat, and I welcomed him as soon as my eyes fluttered open, spreading my legs as wide as I could and moving my hips, searching for more—more of his mouth, his tongue, his teeth, and the way he makes me feel.

"You're taking our girl again?" Lis asks as we walk into the kitchen.

I freeze as Paxton's hand slides around my waist and he presses his lips against my neck before pulling me even closer to his chest.

"Taking her home to be with her husband." I blush at his words and I watch as Lis' face goes soft as he takes me in.

"Home? Or that clubhouse?" Theo asks, his face not soft

at all as he glances at us, his expression unreadable.

"Clubhouse. Don't have a house here, yet," Paxton says nonchalantly.

"Is this something you're going to rectify?" Theo asks.

I wonder when, and *how*, Theo became all dad-like; but it's kind of awesome seeing him stand up to Paxton. I bite the inside of my cheek as I turn to look at Lis with wide eyes. He grins back at me, sitting up a little straighter as though he's ready to watch this show unfold.

"Yeah. My president's wedding is this weekend; got a couple weeks where I'm gonna be gone, and after that, yeah," he announces. I turn around in his arms, looking up at him.

"You're going to be gone for *weeks*?" I ask in surprise.

"Yeah," he shrugs, as if it's no big deal.

"And you want me to stay in your club, alone?" I ask.

He doesn't answer, his eyes narrowed on me, and he clenches his jaw, a muscle jumping in his cheek. Then he leans down and whispers so that only I can hear him.

"We're leaving and we'll discuss what happens, where you stay and what goes on in our marriage, when we're fucking *alone*."

"Paxton," I whisper.

"Get your shit, I'll meet you at the car," he grunts before he turns around and stomps out of the room, slamming the door as he leaves the house.

"Think we pissed him off," Lisandro announces. I look over at him to see he's smiling.

"Why are you smiling about that?" I hiss.

"He's even hotter pissed off," he shrugs.

I close my eyes and fight my own smile, because it's so true. Paxton is so much hotter angry.

"Got this for you yesterday. Mine and Lis' numbers are programmed. You need a phone," Theo murmurs as he takes the device from the table and hands it to me. It's an iPhone 6, and it's rose gold. *Damn, my friends have great taste.*

"This is too much," I murmur.

"It's not. Take it. We want to know you can contact us at any time you need us," he says, his meaning perfectly clear.

"He's waiting for you, sweetie pie," Lisandro murmurs.

I look to him, waiting for more, for anything. If he gave me just one word that he wanted me to say, or if he said that I should, I probably would.

"Lis?"

"You've been waiting for this for over ten years. You need to give it a real shot," he shrugs.

"What if it fails miserably?" I ask, biting my bottom lip.

"Then it will be something that failed; but at least you won't spend your life wondering," he whispers before he stands and wraps his arms around me in a tight hug. "Your life is worth living, so fucking *live* it, sweetie pie. Be wild."

I take a step back, clutching the phone to my chest as tears fill my eyes.

"Be wild?" I ask, tipping my lips up in a smile.

"Be so fucking wild that you would shock the shit out of me," he laughs.

"I'll try," I whisper.

"Go. Don't try, fucking *do*," he urges.

I give my friends a wave before I turn and walk away from them. Wild. *Be wild.* I've never done anything particularly crazy. Only in my head-over-heels falling in love state with Paxton did I do something semi-wild and marry him. Other than that, I've never been wild a day in my life. But

153

maybe that's what draws me to him. He has always been a wild card, since the moment I met him; being with him has always been so freeing.

He's different now. He's wilder, rougher, and a little scarier. He's so opposite of me, it's ridiculous; but maybe that's exactly what I need.

Sucking in a breath, I walk out of the house, wearing the same clothes as yesterday, but feeling a sense of hope that I didn't have before. Paxton is leaning against the passenger side door of his *Ranchero,* his head aimed down at his boots until he hears my footsteps.

I take him in as he lifts his head and gives me a side grin before he pushes off of the car and walks toward me. Once he's closed the distance between us, his hands wrap around my hips as his head dips down, his lips caressing mine gently.

"Where'd you get the phone, baby?" he murmurs against my lips

"Theo and Lis gave it to me, just in case," I admit on a sigh as his teeth nibble on my bottom lip.

"I just bet they fuckin' did," he chuckles, releasing me. He walks over to the car, opening the door as he watches me, waiting for me.

"Are you upset about it?" I ask as I make my way toward him and get inside of the car.

"Nah," he shakes his head. "But as soon as I get back from my job, I'm going to get you a phone, and you can give that back."

"*Pax,*" I sigh.

"Not a pussy, babe. I'm a man. I can take care of you, which means I'll buy you whatever shit you want or need. That bein' said, it's good they thought of a cell. Gotta say, that shit didn't cross my mind, yet. But as soon as I get back, I'll get your shit handled, yeah?" he announces, looking down at me.

"Yeah," I murmur, lifting my chin to look up at him. He grins before he gives me a wink and then closes the heavy door.

I watch as he jogs around the front of the car before getting inside of the driver's seat and starting the roaring engine. Paxton backs out of the driveway, heading toward Shasta. A few moments into our ride, he reaches out to turn up the radio. I reach over and turn it right back down.

"The fuck?" he asks, his eyes shifting to the side to look at me before he moves them back onto the road.

"I don't want to live there, Paxton. Especially not without you," I murmur as we make our way out of the city.

"You think my brothers would hurt you?" he asks, raising a brow.

"I think that you told me because I wasn't tattooed that they could do whatever they wanted to me," I point out, watching as his jaw clenches. "Also, sharing a bathroom is weird. I feel like it's some kind of frat house."

"Then I better get you to the ink shop," he growls ignoring my comment about sharing a bathroom.

"No way in hell," I cry out.

He swerves the car over to the side of the road, taking a dirt path to the middle of nowhere. He stops and throws the car in park with such force, I'm afraid that he's going to break the gear shift. Then he unbuckles his seatbelt and turns to me.

I press my back up against the door, trying to get as much distance between us as possible. Though, since this is a bench seat, it wouldn't take but one strong tug of my arm to be in his space.

"You in this with me? I mean, fuck, I thought we hashed this shit out last night," he shouts.

"Tattoos are permanent, Paxton," I whisper.

"Fuckin' know that, Clee, that's the whole fuckin' point. We're married. You planning on walkin' out the fuckin' door on me any time soon? I gotta worry about you leavin' me?" he asks, narrowing his eyes on me.

"I don't know. I'm trying this with you. We're getting to know each other; but Paxton, we *don't* know each other. In six months, you might hate the sight of me," I murmur, trying and failing to look away from him. His light blue eyes hold me completely captive.

"*Never*. Never could I hate the sight of all that is you, Cleo," he murmurs as he scoots closer to me, his hand gently sliding up the outside of my thigh.

I hold my breath as his hand pushes my skirt up to my hips, leaving me completely bare to him. I didn't have any clean panties to change into. His eyes don't look anywhere but straight into mine as his hand moves to between my thighs.

"There's no fuckin' way all of this isn't meant to be mine, forever," he rasps as he fills my wet center with two fingers.

"Paxton," I mutter as my whole body shivers.

I came less than two hours ago, but suddenly, I want more. I want him inside of me. I don't know if I'll ever get enough. I doubt it. Even the touch of his fingers anywhere on my body sends me into overdrive. It always has. It probably always will.

"You're never leaving me, Cleo," he rumbles.

I hear him shift around before his fingers leave me and he's pulling me on top of him. I sit up, straddling his thighs, and gasp when he wraps his hand around my waist and yanks me down on top of him. His cock fills me full, so fucking full, I feel like I'm going to explode into a million pieces.

"Look at me," he orders. My chin dips down to look into his blue eyes. "Not goin' anywhere, Clee. You're my wife, my woman, and my Old Lady."

His hand slides up my waist, traveling up my body, and wraps around the side of my neck, his thumb running over my bottom lip as he just stares at me for a beat.

"I'm not part of your new life," I admit.

"That's where you're wrong," he whispers. "You're mine. You've always been mine, and you're part of my life. It's different, and it's new, and it's something you have to get used to. You will, just like you acclimated to me being in the military and gone when you joined all those groups. This is no different," he murmurs as his hands wrap around my waist. He starts to roll my hips for me.

"But are you mine?" I ask as I take over, rising and falling on his hard, thick length.

"Was yours the second you looked at me. Those green eyes rendered me speechless, Clee."

"But are you mine, Paxton? Are you *only* mine now?" I ask, as my breath comes out in pants.

Paxton's hands move up my back to fist in my hair. His chin tips down, and he watches me take him inside of my body for a few seconds before he lifts his head and his eyes connect with mine again.

"I'm yours, sweetheart. *Fucking shit*," he rasps as one of his hands slides between us and his thumb presses against my clit. "Give me your pussy, sweetheart. Give me all of you."

My legs start to shake with his words, and I feel my

orgasm climbing before I throw back my head and let it completely take over me. The hand that's still tangled in my hair tightens and yanks my neck back a little farther as his thumb on my clit disappears.

Then he drives into me from his seat. I'm arrested in my spot, unable to move, only able to feel. I let myself digest every single thrust of his cock driving deep inside of me. When he stills, I gasp as he fills me with his cum.

"Paxton," I breathe when he releases his hold on me. I collapse against his chest, my lips finding his neck to place a gentle kiss there.

"Wear my mark, be mine in every way, Clee," he whispers against the top of my hair.

"I'm scared," I admit.

"Not leavin' you again, sweetheart. Our lives begin right now. No more waiting around. I'm so fucking ready to be the husband I promised I'd be all those years ago," he swears.

"We're a mess. *This* is going to be a mess," I mutter into his neck.

"Yeah, but it's gonna be *our* mess—just you and me," he mumbles. His hand tugs at my hair to bring my face away from his sweat soaked neck. "You and me, Cleo."

I nod and bite my bottom lip. I want that. Deep down, I've always wanted that. This is a dream come true. But I know enough about dreams and reality to know that this could crash and burn. He's not the same boy, and I'm not the same girl from a decade ago. I want to be cautious, but he's not really allowing me that.

Then there's this—the way we are together, when no one else is around and nothing else matters. *This* gives me the hope I desire for the future.

"You and me," I nod.

"Yeah, sweetheart," he murmurs. "Now let's get back."

I watch as his face breaks out in a slow grin, and then he moves his hands to my ass and grabs it with a rough squeeze before his lips brush against mine in a slow kiss.

"Can't wait to fuck you again, Clee," he mutters against my lips.

Torch

I watch as her pretty face blushes at my words, and my smile widens as she tries to climb off of my lap. I reach over to my glove box and grab some napkins, handing them to her so she can clean up. Her blush deepens to bright red as she quickly wipes between her legs and then holds the napkins in her hand.

I pull my jeans back up and tuck myself back in my pants before I take the napkins and roll down my window, throwing them into the wooded area at the side of the road. I then put the car in reverse to get back on the main highway.

"You just littered," Cleo hisses.

"It's biodegradable, sweetness. It'll disintegrate in less than a week," I chuckle as I make my way out to the main road.

Before she can buckle her seatbelt back up, I wrap my hand around her upper thigh and pull her next to me. Bench seats were made so your woman sits right next to you, not so she's in the fucking corner all by herself.

"Paxton," she whispers. The sound of her breathy whisper

goes straight to my cock, every single time.

"Tell me about that boss of yours that was a dick, sweetheart," I gently demand.

"There's nothing to tell," she shrugs. I squeeze her thigh a little tighter and she sighs. "I was young and naïve. Obviously, I'd just moved back to Sacramento from Texas. A few sweet words, a lot of little thoughtful actions with some serious coaxing and late nights at the office. One night, it just happened. I was okay because I thought he wanted more; like maybe all the shitty stuff happened, and I was going to end up with this really sweet lawyer, and everything would be okay."

I grip the steering wheel so tight that I fear breaking it in half by the time she's finished the beginning of her little reminiscent story.

"But?"

"But he only liked a challenge. Once he'd bested it, once I'd given in and slept with him, it was as if I didn't exist anymore. He wasn't purposely mean to me. He didn't go out of his way to be rude or anything. But I wasn't significant. I was his secretary and nothing else. I didn't make a big deal about it. He hurt me, but I was stupid, and I wasn't ready anyway," she shrugs, looking straight ahead of us.

"I'm sorry he did that to you, sweetheart," I say through gritted teeth.

In reality, I want to go and find him, beat the shit out of him, and tell him what a fucking piece of shit he is. But really, how fucking hypocritical of me? I left her, too; except, I did it in a much more hurtful manner.

I plan on making it up to her as much as she'll let me. She wants this to happen between us just as much as I do. I'm bringing her completely into my life. Hopefully, she doesn't run away screaming—scared shitless.

"This tattoo you and the other girls were telling me about, where would it go?" she asks, looking down at her lap.

"Where would you want my name, Clee?" I ask, trying to fight my grin.

"Your name, or that other name they call you?"

"Torch is my road name, I doubt anybody even knows my real first name," I shrug.

"Seriously?" she asks, turning to face me.

"Serious, babe. Just like nobody knew my first name when I was in the service. They all just called me Hill. Same goes here, except they know me as Torch. You want Paxton tattooed on your body, too, then we can do both; but Torch is what you need."

"I've never even thought about a tattoo before. I have no clue where I could put one that would look cute," she mumbles.

"Would love it if you put it somewhere that it would be seen," I say as I rub my thumb on the soft skin of her thigh.

We continue to drive in silence for at least another thirty minutes, until I feel her eyes on me, and then she speaks.

"What about my shoulder? That way I could hide it for work, or whatever, but a tank or an off the shoulder shirt would show it off?" she asks.

I can't help the way my chest swells with pride. I don't deserve to have my brand on her, not at this point; and yet, she's willing to do it for me.

"Yeah?" I ask.

"Yeah," she nods.

"So, I gotta go with one of the brothers for work on Monday. I'll leave you my car, and maybe you can stay with his Old Lady?"

"Have I met her yet?" she asks.

"Naw, Genny doesn't come down to the clubhouse much. It's Soar's Old Lady," I explain.

"Soar has an Old Lady?" she asks with wide eyes, confusing me.

"Yeah, his wife, Genny."

"Interesting," she mutters. My hand on her thigh tightens, a-fuckin-gain.

"Nothing happened," she quickly cries out. I release her, not realizing that I had such a tight grip on her leg. "We just talked. I just didn't know he was married. He didn't act like he was."

"Yeah, well, Soar *never* acts like he's married," I chuckle. "You'll meet her at the wedding; then Monday you can stay with her, keep each other company for a couple weeks."

"Yeah, okay," she mutters. I shake my head.

She's thinking, which could be good—but odds are, it probably isn't. Doesn't matter. We're almost at the clubhouse, and I'm about half an hour away from being balls deep inside her cunt again.

chapter sixteen

Cleo

I stretch and reach over to where Paxton should be sleeping, but the bed is empty. Other than him taking me to work yesterday, we haven't done much the past week except have sex. He's kept me holed up in his little room and hasn't wanted me to leave. We eat, have sex, sleep, I go to work, come back, eat, and have more sex.

I ache in the best ways possible. I'm falling for him, at least my body is. My heart? I'm not so sure about. I'm finding it hard to think past my hormones, and I'm too old to lead with that part of me again. I did it once and ended up shattered.

"Hey, you're up," Paxton mutters distractedly as he looks at his phone and closes the bedroom door behind him.

"Where were you?" I ask on a yawn.

"Busy," he shrugs, still not looking up from his phone.

He doesn't tell me what he was busy doing, and that sets me on edge immediately. While we've been having fantastic sex, I also feel like I haven't gotten to understand his life any better, or the people he shares it with.

I feel as though he's segregating me, and I want to know why. I also haven't learned anything new about him. We haven't talked—*at all*.

"I have to work today," I announce.

"You'll be off in time for the wedding, right?" he asks, lifting his eyes for a second to look at me. I nod and he goes right back down to staring at his phone.

"Yeah," I say wanting to do anything but go to this fucking wedding.

A wedding where everybody will know each other. Then there's me, this *woman* whose been holed up inside of Paxton's room. Technically, I'm his *wife*; however, I feel like nothing but his whore.

I can't pretend that I've been learning anything new about him this past week. He isn't opening up, and every time I try to talk to him, he shuts me up. Although, he does it the best way possible, by giving me an orgasm.

"I need to leave here in an hour if I want to make it to the shop on time," I announce as I slide out of bed, wearing nothing but his t-shirt.

I start to walk past him but don't get far. His arm comes out, and his hand wraps around my waist, pulling me to his front. I watch as he tosses his phone onto his bed, and dips his face down, his lips capturing mine.

I melt into him, just like I always do, my hands sliding up his chest to grab ahold of his soft hair while his lips take mine. When his tongue slides inside of my mouth I can't stop the moan that escapes me as I press my body closer to his, my hardening nipples scraping against the shirt I'm wearing and making me wet.

"Cleo," he groans as his hands skim the exposed bottom cheeks of my ass.

"I need to get ready for work," I whisper.

"You *need* to suck my cock," he grunts.

My eyes widen. We've had plenty of sex, but that's something I've never done, not even when we were first married. I can't deny that it's something I've thought about. Back then, and especially now, but I've never actually done it for him. I did with my ex, Brad, a few times, but he acted like he didn't like it. I don't know why, and I honestly didn't care enough to ask. Now, I'm wishing that I'd asked.

"Paxton," I whisper.

"Had a rough mornin', sweetheart. Suck your man's cock and make him feel better, yeah?"

I slowly sink down to my knees, my hands quickly finding his belt and unlooping it before I slowly unbuckle and unzip his jeans. Then I push them past his hips and gently pull his tight boxer briefs down his hips. His cock comes out, jutting straight toward me. I lift my eyes and look up to Paxton. His jaw is set as he watches me, the look in his eyes undecipherable.

"Need to fuck your mouth, Cleo," he rasps.

"Paxton, we've never…"

"Christ, Cleo," he shouts as he takes a step back and pulls up his jeans. "*Fucking shit.* You're a fucking grown woman. How in *the fuck* do you not know how to suck cock?"

My heart starts pounding in my chest, and my face heats,

surely turning bright red at his words. I don't cry, though. I control myself. I stand up as gracefully as I can, in nothing but a shirt and no panties, and I tip my head back to look into his eyes.

"You're an asshole, Paxton. Fucking hell. What the hell is *wrong* with *you*? This push and pull, this I want you and I want us to work, but as long as I don't ask too many questions, as long as I'm exactly the way you want me to be, is obnoxious. Figure your shit out. Jeez." I stomp my foot once before I walk past him, grabbing my bathroom toiletry bag on my way out.

I take a long shower, washing my hair and enjoying the peace and quiet as I do. I'm suddenly extremely thankful that I didn't go right out and get a tattoo of his *name* on my body.

Honestly, I'm not sure if this is going to work out. The sex is phenomenal, but I don't know anything more about him today than I did twelve years ago, except for what his job was in the military. That's it. I'm literally sleeping with a stranger.

Once I'm showered, I wrap a towel around myself and head back to Paxton's room, only to run into Soar on my way down the hall.

"Hey, there," he chuckles as he sways, wrapping his hand around my bicep.

"Hey," I sigh, holding onto my towel a little tighter.

"Me and your man are takin' off for a coupla weeks. You and Genny'll have fun. Just don't get in her way if she's in one of her bitch moods," he chuckles. I look up into his glassy eyes. He's high as shit right now.

"I think I'm going to stay with my friends. It'll just be easier to be in Redding," I murmur.

"Yeah, and then maybe you can let me know how well

that goes over with that man you're married too," he laughs as he walks away.

I hurry back into the bedroom and lock the door behind me only to find Paxton sitting on the bed, his head in his hands.

"Today's the day my dad died, twenty-years ago," he mutters. "I don't talk about my parents because my mom is a piece of shit, and she hates me. She hated my dad, she hates everyone. My dad was so fucking awesome, though. He was a *Notorious Devil* in Idaho, in my hometown. He died when a guy driving a semi fell asleep and drifted into his lane. Head-on collision on a motorcycle with a semi-truck—think you know that wasn't something anyone could walk away from breathin'."

I suck in a breath at his words and hurry to his side, wrapping my arm around his back and resting my head on his shoulder.

"Swore I was gonna be better, do better, for him. He was in the Air Force, but not in a special unit like I was. I did what he did. I joined and I *was* better. I also saw a lot more shit, but it didn't matter. He wasn't there to see any of it, or to help me through any of the tough shit. I'm sorry I was an ass to you, sweetheart," he murmurs as he turns his head and looks at me. There's wetness brimming in his eyes, and it makes my heart ache just to look at him.

"Pax," I whisper.

"It doesn't excuse a fuckin' thing, but what I said, it wasn't nice," he murmurs.

I cup his rough cheek in my hand, noticing this is the first morning he hasn't had a freshly shaven face. I run my thumb along the apple of his cheek, feeling his warmth.

"It wasn't nice, but thank you for telling me all of that. I really appreciate it," I whisper.

"Let's get you ready for work, so you can come to the wedding tonight," he rasps.

"Okay," I agree, unmoving.

"Cleo, baby you gotta get movin' if you don't want me inside of you."

I press my legs together, thinking that's exactly what I want from him. He's given me a slice of his past, and for whatever reason, my body is responding to that with fire running through my veins. My pussy is aching for his dick. It's like his being open and honest freaking turns me on.

Torch

Opening up to Cleo was not my intention this morning. Some shit is better left unsaid; but I was an ass, and she looked about two seconds from bolting. She wants more from me now, so much more than she used to. I don't know if I'm going to be able to fucking cope with that shit.

It's going to be hard as fuck, and I've been ignoring it for so long, putting a band-aide on it with booze and bitches. I pinch my eyes closed and think about the nightmares that are sure to surface in full fucking force. Goddammit, why does she have to be made for me? Why do I want to give her everything, and why the fuck am I such a fucking pussy about it?

"You look about two seconds from either throwing that bottle across the room, or beating some guy's ass," Fury states.

I turn around to face my old President from Idaho. My

friend. He's in town for his dad's wedding. Standing, I wrap my arms around him in a hug and tell him that it's damn good to see him again.

"You got your shit handled?" he asks as he sits down next to me a few moments later.

"Kind of," I chuckle, taking a pull from my beer.

"*Brother*," he grunts.

"I treated her bad before I left her, then I abandoned her. Wounds like that? They don't heal overnight. For now, I got her with me. Things are shaky, but she's here with me," I shrug.

"Can't keep her in the clubhouse like that, not with the women and parties around. You want this shit to really work with her, you have to get a place for just the two of you," he advises.

"You know, Kentlee has made you soft as fuck. Ten years ago, you would have told me to ditch her and go fuck fresh pussy," I chuckle.

"Ten years ago, I didn't have the love of a good woman. I didn't have three kids and one on the way. Livin' this life, you're a lucky bastard if you have half of the love Kent gives to me. What about your woman, what's she givin' you?"

"If I let her know about my entire past, if I let her in?" I ask as my eyes shift back to his.

"Yeah," he grunts.

"Everything. She'd give me fuckin' everything, and be sweet as fuck as she did it all, too," I say, my voice hoarse and just above a whisper.

"Then make that shit happen, brother. Swear to Christ, you won't regret a goddamn minute of it," he rumbles. "Now you gonna drink with me so that I can grow my dick back to replace this pussy I suddenly got between my legs?"

"Shit," I laugh as I finish off my beer. "Can't get too drunk, it's Prez' wedding today."

"I gotta watch my old man marry a woman over fifteen years younger than me—a woman he knocked up. I'm gonna need some fuckin' booze to get through it all," he grins.

"You love seein' your old man happy," I point out.

"Sure as fuck do, brother," he agrees before he holds up his hand to get the prospect behind the bar's attention.

We spend the rest of the day drinking, switching between beer and Tequila while all the Old Ladies help prepare the wedding shit, and then themselves for the big event. I don't worry about Cleo, knowing that the prospect I scheduled to watch over her will bring her back here after she's off work this evening.

By the time the wedding is about to start, I realize that she's not back yet. I send the prospect who's supposed to be bringing her back here a text. His reply makes me see red. She's not only still working, she supposedly doesn't know when she'll be off.

I watch the nuptials of my new president to his new bride. They look happy—blissful, actually—and I wonder if that's what I looked like the day I married Cleo. I remember it well. We'd only been dating a few months, but she was it for me. Sweet as fucking sugar and a virgin. Fuck, I hadn't ever been with a virgin; but she was, and I made her mine.

I knew a girl like her, with the past she had—her parents dying, and then her only other relative dying—that she'd always stay by my side. Was it selfish of me? Yeah. Fuck, yeah. I never claimed to be selfless. I was everything to her, her only family, her only source of income, and her husband.

I close my eyes for a second and feel that burn of pain

slice through me. The way I treated her, I don't deserve to have her back, but she's here. Now she's throwing sass my way, and she's not at this wedding where she said she would be. *That* pisses me off. The longer the reception goes on, and the longer she doesn't show, the more I drink.

Then the prospect texts me with an ETA, stating she'll be arriving in about ten minutes. I make my way to the front of the clubhouse to wait for her. My body swaying with each step I take.

She's mine, and she's going to stay that way.

I'm having her branded before I take off for Denver on my run.

I watch as the prospect's single cab truck pulls up to the clubhouse. I'm so mad at Cleo, I don't even see her face. All I see are shapes and colors. The prospect doesn't say anything to me as he slips by and makes his way inside. Cleo, however, walks up to me, wearing the sexiest outfit I've seen her in. She's got on a skintight skirt and skintight tank with some of the highest fuckin' heels I've ever seen.

I spit on the ground as I place my hands on my hips as I watch her walk up to me.

"You said you'd be here on time," I point out.

"I had to work late," she shrugs.

"Bullshit. You stayed late on purpose. For whatever fuckin' reason, you don't want to be part of my life and the club. It's a wedding, Clee, not a fuckin' orgy. Why weren't you here?" I growl.

"I have a job; and honestly, I'm so mixed up and confused about us—about what *we are*. I wasn't sure I was going to come back at all," she says shifting from one foot to the other. Lying her cute as fuck ass off.

Cleo turns to walk away from me, and I narrow my eyes on her for a moment, spitting on the ground one more time before I stop her. It only takes me a couple of steps to reach her. Wrapping my arm around her waist, I stop her, pulling her back toward me before I spin her around. Her hands fly up to my chest as she tries to push me away, but I don't let her.

Leaning down, I shove my shoulder in her belly before I pick her up, hoisting her over my shoulder. She kicks and punches my back for a couple of minutes before I've had enough of her squirming body, and I slap her plump ass, hard.

"Shut the fuck up," I growl.

I take her to the closest secluded place I can get to, the warehouse, and walk inside. I don't bother with the lights. I can see enough through the one window we have from the party in the distance. Setting her down, I don't let her move an inch before I push her back against the wall, the entire length of my body pushing against her trembling one. I then spin her around to face the wall.

"Paxton," she whimpers.

"There's more. Fucking tell me," I grind out.

"I don't want to go in there looking like your whore," she shouts.

Turning her around, I grab the hem of her skirt and wrench it up over her ass and hips before I tug her panties down. Her body shakes as I slide my hands up the backs of her thighs and grab two handfuls of her ass, leaning down to whisper into her ear as I yank her hips back.

"You're far from my whore, Clee. You're mine. Even if you walked away today, you would still want me, and you'd still wait for me to come and get you. This shit between us, it doesn't just go away," I murmur against her ear. I drop my pants and shove my underwear down to free my cock.

"You're such an asshole," she moans as I move my hand around to cup her tit, giving it a rough squeeze. I let out a moan of my own as I let my cock slide against the folds of her pussy, finding her wet for me.

"You like riling me up, don't you, sweetheart?" I whisper as I align my dick with her wet cunt.

"Don't be an asshole," she grinds out.

"Tell me you want me," I rasp as my hand moves from her tit to wrap around her throat.

"I don't *know* you," she whispers. I know that her eyes are probably swimming with unshed tears.

"You know me, Cleo. You've always known me. Deep down, you *see* me," I whisper as I fill her full of my cock.

"Pax," she whimpers. I yank her neck back, squeezing her slender throat as I thrust up and inside of her tight cunt.

"You aren't pushing me away, Cleo. You aren't taking all of you away from me; not when I'm ready, not when I'm finally fucking ready for you," I roar as I fuck her.

She doesn't say another word, and I don't think it's because she's speechless—it's because I'm fucking her so hard. She physically cannot speak. I feel her pussy flutter around my cock, and it makes my entire body shiver.

"Are you gonna come for me, sweetheart?" I whisper against her ear before I suck the back of her neck—the place she loves—and she groans.

I slide my free hand from her hip to between her thighs, my fingers pressing against her clit. My hips thrust harder and faster as I play her clit, stroking her firmly and bringing her even closer to the edge.

"Come, Clee baby, come all over me," I rasp.

Her body starts to shake a little harder, and I feel every muscle tense before she lets out a long, deep groan, sagging in my arms. I fuck her hard, taking my pleasure from her sated body until it's my turn to erupt, doing it inside of her, and filling her full of my cum.

I stay planted, holding her body up with my hand at her throat, and the other on her hip, inhaling her scent—our scent.

"Paxton," she whispers, turning her head slightly to look back at me.

"No more, Cleo. Enough of the push and pull. I get it. I fucked up years ago. I fucked up by not coming for you when I finally got most of my shit straight. I fucking *get it*, sweetheart. Stop punishing me and let's move the fuck on."

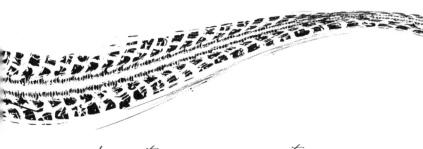

chapter seventeen

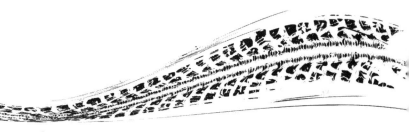

Cleo

Moving on. I have tried so many times, but each time I try, something pulls at a memory of me and Paxton. Each time, I get sucked back into the past. Now, it's as if my past is forcing me to stay there. Except, we're not the same people we were, so it's not really the past, now is it? Maybe it truly is a new future, for us.

"I want to, but…"

I suck in a breath when I lose him from inside of me. Then he spins me around, looking down at me, nothing but concern in his hard gaze.

"You're scared. It's new, sweetheart, and it's so much different than what we had before. We're different, too. But if we keep taking one step forward just to take two steps back, then what's the fucking point of it all?"

"You're right. I'm sorry. I just—I don't know," I say, shaking my head as the tears that have been threatening to spill this entire conversation finally fall.

"Work with me here, baby," he murmurs as his head dips down and his lips brush mine.

"Okay," I say on an exhale. "All right."

"I gotta head out in the mornin'. You gonna be good staying with Genny?" he asks.

"*Pax*," I breathe.

"Get to know the women of this club, Clee. It's a couple weeks, then I'll be home," he murmurs as his fingers wrap around my wrist and trace my skin.

"Okay," I agree before I fix my skirt.

Paxton watches me for a second and then he pulls up his own pants and buckles himself back up. He takes my hand in his and tugs me into his side, sliding his arm around my waist, his hand resting on the outside of my hip.

"You wear shit like that to work all the time?" he asks as we step out of the big metal building and slowly make our way toward the wedding reception, which sounds more like a loud, rambunctious party at this point.

"A skirt and top? Yeah, Pax, you've seen me in my work clothes before," I shrug.

"Everything you got goin' on right now is skin fuckin' tight. I've never seen you wear anything like this," he states, running his hand over my tank.

"I usually wear a jacket. It's cold enough that I should have, but I forgot it back at the shop, today," I shrug.

"Cleo, you forget your coat, you call your man to bring it to you. *Fuck, baby*, it's like thirty degrees out here. You must be freezin' your ass off," he rumbles as we walk into the warm clubhouse.

Paxton pulls me into his arms once we're inside, and though there are people everywhere, I can only see him through the smoky haze of the room. I reach up and cup my hand against his cheek. Looking into those blue eyes that I've always adored, I smile.

"I'm okay, Paxton. Thanks, though," I murmur.

"The second my ass is back here after this trip, we're getting' you branded, sweetheart. Want my name on your shoulder. Want my diamonds in your tits, too," he grins.

"Paxton," I mumble, unable to look away from his face.

"Mean it, sweetheart. No more fuckin' around. I refuse to lose you, to let you walk outta the door and away from me. We'll get our own place, too. You wanna start lookin' while I'm gone, you feel free. Have the Old Ladies help you. They fuckin' love that shit," he chuckles.

"Really? No more staying here?" I ask in surprise.

"We party too hard and need to crash, we'll crash here; but Clee, we need our own place to start our lives together, and to live," he states. I can't stop the huge smile that forms on my lips.

"Yay," I whisper as my arms wrap around his neck. I press my chest to his as my lips brush the underside of his jaw.

"Drink, meet some Old Ladies, and relax," he rasps as his hand slides down to grab a handful of my ass, squeezing me before he lets me go.

We walk over to the bar, and he orders a couple of beers before he takes my hand and tugs me toward a huge table full of people. Everyone is dressed nicely, some in obvious bridesmaid's dresses, and others just in cute, nice dresses. All of the men look about the same, in jeans, long sleeve button down shirts, and their leather vests.

"My Old Lady, Cleo. Cleo, this is my family," Paxton introduces. I can't help but smile at his words.

I get a bunch of chin lifts from the men, and some low waves from the women before the guys turn to talk amongst themselves.

"So you'll be staying with me for a few weeks," a woman says. She's blonde, really thin, with big light blue eyes, and she is perfectly put together, as if she's walked out of the pages of a glossy magazine.

"Genny?" I ask a bit nervously.

"Genny Huntington, Soar's wife," she introduces herself with a tip of her lips.

I feel a bit guilty. Soar flirted with me, and I was a little flirtatious back. Even though it meant nothing to me, he's obviously married. I try to give her a smile, but her eyes narrow for a second before she covers it up and gives me a smile back.

"So do you work or anything?" she asks me after a beat of silence.

I explain to her about how I work at Lisandro's jewelry store and how much I love working for my best friend. She listens politely, but her eyes keep shifting to somewhere behind me, and her brows furrow each time they do.

"Is everything okay?" I ask.

"Not really," she shrugs but doesn't continue on. Colleen, Texas' wife that I'd met a few weeks ago, joins us.

"Oh, Paxton said you guys might be able to help me look for a place for us?" I ask, trying to break the silence and ease the tension that's coming from Genny.

"Oh, house shopping?" Colleen asks.

"Yeah," I nod.

"Definitely. There isn't a ton around here, but I'm sure we can find something," Genny mutters distractedly.

"No budget, sweetheart," Paxton calls out from next to me, turning his head toward our circle.

"There's a budget," I mutter.

"No, baby, there isn't," he insists. I turn to face him, placing my hand on my hip.

I watch as he faces me, and his eyes flick down to my hand propped on my hip. They then move back up to my own before a lazy grin appears on his lips.

"Fight me, baby. Please, sweetheart, fight me on this," he mutters just above a whisper.

"Paxton," I breathe, dropping my hand from my hip as his arm comes out, wraps around my waist, and pulls me into his chest.

"Fight me so that I can fuck that fight right outta you, Clee," he states.

His face dips and his mouth presses against mine. I suck in a breath, and he uses that moment to slide his tongue inside of me—tasting me and rendering me hopelessly speechless, just as he always does. Then he lifts his head.

"Yo, Gen, I'll have her by the house around eight," he calls out.

"Sure," Genny says, sounding distracted.

I try to turn around to look at her, but Paxton doesn't let me. He wraps his hand around mine and pulls me toward the hall.

"Fuckin' hell, brother, where's the fire," a deep voice booms.

I peak around Paxton's shoulder to see a huge man standing in front of him. He's gigantic, built with thick muscle. He has a short beard and short black hair, his blue eyes almost as pretty as Paxton's. His features are harsher, more intense, but I don't know how that's even possible. To me, Pax is totally intense.

"Who's the little mouse in your pocket?" he asks, smirking.

"Sniper, this is Cleo, my wife," Paxton introduces. The man's eyebrows shoot straight up in surprise.

"Wife?" he asks as his eyes flit from me to Paxton and back to me again.

"Wife," Paxton nods. He pulls me into his side and presses his palm against my lower back.

"Bates, what's happening?" a voice says from behind him. A few seconds later, a stunning brunette walks up beside him.

"Torch," she practically squeals.

She's wearing what I assume is a bridesmaid's dress, since it matches a couple other girl's dresses who are in the bar behind us.

"Brent," he chuckles. "How you doin', honey?"

"Better now that I see you're okay; and who's this?" she asks, tipping her head toward me.

"My wife, Cleo. Clee this is Brentlee, a friend of mine from Idaho. Known her since we were kids," he mutters.

I take her in. She's beyond stunning, and thin but curvy. I watch as she curls into the man introduced as Sniper, and she gives me a kind smile.

"Mary-Anne, the bride, is my sister-in-law," she grins. "We came out for the wedding, and Kent and I have been worried about Torch since he left Idaho in such a hurry. We're killing two birds with one stone. Glad to see he's doing really well," she says as she eyes me up and down. Her smile stays kind, but she's sizing me up, nonetheless.

"It's nice to meet you. I didn't get to make the wedding because I had to work," I explain.

"Oh, yeah? But we'll see you around this week, right?" she asks.

"Umm, Paxton leaves tomorrow, so I don't know..."

"She's stayin' with Genny, Soar's wife, while I'm gone. I gotta run I have to go take care of," Paxton says. Brentlee nods just as Sniper lifts his chin.

"Well, come down here once you're all settled tomorrow. Us girls are going to put on a little barbeque. Nothing big, but it'd be nice to get to know you. Kentlee, my sister, she'll want to meet you for sure," she insists.

"Okay, *Tigritsa*, let's let them be on their way," Sniper rumbles. I swear, I do an entire body shiver at the way he says whatever it is that he said.

They walk away, and I have to force myself not to stare at him.

"If you're thinkin' you can get a piece of him, they don't share," Paxton says. I turn my head to look at him, my mouth dropping slightly. "You were pretty affected by him, baby," he chuckles.

"He's huge, Pax," I mumble as we continue toward his bedroom.

"I know—a little too well, actually," he grins as he locks his bedroom door behind us.

"What's that mean?" I ask with wide-eyes.

"Means I've seen all of him, Clee. In this life, you see that—*all* of your brothers," he says, shaking his head.

"Like public sex or what?" I ask, suddenly fascinated.

Torch

She's so innocent.

My eyes take her in, and I can't believe that she's mine. All for me. That she's willing to continue to stay mine, even with the way I've treated her in the past, or even recently. I'm not a man that does grand gestures, flowers and apologies. I'm not an easy man; and yet, she's still here.

"Yeah, sweetheart, public sex," I mumble as I take off my cut and set it on the top of the dresser next to me.

I keep my eyes focused on her as I finish removing the rest of my clothes. Cleo doesn't move. Her eyes drop down to my hard cock, and she watches as I stroke myself in front of her. Without a word, she hesitantly takes a few steps toward me and sinks to her knees. My eyes widen in surprise, especially after the way I talked to her, only hours ago, about this exact subject.

"Clee, no," I protest.

"Let me. I want to," she whispers as her tongue snakes out and tastes the tip of my cock. She's hesitant, and it's sexy as fuck.

Fuck.

Without warning, she takes as much of me down her throat as she can. My eyes widen as one of my hands flies to her cheek, the other to fist her hair. I let her suck me, slowly and hesitantly, her sweet mouth sliding over my cock as her tongue swirls around the head before she takes me in again, the motion causing me to grit my teeth. She's so fuckin' beautiful on her knees, my cock sliding past her lips as she takes me down her throat.

"Gotta fuck that mouth for a minute, sweetheart. Stay real still," I warn.

I move my hand from her cheek to the side of her head, fisting my fingers in her hair just like my other hand. Then I slowly sink further down her throat, watching her reaction. She doesn't look scared or apprehensive at all, so I do it again.

Pulling almost completely out of her warm mouth, I sink back inside, a little further and a little quicker, until I'm literally fucking that sweet mouth of hers.

My strokes are even but quick, and it's taking everything inside of me not to fuck her hard and fast—not to shove myself all the way to the hilt. When I'm about to explode down her throat, I quickly pull out, my chest heaving with my labored breaths.

"Pax," she whispers as she wipes her mouth.

"Didn't feel like coming down your throat tonight, sweetheart. I will, just not tonight," I grin. "Take those clothes off."

I watch as she strips down to nothing. With her body available for me to look at, my cock grows even harder, aching for her tight cunt again. Fuck, I'll never get enough of her, any part of her, *every* part of her.

"Hands and knees on the bed. Face the wall," I instruct.

Staying perfectly still, I watch as she climbs onto the bed, on her knees, bending over, and I can't suppress the groan that escapes as her pink pussy presents itself to me. With her feet hanging off of the bed, her legs spread, and her back arched delicately, I make my way toward her.

Sliding my hands up the backs of her thighs, I grab ahold of her plump ass, spreading her cheeks to get a better view of her entire center.

"Paxton," she whispers as her legs tremble.

HAYLEY FAIMAN

"Fucking hell," I groan, aligning my dick with her wet pussy.

Tipping my head down I focus on the way my cock slides all the way inside of her. Then I lift my eyes and zero in on her tight back entrance.

What I wouldn't give to fuck her there right now.

Christ.

I don't mention my thoughts, knowing there's no way in fuck she trusts me enough to fuck her ass. Her pussy's sweet, and it's tight, warm, and wet, so it'll satisfy me for the foreseeable future—fuck, truth be told, *it'll satisfy me for a lifetime.*

"Oh, *god,*" she moans once I'm fully seated inside of her.

I slide my hand up her spine to twist in her hair before I yank her head back. I want to look into her eyes while I fuck her from behind.

"Pax," she gasps as she looks up at me.

"I'm gonna be rough," I warn. She struggles to nod.

I wrap my other hand around her hip before I pull out and slam back inside, feeling the walls of her cunt surround me. With my eyes focused on her soft green ones, I fuck my wife.

There's nothing else to call this but pure fucking, and I'm going to keep this memory tucked away for the entire trip to Denver and back—until I get to do it again.

"*Pax,*" she hisses.

Her pussy tightens, and I know that she's close, so I lean over a little more and slide my hand from her hip to her clit as I press my lips at the side of her neck. Her body is so tense, wound so fucking tight, that when she comes, I know it's going to be epic.

"Come, sweetheart. Come all over me," I whisper against

her neck. My hips continue to slap against her ass, the sound filling the room with every single thrust.

I feel her shaking as her release starts to consume her. Pulling her hair a little harder, I bring her even closer to me, arching her body to a place that is surely uncomfortable. Right now, I don't give a fuck. Opening my mouth against her neck, I suck her skin and bite down, my cock continuing to drive inside of her tight cunt, feeling her squeeze me and pulse all around me. Then, as if she can take no more, her legs give out and her body completely relaxes.

I release her hair and let her fall forward before I wrap my hands around her hips and pull her ass up a bit, changing the angle as I pound inside of her, harder than I should. I can't fucking help myself.

When I know I'm about to explode inside of her, I jerk her hips back one last time as I thrust and still, my long groan filling the room.

"Oh, fuck that was hot as hell," a voice says from the doorway.

Cleo squeaks and tries to break our connection, but I don't let her. I keep her hips firmly snug against my hips, my dick very much still inside of her.

"My door's closed, means you don't wander inside," I growl to Honey, who is standing in my doorway.

"I'm sorry. It was an accident, but then I couldn't look away. Let me play," she pouts as she takes a step inside of my room.

"Baby, if my woman wanted to play, you would *not* be the bitch she picked to play with. Get the fuck out of my room," I grind out.

I watch as Honey stomps her foot and then walks out of

my room, slamming the door behind her. I let out a grunt of annoyance as I break my connection with Cleo to walk over and lock the deadbolt. When I turn back around, Cleo has picked up my discarded shirt, and she's wearing it, covering her naked body from my view.

"What?" I ask as she stares at me.

"She saw me, and you—she saw us," Cleo whispers.

"Yeah, that shit tends to happen in this place. What's the deal?" I ask, closing the distance between us and wrapping my arm around her waist, pulling her closer to me.

"Nobody's ever seen me like that before," she mutters.

"Nothin' to worry about, sweetheart," I rumble as I lower my face and press my lips to her sweet ones.

"I'm so embarrassed," she mutters.

"Why? She walked in on us. If anyone should be embarrassed, it's her."

Cleo presses her lips together, and it's then that I know this has nothing to do with Honey. I wait her out, my arms refusing to let her go, holding her close, and patiently waiting for her to continue with whatever fucked up shit she's got rollin' around in her gorgeous head.

"She's skinny, and young, and you've been with her. She saw that your wife has dimples on her thighs and ass, boobs sagging down, and probably my stomach, too. I hate that she's seen that, I know you say you like the way I look, but you've been with her, and I'm *nothing* like her."

"Do I need to fuck you again to prove just how much I like all that shit you listed as negative about your body?" I ask. Cleo shakes her head with wide eyes staring up at me. "Not one for skinny bitches, baby. I fucked her because she was there, not because I found her attractive. Makes me a dick, especially since we're technically married; but, sweetheart, you have to believe me when I say that all you have goin' on is sexy as fuck. You're the most beautiful woman I have ever laid eyes on."

"Paxton," she whispers as her eyes fill with tears.

"Not lyin' to you, Cleo. Now let's get some sleep so I can fuck you one more time before I gotta leave tomorrow," I grin down at her.

This woman.

Fucking shit.

She's everything.

chapter eighteen

Cleo

I suck in a breath as I throw my head back and grind down on Paxton's lap. His arm is wrapped around my back, and his fingers are shoved between my legs as he plays with my clit. But the sexiest part of this moment are his blue eyes. They're completely focused on me, and I can practically feel how much he wants to make me come—again.

"You gonna miss me?" he rasps as I climb higher toward my release.

"Yeah," I whisper before he pinches my clit.

"When I come home, we're moving on from the past, completely and totally done with it," he growls.

He thrusts inside of me, stroking me one last time before I fall apart in his arms. He shoves his face in my neck and lets out a long groan. I sag against him and give him the rest of

188

my body weight.

"Okay, Pax," I whisper.

"Fuck, I'm gonna miss you. I'll call you," he murmurs.

I lift my head up and look into his eyes.

"You'll call?" I ask in surprise.

"Yeah, sweetheart, I'll call. We'll talk. You'll tell me about the past eleven years, and I'll try to open up about myself, too," he chuckles as his thumb traces my bottom lip.

"I'd love that," I whisper.

"Know you would, baby; it's why I'm doin' it."

"Thank you, Pax," I grin.

"Hop off my dick, sweetheart. I don't have time to fuck you again," he grunts.

I giggle as he releases his hold on me, and I crawl away from him and off of the bed. I gather my things before I put his shirt back on and start to head for the shower.

"Can't wait until we have our own place. First spot I'm fuckin' you in is the shower," he announces as I step out of the door.

"Sounds fun. I'll keep that in mind while I'm house hunting," I offer with a smile.

"Yeah, sweetheart, you do that," he grunts as his nostrils flare.

"So how long have you and Soar been together?" I ask Genny, taking my small suitcase into her spare bedroom.

"Since I was fifteen. He was eighteen," she shrugs.

I set my things down and then turn around to face her. It's weird. I don't really know her, and yet, I'm going to be living here with her for the next couple of weeks. Everything about her is immaculate, including her house. She seems almost like a porcelain doll, like one wrong move could break her. She's so fragile.

"Wow, that's a long time," I murmur.

"Seventeen years. Probably twelve years too long," she announces as her nose scrunches up.

"You need to talk about it?" I ask.

"No. There's nothing to say. He fucks other women at his *club* while he's so high he doesn't even remember his own name; and I'm here, waiting for him to grow the fuck up. He's thirty-five years old. I've lost hope that he ever will."

I open my mouth to reply to her, but she doesn't let me. Instead, she just walks away, leaving me alone in her living room. I make my way into the kitchen, searching for a glass and then some water. I have a feeling that the next two weeks are going to be really, really long.

***

"Hello," I whisper into the phone.

"Hey, sweetheart," Paxton's voice murmurs huskily from the other line. "How you gettin' along?"

"I'm okay. Just reading in bed," I say with a sigh.

"Everything goin' okay with Genny?" he asks.

It's been three days, and I've only encountered Genny once since our initial conversation. She seems sad, almost as if she's just floating through life, as if she's living it with no purpose at all. It's painful to watch. I don't know what she does in her room all day long, but I didn't go to work today, and she never came out. The only reason I know that she's home is because her car is in the garage.

"Yeah," I sigh.

"She's not always an easy woman, I've heard," he murmurs.

I hum my response but don't say anything. I'm not sure how easy I would be if my husband of fourteen years, who I lived with the entire time, got high and had sex with whores on a regular basis.

"Tell me something about you," I urge, changing the subject.

Every night, Paxton has called, just as he's promised; and every night, he's told me something new about himself. In return, I tell him something about me. Sometimes they're deep, like when he told me about his mother and her horrendous treatment of him; and sometimes he just tells me something simple, like his favorite meal.

"When I was deployed the first time, and you were at home waiting for me," he begins, and I know that it's going to be something deep tonight. "All the guys were getting *Dear John* letters, calls, and emails from friends about their girls being sluts or whatever. I never worried about you. I know I came home and was a dick to you. But honest to fuck, sweetheart, I never once worried that you would step out on me."

I curl onto my side and close my eyes, thinking about the words he's saying and the amount of trust he truly had in me back then. I loved him so much, and I just knew we were going to have a perfect life together.

"You'll never have to worry about me, Pax," I admit.

"Know that, Clee. I came back a fuckin' mess. I knew I would hurt you. After I did what I did, I left and I got drunk, but I got drunk alone. I didn't go out with anyone and I didn't party or anything. I sat in a booth, in a bar, by myself, and I drank and drank and drank some more. I was my mother. I was hateful and cruel and I hurt you for no good fuckin' reason. I knew, baby, I knew that it would happen again. It's one of the reasons I left you. I couldn't hurt you like that again," he murmurs.

I can't stop the tears from flowing down my face. He's said some of this to me before, but I know that right now, he's still kicking himself for the past, and that needs to stop. We'll never move forward if he doesn't stop.

"For a long time, there was nobody else, Cleo. I did another tour, and so much bad shit happened that I couldn't re-up again, not if I ever wanted a chance at not being a complete mental case. I got out and went back to my hometown. It wasn't 'til I saw a buddy of my dad's that I looked into the club. Never had that in me before. The life my dad lived just wasn't really what I ever dreamed about. But Buck saw the demons and he talked to me about the war, about the bad shit, and it helped."

"I'm glad that you had someone to help you," I whisper.

"You would be, my sweetheart."

"I wish that I could have been that for you," I admit, chewing on my bottom lip.

"I know you do. I wish that I would have allowed you to be that for me."

We stay silent for a moment and then Paxton says he has to go. I don't want him to get off of the phone, but I know that he has to.

"I miss you," I whisper before I hang up.

"Miss, you too, sweetheart."

The line goes dead, and I plug my cell into the charger before I curl beneath the sheets and think about him. I can't help the tears that continue to flow at the thought of him eleven years ago.

I can't even comprehend what he must have been feeling.

He was so young—*we* were so young. I have to try and forget the what ifs, because that time is gone. I need to focus on the future and what can be.

Torch

It's been a week since I've seen my woman. Goddamn, I didn't think that I would ever truly yearn for someone the way that I do for her. We've just dropped off our delivery to Ziven, our Russian contact in Denver, and Soar is chatting to him before we head back to our hotel. I watch as Ziven pulls out a phone, and then a few moments, later he grins at Soar and they shake hands.

"Got some pussy and dope for the night. Figured you wouldn't be down. They're sendin' a car to pick me up," he shrugs.

"Have fun. Don't get into trouble," I chuckle as I clap him on the back.

"I ever get into trouble?" he asks, lifting an eyebrow.

"Depends on who's askin'," I laugh.

"Gen doesn't count. She's pissed off because the sky isn't the right shade of blue and doesn't match her eyes." I look at him in surprise and he shakes his head. "Everything pisses, Gen off. Every fuckin' thing. I might as well have some fun," he shrugs.

"Not gettin' in the middle of your marriage, brother," I say, holding up my hands.

"Fuck, *what marriage*? Can't remember the last time I even got tit, let alone fucked her," he growls as a car pulls up.

"I'm out."

I watch as she slides into the backseat of an expensive black sedan, lifting his chin in my direction before the car takes off. I hope that he's back by morning, because there's no way in fuck I want to stay around Denver longer than I have to. It's cold, and I miss my woman.

I'm gonna *kill* that fucker.

It's noon when Soar saunters into the hotel room, as if we weren't supposed to head out of this place five fucking hours ago. I place my hands on my hips and watch him walk into the room. When he sees the steam that's pouring out of my ears, he at least has the guts to look sorry.

"We're leavin', now," I grunt as I pick up my bag and hoist it over my shoulder.

"Need to at least get a shower, brother. I smell like I've been fuckin' pros all night," he chuckles.

"No time," I announce.

"Fine. Fuck it. At least we won't be back in Cali without having to stop at another hotel, so I can wash the hooker off of me before I see Gen."

I grunt, unsure of why he's all of a sudden worried about what Genny thinks. He wasn't worried about it yesterday afternoon when he left, or last night when he was *fucking* the prostitutes themselves. I don't understand what they've got going on, not even a little.

Back in Idaho, we had brothers who fucked whores and were married. They didn't want their wives to find out—not like Soar who, one second doesn't care, and the next second acts as though he's remorseful.

I don't understand it at all.

Driving toward home, we're able to go a little faster, taking main roads and not having to avoid any. Our truck is completely empty of anything illegal, and I'm glad for it. I miss my woman, and last night she informed me that she'd found a place for us.

Colleen, Texas' Old Lady, took her house hunting, along with Mary-Anne and Teeny. They even put a deposit down to hold it. Cleo was so excited, there's no way I could say no, even if I tried. There's a pool, and she's thrilled to be able to sunbathe. Honest to fuck, I'm *thrilled* to be able to watch her do it.

"When we stop for diesel, I'm gonna need to ride passenger and you're gonna need to drive. My head is killin' me," I grumble.

"Yeah, sure," Soar shrugs.

It's been two days since he came back smelling like a brothel, and he's rested up. His eyes are no longer rimmed red from drug use. Soar's not a bad guy. He's a great brother, but I can see there's something larger than pussy and dope working behind his eyes.

It takes a guy with demons to spot another. He tries to play off like he's this happy go-lucky guy, that nothing bothers him, but I can see past that to the pain that lies beneath.

"Oh, fuck," Soar shouts as the truck starts to slow down.

What seems like minutes later, I sit up, my vision hazy from sleep.

"What's happening?" I ask, looking around.

"Fucking pigs, goddamn," he growls.

I don't know what he's so worried about. We have a hidden compartment where we stow our guns while we're traveling, for this reason alone, and all of our product is gone. I don't get a chance to ask him why he's starting to sweat and look really fucking guilty because the officer is already at his door.

He asks both of us to get out of the truck just as another officer pulls up. One has Soar and another has me. He asks me shit like where we're headed and where we came from. I tell him the story that we're always supposed to tell anybody who asks.

We helped a friend move to Denver. We're on our way back to California.

The cop questioning me totally buys it, but something isn't right with Soar. He's being patted down, and I know that he's holding something just by the way his head drops back as he closes his eyes. Fuck.

We're only an hour from home. One hour. Goddammit.

I watch as the cop throws some baggies on the hood of his car. Then he hooks Soar up with cuffs.

"Your buddy's getting arrested and booked with intent to sell those narcotics he's got on him. We gonna find anything in the back of that truck that will hook you up, too?" asks the cop that's been questioning me.

"Take a look around. I got nothin'," I shrug. I swear to fuck, if Soar has more in his bag and I go down for his shit, I'm gonna shank his ass in prison.

It only takes a few minutes for the two cops to search the truck and come up with a whole lotta fuckin' nothing. Begrudgingly, they let me go. I turn on my speaker and dial MadDog as I make my way toward the clubhouse.

"Yeah," he mutters into the phone.

"Got pulled over an hour outside of the county line. Soar got hooked up with intent to sell," I say, cutting to the chase.

"Fucking shit. That guy and his goddamn dope," MadDog roars.

"I'm on my way to the clubhouse, but someone's gotta tell Genny," I grumble. No way in fuck do I want to be the one who tells her.

"Christ. That bitch is going to go off the rails," he says.

I nod, like he can see me, and tell him that I'll be there in an hour. He tells me that he'll call the girls and have them come to the clubhouse.

Fucking hell.

Pulling up to the clubhouse an hour later, I see that the parking lot is full of cars and bikes. My eyes catch my *Ranchero,* and I know that Clee is inside waiting for me. I pull the truck into the warehouse and then hop out, slamming the door behind me before walking into the club.

Opening the door, I'm met with the angry glare of Genny. "What did he have?" she asks.

"I'm sorry, babe, I don't know. I only know they hooked him up and carted his ass off," I say, my voice soft and gentle.

She nods once, and I watch her—the whole fuckin' room watches her—waiting for her to flip her shit. But she doesn't. Instead, she looks around and catches MadDog's eye.

"I'm leaving. I'm not coming back. I'm going home to my family. I'm sorry, but I'm divorcing his ass," she announces.

"Now, Genny. We don't even know if the charges will stick," MadDog explains.

"No, fuck that. He doesn't give a fuck about me. He cares about the club and the drugs and the whores. I'm not anywhere on that list. So he can have it all, and he doesn't have to worry about me anymore," she says as she starts to take a step toward the front door.

"Babe, you know that's not true," Colleen says.

"Do I?" Genny asks, arching a brow. "I know he doesn't come home for days, sometimes even weeks. I know he'd rather fuck those whores then come home to me. I know that what I want, it doesn't fucking matter."

"What do you want?" Colleen asks. I feel embarrassed for Genny. She doesn't seem like an open person, and here she is, laying her shit out in front of the club.

"Everything," she practically whispers.

"That's too much," Colleen whispers back.

"Then. Fuck. *Him*." Genny growls before she walks out of the door, slamming it behind her and leaving us all pretty fucking stunned.

chapter nineteen

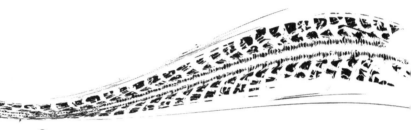

Cleo

"I feel like I should chase after her," I whisper to nobody but myself.

"Don't, I'm going to," Mary-Anne says next to me. I watch her storm after Genny, MadDog close behind her, with a grunt and a low murmur that I can't quite decipher.

"Clee," Paxton's voice rumbles, taking my thoughts from Genny as I turn to him.

He's standing too far away, looking at me with something I can't read, but I don't care. After weeks, he's here. *Here*. I start to move my feet; then they carry me in a run, and I jump in his arms, wrapping my thighs around his waist and my arms around his neck before my lips crash against his. Paxton catches me with a grunt and wraps his long fingers around my ass, giving me a squeeze.

"I missed you," I breathe as cat calls erupt from the room.

"Missed you, sweetheart," he whispers before his lips brush mine and he starts to walk away from the crowd.

"Paxton, they're all watching," I say, shoving my heated face into his neck.

"Yeah, and they all know I haven't had my woman's pussy in two weeks, so they know not to bother us for a few hours," he murmurs, making my breath hitch.

Once we're inside of his room, he slams the door closed and I hear the lock flip before he unwinds me from his body, gently forcing my feet to land on the floor.

Lifting my head, I look into his blue eyes and take him in. His face is scruffy from not shaving, his jaw clinched hard, and his eyes are focused on me—nothing but me.

"Paxton?"

"You okay with all the shit I told you?" he asks. It makes me fall a little deeper for him, just the fact that he's asking.

"More than okay," I whisper.

"Don't deserve even an ounce of you, sweetheart. Not in a million years could I be a good enough man to deserve the woman you are."

I reach up to his face, cupping his cheeks with my palms as I smile up at him.

"I have a feeling, no matter how long we're together, you'll always think that. Which means you definitely deserve me," I grin.

"You're a fuckin' crazy woman," he smirks as he turns his head and places a kiss on my palm.

"I'm *your* crazy woman," I murmur.

"Fuck, yeah, you are."

Paxton wraps his fists in my shirt and pulls it apart,

sending the buttons of my satin blouse all over the room and causing me to gasp before he wrenches it down my arms and lets it fall to the floor.

Next, he unhooks my bra and lets it fall. Without a word, he dips his head and sucks one of my nipples into his mouth. I moan as my hands fly to the back of his head to hold him against me, feeling his warm, soft, tongue swirl against my skin teasingly.

His hand skims down my side, his fingertips gently brushing my skin and leaving a trail of goosebumps in their wake, until he reaches the waistband of my cotton skirt. Without skipping a beat, his fingers travel beneath the waist and cup my center over the top of my panties.

"This pussy, hot and warm. Fuckin' missed it, Clee."

"I missed you, too," I whimper as his finger moves the center of my panties to the side and grazes my slit.

"You want me?" he asks as his mouth kisses over to my other breast while his finger continues to gently touch me.

"Yes," I say as my thighs shake.

"Goddamn, you are so sweet, baby," he murmurs, his finger thrusting inside of me.

I throw back my head with a long whimpered moan as he fucks me with his finger, his mouth owning my breast. His other hand grabs ahold of my waist and he squeezes me. Paxton is all around me, consuming me, making me dizzy and completely breathless.

Rolling my hips, climbing toward my release, I let out a cry when he pulls his hand out of my skirt and takes a step back from me. His hair is as wild as his eyes, and he grins before he lifts his chin toward the bed. I don't bother asking him what he wants from me. I shimmy my skirt over my hips and let it drop to the floor. I then step out of my shoes and pull my panties down to join my skirt before I walk toward the bed.

"You can't move," he announces.

I turn to look at him. He's shirtless now and his muscles move as he unbuckles his pants before they slump down his legs and hit the floor. I'm lost in thought about his muscles, how sexy they look, how I can't wait until he's using them with all of his strength to bring me pleasure.

"Why not?" I ask.

"Be a good girl. Do what I want," he says, pinning me with a look that I can't read.

He looks almost scary. I nod once, afraid to say anything else as I crawl onto the bed, staying on my knees as I wait for him.

"I'll make you feel good. Swear it," he murmurs.

His hand gently wraps around my neck before he lets it fall between my breasts, down my stomach, and to my center, where he swirls his fingers around my clit and then fills me with two of them.

I sigh as I spread my thighs wider, his fingers filling me over and over, curling inside of me every so often. Then his palm presses against my clit, and I can't hold back the moan of pleasure.

"Always, I'll always make you feel good. Now lie down and spread your legs for me," he orders.

I bite the corner of my lip and nod. Moving to lie on my back, I close my eyes and spread my legs. It isn't far enough, because his hands wrap around the inside of my thighs and he pushes them further, to a point where my muscles burn. Then his hands wrap around my waist as he pulls me closer to the edge of the bed.

Paxton fills me quickly, with one abrupt, hard thrust, falling over me as he plants his hands on either side of my head, his arms locked so that no part of him, other than his cock and pelvis, are touching me. I lift my hands to wrap around his neck, and he gives me a sharp shake of his head.

"No touching me," he announces.

I don't understand why he doesn't want me to touch him, but I comply with his demand and fist the bedding beside me, instead. Paxton doesn't slowly pull out of me or ease back inside—rather, he fucks me *hard*, brutal, and with a force I've not felt from him before.

My eyes widen, each thrust harder than the last, and I force myself to relax, to exhale a breath and just accept him and the way he's moving inside of me.

"Goddamn, *fuck*," he grinds out as a sheen of sweat breaks out on his forehead. "Stay still."

I bite my bottom lip, keeping my trembling legs as still as possible as I let out a breath from my nostrils. It's getting hard to stay mannequin still as each thrust of his jars my body.

Each time his pelvis grinds against my clit, it feels so damn good, I want more. I want to roll my hips to search for more, and I bite the inside of my cheek to keep from doing just that.

"Pax," I whimper.

One of his hands leaves its spot next to my head and wraps around my throat. He squeezes firmly, yet gently, as his eyes zero in on mine.

"This cunt is mine," he grinds out.

"Yes," I rasp.

"You're *mine*, Cleo."

"Always," I whisper.

"Goddamn right, always," he growls as his hips buck wilder, his rhythm completely broken. "Always, sweetheart. You'll be mine always," he whispers as he throws back his head and squeezes my throat a little tighter, letting out a long groan. His cock twitches inside of me as he comes.

"Paxton," I rasp when he finally lets my throat go.

He doesn't say anything as his hand moves between us and he starts to play with my clit.

"Move, sweetheart. Take from me," he demands.

He doesn't have to ask me twice. I wrap my legs around his waist and finally move, my orgasm already on the brink, and I take from him. With my eyes focused on his, I arch my back and I come with nothing more than a whimper.

Paxton lowers his face and continues to stroke me as he fills my mouth with his tongue, fucking me as his hips gently thrust into my pulsing pussy. When he stops moving, he rips his lips from mine and moves his hand from between my legs only to wrap it around the side of my neck.

"Missed you," I whisper.

"Missed you, too," he chuckles.

He starts to push off of the bed, but I wrap my shaking legs around his waist and hold him to me.

"Please stay," I whisper.

"You need that, sweetheart, you fuckin' got it," he mutters as his nose skims my chin and his lips touch behind my ear.

I take in a deep breath and then I ask him what I tried to earlier. "Why do you make me be still, sometimes?"

Paxton lets out a long breath against my neck before he speaks.

"Control. I like control, especially during sex. But it's more than that. When I was in the military, the job I did.

Sometimes if you moved the wrong way you or your men could die. That shit leaked into my head and if I feel like I don't have control, if I feel like anything is off, then I gain it the only way I know how."

"By demanding I stay completely still?" I ask as I run my fingers over his warm back.

"Yeah, sweetheart. If you're still, you're breathin'," he explains.

I don't fully understand him, but I respect his needs so if me being statue still, sometimes, helps him then I'll do it. And he always feels good and makes me feel good, so it's not a complete hardship.

"I don't like you leaving me," I admit after a few minutes of quiet.

"It's only a couple weeks, and it's only every couple of months," he murmurs against my neck, his lips grazing my skin.

"Rationally, I know that. Irrationally, I'm afraid you won't come back at all," I admit.

"Sweetheart," he moans as he lifts his head to look at me. I watch as sadness crosses his features. Then he smiles, also sadly, before he speaks. "I'm ready now, for everything. I'm ready for the good, the really fuckin' great, the bad, and the really fuckin' ugly. Not goin' any damn where, baby."

I burst into tears, losing him when I let out a sob that makes my entire body jump. Paxton acts as though I don't affect him. He stands and picks me up, cradling me before he crawls, with me in his arms, to the center of the bed. With his back against the headboard he holds me.

"Sweetheart," he murmurs as his fingers comb through my hair.

"I just—I never thought I'd have you again, and, and, and I'm afraid I'm going to lose you all over again; and I've been a bitch, and I've been standoffish, and I'm a horrible person," I blubber incoherently.

It's Paxton's turn to burst into emotion, but instead of crying, he throws back his head and starts laughing. I lift my head and watch him, half in awe of how gorgeous he is when he's laughing, and half pissed off that he's laughing at me.

"Clee, baby, you're crazy as shit, woman," he grins once he stops laughing.

"What?" I whisper.

"You're batshit crazy, Cleo. You been a bitch for about half a second, I deserved a fuck've a lot more attitude for what I did to you, and for the amount of time I did it, too. I also know where you're comin' from when you say you're afraid I may not come back. You don't fully trust me yet, and I don't expect you too, either. We'll get moved into our place, get a regular routine goin', and we'll settle. All of this shit will be just a really fuckin' bad memory."

"I hope you like the place I picked," I say, changing the subject as I wipe the tears from my eyes. I don't want to talk about the past a second longer, or how absolutely *batshit* crazy I feel.

"Nice segue," he chuckles as he presses his lips to mine and nibbles on my bottom lip for a moment. "Let's get some sleep. Drivin' like that, and all the shit with the cops and Soar—goddamn, I'm worn to shit," he mutters.

"Okay, Pax," I whisper.

We crawl beneath his sheets, both of us completely naked, and then he pulls me against his chest, my head resting on the hard muscle of his peck, and my arm curled around his middle.

I let out a contented sigh as he strokes my hair, soothingly combing his fingers through it like he did while he was trying to calm me down. I find myself being lulled into sleep almost immediately.

Torch

I don't fall asleep immediately, though I'm tired as shit. My mind won't shut off. I keep thinking about Cleo's fears and how she's not all that crazy for thinking them. Honestly, I wouldn't have ever even looked for her had *The Cartel* not been a plausible threat to her. And originally, I was going to keep her safe and then get my ass back to Idaho.

Closing my eyes, I let out an exhale of breath. I can't leave her now, even if I wanted to. I don't think I could. She's so much more than the girl I remember. She's stronger, fiercer, and yet still that sweet, vulnerable Clee from all those years ago, all rolled into one. She's Old Lady material, flat out, Old fuckin' Lady material. And I'd be a liar if I said I wasn't excited for our future.

Moving her hair to the side, I freeze when I look at her shoulder. I can't believe I'm just noticing it, and my eyes widen when I realize what is tattooed on her body. Without a thought, I shake her awake and her eyes pop open as she sucks in a breath of air.

"What the fuck did you do?" I ask, narrowing my eyes on her.

"What?" she asks with wide eyes.

"Your arm?"

"Oh, that?" she whispers.

"Yeah, baby, *that*," I growl.

"Is it not right? I went to the person Mary-Anne went to. She said he did all the Old Lady's tattoo's," she rambles.

There, on her shoulder, delicately and beautifully, is my road name. *Torch*. It's written in a circle; and if you didn't know what you were looking at, it really just looks like circle of swirls. But it's my name—my fuckin' name etched in her skin, permanently.

"I should be pissed as fuck," I grunt as my fingers gently trace her skin.

"Why? Do you not like it?" she asks as her bottom lip starts to tremble.

"Fuckin' love it, sweetheart. I should be pissed that you went without me. It's tradition. Your man takes you for your brand," I explain. I then watch as her eyes well up.

"I wanted to surprise you," she whispers as her tears fall.

I roll her onto her back and press my lips to hers, shoving my tongue inside of her, fucking that sweet mouth of hers until her legs spread and her hips start to move. Then I gently lift my hips and slide my cock inside of her.

"I thought you could take me for my nipple piercings," she breathes as she wraps her legs around my waist.

"Yeah?" I ask in surprise, my hips gently thrusting. I take her soft, seeing as I fucked her harder than I ever have before just a few hours ago.

"Mmmm," she hums as her back arches.

"My Cleo, wearing my brand, then wearing my diamonds in her gorgeous tits," I growl before I shove my face into her neck.

"Just in my tits?" she asks breathlessly.

"Want a ring, sweetheart, go pick one out at work. I'll buy it for you," I moan as my dick continues to take her, slower and gentler than I want to.

"Yeah, I want to wear your ring, Pax," she says with a hitch to her breath.

"Whatever it is you want, sweetheart, anything at all, it's yours, baby," I moan, meaning every fucking word.

Slipping my hand between us, I stroke her clit with my thumb, feeling her wetness grow around me as I do. Then her pussy clamps down, and I let myself go, gently easing in and out of her until my balls tighten. With a pinch of her clit, I bring her over the edge as I allow myself to fall at the same time.

"*Paxton*," she cries.

"Fuck, yeah, whatever you want," I growl against her neck. My teeth sink into her skin, my cum filling her tight cunt. "*Whatever*."

"It's practically suburban," I mutter as Cleo opens the front door.

The house is newer, in a nice neighborhood, and I'm assuming the neighborhood watch isn't gonna like my bike roaring down the street at all hours of the day and night. But the way Cleo is looking, her excitement practically oozing out of her, I can't deny her a fuckin' thing. If my woman wants to live in suburbia, so fuckin' be it.

"You have to see the backyard. It's what sold me," she giggles as she wraps her hand around mine and pulls me toward the back.

I don't even see the living room or kitchen, as they're a blur when we walk past them. Cleo throws open the sliding glass door and then stops, causing me to almost run her over. I look up and my eyes widen. Her pool.

"I'm so excited to have a pool," she whispers.

I grin, wrapping my hand around her belly and pulling her back into my chest as my head dips down and my lips skim her neck.

"It doesn't really get hot enough for a pool, sweetheart," I whisper against her skin, hating to burst her bubble.

"I don't care," she says. She turns her head, then her body, in my arms, forcing me to lift my head from her neck.

"I just want to lie by it, soak up the sun, and maybe have a party or two," she grins. It's infections, and I find myself smiling down at her as her arms wrap around my neck.

"Okay, sweetheart. Pool parties, suburbia, and you in a bikini. I'll fuckin' take it," I say with a laugh. "Who do I pay for the deposit and shit?"

"I already paid," she shrugs.

My eyebrows shoot straight up and then I scowl. No woman of mine pays for shit, and I tell her as much. She was just supposed to put something down to hold it, not pay for it all.

"You were gone, and I didn't want to lose it," she defends.

"Who's on the lease?" I ask, taking a step back from her and putting my hands on my hips.

"Me," she shrugs.

"Fuck *that*. We're goin' down to the landlord right fuckin' now and changing that shit," I announce.

"*Paxton*," she hisses.

"No woman of mine pays for shit, Cleo. That's nothin'

new to you," I growl.

I watch as she actually rolls her eyes at me before she throws up her hand.

"Well, we better do it today then, macho man, because I have to work tomorrow."

She skirts past me, and I can do nothing but watch her ass as she goes. I'm shocked as shit she's not fighting me. A smile tugs on my lips as I shake my head at my crazy woman. Then I look back at the pool and imagine her in a little bikini, my smile widening at the thought. Yeah, I'll survive livin' in suburbia for that sight.

"Are you coming?" she asks, poking her head out of the door.

"Yeah, baby," I murmur, turning to make my way toward her.

"When can we move in?" she asks as we walk toward the *Ranchero*.

"I'll get my shit moved over while you're at work tomorrow, then you and the other Old Ladies are gonna have to go shopping to furnish the place. I don't have much," I grunt.

"And you'll be paying for it all, I assume?" she asks, scrunching up her nose.

"Bet your sweet fuckin' ass."

"Macho man," she mumbles.

I reach back and give her ass a slap, telling her *damn right* before she slides into the passenger seat of the car. I drive us straight to our new landlord to get her money back and pay for the deposit, rent, and add my name to the lease.

We're married, but I'm a man—I'm her man—and I'm going to take care of her, the way I should have been doing the past fuckin' decade.

chapter twenty

Cleo

The last two weeks, I've felt *settled*. I don't know how it happened, but Paxton and I have found ourselves in a routine. He's taken some of the safety precautions down a notch, since nothing has happened to anyone. He allows me to drive to and from work in his *Rachero* alone; but I'm only allowed to be scheduled for work when Lisandro is there as well, which I don't mind even a bit.

"You want lunch?" Lis asks.

"No, I'm not feeling well," I murmur.

"It's the giant ring weighing on your finger. It's making your equilibrium off," he chuckles, lifting his chin to my new wedding ring.

The ring is a bit much, a little ostentatious and absurd, but I love it, nonetheless. I didn't want a traditional wedding set. I'd had a small white gold wedding band for our original marriage that I keep in my makeup bag, but we're not those same people anymore.

I decided to pick something different, yet beautiful. Lisandro just started carrying *LeVian,* and I fell in love with a cushion cut, peach Morganite stone ring. It sits in a *strawberry* gold band, with *vanilla* and *chocolate* diamonds surrounding it.

"Do you think it's too big?" I say with a frown, looking down at my hand.

"Not in the slightest. It's gorgeous, and I gave him wholesale. If you're worried about price, don't be," he smiles with a wink before walking up to me. "You sure no lunch?"

"I'm sure," I sigh.

"This because you're going to one of their parties tonight?" he asks as he gathers his things to head to lunch.

"No," I lie. Lis rolls his eyes and walks out of the shop.

I've become friends with the Old Ladies I've met, and I really like them. But tonight is different. It's a party, and not a family barbeque. Paxton has already warned me what it's going to be like, and I'm more than just a little nervous.

I'm so nervous I'm sick. I shouldn't be. It's not as though Paxton will do anything or let anything happen to me, but it's the unknown and the whores. I'm still not comfortable with the fact that Paxton has slept with at least one of the whores at the clubhouse; and I honestly never want to see *Honey* ever again.

"What a surprise to see you here," a man's voice says. I look up in shock.

It's Mr. Garcia, from my old job. I feel that unease wash over me at seeing him again. He creeped me out, totally creeped me out. He seemed really nice the first time I met him, although his gaze was a little intense, but it was the way he asked me out; that made me completely uneasy.

Now that he's in front of me, it's even creepier, I don't know how the hell he even found me. His beady eyes roam from my waist up to my face and then settle on my breasts with a grin before he lifts them to my eyes again.

"How can I help you?" I ask.

"You stood me up," he grunts, stepping closer to me.

"I—I'm sorry. My husband and I got back together," I truthfully admit.

"Husband," he states as his eyes dart down to my hand.

"We were separated," I explain.

I don't know why I feel the need to explain a damn thing to him. I'd already told him we were estranged when he asked me out.

"Hmmm," he hums as he starts walking around, looking at the display cases.

He shoves his hands in his pockets but doesn't say anything else. He just roams around the store, whistling as he does, making my heart race with each step he takes.

"I don't see what I'm looking for. It was lovely to see you again, Cleo," he murmurs before he walks out of the store.

My shoulders sag as I let out the breath I had been holding, then my mind starts racing. No way could that have been a coincidence. We're several hours out of the city, and I haven't been back. As far as I know, my landlord has dumped everything in my apartment and someone else is sleeping in my old bed.

"You look really sick now," Lisandro says. I blink, unaware of when he walked into the shop.

"I just, can I go into the back and rest a little?" I ask.

"Yeah, sweetie pie, go right ahead."

I ignore the look of concern that crosses his features and make my way to the back of the shop. I feel unsettled and scared. I haven't ever felt this way before, not since Mr. Garcia asked me out. He's not right. There's something in his gaze that frightens me.

By the time that I'm calmed down, I've decided that I'm overreacting. A lot of people come to Redding from the city, to get away or whatever. That must have been what he was doing.

I overreacted, *again*, just like I did when I ran away to Lis and Theo's in the first place. Absolutely nothing has happened, and even Paxton's club hasn't seemed concerned about anything at all. It's just me being a complete scardy cat, as usual.

I nod to myself, then go back out on the floor, assuring Lisandro that I'm feeling much better. He eyes me wearily throughout the rest of the day, but he doesn't say anything else to me.

"I'll see you Monday morning," I announce as I grab my purse.

"Next weekend at your place still?" he asks.

I smile, excited to host our first party at our new house. It's pretty much all set up now, but I still have some things to hang on the walls. We're going to have a low-key barbeque with Theo and Lisandro, plus all of Paxton's friends.

"Yeah, Saturday after work until whenever. But you guys are staying with us, right?" I ask.

"Planning on it, sweetie pie," he laughs with a wink.

"We'll sip mimosas by the pool Sunday morning," I squeal.

Lisandro grins and shakes his head, but I can tell he's really excited, too. I leave work with a wave back at him, and then I head home to Paxton, to this party that he wants me to go to—this party I definitely *don't* want to attend.

Four weeks later I find myself looking into a mirror. I suck in my stomach and turn to the side. The mirror doesn't lie, and the person looking back at me looks sexy, but I don't *feel* sexy. Paxton should be here any minute to pick me up, and I fluff up my hair before I apply more lipstick.

I'm wearing a pair of skin tight black jeans, with rips and tears in the knees. Mary-Anne talked me into buying them. I've also got on an off the shoulder, light grey sweater that hits right at my hips and hangs loosely on my body, showing off my shoulder tattoo, but leaving my curves more of an illusion instead of highlighting them.

Stepping into the nude high heels, I fluff up my dark red hair, which seems to stand out even more in the neutral outfit, before I suck in a deep breath and turn my bedroom lights off.

"Clee, baby, you ready?" Paxton calls out as the front door slams.

I step out into the living room and take him in. He's got his phone in his hand and he looks like he's texting. He's wearing a pair of faded blue jeans, a tight black shirt, which hugs his chest, and his, vest, which I learned is called a *cut,* over his strong body.

Black motorcycle boots, of course, finish his look, and his hair is messed up, probably from his helmet. He shouldn't be riding his bike in this cold weather, but I've been using his car. I really need to get my own. It's not safe for him to be on his bike.

"I'm ready," I murmur.

Paxton lifts his head, and I watch as his eyes scan me from head to foot and then back up before they connect with my eyes.

"Sweetheart," he murmurs.

I press my lips and my legs together at the same time. We haven't had any rough sex in weeks. Not since he took me to get my nipples pierced. It's been four weeks, and they're almost completely healed. Paxton did exactly what he said he would. He bought me nipple bar piercings with diamonds on each end. They're sexy as hell, sexier than I thought they would be, and I don't regret it at all—except that he hasn't been able to really touch them in weeks.

"Stop lookin' at me like that or I'm gonna have to fuck you before we go," he warns.

"That's a bad thing?" I ask.

Without a word, he stalks up to me, his hands finding purchase on my ass as he pulls me against his chest. I moan as my sensitive nipples press against my lacey bra, and my eyes roll in the back of my head. He doesn't kiss my lips, probably because he doesn't want to get my deep berry lipstick on his face, but instead, his lips suck on my earlobe.

"You need me to fuck you?" he rasps against my ear, his hot breath fanning over my skin.

"Pax," I whimper.

"You're gonna have to tell me, Clee. What do you want?" he asks.

I don't say anything. Rather, I unbutton his pants and shove my hand down his boxers, wrapping my fingers around his cock. I stroke him hard and fast a few times before he moans and backs out of my grasp.

"On your knees, sweetheart," he orders.

I fall to my knees without hesitation, pulling his jeans down on my way. Paxton's cock juts out toward me, and I can't stop myself from licking the tip before I swirl my tongue around it. His hand flies to my hair as he applies pressure to the back of my head, silently urging me to take all of him into my mouth. Then he lets me go, and I look up at him in confusion.

Taking my sweater, he lifts it up over my head with a whoosh before he unclasps my bra within seconds, tugging it down my arms and tossing it behind me to join my sweater that he so casually threw off.

My entire body trembles as he lowers and his fingers gently dance over my nipples, touching the bar piercings on each one before he stands up straight and wraps his hand around the back of my head again.

"Open."

My mouth falls open and he gently sinks down my throat, his blue eyes staying focused on mine until he's as far down as I can take him. I breathe through my nose, relaxing my throat as he sinks a little further, and then he grins before he bites his bottom lip.

"My name on your shoulder, my diamonds in your tits, and my ring on your finger as you wrap your red lips around my cock. Most beautiful fuckin' sight I have ever seen, sweetheart," he rasps.

I stay still, the way I know that he likes, and he slowly starts to fuck my mouth. His jaw clenches as his eyes continue to roam over me, dancing along my breasts, to my shoulder, and then to my eyes. I've never felt so desired and beautiful and sexy all at the same time.

"I'm comin' down your throat, then tonight I'll take care of you," he growls as he picks up his pace, fucking my mouth, his thrusts picking up their pace. I whimper, so turned on that the thought of waiting until later this evening feels almost agonizing.

"Fuck," he hisses.

His cock grows larger in my mouth as his hips buck, and then he buries himself all the way down my throat and comes on a long moan. He doesn't stay buried for long. He quickly pulls himself out and then moves his hand from the back of my hair to cup my cheek.

"You're so goddamn beautiful, Clee," he rasps as his thumb wipes my mouth clean. "Go get yourself put back together and we'll leave."

"Paxton, you're really making me wait?" I ask on a whine.

"Yeah, you're gonna wait, Cleo. I'll take care of you," he practically whispers. I can't help myself, and I pout. "C'mon, sweetheart," he chuckles as he moves his hand and holds it out for me to help me up.

"You're awful."

"I'm gonna get my wife drunk, and then I'm gonna fuck her until the sun comes up, how's that sound?" he asks. I sway in my spot.

"Really?" I breathe.

"Really, sweetheart," he laughs lightly as he lowers his head and places a kiss on each of my nipples. "How they feelin'?"

"Good. They're practically healed," I whisper.

"I'll play a little tonight, but I'll make sure I'm gentle," he murmurs. I bite my bottom lip trying to keep from begging for his touch, for more of him, for all of him right now. "Run now, baby."

I turn away from him and grab my bra and sweater as I make my way back to the bathroom. After I slip on my clothes, my eyes widen at the sight of my face. I'm flush, and my hair a little wilder than before, which is all super sexy, but my lips are smeared. I hurry and fix myself before I shuffle out of the bathroom and back to Paxton.

"Ready now?" he asks, lifting a brow.

"Ready," I mumble solemnly.

"Hey," he calls as he wraps his arm around my waist to stall me. I look up at him, still pouting like a child. "You'll have fun, and we'll end the night in bed, naked."

"Okay," I shrug.

"What do I have to do to make my girl smile?" he asks with a grin.

"Make me come?" I ask lifting a brow.

"Sweetheart," he groans as his hand smacks my ass. "Later. Swear it, babe."

I huff out an exasperated breath, overly exaggerated of course, and walk toward his car. I wait for him to open the door, something he schooled me on a few weeks ago. Apparently, my husband is a gentleman, a *biker* gentleman.

Torch

The air around the clubhouse is *charged*. Everyone is celebrating, but only the brothers know why. Tonight, four major players of *The Cartel* were brought down in New York by our friends in the Russian Bratva.

MadDog's contact down south, Kirill, told him of the plan, and tonight it was to be executed. It's a reason to celebrate as much as it's a reason to ramp up our vigilance. There could be blowback, but we're all fairly certain it won't be toward us.

"You want a beer or something else?" I whisper against Cleo's temple.

"Something stronger," she announces.

I look down at her in surprise. Cleo usually drinks a fancy vanilla beer at night, or a glass of white wine. Since we've been together, I've never actually seen her consume anything harder, even twelve years ago. She's staring at something, and I turn to follow her line of sight and groan.

Honey is dancing on one of the tables, her top off, wearing a pair of high heels and a g-string.

"You gotta ignore that shit, sweetheart," I murmur against her ear before I start to walk us toward the bar.

"That *trainwreck* is impossible to ignore," she says. It makes me laugh.

"Tequila, two glasses," I call out to the prospect behind the bar before I turn to her. "She's just doin' her job. And she's on the complete opposite side of the room."

"Has she hit on you at all since we've been together, since we moved out of here?"

I grab the bottle of tequila and the two glasses with one hand before wrapping my other hand around hers and tugging her toward the group of Old Ladies that I know she's become friendly with, hoping to end this conversation.

"Paxton," she calls out. I stop, turning to face her.

"Yeah, sweetheart, she has. I turned her down, so I didn't bother mentioning it. It wasn't worth it. *She's* not worth it," I inform her before I turn around, dropping her hand and walking away, hoping she'll follow me. I'm not wrong, and I can feel her tits pressing against my back a few seconds later. Then we're with our friends.

I drop the bottle of tequila on the table and fill my shot glass before I down it in one swallow. I watch in surprise as she does the same. I wait for her to cough, but she doesn't. Instead, she grins.

"You're fuckin' crazy," I mumble as I wrap my hand around her hip and tug her closer to me.

"I could list all the things you are, but I won't," she mutters as she fills both of our glasses again.

"Damn right you won't, not if you want to come later," I whisper against her tatted shoulder before placing a kiss there. She stomps her foot, and I can't stop the smile from appearing on my lips.

"Are you all moved in?" Mary-Anne asks, looking between us. I watch as MadDog wraps his arm around her waist and places his hand on her small, round baby bump.

"Yeah, the rest of our furniture was delivered a couple days ago. I think we have everything we need now," Cleo says, nodding her head.

"Better have it all, as much as all that shit cost me," I grunt.

MadDog grins and shakes his head once.

"Brother, just wait until you add kids," he chuckles. "Better not even ask the price, just hand over the cash."

"Max," Mary-Anne hisses as she turns her head to look up at him.

"Sweetness, we're buyin' shit I've never even heard of

before. Pretty sure Pierce didn't have half of the shit this new baby's got," he grunts.

"We can just take it all back and put the baby in a dresser drawer in our room, I guess," she says. I look down at my boots, trying not to laugh.

A few seconds of silence has me looking up to them, and I see that Prez is whispering into his woman's ear as his hand rubs her belly. I then watch as a lazy smile appears on her face. I squeeze Cleo's hip and look down at her.

"You good, sweetheart?" I ask.

"Yeah," she whispers, looking up at me, her dark lips plump and inviting.

I reach beside us and hand her her full shot glass before I take my own. Once we clink glasses together, we down it.

"I'm gonna need that whole bottle," Ivy says as she walks up behind us.

"What's wrong?" Cleo asks her as Camo laughs, grabbing a handful of his woman's ass.

"My brother is fucking that Serina girl again. It's so gross," she says as she gags a little.

We all look over to where the brothers are getting wild with the whores. Sure enough, there's Grease, Ivy's brother, with Serina bent over the pool table. It looks like he's fuckin' her in the ass, which would seem par for the course. That bitch absolutely loves taking it up the ass.

We spend the rest of the evening drinking, talking, laughing and just having a good time. Prez and Mary-Anne leave first, Mary growing tired quickly from her pregnancy. But then the rest of us continue on the evening, and I can tell that Cleo is having fun.

I press my lips behind her ear before she giggles at

something that Ivy says, and Colleen rolls her eyes, curling closer to Texas' side.

"Ready for bed, sweetheart," I whisper.

"Really?" she breathes before she turns around and smiles up at me lazily.

"Yeah, really," I grind out, clinching my jaw together, trying to keep from fuckin' her right here in front of everyone. She looks so goddamn sweet.

"Bye everyone," Cleo calls out with a wave, wrapping her hand around mine and hurrying toward my room.

I laugh the entire time. I also watch her ass in her tight jeans, knowing that I'm going to be fucking her in just a matter of minutes.

This fuckin' crazy woman.

Goddamn.

I love her.

chapter twenty-one

Cleo

I can't wait to have Paxton's fingers on my bare skin. As soon as I walk into his bedroom, I'm stripping off my sweater and unhooking my bra, flinging both somewhere across the room. Then I kick off my high heels and unbutton my jeans before I turn around to face him.

"Keep goin," he chuckles.

I shimmy my tight jeans down my legs and kick them off before I discard my panties, leaving a tornado effect with all my clothes, but I don't care.

"*Paxton*," I breathe. "Touch me, please," I beg.

"What if I want to watch?" he asks, arching a brow as he slowly starts to take his clothes off.

His cut is first. He folds it neatly, placing it on the top of his dresser before he strips his shirt off and tosses it onto the floor to join my discarded clothing.

"I need you," I shamelessly beg.

I lick my bottom lip as he steps out of his boots and drops his pants to the floor, walking out of them and making his way toward me in nothing but his boxer briefs. I place my hands on his hips when he's close enough for me to touch, pulling the waist of his boxers down and letting them fall as my eyes stay connected to his cool blue ones. He looks down and chuckles before his eyes meet mine again.

"That pretty lipstick's still on my cock," he grins. "Fuck, you looked so goddamn pretty on your knees earlier tonight," he whispers before he dips his head and his lips brush mine. "But now, it's my turn. Be a good girl and get on your hands and knees on the bed for me, sweetheart."

My entire body shivers before I turn around and crawl onto the bed, spreading my thighs and bending over for him. I have no shame tonight. I'm so turned on, I could scream. I let out a gasp when I feel his tongue slide through my center before it swirls around my ass and back.

"Paxton," I moan, pushing my hips closer toward him.

He chuckles, "you like that?"

"Baby," I murmur when he does it again.

"I like it when you call me baby," he murmurs before his tongue flicks my clit from behind me.

I feel his thumb press against my back entrance while his tongue continues to bring me more pleasure than I've ever felt by anyone's mouth before. I don't know if I'm feeling differently because I'm completely drunk, or if he's really *that* good tonight—not that he isn't phenomenal every single night.

"*Shit*," I hiss as I push back against his thumb and his tongue, letting both fill me with pleasure, simultaneously.

I come on a whimper, and I try to crawl away from him. The sensitivity is too much for me to handle, but his hand clamps around my waist, holding me still while he continues to eat me through my shaking orgasm. I collapse on the bed and he places a kiss on my ass, removing his thumb from my entrance as he crawls up behind me.

"I'm gonna fuck your ass one of these days, Clee," he whispers against my shoulder as his teeth sink into my tattoo.

"Paxton, stop torturing me," I whimper, completely out of my mind.

"Not when you're drunk," he chuckles. "Now, you're gonna ride me."

"I'm so tired," I hum. Then I yelp when I feel a sting against my ass from his hand.

"Nope, it's time to ride my cock, sweetheart. Cover all that lipstick you left behind with your cum," he grins.

I exhale before I say, "you're gross."

"That why your nipples went rock hard as soon as I said it?" he asks, arching a brow. "Climb on up, sweetheart," he rumbles. I don't even pretend that I'm not turned on.

I climb up his body, wrapping my fingers around his cock and lining it up with my center before I move my hand and sink down on him. I take him completely inside of me with a hiss of pleasure as he stretches me.

"Cleo," he moans as his hands span my waist and then move up to my breasts, cupping them as his thumbs slide over my nipples.

My hips roll as I throw my head back, enjoying the warmth of his hands on my body. I whimper when he gently pinches my achy nipples, sending pleasure through my veins and urging me on. I move faster, gliding up and down on his dick, before I grind against his pelvis.

His fingers spasm and grip me tighter, bruising my breasts with his tight hold against my sensitive flesh. "*Shit*," he curses.

"You feel so good, baby," I whisper as I drop my head and look down into his eyes.

"You gonna make that pussy come for me again, sweetheart?" he grinds out through clenched teeth.

I wrap my hands around his wrists, which are still tightly gripping my breasts, and start to ride him harder, chasing my climax with each move of my hips. Paxton groans, but I can't stop. If I tried, I feel like I might actually die.

"C'mon, Clee, *fuck* me," he growls, squeezing me a little harder as my thighs shake around his hips.

I bite my bottom lip, feeling everything, *every single thing*. The way his fingertips grip me, the way his cock stretches me, and then the way he's looking at me, as if I'm a mirage; like I'm not real, or that maybe I could vanish at any second right before his eyes.

"Pax," I whimper.

I gasp and slam down on him, my pussy clenching him tightly. He thrusts up inside of me a few times while I ride the wave of my orgasm before he lets out a long groan and finds his own release.

"Fuck," he rasps as his hands move to my back and pushes my chest down against his. My face goes directly into his neck after I fall forward.

"Mmm," I purr against his skin as I press my lips to the side of his sweaty neck.

"Fuckin' shit," he mutters as his fingertips trace my spine before moving down to my ass, and then back up again. "Your nipples okay, sweetheart?"

"I feel absolutely wonderful," I sigh as I squeeze my pussy around his cock for emphasis, making him groan.

I fall asleep on top of him, his dick inside of me, and his arms wrapped around me. I've never been more content than I am in this exact moment, not even when I had him all those years ago.

I've discovered that I didn't really have him back then.

I had pieces of him, but I never had the version that I have now. I didn't have his vulnerability, the background of his life, or just *him*. I had the pieces of him that he wanted to show, but not the ugly parts of him.

Now, I feel as though I have it all, and there's something completely out of the world about it. It's as though I cherish the little parts of him in a way where I never have before; perhaps because I've never actually had all of him before, not this way.

This is the way we were always meant to be. It's been a long road, but the way I feel right now, I would endure it all over again.

I feel myself flying across the room, and I land on the floor with a thud, my eyes opening and my heart racing from the sudden move and fall.

Then I hear an agonizing scream and a long moan. It sounds like a wounded animal, and I stand up to see that it's Paxton. He's thrashing around in the bed, moaning and talking, but it's guttural and animalistic. I can't make out a single word he's saying.

Slowly, I approach the side of the bed and sit down, placing my hand on his arm and giving him a gentle squeeze, careful not to jar him too much. I know you're not supposed to wake someone up from a nightmare, but the way he's thrashing around, I'm afraid he's going to hurt himself.

"Paxton," I whisper, squeezing his arm again.

His head turns to face me, and his eyes open but I can tell that they're completely void. He's not awake. His eyes are wide and alert, but there's nothing working behind them. I start to stand up, to step away from him, but his hand wraps around my wrist, and he tugs me down on top of him.

I struggle to move off of him, but he rolls so that he's on top of me. He spreads my thighs with his knees before he slams his cock inside of me, never saying a word, but his gaze completely focused on me. I let out a cry of pain, but he doesn't seem to notice as he starts to wildly pound inside of me. He groans, and no matter how scary he is, my body reacts, growing wetter with each stroke, until he starts to feel really *good*.

Wrapping my arms around his back, I meet his thrusts with my own, hoping that I'm helping whatever he's going through in his mind, and not causing him more harm. He grunts, shoving his face in my neck while he continues to pound hard and fast into my body, no doubt bruising me.

"Come, baby," I whisper against his ear.

He growls something against my skin before he moves his arms around my back and holds me even closer, his hips unstoppable as they continue with their punishing thrusts.

I come, it hits me suddenly and like a freight train, but I'm unable to enjoy it because Paxton doesn't even skip a beat. He fucks me even harder. I didn't think it possible, and tears start to stream down my face at the rapid impact of his cock drilling inside of me.

"Please, Paxton, *please* come," I beg through my sobs.

I watch as he sits up and then his hand wraps around my neck as he squeezes me, harder than he ever has, making me gasp for air. I close my eyes, moving my hands from his back to his wrist, and I hold on. Then he stills inside of me and comes on a long guttural roar.

I wait for his fist to release my neck, but it doesn't. I can see spots forming in my vision, so I do the only thing I can think of to wake him up. I reach back and slap him as hard as I can across his face.

"Fuck," I hear him say somewhere in the distance. Then I suck in a deep breath of air as he releases my neck.

"Holy fuckin' shit," he moans.

Weightlessly, my body moves around, and then I feel my head land on his shoulder and his arms are surrounding me, his fingers combing through my hair as he rocks me.

"Please tell me you're okay, sweetheart," he whispers.

Once I've caught my breath, I lift my head and look into his eyes. He's crying, tears streaming down his face, and his pretty stormy eyes look panicked and frightened as they take me in.

"I'm okay," I rasp.

"Fuck, I hurt you. I could have killed you," he whispers.

"I tried to wake you up. You were dreaming," I say as I place my palm on his cheek, using my thumb to wipe the wetness under his eyes away.

"I raped you again, holy fuck," he moans.

"You needed that. Baby, it's my job to give you what you need," I whisper as tears fill my own eyes.

"No matter what I need, it should never include hurting you," he mutters. "I love you so fuckin' much."

The tears that were filling my eyes fall at his words. He hasn't said them to me in over a decade, and I'm not sure he truly knew me enough to love me back then. I think he loved the idea of me, but not *me*. Now, though—now he knows so much more about me, and I know more about him.

"I love you too," I rasp as I lean forward and place my lips against his.

He moves his hands to fist the back of my hair, tilting my head to deepen our kiss, shoving his tongue inside of my mouth and tasting me. I moan as he swirls his tongue, moving my hands to wrap around his neck and press myself even closer to him.

"I'll go back on my meds. I hadn't had a bad episode for so long that I thought I was good," he murmurs against my lips.

"What meds?" I ask.

"*Prazosin*. It helps with the nightmares. Nothing gets rid of them completely, but that shit helps," he shrugs.

"Paxton," I whisper.

"Sweetheart, had I not woken up, I would have killed you. I was not in my right mind, and we live together. Unless I start locking myself in the guest room to sleep, or staying down here, I can't sleep next to you and have nightmares like that."

"You are *not* sleeping down here," I practically growl. He laughs lightly as he leans back, and his eyes search mine.

"The meds aren't gonna hurt me, sweetheart. I shoulda never stopped taking them. I was self-medicating with booze and dope, but I haven't been doing that at all the past month, so the nightmares reared their ugly head," he murmurs as his hands wrap around my waist.

"Just don't, don't come down here and sleep here, leaving me at home," I whisper, feeling irrationally emotional about the fact that he would be here alone with whores.

"It's only you, Cleo. Swear to fuck, it's only you," he rasps. "But I'll call the VA this week, get an appointment, and get on meds again."

"Okay," I whisper.

"You okay, sweetheart? Honestly, tell me how bad I hurt you," he says, furrowing his brows in worry.

"I'm okay, Pax. Let's get some sleep, baby," I murmur.

He nods his head, but I can see that he doesn't believe me at all. We crawl between the sheets, and I sigh with content-ment when he pulls my back against his front and wraps his arm across my breasts, holding onto my boob with a gentle squeeze before his lips touch my neck.

"You're too good for me," he whispers against my shoulder.

"I love you," I breathe.

"Sleep, sweetheart," he mutters.

Torch

The knock on my door breaks me out of my sleep. I look down at Cleo to see that she's still knocked out, her red hair fanned all around her, and she looks fuckin' beautiful. There's another knock, and I groan, pressing my lips to her shoulder as I gently remove myself from her sleeping body and stum-ble toward the door. I open it just enough to stick my head out and see that it's Grease, the Vice President, standing on the other side.

"Emergency church, now," he grunts.

"Fuck. Yeah, be there in a sec," I rumble.

He walks away without another word, and I grab a pair of jeans off my floor before making my way back to Cleo. Once my jeans are pulled over my hips, I press my knee into the bed as I lean down and kiss her cheek, whispering in her ear for her to wake up.

"What's wrong?" she groans.

"I got a meetin', sweetheart. I'll be back as soon as I can, but I didn't want you to get worried when you woke up and I was gone," I explain. I watch as her eyes open and a lazy smile appears across her face.

"Okay," she whispers, lifting her hand to cup my cheek, the way she always does. I fuckin' love it every time.

"Be back soon as I can, sweetheart," I murmur, turning my head to place a kiss on her palm.

"I'll be right here," she says, snuggling further into the bed.

I reach around and grab a handful of her ass through the sheet before I bring the comforter over her body and grab my socks and boots. I pull them on and then throw my cut on, sans shirt, before I turn around to look at her. Gorgeous, made up, sleeping, or just doing a whole fuckload of nothing—that's my Cleo.

I almost hurt her last night, and I hate myself for it; but I can't deny that I'm a selfish man. Even in suggesting it, I never once actually thought about sleeping away from her. I'll take my meds, I'll drink myself to sleep, I'll smoke, I'll do whatever I need to so that she's safe with me—always safe with me.

"What the fuck, man, I was getting ready to get my cock

serviced," Roach whines as soon as I walk into the clubhouse.

"You shouldn't talk about your wife like that, brother," one of the other guy's mutters.

"Don't be a pussy," Roach grunts, slumping in the chair.

Shaking my head, I walk over to my own chair and sit down. My head is fucking pounding, but it's not from a hangover, it's more from lack of sleep and my actions from the night before playing on a repeated loop inside my head.

"We got problems. It's why I called you all here," MadDog announces as he takes his seat at the head of the long conference table.

We all sit in silence and wait for him to continue. *Problems* could be a number of things, so I wait until he clarifies.

"One of the Russians turned traitor last night. Got a call from Kirill this morning. When they were supposed to be taking out the top tier of *The Cartel*, they had a shootout at the actual wedding of a Bratva princess. He's dead, and so are a few of *The Cartel* that were gunned down in their beds, but this is not over, not by a long shot, not like we all anticipated."

"What's this mean for us?" Texas asks.

"Not sure yet. Could mean nothin', but *The Cartel* knows we're friendly with the Russians. My guess is there will be blowback. What kind? I'm not sure. I do know that they're sneaky fucks, and their whole deal has been trying to get women and children for sex trafficking. If I were a betting man, I'd say that's where they're going to be hitting us. What club? I don't know. When? No fuckin' clue. We just have to stay vigilant and put a tighter rein on the women and children again," MadDog announces.

Nobody says a word. Many of the men have Old Ladies, but even more of them have kids. The threat of the unknown enemy is scarier than the enemy you know. *The Cartel* hasn't ever truly struck us before. We can guess where they will strike when they do, but we can't guess anything else. We're all walking around with our hands tied. It makes me fucking twitchy.

"If we find out where any are around here, can I count on you, Torch, to do your thing?" MadDog asks, interrupting me from my thoughts.

"Blow them up?" I ask, arching a brow.

"Yeah," he grunts.

"Tell me when and where."

"Okay. For now, we'll keep an ear to the ground. I'll talk to the Russians and their IT guy, see what kind of activity they've got going on. I'll also call all the other clubs and talk to the presidents, issue warnings and shit," MadDog states before he slams his gavel down.

We all disperse and go back to our women, some of the guys walking straight over to the bar. I make my way to Cleo. Walking through the doorway of my room, I lock the door behind me and shed my clothes before I crawl in behind her and hold her to me.

"You're back," she sighs.

"Go back to sleep, sweetheart," I whisper as I hold her a little tighter.

"Love you," she whispers.

"Never stop," I rumble as sleep takes me under.

Though the threat toward the club is serious, I don't have to worry. I'll never let anything touch my sweet Cleo.

chapter twenty-two

Cleo

"Your party is tonight. Do you need anything special?" Lisandro asks as we clean the counters at the store.

It's been a week since the party at the clubhouse; a week since getting completely trashed; and a week since Paxton had a nightmare. He never did talk to me about what his dream entailed, but I can guess it was about one of his tours overseas.

I haven't pushed him to talk about it, even though I personally think that it would help. He has an appointment with the VA next week for his medication. I don't think he's been sleeping well, though. I think he's afraid to hurt me again. I hate that he's so scared. He's been through so much. He shouldn't fear falling asleep next to me.

"Clee?" Lis says, interrupting me from my thoughts.

"Oh, sorry. No, just yours and Theo's beautiful faces," I grin.

"Okay, he should be home by now. I'm going to pick him up and we'll be just a few minutes behind you. Bye, Gina. You call me if there's a problem," Lis calls out as he scoots out of the front door.

"You sure you're okay to close alone?" I ask Gina as I gather my purse in my hand.

"I'm fine. My boyfriend is going to pick me up, so he'll be here watching the doors while I lock up," she says with a reassuring smile.

"Okay. See you Monday." I wave to her as I walk out of the front door.

I'm digging through my purse, getting Paxton's car keys out of my bag, when I feel a presence behind me. The hairs on the back of my neck stand up, and I turn around slowly, but there's nobody there. I shake off the bad feeling. It's only three in the afternoon. Its sunshiny and beautiful, and I'm just being paranoid.

I open the door to the *Ranchero* and slide into the driver's seat, starting the engine and hearing it roar to life. I feel safe now, in his car and away from whatever creepy feeling that was behind me in the parking lot. I put the car in reverse and scream when the passenger door opens and slams closed.

Mr. Garcia is sitting next to me, pointing a gun in my face, a maniacal smile on his face.

"You really should have just gone on the date with me, then we could have avoided all of this over the top dramatic bullshit," he states, almost bored sounding. "Now you're going to need to drive back to Sacramento, please."

I stare at him for a moment too long. His free hand shoots

out and slaps me across the face before he screams in my face. I throw the car in drive and aim it toward the city. I glance in my rearview mirror, hoping that Paxton had a man on me today. He doesn't always. He's never consistent with sending someone to watch after me, but I can only hope and pray that today was a *watch Cleo day*.

"You're a very beautiful woman, Cleo," he states as my fingers grip the old steering wheel.

"Thank you," I whisper, not wanting to answer him, but also not wanting to be hit again.

"The moment I met you, I knew that you would fetch a high price. Natural redheads are always desired. I asked Voight if you were natural. He, of course, supplied me with the knowledge that you were indeed. Though he didn't go back for seconds, and I'm curious as to why. Your body is absolutely delightful; perhaps a little too full for most of my clients' taste, but I have a wide variety of clients. Some prefer chubbier girls," he shrugs.

The color drains from my face as I register what he's actually talking about. Clients, sex, my body and pricing. Selling me. *The Cartel*. There's no other explanation. Paxton warned me, and he was absolutely right to do so. I curse myself for not telling him about Garcia's visit a week ago.

We sit in silence for the rest of the ride to Sacramento. Garcia plays on his phone with one hand while he points the gun at me with the other.

When I'm only twenty minutes from hitting the city line, I know for certain that today was not a *watch Cleo day*. There are no motorcycles in sight. I immediately make an executive decision. What I do next could get me killed, but honestly, I would rather die than be *sold* to whatever freak show Garcia has lined up for me.

"Go down to your old office, to Voight's office. The trade will be in the parking garage," he mumbles.

"Okay," I whisper my lie.

I glace over to him as I bite my bottom lip. He's not really paying attention to me, and I take that into account as I drive toward the downtown Police department. Heading down I-5, I hope that he doesn't look up at the street signs anytime soon. I'm almost there, so close that I can see the police department ahead of me.

If I have to drive past it, I know that the US Marshals office is also nearby, as is the jail and the sheriff's department. They're all in this small square within a few blocks of each other.

I send up a prayer that I'll be able to at least drive to one of them and be able to get out of the car and run into a building.

"What the fuck?" Garcia screams as I press on the accelerator, inching closer toward the police department building. I can see it, I'm so close.

He reaches over and throws the car into park, in the middle of the street, before he points the gun at me and pulls the trigger. My scream is drowned out by the sound of the gun firing in the small space of the car, and then everything goes black.

Torch

"Hey, brother, where do you want this heater?" Camo asks as he pulls the tall outdoor patio heater through the backyard to set up on the porch.

"Let's put one under the porch and the others by the pool," I say, turning around to see if Cleo has arrived home yet. It's getting closer to party time, and she should be here by now.

"I brought wine and my fabulous self. What can Theo do to help?" Lisandro shouts as he walks into the backyard from the side of the house.

I furrow my brow, looking past him to Theo, and then past Theo, expecting to see Cleo—but she's not there.

"Where's Clee?" I bark, my eyes focused on Lisandro.

"She's not here yet?" he asks, looking confused. "She left about an hour ahead of me."

My heart starts to beat rapidly in my chest at his words, and panic floods me as my veins fill with ice.

"Camo," I yell.

"Yeah?" he asks as he places a patio heater by the pool, like I asked him to.

"Get on your phone, make some calls to brothers. I'm calling MadDog. Cleo's missing," I say as I pull my phone out.

"Wait, why do you look so worried?" Lisandro practically whispers.

"I didn't have a man on her today. I figured she was gettin' off early and coming straight here, and you were there. Shit went down a few days ago, but I didn't think it would really leak here," I explain as I scroll through my phone and find MadDog's number.

"On our way," MadDog says. I can tell he's smilin', probably at something Mary-Anne's said to him.

"Cleo never made it here from Redding," I rumble.

"What?" he asks, his voice going hard.

"Her friend just showed, and he said she was an hour

ahead of him. I'm getting on my bike and riding to Redding, Camo is makin' calls," I say as quickly as I can.

"Grease'll stay at the clubhouse, you tell her friends to stay at your place, and I'll meet you out front. All the Old Lady's need to be at your place, and we'll leave all the prospects there," he mutters.

Hanging up the phone, I turn to Camo and start giving orders. Then I tell Theo and Lisandro what's going to be happening here.

"Let me follow you guys in my car," Theo offers. I shake my head.

"We can get where we need to be faster on our bikes. I'll keep you updated. You guys stay here with the women and keep an eye out. Keep your phones close in case she calls," I mutter.

"Fuck that. I'm not staying with the women," Theo grunts.

"Excuse me?" Lis protests.

"I don't have time for this shit. Fine, Theo you follow us; Lis you stay here with your phone in hand," I grind out.

I don't listen to anything else. I lift my chin at Camo and jog out of the backyard. I can hear Camo's boots behind me, and Theo as well. I find my bike and straddle it, not wanting to wait for MadDog, but knowing that I have to.

The second's tick by, and they feel like long minutes, but I know they're not. MadDog pulls up on his bike, along with twenty other brothers, and then I see the long line of cars behind them, filled with Old Ladies. I watch as the women exit their cars and hurry inside, except for Ivy, who rushes to Camo's side to give him a hug and kiss.

"We're gonna find her, brother," MadDog murmurs, slapping me on the back.

"Theo is going to follow us in his car," I say, ignoring his words.

"Sounds good. Let's go find Cleo," he calls out.

We all start our bikes together. Two by two, we pull onto the street and head toward Cleo. A million different scenarios run through my mind as we make our way out of Shasta and head toward Redding. Once we're in the mountains, we slow down, not because we need to, but in case my *Ranchero* was run off of the road.

Nothing.

There's absolutely no trace of her. By the time we make it to the jewelry shop, I'm feeling dread climbing up my throat. We all park our bikes, and I pull out my phone to check messages, but there's nothing.

Fucking nothing.

I stand and start to walk toward the store, but it's empty. Completely shut down.

"I called Gina on my way over, she's the one who closed. She told me that Cleo left just a couple minutes after Lis. When she closed up, the car was gone," Theo says as he walks up behind me.

"Where the *fuck* is she?" I ask, tipping my head back to look at the sky.

"We're gonna find her, brother," MadDog assures me as he claps his hand on my shoulder.

"Who has her?" Theo asks quietly.

MadDog and I share a look and then Theo nods.

"She told us. I mean, she said you'd warned her. I didn't really think that it could have been a real possibility," Theo mutters, almost to himself.

"*Fuck*," I roar looking at the sky again. "Goddamn,

mother fucker."

"I'm calling Oliver," MadDog announces.

"The Russian IT guy?" I ask.

"Yeah, maybe he can do some super special hacking if she's got her phone on her. Fuck if I know what all he can do," MadDog says. "It's better than doin' nothin'."

I nod, because I can't *not* agree with him. Anything is better than nothing. I hold my phone in my hand and stare at it. MadDog walks away with his phone pressed to his ear, and all I can do is close my eyes and think about Cleo.

I've hurt her so much over the years. Before I left her, then by leaving her, then by being gone as long as I was, and finally when I came back.

I pushed her.

I've always pushed her. Even when we got married, I fucking pushed for it. I'm always fucking pushing her.

"She's at the police station," MadDog calls out.

I turn and face him, unable to hide the look of surprise on my face.

"In Sacramento, or at least that's where her phone is."

We run, all of us. We jump on our bikes, throwing our helmets on. Theo jumps in his car, and we start our bikes, our engines roaring to life before we speed down the street.

I don't give a fuck about obeying the traffic laws. I have one thing on my mind, one mission, and that is to find my Cleo.

Cleo

"We got you miss," a deep voice assures me as my body is being jostled around.

I whimper in pain, and I feel strong arms hold me a little tighter.

"I got you, babe," he mutters against my ear. I don't know the voice. It isn't familiar, but I can't open my eyes to see who is holding me.

Darkness takes over again, the pain radiating through my body, and I hope that I'm going to a hospital and not back to Mr. Garcia.

Torch

The streets surrounding the police department in downtown Sacramento are all blocked off, and a sinking feeling settles in my gut. I park my bike, leaving it with my brothers as I march toward the crowds. When I finally push my way through the gathering, I freeze at the sight before me.

My car is just sitting in the middle of the street, and there are police running around everywhere. I see an officer standing to the side, and I try to walk under the tape, but he stops me.

"That's my car," I growl.

"You can't cross police tape sir," he repeats.

"That's my car, my wife was driving it—where the fuck is my wife?" I scream, unable to control myself and the panic that is flowing through me, not to mention the adrenaline.

"Just—hold on, one second, sir," the officer says shakily. He looks like he's about to piss himself.

I don't bother holding on after he walks away. I duck beneath the police tape and start walking toward my car, toward the mass of police officers that look like they're just standing around with their thumbs up their asses.

"Uhh, he's here, Captain," the officer whispers loudly.

I watch as one of the policemen turns around and eyes me up and down, his lips snarling before they straighten out.

"You say your wife was driving this car?" he asks, arching a brow.

I'm two seconds from beating the shit out of him, not giving one ounce of fucks that he's a cop.

"Yeah, this is my car, registered to me. She was supposed to drive from Redding to our home in Shasta. What the fuck is goin' on here?" I demand.

"Can I see some identification?" he asks, almost condescendingly.

I quickly pull out my wallet and hand him my driver's license. He looks it over, studying it for a moment while someone else looks at it over his shoulder.

"That's him," one of the cops announces.

"Can you come inside so we can talk to you privately?" the captain asks, handing me back my license.

I signal to my brothers who are all now standing right behind the tape, their arms crossed and their eyes focused on us. MadDog ducks beneath the tape and stomps toward me.

"As long as he comes with me," I say.

"Sure," the captain grunts.

We all walk toward the station, the captain, a couple other officers, MadDog, and me. I don't know what's going on, but I'm not going into a police department on my own. I want my president at my back for whatever the fuck happens in there.

They lead me to a room, and I feel like I'm under fire. I haven't done shit—not lately, and not in Sacramento—so there's no valid reason for me to feel this way; but I'm in a police station surrounded by cops. I'm jumpy.

"Can I get you anything?" the captain asks as he sits down across from me, another officer to his right.

"My wife," I state.

"Right. Well, do you know a man by the name of Juan Garcia?" he asks.

I look to MadDog who shakes his head once and then I tell the cop, no.

"She was with him. We don't know why. We don't know anything, because he isn't talking," he explains.

All that is going through my mind is *why didn't they ask her?* I don't ask the question out loud. I wait for him to finish. If I ask that question, I might not like the answer.

"He shot her, Mr. Hill. Close range," he states. My entire body starts to vibrate with a mixture of anger and fear.

"She's dead?" MadDog asks on a whisper.

"No, we don't know the status. She was taken to *Mercy General*. One of our officers went with her and has been sending us updates; but right now, all he knows is that she's in surgery," he explains.

I don't say a word to him. I stand and sprint out the door, vaguely hearing MadDog's voice saying thank you, and giving them his number to contact me further. I don't give a fuck about them, or anything except Cleo. They had me in that fucking room for at least thirty minutes, and she was alone in the hospital, shot—fucking shot.

My beautiful wife, *bleeding*.

I run past my brothers to my bike, ignoring their

247

questioning looks. Once I'm on my bike, I start the engine and slap my helmet on before I take off down the street in a tear, with squealing tires and smoke. I have one mission, and one mission only—*my wife.*

chapter twenty-three

Torch

The hospital smells like all hospitals as I walk inside, and I close my eyes for a moment, sucking in a deep breath before I make my way toward the nurse's station. There's a woman filling out paperwork behind the desk, ignoring me. I clear my throat and wait for her to look up, but she continues to do her paperwork, which means she also continues to ignore me.

"Listen, my wife, she's been shot. I need to know where she is," I say, dipping my voice low.

"Then you should go down to reception and ask them," she says, not looking up from her papers.

"Goddammit, you cunt! Tell me where my fucking wife is," I roar.

She looks up and narrows her eyes until her gaze lands

on my cut, my patches, and then moves up to my hard face.

"Uh, um, what's her name?" she whispers.

"Cleo Hill. She was brought in with bullets riddling her body. Think you can fucking figure out where the goddamn fuck she is?" I growl.

"Torch, brother," MadDog mutters from next to me.

I barely hear him. Blood is roaring through me, and I only see red, like the blood my wife has spilled. It's my fault. I don't know Juan Garcia, but I have no doubt that he's part of *The Cartel.*

"C'mon," MadDog says, giving my shoulder a shake.

"What?" I ask, turning to look at him.

"This nice lady gave you Cleo's room number," he mutters.

I turn to look at the nurse, and she's white as a ghost and shaking. I lift my chin to her and follow MadDog to the elevators. I'm nervous. I don't know what to expect, and it feels like everything is crashing down around me. MadDog doesn't say anything to me, and I'm grateful for the silence. When the elevator pings, I step off first, even though I have no clue where we're headed.

"She's not in a room yet, but her surgery is on this floor. The nurse said to stay in this waiting room and a doctor would come out," MadDog mutters.

Walking into the room, I notice there are a few people around but not many. One person that stands out is a cop. I vaguely remember the police captain telling me that an officer was with Cleo.

MadDog turns to call someone on the phone, I'm assuming to tell the brothers where we are, and to call Lisandro and the Old Ladies for an update.

I use the opportunity to walk over to the officer. He's

young, about my age, fit, tall and he's covered in blood.

"You the one who came here with a woman that'd been shot?" I ask, finally finding my voice.

He tips his head to the side, eyeing me up and down until he sees my cut, then his eyes go hard.

"Who wants to know?" he asks, arching a brow.

"Her husband," I grunt.

"Her *what*?" he asks as his brows shoot straight up.

"Husband. I'm Cleo's husband, Paxton Hill," I introduce.

"I had no idea," he mutters to himself. We stay silent for a moment and then he nods as he lifts his eyes. "Doctors took her back for surgery, but I haven't heard any updates on her."

"Thanks," I sigh.

"She was shot in the chest," he whispers.

I close my eyes and bite back the roar that's threatening to escape. I don't know much about medical shit, but being shot in the chest, fuck, I don't think she can survive that. MadDog was shot in the gut not long ago, and he almost didn't make it.

"How's Cleo?" MadDog asks, walking up beside me.

"Shot in the chest," I murmur.

"*Fuck*," he curses. "Brothers are on their way up. Old Ladies, too—plus Lisandro, and the prospects are on their way down," he rumbles.

"Yeah," I nod.

"You the cop who brought Cleo in?" MadDog asks. The guy jumps next to me and gives a jerky nod.

"Paxton probably didn't thank you, his head's not in the right place, but I'd like to thank you," he says, holding out his hand for the officer to shake.

The cop shakes MadDog's hand, and I give him a jerky nod and mumble my thanks as well. It's hard for me to truly

251

thank him, since it seems like he's got a hard-on for my wife. The amount of deflation he suffered from finding out she was married was painfully obvious.

The room grows loud as Theo and the twenty brothers start to trickle in. Theo wraps his hand around my shoulder and gives me a squeeze. I murmur to him what happened, and that we don't know anything, and I watch as his eyes get all glassy with tears. He fights them back, probably not wishing to cry in front of all these hard-assed bikers. I could give a fuck; this situation is fucked, and it's goddamn sad.

The hours tick by. The Old Ladies arrive and bring food for everyone. I don't eat. I can't. Instead, I pull out my phone and I call Fury, my old president, my friend.

"Pops called me," he says after the first ring.

"Fucked up," I mutter.

"How? You didn't hurt her. That piece of shit did, and he's lucky he's sitting in jail right now," Fury growls.

"Spent so many years away from her—lost inside my own head, fucking other bitches, drinking, smoking. Fucked up."

"Could be worse. She coulda had your kid and you ignored her for years," he says, speaking from experience.

"How do I fix it?" I ask.

"She still giving you shit over it?" he asks on a chuckle.

"No, she's got my brand on her body. She's all in," I admit, looking down at my feet.

"Then you've fixed it for now, and you keep giving her all the good you've got to give. Make each day better than the one before, and never believe that you deserve her, because you sure as fuck don't."

"Never did," I admit with a shake of my head.

"Keep us updated on her, yeah?" he asks.

"'Course. Me or MadDog," I say.

"Yeah, hang in there, brother."

I end the call, unable to say anything else. There are way too many emotions running through my body. I need to see her. I need to know that she's going to be okay. I can't lose her. If I lost her, I wouldn't be able to go on. I've never been as happy as I am with Cleo at my side. I love her, honest to fuck, I fucking love her.

"Family of Cleo Hill," a doctor calls out.

I stand and practically run over to him.

"I'm her husband," I shout on my way. "How is she?"

"Your wife has suffered a traumatic injury. Now, she's going to be in a medically induced coma, for lack of better words, for a couple of days. Then we'll slowly reduce her medication. This is so that her body is calm and she has time to heal. The bullet didn't hit anything major. She's very lucky. Now we just wait for her body to heal," he explains. I let out the breath I'd been holding while he talked.

"So, she's going to be okay?" I ask.

"She looks good. She's young and healthy; I don't foresee her not making a full recovery."

"When can I see her?" I practically beg.

"They're just setting her up in her room. I'll send a nurse out when she's all settled in," he smiles. "I'll also be watching her monitors, and I'll be popping in from time to time throughout her stay here."

"Okay. Thanks, doc," I say, shoving my hand out to shake his.

He takes my hand with a grin and we shake. I watch as he walks away before I turn to the waiting room full of people. I open my mouth to speak, but before I can even get a word out, the cop from earlier is in front of me.

"She's gonna be okay. Bullet's missed everything major. They're keeping her in a coma for a while, but the doctor said he thought she'd make a full recovery," I explain before he can even ask.

"Good. I'm really glad. I'll tell my captain," he mumbles before he puts his head down and walks away.

I was right. He had a hard-on for my wife. I can't really blame the dude. My wife is stacked and gorgeous. If he knew her, he'd like her even more. She's the sweetest fuckin' woman on this planet.

Facing the room full of my friends, men and women I also consider my family, I tell them what the doctor told me. I watch as Lisandro turns into Theo's chest, and his body starts shaking with sobs. I can't blame him. I feel like crying, too. I won't, but I feel like it; I'm so fuckin' happy.

Cleo

I try to open my eyes, but the pain shooting through me is too much. I moan and turn my head to the side, attempting to call out for help. I don't know where I am or what's happening, but I know I'm in serious pain. I imagine I'm locked in some creepy dungeon with creepy Mr. Garcia. Then I hear the sweetest sound in the entire world.

"Relax, sweetheart. I'll get you something for the pain," Paxton whispers.

I whimper again, not because of the pain, but because I know that it's only my imagination playing tricks on me.

Paxton isn't here with me. He's at our house, probably panicking because he doesn't know where I am. And me? I'm going to be *sold* to the highest bidder.

"Baby, don't get all worked up, the nurse is comin'," his voice rumbles through the quiet room.

A few seconds later, I hear another voice, a female, and then the pain floats away and I'm pulled under again. Hopefully, I won't ever wake up. I don't want to live through whatever nightmare awaits me.

Torch

"What the fuck is going on with this Garcia guy?" I growl into the phone.

I'm standing outside of Cleo's room. I don't want to talk about this in front of her, just in case she can hear me. The last thing I want her waking up to is my angry voice.

The doctors told me that she could probably hear what was happening in her room; at minimum, she can feel the vibe of the people in there, and right now my vibe is fucking pissed the fuck *off*.

"Oliver did some digging. He had to dig fucking deep," MadDog murmurs. "It's ugly."

"Don't care. I didn't think it was going to be pretty, since my woman is lying in a hospital bed, in a goddamn coma, man," I growl.

"Fuck. Her boss, the attorney, he was in on it. At least on the major aspect of Garcia's work. I don't know if he had anything to do with Cleo specifically. Apparently, Garcia is a client of his. Voight has represented him for different things, and they're friends. I don't know what that means, or what Voight is into, but I do know that he brought Garcia into his office just a few days before Cleo vanished to Redding. Cleo was on a buy list, Torch." He mumbles his last few words, as if saying them like that will make it less true.

"What the fuck do you mean, a buy list?" I ask, my eyes watching her through the window.

"Garcia was taking her to sell her; he had a buyer lined up already. I don't know who, and Oliver hasn't figured it out yet."

"He's lucky he's locked up," I state.

"We have guys on the inside. When he gets transferred to prison, we have guys," he informs me.

"What about Soar?" I ask.

"Happens to be in the California State Prison, located in Sacramento, for the next couple of years," he states.

"Sucks for him, but could be beneficial for the situation," I say, thinking aloud.

"Exactly."

"What's this mean for the rest of Garcia's friends?" I ask, speaking of *The Cartel.*

"Oliver's hacked his shit, now that he knows who he is. His local friends are going to go down here in a couple days. Kirill, my Russian friend, is heading this way, and we're going to have a chat," he explains.

"I want in," I grunt.

"You stay with Cleo, keep your hands nice and sparkling clean," he says. I know that it's more than just words. It's a fucking order.

"You'll keep me updated?"

"Always, brother."

MadDog ends the call, and I let out a breath before I walk back into Cleo's room. My woman. She's fucking helpless right now, but revenge will be dealt, and with a fucking smile. She's not just my woman. She's my wife, my Old Lady, which means she has the protection of the *Notorious Devils*. They're ruthless when it comes to women and children under their protection.

A few minutes later, the door opens, and Mary-Anne walks inside.

"How is she today?" she asks, handing me a bag from In-N-Out Burger.

"Same as yesterday," I grumble, taking the bag that I know is filled with a double-double and animal style fries.

"Why don't you eat and then take a shower. I'll stay with her for a while," she suggests.

"Yeah," I mumble as I pull the food out and start shoving my face.

"She's going to be okay," Mary says. She's not talking to me. She sounds more like she's talking to herself.

"She is."

"Genny is gone. She left. The house is untouched, but she's gone," she says, telling me about the latest happenings of the Genny and Soar drama.

Genny didn't show up to the short sentencing. Soar didn't have a trial. He plead out and he got five years. Maybe he'll be out in three with good behavior, but this shit was not his first strike, and the judge was not one of ours. He's a hard ass who was making an example out of him.

"Maybe that's what she needs to do. They didn't seem happy," I shrug.

I don't really give a shit about other people's relationships, but I can't think about *The Cartel* and why Cleo isn't awake yet, even though she's off of the medicine that kept her in a coma like state twenty-four hours a day.

"Yeah, makes me sad. They were a pretty couple," she says with a shrug.

"Soar said they'd been together since high school. Seems like they just went in different directions as they grew up. That shit happens sometimes."

"Yeah, I guess so," she mumbles.

I know she's probably thinking about her brother Sniper and his woman Brentlee. They were high school sweethearts, too. He left her, joined the military, and she married an abusive piece of shit. They're back together now, happy and poppin' out babies left and right; but for a long time, they were miserable and living a lie, both of them.

"If they're meant to be, they'll find their way back to each other," I say.

"I like this part of you, Torch," she smiles. I look at her in confusion. "This happy part of you. This part of you that's in love with a woman; and not just any woman, but the woman that you have always wanted. It's a beautiful thing, what you two have. I love that for you. I don't know everything you went through in the military, but I can tell it wasn't pretty. I think you deserve all of this beauty that Cleo gives you."

"Mary," I grunt.

"Go take a shower," she grins.

I shake my head but do as she suggests. A hot shower is something I don't only *want* right now, I fuckin' need it.

chapter twenty-four

Cleo

"C'mon, sweetheart, it's time to wake up now," Paxton's rough voice murmurs.

My eyes flutter open in hopes that it's not my imagination, but the real thing. I turn my head, expecting to see Mr. Garcia. Instead, I'm met with the sweetest vision I have ever seen in my entire life.

Paxton.

"Are you real?" I ask, lifting my hand to touch his cheek.

"Yeah, sweetheart. I'm real," he whispers.

The room is dark, but there's a beeping sound that fills it. It smells like a hospital, and I know that I must be in one.

"What happened?" I ask.

"You were shot, baby," he chokes before he clears his throat.

I take in his features and furrow my brow. He's got a full beard on his face, something I've never seen before, and his eyes are sunken in deep, as though he hasn't slept in weeks.

"How long have I been here?" I rasp.

"A month, sweetheart. Never thought you'd fuckin' wake up," he says hoarsely before he lets out a cough. "Called the nurses to come and see to you."

Before I can say another word, Paxton steps away, and my room is filled with doctors and nurses. I'm asked a million different questions, and when I admit that I'm in pain, I'm given medicine in my IV. I start to feel lightheaded, but I don't want to fall asleep before I can see Paxton again, so I try as hard as I can to keep my eyes open.

Once the doctors leave, his tired face fills my vision again. I grab his hand with mine and give it a squeeze.

"I love you, Pax," I whisper.

"Love you so fuckin' much, Cleo," he says gently as he squeezes my hand. "Rest. I'll be right here when you wake up."

My eyes flutter closed. No matter how hard I try to keep my lids open, I fall asleep, Paxton's hand in mine and the image of his handsome, but tired face in my mind.

Torch

"How's she doin'?" MadDog asks. We're standing in the hallway of the hospital, an hour after Cleo woke up and then fell back asleep.

I turn my head to look at her in her bed before I face

MadDog.

"She's tired and out of it, but she could talk, and she seemed coherent as far as what was happening around her. She was confused, but she knew who I was," I admit.

"Good. You know all the Old Ladies are gonna be down here as soon as they know she's awake," he chuckles.

"Tomorrow?" I ask.

"Yeah, I'll try to hold Mary off that long," he laughs. "I'll start makin' calls."

"I'm calling Lisandro right now," I inform him. He lifts his chin to me before he walks away.

"What happened?" Lisandro screams in my ear. He does this every single fuckin' time I've called him to give him an update, or lack thereof, until this point.

"She woke up," I admit. "She talked, and she seems good," I grin.

"I'm there as soon as I can be," he announces.

"She's sleepin' right now, but yeah, come on down tonight. Wait 'til Theo gets off work. He'll be pissed if you leave without him," I warn.

The past month, I've become close with Theo and Lisandro. I've discovered that they're good men. They care about Cleo, but they care about me, too. I feel like I don't deserve to have them as family, because that's exactly what they've become. I'm completely grateful for them, for their compassion toward me and their love of Cleo.

"You're right," he grumbles.

"See you tonight," I chuckle.

"You want me to bring you dinner?" he asks.

"Fuck, yeah," I grunt.

I haven't left the hospital once since I walked in here a

month ago. Mary-Anne brought me a duffle bag of clothes, and sometimes a brother or Lis will bring me food, but I've been mostly survin' on shitty hospital food and coffee.

"See you soon," he sings.

I'm glad that he's happy again. He's been a fuckin' mess. We *all* have.

I watch television, waiting for Cleo to wake up again, hoping to get a little more time with her before Lisandro and Theo arrive, but I don't want to wake her up. I know that she needs rest.

"Are you watching *Fixer Upper*?" Cleo's hoarse voice mutters. I walk over to her bedside, pulling a chair with me and taking her hand in mine as I do.

"I was," I chuckle.

"Love that show," she breathes as her eyes flutter open.

"How you feelin', sweetheart?" I ask as my thumb makes circles on her hand.

"Tired and sore, but better than when I first woke up," she admits. I can't help but smile.

"Lis and Theo will be here soon," I inform her.

"Yay," she cheers softly.

"Fuckin' hell, baby, you scared the shit outta me."

"I'm sorry, Pax," she whispers.

"Don't be. Not your fault, not even a second. You did the right thing. So fuckin' proud of how you handled the situation, baby," I mutter as I cup her cheek with my hand.

She smiles at me, and it's like a goddamn punch to the gut. She's stunning, and I missed her gorgeous smile—I missed her even more than I realized.

"Missed you, Clee," I admit, sounding like a pussy.

"I love you," she replies.

"Yeah, sweetheart, love the fuck outta you, too," I grunt.

"Where is she? Where's my girl?" Lisandro cries. I turn my head, chuckling as I do. "Oh, my *god*, I swear I haven't slept a wink in a month. Do you see the bags under my eyes?" he asks as he hurries to her side.

I stand and wink at Cleo, and she rolls her eyes before I walk away.

"Gonna make a phone call," I mutter.

Theo and Lisandro both wave absentmindedly at me as I walk out of the room. I head over to the window and I watch my woman with her family, her best friends, as I pull out my phone and call MadDog.

"Didn't ask you earlier, how's the situation?" I question him before he can even greet me.

"Handled. He was brought in four days ago, and was gone as of shower time this mornin'," he explains.

Without saying the words, his meaning is perfectly clear. Soar killed Garcia this morning in the showers. I grin at the information as my eyes roam over Cleo. She's smiling, talking to her friends. Lisandro's hands wave around in excitement, and I can tell that he's finally breathing easy.

Lisandro's been beside himself, been a wreck, emotionally and every other way he could be. His obvious love of my woman makes me realize that he is special, he *is* family and he is part of our circle from now until the end. Him and Theo are under the *Notorious Devils* protection, and under my protection.

"She looks good," Theo says, walking out of the room to join me.

"He's been taken care of," I state, not looking at him, my eyes unable to move away from my Cleo.

263

"Thank fuck," Theo rumbles. I've kept him informed of *everything*. Probably not the wisest decision I've ever made, but a decision that I made anyway. Smart or otherwise. "How'd it happen?"

"The shower," I grin as I turn to face him.

"Seems fitting," he smiles widely. "Now we heal our girl."

"We do," I nod.

"You're up for the job? I have a feeling it's going to be a long road ahead of you," he states.

"Been sitting by her side every single day for a month. Hardly eating and sleeping. I'm up for it," I say lifting my chin.

"You're gonna give her the life she's always deserved."

"Nope," I grunt. His eyes narrow and I continue. "She deserves more than I could ever give her. So, no, I can't give her the life she deserves, never could. I'm gonna give her the best fuckin' life I can. Gonna make her smile every day, kiss her every day, and hopefully fuck her every day," I grin. "Then, I'm gonna fill her with babies when she wants 'em, however many she wants, too. Build a life for her, and with her. Tell her every single fuckin' day that I love her, and only her."

Cleo

I watch as Theo and Paxton walk back into my room and wait for some kind of crazy lecture. Things were looking tense through the window as they talked, but it seems as though everything is okay now. They both smile and Paxton even gives me a wink.

"I have to work tomorrow, but I'm here all day Saturday," Lisandro explains.

"Okay," I murmur as my eyes grow heavy.

"We'll head out, but we're so glad you're awake now," Theo says as his hand wraps around mine, giving it a squeeze. He leans down and presses a kiss to my forehead.

"I'll bring antipasto Saturday," Lisandro rambles as he places a kiss on each of my cheeks.

"Okay," I say with a nod.

They leave a few moments later, Theo having to practically drag Lis out of the room. Now it's just Paxton and me, and I'm so grateful. I'm also so tired.

"You, okay?" he asks, sitting down in the chair next to my bed.

"Yeah," I sigh.

"Love you, Clee," he mutters. "Missed you."

"It was all awful; but Paxton, I've never been happier to have you back in my life," she whispers.

"Your safety will never be compromised again," he announces.

"Baby, you can't promise that," I say, shaking my head.

"The fuck I can't."

"Paxton," I exhale.

"I'll protect you until my dying breath. You're mine, my wife, my woman, and my Old Lady. You're gonna be the mother to my children, too. So, yeah, I can fucking guarantee that nobody will ever harm you again," he growls.

"Okay," I say, not believing my words, but saying them because he believes *his* fierce words.

"Mean it, sweetheart. Nobody will ever hurt you again," he growls.

"You can't know that, Pax."

"The last piece of the puzzle is eliminated," he chuckles.

"What's that?" I ask.

"Garcia's no longer an issue," he shrugs.

"What exactly does that mean?" I ask, my eyebrows kitting together. Paxton just shrugs and my imagination takes over, my eyes widening as he grins.

"No more talk of him, yeah?" he asks, giving me a wink.

"Paxton," I whisper.

"I was sitting right here, sweetheart. I didn't do shit," he grunts.

"Garcia?" I ask.

"Interesting thing, he was eliminated in prison just this morning," he shrugs.

I close my eyes for a second and let out an exhale. I'm not happy that this man has been, as Paxton put it, *eliminated*, but I also can't stop the immense amount of relief that fills me, either.

Maybe that makes me an awful person, I don't know, but he's gone—forever. There's a solace to the fact that I never have to worry about him ever again.

"Sleep, sweetheart," Paxton whispers.

"Okay," I breathe as sleep pulls me under.

chapter twenty-five

Cleo

"Paxton, I need to get out of this house," I explain.

I've been stuck inside of our home for the past two weeks. I'm not feeble. I can walk around, talk and even shower on my own now. But Paxton won't let me out of the house or out of his sight. He stays in the bathroom while I shower, only giving me privacy to use the facilities throughout the day. It's driving me insane.

"You're not going," he growls.

"It's girl's night at Mary-Anne's. Nothing is going to happen to me there," I say again.

It's probably the fifth time I've tried to tell him that nothing is going to happen and that I'm going to be fine. I'm about two seconds away from getting on my knees and begging.

"Not tonight," he murmurs as he walks over to me.

Wrapping his hand around my cheek, his thumb caresses my bottom lip and sends my body into overdrive. We haven't been intimate, something that didn't bother me until this exact moment. Suddenly, I feel as though I'm on fire for him. I whimper, unable to hold it in and he gives me a small lopsided grin.

"Pax," I whisper.

"I'm not trying to be a dick or to keep you from your girls, but, sweetheart, not tonight?"

I nod when his phone rings, and I poke out my bottom lip in a pout when he steps away from me to take the call, but not too far. I shamelessly listen in on his conversation. I'm bored as hell.

"Tonight, thought we were doin' that shit tomorrow?" he asks. "Yeah, I'm ready. I got all my supplies at least, just have to finish up a few things. Why didn't I get more notice? Yeah, he arrived about an hour ago, he'll be tired as fuck though. Yeah, see you soon."

I hold my breath when he turns to me, his brows furrowed before he speaks.

"You're goin' to girl's night," he announces.

I don't know what Paxton has to go do, and I don't care enough to ask him. I'm way too excited about going over to Mary's and seeing the rest of the girls. Our plans were to start planning Mary's baby shower, along with cocktails and dinner.

"Okay," I shrug as if I'm not completely and totally over the top excited.

"You gonna gloat?" he asks on a chuckle.

"No," I say, shaking my head with wide eyes.

"When do you go back for your checkup?" he asks,

changing the subject.

"Next week."

"You gonna ask him when you can fuck your husband again?" he asks, closing in on me and wrapping his hand around my waist, pulling my chest into his.

"Pax," I breathe, pressing my legs together.

"You do this night with your girls. You ask your doctor that, and next weekend—all weekend—we're in bed. No interruptions, just you and me," he whispers, his breath tickling my face.

"Yeah," I exhale.

"Hmmm," he breathes as his nose slides alongside mine and his lips press against my own in a gentle kiss. "Go get ready to leave."

"I want you," I admit.

"I'm not going to do anything that could hurt you, sweetheart. I know what you went through has nothing to do with that part of your body, but I don't fuck soft and gentle, and I don't want to damage your wounds," he rumbles.

I grin, rising to my toes to press my lips to his before I walk back to our bedroom to get ready. I don't have to look behind me to know that he's right on my heels, my shadow for the past two weeks. I can't deny that he's a fabulous nursemaid. He's followed the doctor's orders to a T, but I still need to breathe a little.

"You need help getting dressed?" he asks while he thumbs through his own clothes, grabbing a black t-shirt and taking his white one off to replace it with the black.

"I'm just going to do this dress, I think," I shrug, holding up a plain dark purple, cotton dress.

"Looks short," he grunts as he walks toward me.

I suck in a breath as he helps me out of my shirt, then tugs my sweatpants off. I try not to look at the scar on my chest in the mirror. Paxton distracts me causing me to moan when his fingertips trace the swells of my breasts peeking out from my bra.

I close my eyes when his head leans down and his lips touch the top of each breast before he pulls my dress over my head. Silently, he helps me thread my arms through the long sleeves, then his hands wrap around my waist, his head tipped and his eyes focused on mine.

"I love you, Cleo," he whispers.

Something has changed inside of him in the last few minutes. I can't put my finger on what it could be, but his demeanor is different; and the look in his eyes is nothing short of somber.

"What's happened?" I ask, cupping his cheek.

"Just got some shit goin' down. I don't like leaving you. Now that I have shit I gotta do, that hopefully won't but could cause more war..." he shakes his head once before he settles his eyes back on mine. "Don't want to be away from you, not for even a second."

"I'll be okay," I murmur.

"Know you will, sweetheart. You'll have four prospects and two brothers watching you. Doesn't mean that I don't worry."

"I love you so much. How did I get so lucky to have you waltz back in my life?" I whisper as tears fill my eyes.

"Lucky? Look what bein' with me has done to you. I don't call that shit lucky," he grunts.

"That doesn't matter. Not really. I have a man that would kill for me, that loves me so much he tells me so often that I don't think I could forget that love even for a second. I have a man that takes care of me, and looks at me as if he doesn't deserve me at all. I'm so damn lucky," I murmur.

"I'm the lucky one," he grins before he dips his face even lower and presses his lips to mine.

His tongue snakes out and tastes the seam of my lips. I gasp in surprise, and he takes the opportunity to slide his tongue inside of my mouth, filling me, tasting me, and seducing me. I wrap my arms around his waist and press my chest against his, which causes him to moan. He doesn't kiss me for long before he's pulling away, his teeth nibbling my lips as he steps back from me slightly.

"Gotta head out, sweetheart," he rasps as he drops his forehead against mine.

"Okay," I sigh.

We arrive at Mary-Anne's a few moments later. The house looks like it's under heavy guard with the amount of bikes and men that surround it.

"What exactly is going on, Pax?" I ask as I look around.

He ignores my question as he helps me out of the car, and we walk up to the front porch together. Colleen opens the door before Paxton can ring the bell and greets us with a warm but concerned smile. She doesn't say anything, just turns around and walks back into the house.

"That's weird," I mutter as I turn into Paxton's arms.

"Not everyone reacts to being on semi-lockdown all that well, Clee," he states.

"Semi-lockdown?" I ask in confusion.

"Lockdown is when all the women and children are brought to the club and literally locked-down. This is semi. You're all together, the kids are all together in a different house, and you're all under guard," he explains.

"Why are we separated?" I ask.

"Don't know. That, sweetheart, I was not privy to," he says with a grin.

"I'm a little scared now," I admit.

"Don't be. You'll be safe here. Now, go inside and have a good time. I'll be here to pick you up later tonight," he murmurs before his lips brush mine.

"I love you," I whisper.

"Love you, sweetheart."

I hurry inside of the house and close the door behind me. Turning around, I notice that all of the other women are feeling the same kind of melancholy and somberness that Colleen greeted me with. Mary-Anne gives me a wobbly smile, and I know that something is really, really wrong.

"Tell me," I whisper.

"We don't know exactly what's going on," she whispers. "But we've all pieced together conversations, and it seems like they're going to do something to *The Cartel* tonight." I blink at her words and find an empty chair to sit down in, feeling unnerved by her words.

"Everything's going to be just fine," Ivy says with a nod.

"Yeah, it will, for sure," Teeny mumbles, nodding as well.

"Anyone heard from Genny?" Bobbie asks, changing the subject.

I'm thankful for the change of topic, but I can't stop the thoughts I have from swirling around in my head. This is all my fault. Garcia found me, and he didn't even know my connection to Paxton when he did; at least, I don't think he did—not at first, anyway.

I can't help but feel like whatever happens tonight, and

whoever gets hurt because of it, that's on me. My fault. Totally and completely my fault. If I had never come back here, if I hadn't given in to Paxton and gotten back together with him, nobody would be in danger right now.

"Get that out of your head," Mary-Anne says.

"Hmm?"

"None of this is your fault," she states.

"How is it *not*?"

"You are not in control of other people's actions, neither are you responsible for anybody's *re*actions," she shrugs.

I think about her words, letting them replace my thoughts of fear and guilt. I send a silent prayer that, by the end of tonight, everybody comes home safe to their families.

Torch

I stick my lip out in concentration as I combine the deadly ingredients that make up the bomb we're going to use tonight. These fucking *Cartel* fucks think that they can target our friends, the Russian's, and that they can target our women, they have another fuckin' thing coming.

We are done fucking around.

Maybe this will bring on more war and bloodshed, but at this point, our hands are tied. I'm not going to do a shootout in fucking public like that shit they pulled in New York. This is not the wild west.

I'm going to do what I do best and help my brothers, and my family, plus get a little retribution for that piece of shit who tried to hurt my Cleo.

I'm in the room where we hold church and I'm building a fucking bomb. I thought that I was done with this shit years ago, but apparently, my skill set is still desired even after being out of the military. At least for today.

My job in the Air Force was Explosive Ordinance Disposal, finding bombs and destroying them properly. However, in order to understand how to do that, you have to know about the components of bombs, and also how they're built.

"You ready?" MadDog asks.

"Almost. This shit is touchy. We have to be careful," I explain.

"How careful?"

"It's chemical, and it's not stable," I shrug as I back away.

"Torch," MadDog rumbles.

"It's going to get shit done, and you said that's what you wanted—without being suspicious and fingers being pointed in our direction," I clarify.

"Fuck, what is this shit?" he asks as his eyebrows furrow together.

"*TATP*. It's not quite as strong as TNT, which was my original thought, but these components are easier to get ahold of under the radar. It's been used a lot, recently in the Paris attacks last November," I explain.

"Fucking hell, Torch. You're gonna have the Feds swarming around us like piranha," he grunts.

"You want it done? I'm handlin' shit. You wanna pussy-foot around, then I guess I could sit and wait for them to actually succeed in taking one of our women, our children, or shoot us up like they did the Russian's at a wedding at the fucking *Plaza* in New York."

"Don't get yourself killed," he mutters as he walks away.

I won't get myself killed. This isn't my first rodeo.

"You ready?" I ask the seemingly empty room. I load up my bag, careful not to jumble around the explosives too much.

"Got my shit set up. Just us two?" he asks.

"Yup."

"You really are a crazy fucker," he grunts.

"Takes one to know one, Sniper," I chuckle.

Together, *alone*, Sniper and I straddle our bikes, starting their engines before we head toward our first destination. I called Sniper yesterday and asked him for help. Sure, MadDog has his own guy who he uses as a sniper for attacks, but Sniper is my brother from home, and I know his work. We work well together, and I need to fully trust the man who is going to be with me tonight.

We park our bikes a few blocks away from the neighborhood we plan on igniting. *The Cartel* is really fuckin' stupid. They buy entire neighborhoods and plant their highest men in them. I say as much to Kirill, who has driven from Los Angeles as added aid.

"We do it, too, sometimes," he shrugs.

"If you're spread out, it's harder to attack all at once," I explain.

"I can appreciate that tactic. More than one of our men have escape tunnels to adjoining houses or to a different location, sometimes a different house on the next street," he explains. My brows rise in surprise.

"Yeah?"

"Yeah," he grins. "It's come in handy more than once."

"I bet it fuckin' has," I chuckle.

"What's the plan?" he asks, all humor gone. Now, he's in business mode.

"Sniper's gonna stay up on the roof in case something happens, then I'm going to break in and drop the explosives," I say.

"That's your plan?" Kirill asks in surprise.

"Got somethin' better?" I ask.

"It's going to take you too long to break into every house. By the time the first explosion happens, the other guys will be out of bed," he says. I nod. I didn't want a bunch of men in on this, so my execution is pretty fucking bad.

"Let my men get the doors open, and we'll all throw the shit at once," he suggests.

"It's unstable and dangerous," I explain.

"This is not a one-man job. Us being *us* means that we're dangerous and unstable. You tell us how to handle it, and we'll handle it," he offers.

"Goes for us, too," MadDogs deep voice growls from behind us.

"The fuck?" I ask, turning to face him.

"You're our brother. We don't leave any man alone. Not like this," he explains.

I shake my head as men start surrounding me, around thirty in total, between the Russian's and my brothers. I let out a puff of air before I give them detailed instructions on how to handle the *TATP*. Then I watch as half of them walk along the shadows of the street and start to open the doors of the known Cartel members that are just waiting for instructions on when and how to attack us.

"They got women and kids in there?" I ask Kirill.

"You really want to know?"

"I'm not sure, but I feel like I should," I say.

"Their families aren't in there. They're in wherever their permanent hidey-holes are. They're living in these crash pads waiting for orders. That doesn't mean they won't possibly have a whore for the night; no way to know that shit for sure," he shrugs.

"Okay then," I mutter.

"Fireworks time," he announces, looking down at his phone.

The men texted him each time a home was opened. Now it's the Devil's turn to blow some shit up. I look over to MadDog and he grins.

"Time for some fuckers to die," he says.

"You're ruthless, man," I laugh.

Together, ten of us walk in the shadows, just like the Bratva men did, to get to our designated houses. The plan is to throw and run, then load on our bikes and head to a bar—a local bar where we'll be noticed.

The Russian's won't be joining us, though. They'll be headed back home to Los Angeles. My phone buzzes and I know it's time. I take my small bag and I throw it, running as hard as I can, feeling the heat at my back, and hearing the loud explosion as I do.

As quickly as we can, we load onto our bikes and tear out of the neighborhood, hopeful that the explosions were enough distraction from our loud bikes cruising away from the hysteria.

"That was fucking crazy. You're a genius," Camo says breathlessly as we suck back pulls of our beers a few minutes later.

"Fuck," I hiss. "I haven't done anything like that in so long," I grunt.

"Last time was when The Bastards were still around," Sniper chuckles.

"You're right," I grin, reminiscing about the hand grenades I made to fuck up their clubhouse.

"How're you doin', brother?" Sniper asks after a few beers.

Most of the men are off flirting with women, playing pool, or throwing darts. Sniper and I both just observe.

"Good. Really fuckin' good," I practically whisper.

"Girls've been all worried about your ass. Promised Brent I'd check up with you while I was here," he laughs.

"I'll bring Cleo up for a visit soon. They can get to know her better, and see with their own eyes that I'm good," I offer with a shrug.

"That works."

chapter twenty-six

Cleo

I feel lips touch my hip, then gently kiss a path from that hip to my shoulder. Next, hot hands travel the same path, except they skip my shoulder and wrap around my breast. I feel a hard length press against the crack of my ass, and I groggily try to open my eyes.

Last night, Paxton didn't come and pick me up from girl's night until three in the morning. He wasn't in a bad mood, but he wasn't in a good mood, either. His mood was somber, and I could tell that he didn't want to talk about whatever he'd done. I gave him that.

We fell asleep, me pressed tight to his side and him just holding me. I wasn't really sure how I felt about him not even trying to make love, but I didn't want to push anything either, especially since he said he wanted to wait until I had clearance from a doctor.

"Need you," he whispers against my shoulder as his hand falls down to behind my knee and he spreads me wide. I suck in a breath when he enters me from behind in one swift thrust.

"Pax," I breathe, lifting my free arm to wrap it behind his neck.

"My heaven," he rumbles against my shoulder as his hand under my body moves to between my legs. I feel his fingers against my clit.

"Paxton," I whimper.

"You are, Cleo. You're my heaven," he rasps. He moves inside of me while his fingers play my clit with lazy precision.

I close my eyes and relax my back against his chest. Paxton surrounds me, he fills me, and I've never felt so close to him in my life. My need for him rivals his need for me. There is nobody else on this earth for me but him. He's my everything. He's my heaven, too.

"Thank you," I whisper as I feel my body climbing closer toward my release.

Paxton grunts behind me as his fingers tighten around the back of my knee, and he thrusts harder, his cock pounding me from behind, his fingers playing me exquisitely.

"For?" he asks on a growl.

"For being my everything," I whisper before I arch my spine and push back against him with a long whimper as I come. I come so hard that my body is frozen still.

"Fuck," he hisses.

I feel myself being rolled onto my stomach, and then he wrenches my hips back before he starts fucking me, hard and fast. He moves inside of me with such precision and strength,

I know that I'll feel him between my legs for at least a whole day, maybe two, afterward.

I reach forward and fist the bedding in my hands as I rear back, meeting his thrusts. I'm climbing again, climbing toward a second release, and I want it—I need it.

"Fucking shit," he growls as his hand fists in the back of my hair. He yanks me toward him as he pushes into me.

I slip one of my hands between my legs to bring myself closer toward my building release, wanting nothing more than to topple over the edge again. I need it. I need it like I need my next breath.

"Come, sweetheart, come around me," Paxton urges. It's as if his words alone push me closer. When I fall over, I do it with a scream.

"Shit, fuck, shit," he curses.

His fingers tighten around my hips. He jerks me back into him two more times before he stills with a moan.

In my next breath, I feel his chest press against my back. His cock is inside me, his body pressing mine into the mattress, his lips on my *Torch* tattoo—it's bliss.

"I didn't get to play with your pretty piercings," he whispers against my skin as he continues to glide in and out of me.

"Next time," I promise.

"Yeah, sweetheart. Next time. I didn't hurt you, did I?" he murmurs.

"I'm perfect," I sigh. "Everything go okay last night?" I ask as I reach behind me and slide my fingers through his hair at the nape of his neck.

"Yeah, baby, it all went good."

"I'm glad. I was worried," I whisper.

"Love that you were worried about me, Clee."

"What happens next?" I ask.

"We live our lives, sweetheart. You here with me, in my life, in my bed; and soon, having my babies."

"Pax," I exhale.

"You got work today?" he asks.

"No," I whisper.

"Then we fuck all day. Need to be inside my sweetheart all fuckin' day," he grunts, pushing his hips against me.

"All day?" I ask.

"Gonna fuck you, eat you, fuck you some more. You're gonna fuck me, suck my cock, and fuck me some more."

"Paxton, I won't be able to walk tomorrow," I giggle. Unfortunately, I lose him when I do.

"Good. You can't move tomorrow, we'll just play today on repeat."

"You're crazy," I say, rolling beneath him so that I can look into his stormy blue eyes.

"Crazy, and crazy *for you*, Cleo," he grins, pressing his lips to my nose. "Spent too many years bein' a dumb fuck. Now I want back inside my baby as often as I can be."

I bite my bottom lip at his words, trying and failing to hide my smile. He grins back at me, and his lips brush against mine before he kisses down the column of my neck. When his tongue touches one of my nipple piercings, I shiver as I arch my back closer to him.

"Baby," I sigh, spreading my thighs even wider.

"Goddamn," he groans.

He lavishes my other breast with the same attention he gave the first, gently tugging on my piercing before his mouth descends down the center of my stomach, then his tongue touches my clit.

"Paxton, no," I beg as I try to put my hands between my legs.

"Stop," he grunts.

My hands freeze next to my hips, and I watch as he rises slightly. Then he pushes two fingers inside of me, curling them when he does. It makes my eyes roll in the back of my head.

"You look so fucking beautiful with my cum leaking out of your pussy," he whispers.

Then he pulls his fingers from inside of me and lines my lips with them before he shoves them in my mouth. I moan as I suck the evidence of our sexy morning from them, our mixture tasting better than I imagined.

"Get over here and suck me until I'm hard so I can fuck that tight pussy again, sweetheart," he growls.

I don't even hesitate. I adjust myself so that I'm on my knees, and I lower my face, my tongue snaking out to taste the tip of him.

"Love you," I whisper, looking at him through my lashes.

"Never loved anybody the way I love you, Cleo," he rasps.

We spend the entire day exactly as he wanted to—in bed, having sex. We have so much sex that I feel it for the next week in every move I make.

I love this man, and I never thought I would have him again. Then when I did, I never thought that I would have all of him. Now that I do, I'm so happy that it's almost terrifying. If something happened, I don't know what I would do.

Torch

"You packed up, babe?" I ask as I walk into the bedroom.

Cleo is standing in nothing but a pair of panties and her bra, her wet hair hanging down her neck and back, an open suitcase on the bed.

"I don't know what to pack," she explains.

"Clothes, sweetheart," I chuckle.

"Yes, but what kind? I've never been on your bike, and now you're saying we're going all the way to another state on it. What do I pack?" she whines.

"Sweetheart. There're stores in Bonner's Ferry; not many, but a couple. There's also a whole slew of Old Ladies that will help you out if you need somethin'. They know we're comin' on my bike, so they know you won't have everything you need. We're not going to any fancy balls. Shorts, jeans, some tanks and a coupla shirts will be fine," I mutter as I wrap my arms around her from behind.

"I can't talk to you," she sighs.

"Why?" I ask, chuckling against her neck.

"You're not a woman. You don't understand. I'm going to be meeting your childhood friends, Paxton. I can't look lazy, I have to have cute stuff to meet them in."

"You think Brentlee, Kentlee and all of them give one fuck how you dress?" I ask in confusion.

"Uh, yeah, I do."

"You're fuckin' crazy, my crazy woman," I grunt.

"I'm not crazy. I want to look good, but I don't have anything," she sighs. I turn her around in my arms. "They all look comfortable, like complete biker babes, and I'm just… *not*."

"Biker babe?" I ask fighting a smile.

"Lisandro reminded me that I look nothing like the other Old Ladies. I wear pencil skirts and satin blouses and work in a high-end jewelry store. I don't really look like an *Old Lady*," she explains. My eyes widen.

"Sweetheart, Kentlee is girlie. Bentlee is even more girlie. Hattie's a young, cute little thing, but she's girlie. None of them look like biker babes," I explain. "The Old Ladies here don't look like biker babes, either," I point out.

"Colleen does," she states.

"Calm down, just be you. I don't love a badass biker babe, I love you, Cleo Hill, my sweetheart."

"Damnit, that was really sweet," she whispers, wrapping her hands around my neck and pressing her soft tits against my chest.

"You look at me like that a second longer, I'll show you how sweet I'm not," I warn as I drop my hand and squeeze her panty covered ass.

"I need to pack," she grins.

"Yeah, baby, you do," I grunt. "I'll be back in ten. Be ready to roll."

I walk out of the bedroom, mainly because if I don't, I'm gonna fuck her again. We need to get on the road. We're heading to Idaho today; but since this is the first time Cleo will have been on my bike, I'm taking the trip slow.

She groans as she falls face first on the cheap hotel comforter. I can't help but chuckle, though I do feel badly for her all at the same time.

"Don't laugh," she says, turning her head to glare at me.

"Shower and I'll give you a massage," I rumble.

"No, you gave me a *massage* last night, and we both know how that turned out," she smarts off.

I did give her a massage last night. About two seconds into massaging that full ass of hers, I couldn't help myself. I ate her from behind until she came; then I fucked her until we *both* came.

"You bitchin' about two orgasms?" I ask, lifting my brows.

Cleo rolls her lips and shakes her head slightly. I grunt and take my clothes off, irritated that she'd bitch about getting' fucked so good she came twice. I decide to leave her alone, hoping it's only her sore ass from the ride that's making her bitchy.

I let the warm water from the shower wash over me, washing my hair and massaging my own tired muscles. Then there's a burst of cool air, and small hands wrap around me from behind.

"I'm sorry," she whispers as she places her lips against my back. "I've never traveled like this before. I've never been this sore and uncomfortable before, and I'm sorry."

I grunt and turn around in her arms, the water now cascading against my back. My head dips down and my eyes focus on hers. Without saying a word, I press my lips against her mouth as my fingers wrap around her waist, and I pick her up, pressing her back against the shower wall.

"*Paxton*," she whispers as her head falls back. One of her hands grasps the hair at the nape of my neck while the other holds onto my shoulder as her legs wrap around my middle.

Moving one of my hands from her waist, I cup her tit and give it a hard squeeze, watching her eyes widen. Then the sexiest, throaty moan escapes from her lips. My rock hard cock presses against her entrance, and I guide myself inside of her, letting her tight, wet heat surround me.

"Cleo," I groan as I stay planted deep inside of her.

"I was a bitch," she whispers.

"Fuck that, you been ridin' hard, sweetheart," I murmur before I pull out and thrust inside of her.

She feels so fuckin' good wrapped around my cock, I don't want to ever leave this spot. I gently tug her nipple right before I squeeze the little pink bud hard, my hips moving so that my cock glides in and out of her with long, precise strokes. I don't want to blow my load immediately; though with her, it would be pretty fuckin' easy to do.

"You feel so good," she says as her head rolls to the side.

"You do too, baby," I mutter as I press my lips against hers.

I take her a little harder, my pelvis grinding against her clit as I do, listening to the whimpers that fill my mouth with each thrust. Goddamn. How I even went without this for so fuckin' long, I'll never know. Her fingers tighten in my hair, her body locks around me, and that's when her pussy spasms and clenches even tighter with her release.

I pound into her body. Her pussy is still clamped tightly, squeezing me with each thrust, trying to keep me inside of her. Tearing my lips from hers, I shove my face into her neck. My balls tighten, and I come on a groan. She lets out a shuttered breath as her body shakes slightly. Regretfully, I pull out of her before I let her place her feet on the warm shower floor.

Without a word, I take the shitty soap they supplied us with, and I wash her body, taking care of her still healing nipple rings, then playing with her ass and pussy, gently.

"Pax, I can't, not again," she whispers.

"You lie," I chuckle, but I don't push her further. She's beat fuckin' tired, and sore, but she could come again.

"I know," she whispers as she bites the corner of her lip.

"I'm gonna get some food. Finish your shower, and I'll be back," I grunt as I open the curtain and take a step out.

"Okay."

I shake my head. *Gorgeous.* Every bit of her is absolutely beautiful, and I'm so fucking blessed that she's mine again. Though, maybe I shouldn't think that. She was always mine, wasn't she?

Fuck yeah, she was.

chapter twenty-seven

Cleo

We pull into the miniscule town of Bonner's Ferry, Idaho, and I wonder if Paxton just really loves small towns. Shasta is small, too. I'm surprised there are stoplights in this town, even if it's just two. It's *that* small.

When we pull up to a gate, it opens without him having to do anything, and then we ride into a dirt parking lot, up to a building that looks very much like the plain clubhouse building in California. There's a man standing outside, and he grins before he starts walking toward us.

We discard our helmets, and I fluff out my hair as Paxton steps off of his bike. Once I'm situated, I follow behind him. His hand wraps around mine and he gives me a wink before he turns to the man who's now standing in front of him.

"Dirty," he grins.

The man throws his cigarette down, grinding his toe in it before he give's Paxton a grin and pulls him in for a manly hug. He's skinny, handsome in a really rough way, and covered in tattoos. He's wearing only a white tank and really beat up holy jeans. It's not freezing cold and snowy, but it's early spring and still plenty chilly outside. I don't know how he can stand it.

"Who's the little thing behind you?" he asks with a sparkle in his eyes.

"This is my wife, my Old Lady, Cleo," Paxton introduces, tugging me into his side.

I hold out my hand to shake this stranger's, but he gives me a shake of his head with a grin and grabs my hand. Tugging me into his body, he wraps his arm around my shoulders in a side-hug.

"Good to meet you, honey. The girls and kids'll be here within the hour. They're all fired up to throw you a party," he chuckles before he releases me back to Paxton.

"Oh, no, we don't need anyone to throw a party," I protest.

"You can't stop Kentlee from throwing a welcome party. Don't even try," he grunts with a smirk. "C'mon inside and get a beer or a shot."

"Yeah," Paxton mumbles as he wraps his hand around mine and tugs me toward the door.

We only rode on the bike for a couple of hours today, so I'm not exhausted, but I'm still sore. Maybe a couple shots would ease the pain in my backside. Paxton's hand travels down to my ass and gives it a squeeze right before we walk over the threshold of the clubhouse. I bite back the groan of pain as he laughs. I narrow my eyes on him, but he ignores my death-glare.

"Let's get you some booze, sweetheart," he murmurs.

"Yeah."

We spend the next hour chatting with the various men who walk up to him and shake his hand, welcoming him back and informing him that he's been missed.

I bite my bottom lip, feeling guilty. He's loved here, well and truly loved. He left all of his close friends and people he thought of as his family for me, to protect me. He's done way too much; but if I tell him to come back here, it means I'll be coming with him, and that means leaving Lis and Theo behind.

"Oh, shit," Paxton chuckles from beside me.

I look up, but his head is turning and he's watching the door. I turn and see three beautiful women walking through. I recognize one from the night of MadDog's wedding, but the other two are strangers. Blonde, dark brown hair, and light brown hair. All three are built differently, but all beautiful in their unique way.

I was supposed to meet up with these women when Paxton left for his run, but I stayed holed up at Genny's and worked extra hours instead. Now, I feel extra shitty because they're important to Paxton. I should have gotten to know them, instead of being lost inside my own shit.

Two handsome men follow behind the women. I recognize one of them, too—the bearded one. I think Paxton introduced him as Sniper. The other one is sporting a beard and blond manbun. He looks so much like Paxton's president, MadDog, I know for certain they're related somehow. Then the man Dirty, whom I had been talking to earlier, walks up to the third woman and kisses the side of her neck, making her giggle.

"That's the Old Ladies. Well, some of them," Paxton says. He doesn't look away from them.

He stands up and walks over to them, leaving me exactly where I am. I think about following him, but I don't. I choose to watch him from afar and give him the opportunity to greet his friends in private. I feel like even more of an outsider here than his other club. They all know him so well, and they love him, and I took him away.

Paxton gives the pretty blonde a hug, and then shakes MadDog's relative's hand before he moves down the line, hugging and then shaking until he reaches Dirty. He doesn't give him a handshake, but he does throw back his head in laughter at something that he says.

I take another shot, my eyes glued to them when a man sidles up next to me. I look over to him and my eyes widen. He looks like a giant grizzly bear.

"Never seen him so happy," he mutters.

"Excuse me?" I ask.

"Torch. Never seen him smile like the way he's been smilin' since he walked through those doors with you. You're fightin' some kind of battle, but you don't need to," he rumbles.

"I'm Cleo," I whisper, holding out my hand to him.

"Know who you are," he chuckles. "I'm Grizz. Don't want you thinking that he regrets leaving this place to get you back, because he don't."

"How do you know?" I whisper.

"I can see it in his eyes. Those demons, they're not completely gone, but gotta say, babe, they're just a glimmer now."

"He's on some medication for his nightmares," I respond. He throws back his head in laughter.

"Girl, only medication that's doin' any good is what's

between your legs," he grins before he winks. I gasp in surprise at his words, which only makes his smile grow even wider.

"What kind of bullshit are you tryin' to sell my Old Lady?" Paxton asks from behind me. I can tell he's got a smile on his face. I can hear it in his voice.

"Just introducing myself," Grizz chuckles before he stands.

"Don't listen to a word he says. He's just tryin' to get in your panties," Paxton murmurs before his lips brush mine. "I want you to meet some people."

"Okay," I mutter before I press my lips to his and stand.

Paxton wraps his arm around my waist and pulls me closer to his side as we walk over to the people who came in just a few moments ago.

I blink when I see a whole gaggle of kids run in past them. They're all different ages with various hair colors, but there is no denying that they feel as though this clubhouse is home.

"You already know Dirty Johnny, but this is Kentlee and her sister Brentlee, who you met at MadDog's wedding. We all went to high school together," he announces. I smile at them. "This is, Cleo, my wife."

"We're so excited to finally meet you," the blonde, Kentlee, says as she pulls me into her for a warm hug.

I go down the line, much like I watched Paxton do a few minutes ago, and I meet Fury, Sniper, Brentlee, and Hattie. They're all kind, and I get hugs form them all, including the men. Then a few minutes go by and all the men walk away, even Paxton, leaving me alone with the girls.

"Thank you," Kentlee says.

"For?" I ask in confusion.

"For giving him another chance, for making him happy, and for not being a screaming bitch. It's nice to have fun Old Ladies to hang out with," she grins.

"We've known him forever. We knew the boy he was, and then the man he became. But none of us knew what happened in those years he was gone. Obviously, it was huge, because the man he became was solemn and angry," Brentlee adds.

"He said he had a bad home life," I murmur.

I wonder if these women know any more about him than he's told me. I feel like I've had all of him, but any extra insight would be amazing.

"His mom," Kentlee shakes her head. "She's still around. I don't know much, but I do know she never showed up to anything at the school."

"He keeps it buried," I murmur.

"They all do," Hattie announces. She's young, really young, but her eyes speak of experience. "Johnny had a horrendous childhood, and I didn't know much about it until it was something he couldn't keep from me anymore. I don't know why they don't share it with the women they love; maybe they don't want to burden us with their stories, but you have to take them as is, Cleo. That's the only way they come."

"Man, we taught you well," Brentlee says with a grin. Hattie smiles back with a shrug of her shoulder.

"I've loved him since I was eighteen," I admit.

"Then he'll open up more, when he's able," Brentlee says, taking my hand in hers and giving it a squeeze.

A few minutes later, Fury announces that the grill is ready for food. Kentlee jumps up and grabs trays of burgers and hotdogs, which were somehow all ready to go, from the kitchen. We spend the rest of the afternoon grilling, eating, talking, and drinking while a whole slew of kids run all around the clubhouse grounds.

"You doin' okay?" Paxton asks me when the sun starts to set. He sways slightly, and I can tell he's drunk off of his ass.

"Yeah," I grin up at him.

"Can't wait to fuck you all night long, sweetheart."

"You're crazy," I giggle.

"Shit, yeah. Crazy about that sweet pussy of yours, baby."

When the whores come out, after the children have left, the party gets *wild*. We don't stay much longer, both of us tired and ready for the all night fuck-fest that Paxton promised. Telling everyone goodnight, we stumble and sway to an empty bedroom.

"My old room," Paxton grunts as he starts to undress.

I quickly strip my own clothes off, feeling no pain from our ride, and wanting to do a much different kind of ride for the rest of the evening. Once Paxton is completely naked, he stalks toward me. I'm kneeling in the center of the bed, naked, and waiting.

"I want to be on top," I whisper.

"Fuck," he groans as he falls to the bed before he reaches for me and drags me up his body. "Ride me, sweetheart," he whispers before his lips touch mine.

I position myself over the top of him and slowly sink down, taking all of his length inside of me. I ride him for as long as he lets me, coming before he changes our positions and makes me come again. Then he eats me before he changes positions, yet again, and I scream out in pleasure as he does exactly what he promised—fucking me, all night long.

Torch

My head pounds as I stand outside of the shitty house. I haven't been here in years, but I have shit I need to end with this bitch. Maybe it's fucked up that I refer to my own mother as a bitch, but the cunt is. She made me and my dad fucking miserable, and then she made just me fucking miserable.

I walk up the cracked sidewalk and pound on the front door. The paint is peeling, and it should be stripped, sanded, and repainted, but fuck *that*.

"Wondered when your sorry ass would show up here again," she growls as she opens the door.

She's rounder than she was the last time I saw her; her hair now longer, still jet black, but mostly salt and peppered in coloring. Her dull blue eyes rake over me as she lights a cigarette before she walks back into the house. I follow behind her, turning my nose up at the smell of stale cigarettes and rotten food.

"What do you want?" she asks as she sits in her rust colored recliner.

Fuck, it's the same recliner that was here when I was little. In fact, nothing in this house has changed at all.

"Moved to Cali, thought I should let you know," I shrug.

"Why would I give a fuck? Didn't give a fuck about you when you were here; don't give one now that you're gone," she announces.

I try not to let her words penetrate, but they do. They always fuckin' do.

"Married, too," I say, trying to gloss over the hurtful words she's slinging in my direction.

"One of those biker sluts you hang out with?" she asks, arching a brow. I'm not sure why she's calling them sluts, since she met my dad down at the clubhouse, herself.

"Nope. Nice girl, works at a jewelry store," I shrug.

"She'll leave you. Don't get comfortable," she murmurs as she picks up the remote control and flips the channel on the television.

"You gonna stay a nasty bitch the rest of your life?" I ask. She turns her head and her narrowed gaze lands on me.

"Not my fault. Your father is to blame," she announces, glaring at me.

"Dad didn't make you nasty. You've always *been* nasty; and dad's been gone for years."

"Your dad fucked around on me, all the time. Know what that does to a young girl? He was fucking some whore the night you were born. Did you know that? I'm pushin' his fuckin' kid outta me, and he's got his dick buried in some skinny little bitch."

"How's this my fault?" I ask.

"I always had to take care of your ass while he was out fucking around. Then when you got old enough that he could take you, he took you *everywhere*, left me here alone."

"So you were jealous?" I ask in disbelief.

"He loved you," she almost whispers.

"Woulda loved you, too, if you weren't such a fuckin' cunt to him. He couldn't stand to be home with you because you were so fucking awful, all the damn time. Angry and bitter," I say.

"You don't understand because you're one of them. You're just like the rest of them. There's no point in even talking to you," she shrugs.

"I could understand you bein' pissed at dad. He fucked around, and he did, and I always knew he did. But you were mean to me since I was a little kid. I was innocent."

"You have a dick. You were born the exact opposite of innocent," she yells.

"Fuck this. You're gonna die alone in your anger and bitterness, honest to fuck," I growl.

I walk out of the house, slamming the door behind me, not waiting for her response. I could give a fuck. She's a shit excuse for a person, and as a mother? She's completely worthless. She's alone, bitter, and angry about shit that is not in my control and never was.

I start my bike, bringing the engine to life before I ride back to my woman. A woman who looks at me with soft gentle eyes; a woman who whispers her love for me, and takes me just as I am, never expecting anything but my loyalty and love. She's got it, too. Cleo has everything I can give her. She's my everything.

chapter twenty-eight

Cleo

Paxton walks through the door just as I lean over the bar to grab the bottle of water that a prospect hands me. His eyes connect to mine, and I see him glower before his eyes harden and a muscle in his cheek jumps.

Then, without a word, he stomps toward me, walking right past me and toward the bedrooms. I thank the prospect for my bottle of water and slide off of the stool, hurrying after my husband.

Walking into his room, I freeze when I watch him throw the rickety lamp that was sitting on his dresser across the room, gasping when it smashes against the wall. He then turns to me, and he looks cold, mean, and scary.

"You been hangin' around flirting with all the men in the bar, or just that prospect?" he growls.

"Paxton, I wasn't flirting with anyone. What is wrong with you?"

His eyes soften a touch and he shakes his head before he sits down on the bed and runs his fingers through his hair. He tugs on the strands before he runs his hands over his face. I walk over to him and sink down in front of him, placing my hands on his knees and giving them a squeeze. I haven't seen him like this since the night he came home from the desert, all those years ago.

"Went to see my mother," he rasps.

"You didn't want me to go?" I ask, feeling hurt.

"Fuck no," he shouts. I lean back at his anger.

He reaches down and puts his hands under my armpits, bringing me to my feet before he twists and practically throws me onto the bed. He crawls over the top of me, and his gaze, though still pretty pissed off looking, is equally as intense, but much less scary than it was a few moments ago. I cup his cheeks with my palms, and his clenched jaw relaxes slightly.

I feel his fingers at my shorts, and then my shorts and panties are gone and his bare cock is pressed against my entrance. I don't know when his pants were unzipped, but I know they're still on, because I can feel the rough denim against my legs.

"Paxton," I whisper.

"Need this," he grunts as he pushes inside of me.

I'm not ready, not even a little, but the look in his eyes, its heartbreaking. I can see that *need* in him. I nod my agreement and spread my legs wider as he pushes inside of me. I pinch my eyes closed at the pain, and then his lips touch mine, his tongue sliding inside of my mouth as he kisses me, consuming me, like only he can.

His hips start to move slowly, and I can feel myself getting wetter with each stroke of his cock, while his mouth devours mine. I move my hands to wrap around his shoulders, and then down to the hem of his shirt, dipping them beneath the fabric to feel his warm skin.

"Cleo," he groans as he starts thrusting inside of me a bit harder, his teeth nibbling my lips.

"I love you," I whisper against his mouth.

"Love you more than you could ever know," he murmurs as he continues to glide in and out of me, moving a little harder and faster with each stroke.

His hand wraps around my throat, loosely at first. The harder he fucks me, the more his fingers tighten.

We don't say another word. Our eyes connect and stay that way as we both climb toward our release, searching for it every time our bodies crash together. His hand moves from squeezing my throat to tangling in the back of my hair as he grinds hard against my clit. It causes my breath to hitch.

With a growl, he slams into me so hard it forces me to close my eyes, then I come with a whimper. He doesn't slow down or stop when he knows I've come, too consumed in his own desire for relief. When he comes, he throws his head back, and I stare at the column of his handsome throat until he sags against me and shoves his face into my neck.

"Tell me what happened," I urge. His body locks up, but he doesn't move. He stays planted inside of me, his face in my neck, but his muscles are tight.

"Paxton," I urge.

"She's a bitch. A mean and nasty bitch," he announces as he slides out of me. He lifts his jeans up his hips before he stands and walks over to the window.

"Tell me," I repeat, turning to my side to watch him.

"She just spewed hateful shit, like she always does. I let it affect me, like I always do," he rumbles.

I amble off of the bed, grabbing my panties before I pull them on. Ignoring his cum that's leaking out of me, I walk over to him.

Wrapping my arms around his waist from behind and resting my cheek on the back of his cut. I pinch my eyes closed, trying to imagine the pain he must be feeling.

"It shouldn't even affect me at this point," he shrugs, turning around in my arms and pressing his lips to the top of my hair.

"It's your mother. Of course, it affects you," I whisper. "If you want to talk more about it, I'm here."

"Thank you, sweetheart," he rasps as one of his hands slides beneath my panties and squeezes my bare ass. "I might take you up on that one day. Did I hurt you?"

"No," I grin, shaking my head as I look up at him.

"I'm glad," he smirks before he dips his head and presses his lips to mine.

"We leave tomorrow. I got another run in a couple days," he informs.

"Two weeks, again?" I ask in surprise.

"Yeah," he shrugs.

"Maybe you could give me more notice next time, you know? Instead of a couple days?"

"I'll try to be better," he mutters as his hand massages my ass and his lips gently caress mine.

"See that you do that," I breathe, melting into him.

"Take care of him," Kentlee whispers as she hugs me tightly. Well, as tightly as she can, since she's pregnant.

"Always," I grin.

"When MadDog comes back for visits, we want you guys tagging along," Brentlee says with a wide smile.

"You know it," Paxton grunts with a grin of his own aimed right at her.

We give everyone one last wave before we climb on Paxton's bike. He starts it with a roar, and then we're off. My ass already hurts in anticipation of what's to come, especially since he informed me that this trip was only going to be two days, instead of the three we took when we drove here.

I close my eyes, feeling the air against my skin and hugging Paxton closer, loving the way he feels, his body hard but relaxed as he rides. He loves it, really loves it, and I can tell just in the way he maneuvers the bike on the road.

After six straight hours of riding, we finally stop for the night, and I can't help but cheer as we pull into the hotel's parking lot. Paxton chuckles and helps me take my helmet off before we check in. I'm thankful that I was able to wash my clothes at the clubhouse before we left, so I have all clean stuff to wear for the ride home.

"I'm going to shower," I inform him as I head toward the bathroom.

"Yeah, I'll get some food," he grumbles, flashing me a smile before he leaves.

I don't spend a lot of time in the shower. I'm sore and tired, and I just want to curl into bed and go to sleep. I could actually skip food and I'd be just fine. Once I'm finished cleaning the road dust and dirt off of me, I slip my cotton panties on and an oversized shirt of Paxton's. I do exactly as

I've been dreaming of, sliding beneath the sheets and curling into a ball, unable to keep my eyes open a second longer.

"Sweetheart," his rich voice mutters, pulling me from my sleep. My eyes flutter open and I see him standing in front of me, a bag of fast foot dangling from his fingertips.

"I fell asleep," I whisper. He grins and gives me a wink before he mutters an, *I know*, and holds out his hand to help me sit up.

We eat mostly in silence, and I can't stop from glancing at my handsome husband, a question on the tip of my tongue, but a little scared to actually ask it.

"You gonna ask me or just stare at me?"

"Do you want to move back to Idaho? I want you to be happy, and I have Lis and Theo back home, but you looked so happy with all of your friends. I don't want you to be miserable or regret being with me because I'm not there—but I don't know if I can leave California," I ramble.

"Calm down. Take a deep breath," he smiles. "I love my club in Idaho. I love the brothers there, and its comfortable. My dad was a member and I grew up with almost everyone there."

I suck in a breath and bite my bottom lip, looking down at my lap. Paxton wraps his hands around mine and gives them a gentle squeeze, which makes me lift my eyes to look at him.

"They're my friends; and, yeah, to an extent, they're my family. But, baby, you're my wife. *You're* my family. I go where you go, and your happiness lies in being close to your boys. You're making girlfriends in the club, and that makes me happy as fuck. I'm not pulling you away from Lis and Theo. They've taken care of you for over a decade."

"Your club's taken care of you for your whole life," I whisper.

"Fuck no, they haven't," he chuckles. My eyes widen. "Nobody's taken care of me the way that you have. You're my sweetheart, my wife, and my life. We're stayin' in Cali and that's where we're plantin' down roots, baby," he states with a nod.

"Really?" I breathe.

"Really, sweetheart," he grins before he leans down and presses his lips to mine in a hard, closed mouth kiss. "Let's get to bed. We have a long day tomorrow," he murmurs.

"Okay," I sigh.

I fall asleep the instant my head hits the pillow. Paxton's arms are wrapped around me, and I've never felt more content in my entire life.

How did this happen?

How did I end up this damn happy?

I'm afraid to question it too hard, afraid that if I do, it may disappear.

Torch

I press my lips to the side of her head before I walk out of the hotel and close the door behind me, testing it to make sure that it's locked. Then I head to my bike to grab Cleo and me some breakfast. I can't help the grin that appears on my face as I recall our conversation from the evening before.

Cleo was so worried I was giving up the people I loved to be with her. She probably would have packed all her shit and moved to Idaho today had I said that's what I wanted her to do. But I don't. I'm happy in Cali, tucked away in the woods with my brothers and their families.

I have Cleo, she still has her friends close, and she's opening up to the possibility of new friends, too. It's important in this life to be friends with other Old Ladies. They can hold you up when you need it, and keep you together when shit goes down.

I shake my head, thinking about Genny and Soar. Had she stayed, the club would help her anyway she needed help—money and emotional support alike. She was done, though, and maybe that's what she needed.

Fuck, god knows she doesn't need to turn into the bitter and angry woman my mother turned into. I could see the writing on the wall with that, too.

Genny was already angry and bitter, but I could still see hurt and love in her eyes when she looked at Soar. She wasn't gone yet, like my mother was.

Being in love and being happy is making me a goddamn woman. Like I should give a fuck about Genny and Soar's happiness. I roll my eyes at my fucking pussy assed self as I pull into the shitty fast food place.

Once I have food for the both of us, I ride back to the hotel. I unlock the door and walk inside.

"Clee," I call out, freezing at the sight that greets me.

The entire room is trashed. Every piece of furniture that isn't nailed down is turned over or thrown across from where it originally was. Dropping the bags of food, I pull my gun out of my waistband, and I clear the room and bathroom. She's gone. Her shit is still in the corner and her clothes are still inside, which means wherever she is, she's without shoes and pants.

I pull my phone out of my pocket and contact MadDog.

"Cleo's gone," I say, my voice thick.

"What do you mean?" he asks.

"I went out to get breakfast. She's gone. The room's trashed but empty."

"Where are you?" he barks as I hear rustling.

"Salem, Oregon," I say, pinching my eyes closed, knowing it will take him at least six hours to get here. It would take Fury just as long.

Fuck.

Goddamn it.

Son of a bitch.

"On my way. Call Oliver, see what he can discover with his genius hacking abilities. Call Fury, too."

The call ends and I walk over to the bed and sink down before I start making phone calls. Oliver tells me he'll tap into the streets around us and their camera systems, and see if he can get a visual of her somewhere. Then he tells me to sit by my phone in case whoever took her tries to call me.

Fuck.

Cleo

My eyes flutter open, my hands tied behind my back, and my ankles tied together. I loll my head to the side and take a good look at one of the men who broke into my hotel room. He chased me and threw me down, causing me to slam my head against the hard ground.

Then they tied me up and threw me in the backseat of

307

the SUV, with no pants. I squirmed, which was the wrong thing to do, because I felt something sharp in my neck. I have a feeling it's drugs, and the reason behind why I'm about two seconds from falling asleep.

"Who are you?" I slur.

"Your man's club fucked with the wrong people," he says before he grins. "You're a pretty little, white redhead. They'll all like you a whole hell of a lot. You'll be a great addition to our stable," he mutters before his blue eyes wink at me.

I open my mouth to ask him what he means, but it won't move. No part of my body will move, and then the world fades to black around me before it takes me under.

chapter twenty-nine

Torch

My phone rings, and I answer it without looking at the caller ID.

"I have news," Oliver's voice mutters distractedly.

"Yeah," I grunt.

It's been three hours, and I've heard nothing. Not a fuckin' thing. I'm starting to go beyond batshit crazy.

"You guys ever have dealings with the Aryans before?" he asks. I hear typing on his keyboard keys.

"Yeah, back years ago. We ended their contract, they tried to kidnap Kentlee, Fury's wife. We killed a whole fuckin' bunch of them, but we haven't heard anything in years," I explain.

"Well, they're crazy, so it doesn't surprise me they hid and waited," he grumbles.

"That's who has Cleo?"

"Yeah. I have grainy video of some guys dragging her out of the room and throwing her into a dark blue SUV. I'm trying to find the SUV to see where they're headed. Luckily, I got a perfect picture of the license plate. I'll send you the owners info via text, but I have no way of knowing if it's stolen or not right now, so I'm not sure if it's helpful," he explains.

"How do you know it's Aryan's?" I ask.

"White guys, no hair, and I recognized their tattoos. The video is grainy, but I zoomed in when I saw the ink," he explains.

"Give me everything you have. I'll send some men to check it out," I say, feeling like I'm going to jump out of my skin.

"All right, sending now. I'm on standby and still researching," he says before he ends the call.

A few seconds later, my phone sounds with the information. The car is from a little town in California, right on the Oregon and California border called Tulelake. *Fuck*, it's four and a half hours away and they have a three-hour head start, which means they could be almost fucking there.

I send a group text out with the information I have as I rush to my bike. I don't give a fuck if I go it alone. I'll die before I sit back and let those bastards fuck with my woman.

I race, hauling ass, and not giving a fuck as I do, toward the address Oliver sent me. Maybe I'm going out of my way, maybe I'm making the wrong choice, but this is the only lead I have, and I'm following it.

I've made record time, shaving forty-five minutes off of the drive by the time I find the street. I don't pull straight up to the house. Instead, I park and check my phone under a tree at the end of the street.

"What do you know?" I ask as soon as the phone connects.

"They didn't steal the car. That man the SUV is registered to is the new leader. He came out of hiding about six months ago, but he hasn't done anything, absolutely nothing. He's held meetings, but they haven't been buying or trading, guns, drugs, or anything of the like."

"Thanks, Oliver," I murmur as my eyes stay glued to the house where I know this bastard lives.

"Be safe, and kill those Nazi fucks," he practically growls.

I pick up my phone and call the Cali clubhouse to check and see where the guys are when I hear motorcycles coming up behind me. I end the call as I turn around and see fifteen brothers rolling up to me.

"She there?" MadDog shouts above his engine noise before he shuts it off.

"Don't know, but this guy's an Aryan. Oliver just confirmed they didn't steal the car," I explain.

"We go in through the back, but leave a couple guys on each side and the front. We are not letting these fuckers out," he growls.

"This have to do with all that shit back a few years ago? Or somethin' new?" I ask as my brows furrow.

"No fucking clue. Maybe it's just because they're crazy fucks. Maybe it's because they heard what we did to *The Cartel* and they thought it was a good opportunity to extract their revenge. Fury'll be here any minute. We'll wait for his men as extra enforcement," he says, although it's as if he's speaking more to himself than anyone else.

"But why me? Why Cleo?" I ask in confusion.

"Fuck if I know. Those bastards are whacked as shit. Too

much fuckin' meth," he grunts.

About ten minutes later, the rumble of bikes makes us all turn our attention, and I grin when I see Fury and my brothers ride up.

Cleo was right in the fact that I do miss them. They're my family, and I love them, but that's more my past, and she's my future. I like MadDog's club, the men and women that are there, and, in general, they're good fuckin' brothers to have.

"Let's fuck these assholes up. I'm about sick of them," Fury growls as he marches up to me.

"They been botherin' you?" I ask as my brows shoot up.

"Didn't think anything of it," he admits.

"Of what?" MadDog growls.

"We've been focused on *The Cartel*, on their shit, not this."

"We have to be able to multi-task. Tell me," MadDog orders.

"Got a few threatening phone calls. I've been keeping extra protection on the women anyway, because of *The Cartel*, so I kind of ignored them and nothing materialized," Fury admits.

"Fuck," MadDog says, looking up at the sky.

"Wouldn't have mattered anyway. We had no way to know they'd take someone other than Kentlee," I say.

"This isn't a coincidence," MadDog grumbles.

"Do you think… no," I say, shaking my head.

"What?" both Fury and MadDog ask at the same time.

"Do you think that they're the ones that were buying women?" I ask. "Clee was on their list. She'd been picked for someone. There was a buyer for her already."

"Fuck," MadDog hisses.

"Maybe it wasn't *The Cartel* wanting to take our women,

but maybe it was the Aryan's that wanted to buy them, an ultimate fuck you to us," Fury suggests.

"Let's get your woman back. We'll torture the info out of them," MadDog says with a grin.

I lift my chin and we start to walk toward the house, splitting up. Half of the guys go down the next street to come up through the back. Another group of guys get on their bikes and ride to the end of the street on the opposite side, so in case shit goes down, we have all exits blocked.

"You ready? Shit could be pretty fuckin' ugly in there," MadDog asks the closer we get to the house.

"I'm ready to get my woman," I growl.

"May not be that easy," he murmurs.

"Fuck, brother. I know what the fuck I could be walkin' into," I bark, getting fed up with his warnings.

"All right."

I walk right up to the door, looking from side to side to make sure my brothers are ready as I pull my handgun out. Then I bang on the door. It's silent for a few seconds before I hear a loud whimper, some shuffling and moving around, then the door opens.

My eyes widen at the man standing on the other side.

Cleo

I'm trapped in a room, still tied up, but I'm at least not alone. There are eight other women who look much like me, tied up by ankles and wrists, in different stages of cleanliness. The only thing we all have in common is our pale skin. I press my lips together and try to keep from crying.

"Who are you?" one girl asks.

"Cleo," I whisper.

"What chapter is your man from?" she asks. My eyes widen.

"We live in Shasta," I admit.

"The original charter. Oh, shit," another girl whispers.

"What does that mean?"

"It means they're either really brave, or *really* stupid. Your man's club is the main club, the one that makes all major decisions—the one that all the other *Notorious Devils* have to answer to," she explains. "I'm Ginger, by the way."

She's pretty—light blonde hair, big brown eyes, and delicate features—but she looks dirty and worn.

"Why do they have us?" I ask, afraid to know the answer, but needing it.

"Revenge on the *Devils*. They want to breed us. We were stolen by *The Cartel*, then sold to them," a pretty brunette murmurs.

"Shit, who's *they*?" I hiss.

"The Aryans. Do yourself and everyone else a favor—don't fight them. Just accept it when it's your turn," Ginger advises.

"Seriously?" I say with wide eyes.

"They take it out on everybody when you fight. We've all tried it and we've all ended up bleeding from several places. It's not worth it," the brunette whispers.

Shit.

My heart starts to beat wildly inside of my chest, and my bottom lip trembles as I'm now officially on the verge of tears.

"They're never going to find us, are they?" I ask as my eyes go from woman to woman in the room.

"I've been here for a year," the brunette rasps.

"Oh, fuck," I say as tears start to stream down my face.

"They don't know I'm infertile. Once a girl gets pregnant, she's taken away," she whispers.

I pinch my eyes closed so tight that I see stars. I want this nightmare to disappear. I want to open my eyes and be in my bed, lying next to Paxton. I don't even care what bed, the clubhouse, our house, anywhere but here.

"The sun is starting to set," Ginger whispers.

"What's that mean?" I ask, opening my eyes to look around.

"It means it's almost time," the brunette says in a warning tone.

I don't ask anything else. I don't need that clarified. Not in the slightest. I suck in my lips to keep from whimpering as I bring my knees up, resting my cheek on them as I await my fate. Whatever that looks like.

"It's time to break in the new girl," a voice calls out as the door flies open.

I look up and my eyes widen at the man in front of me. I've met him before. Just a few days ago. He's a member of Fury's club, and one of the men that Paxton trusts.

Holy shit.

"Drifter?" I whisper, looking at the man who was introduced to me as Fury's Vice President not very long ago.

"Surprise, cunt," he grins.

"How, why?"

"Not your fuckin' business," he growls as he stalks toward me.

Drifter bends down and wraps his hand around my bicep before he pulls me roughly to my feet. He then shoves his shoulder into my belly and picks me up over his shoulder. He turns around and starts to walk me out of the room.

I look up and make eye contact with all of the women. They all look at me with varying degrees of pity, and I know that this, what comes next, is going to be horrendous.

I keep my lips pressed together as he lets me fall to my feet. I sway when he bends down and unties my ankles. Then he rises, and his hands dive into my hair before fisting tightly, making my scalp pull. I try not to wince at the pain.

"The club thought they'd be cute. They thought they could cut off contracts, and they all thought that it would just go away," he growls.

"So you betrayed them?" I ask, trying to keep him talking. The longer he talks, the longer until he rapes me.

"Been playing both sides of the fence, darlin', my whole fuckin' life. Dad was an Aryan. I prospected with the *Devils* the day I turned eighteen," he grins. "Now, it's time to play."

I suck in a breath when he reaches for me. Unfortunately, there isn't much fabric between us, and Drifter grabs the hem of my t-shirt with each hand and rips it in half up my body. I shake, unable to stop myself as I'm standing in just my panties and no bra in front of him. His eyes scan me and he grins.

"Nipple rings. *Nice,*" he grunts as he reaches out and touches each ring.

I dig my fingernails into my palms, fighting a shiver in disgust, keeping my face impassive, and trying to keep the bile from rising up my throat.

"Does the carpet match the curtains?" a man's voice asks from somewhere behind me.

"Let's find out, shall we?" Drifter asks as his fingers reach for my panties.

I feel heat at my back, but since my hands are still tied, I can do nothing but stand and wait for whatever comes next. Then a knock on the door has Drifter's head popping up, and he takes a step back from me.

I watch as he pulls a gun out of his waistband and walks over to the door. Three more men suddenly appear, and the man who was behind me wraps his arm around my neck, pulling me into his chest. His arm moves and his hand squeezes my breast before his rancid breath hits my face.

"Can't wait to play with you," he whispers.

I don't make a move or a noise, trying my hardest to keep absolutely still and show no emotion at all to his words.

I hear Paxton's voice, and then there's a shot that rings out, but I don't see who falls. The man holding me whirls me around from the front door. I scream out in pain as my ankle twists, and I try to struggle to get away from him. His grip is tight, and his hand has moved from my breast to my neck. He squeezes, and I stop screaming, but I don't stop struggling against him with all that I have.

chapter thirty

Torch

Drifter stares back at me when the door opens. *Drifter, my own fuckin' Vice President.* The man we trusted to run our club when Fury was locked up a few years ago; the man I trusted as a brother, as my family.

"Drifter?" I ask, my gun at my side.

"The fuck you doing here?" he barks. I watch his arm move.

He's got a gun in his grasp, and I jerk to the side, a bullet going through my shoulder. I hear another shot ring out and watch Drifter fall, Fury appearing and walking through the door, another shot, and another.

My eyes aren't on any of the action. Instead, my eyes are focused on Cleo. I lift my gun in my other hand, my non-dominant one, and point it at the fuck whose hand is wrapped round my wife's neck.

"You try and shoot me, I'll choke the life outta her," he growls.

I don't speak. I continue to walk toward him. He's squeezing her neck, and she's turning an ugly shade of red, but I don't give a fuck right now. He can't kill her by the time I point this gun to his pussy face and pull the trigger.

His eyes are wide and he's searching for something, but I don't give a single fuck of what it could be. He's backed himself up against the wall, and I can hear my brother's heavy boots stomping around the house. All his little buddies are dead.

"Let her go," I growl with my gun pointed at his temple.

"Fuck you, spic," he screams.

My eyes widen in surprise, and then I grin.

"I'm half-Persian, half-mutt, none of those being Hispanic, you fuckin' idiot," I chuckle before I pull the trigger. His body immediately falls to the floor, as does Cleo, who rolls to the side after I've kicked the disgusting fucker away from her.

I sink to my ass and pull her into my arms, my fingers touching the side of her neck, praying for a pulse. When I find it, I let out a sigh of relief.

Fury

I walk into the bedroom, anticipating to clear it of more sick fucks, but then I freeze in my tracks. Women, a whole room full. I count—eight. They're all skinny, dirty, and white, of

319

course. They look up at me, and one of them smiles.

"Holy shit, you guys came," one girl with long blonde hair and brown eyes says. "I'm Ginger. My Old Man is Snake, from Canada," she says.

My eyes widen in surprise and I take in each woman. They're all barely dressed and look vastly different, but they have something in common. They each have brands. Ginger's is across the side of her neck. Proudly on display, it says *Snake* in cursive.

"What the fuck?" I rasp. "He never told me his woman was gone," I mutter, thinking about my friend.

"We'd been separated for a few months," she says, her lip trembling and tears filling her eyes.

"What the fucking shit is this?" my Pops whispers from behind me.

"They need medical attention," I inform him.

"Fuckin' shit. We got a van comin'. Let me call ahead to the clubhouse, see if we can get doc there. It's a couple hours drive," he murmurs.

"Get somethin' set up for nine women and Torch, he's got a flesh wound he needs sewed up," I grunt.

I call out for a couple guys to help me with these women.

"There anymore of you?" I ask as I pick up Snake's Old Lady.

She's nothin' but skin and bones, and it makes my body vibrate with anger.

"I don't think so," she whispers. "Please don't call him," she begs.

"Why the fuck wouldn't I call him?" I ask as my brows shoot straight up.

I'm careful not to jar her tiny body too much as I carry her to the van. She winces with each step that I take. My eye's catch my VP, the man I fuckin' trusted with my life for years, lying in a pool of his own blood on the floor. Blood that was put there with a bullet that I fuckin' shot, right in his goddamn traitor face.

"I don't want him to know," she whispers.

"Sorry babe, gonna call him. His names on your body, would make me no better than my piece of shit ex-VP if I didn't give him the opportunity to take care of his Old Lady," I rumble as I set her down in the open van.

"He won't care," she whispers.

"Know Snake, babe; known him for a lotta years; know he'll fuckin' care," I grind out. She closes her eyes, and I watch as nothing but pure pain crosses her features. "We'll get you all cleaned up. You'll feel different."

"I won't," she rasps.

I don't get a chance to say anything else. The other women are set down in the van, and then I watch as my Pops carries an unconscious Cleo, with Torch looking ready to kill walking behind him.

"Wanna torch the house?" I ask, turning to him.

"Fuck yes," he growls.

"Figured this could go down like that. There's accelerant in the van," I shrug.

"Might have to help me. My arm's lame," he chuckles.

"First, we take Drifter's cut," I grin.

"Fuck, yeah," he grunts.

We take Drifter's cut from his body before we douse the house with a can of gasoline, something we always have in the van. Then Fury throws in a match and runs away.

The house goes up in a burst of flames. The brothers load on their bikes; Torch's bike is loaded into the back of a pickup truck we brought just in case. The van, with the women and Torch, driven by a prospect, takes off; and my Pops and I walk toward our bikes.

"Never woulda pegged him," my dad mutters.

"No shit. He held down the fort while I was locked up, like a well-oiled machine," I say, shaking my head with disbelief mixed with disgust.

"Let's get these women taken care of," he grunts before he starts his engine.

We ride down to Shasta, my Pops probably equally antsy to get home to his Mary-Anne, to ensure her safety after seeing what we saw today.

As soon as we pull into the clubhouse, I make a much needed and difficult call.

"Snake," he growls into the phone.

"It's Fury," I announce. He chuckles.

"Shit, man, I didn't even look at my caller ID. What's up, brother?"

"Shits me to have to do this, make this call," I say.

I close my eyes, not able to watch the men carry the women from the van to inside the clubhouse, where there's surely a doctor ready to help them.

"The fuck, man? What's up?"

"It's Ginger," I murmur.

I can practically feel the electricity from him spark through the phone.

"What's Ginger? That bitch ran out of town two months ago," he growls.

"She didn't."

"What the fuck aren't you telling me?" he practically whispers.

"Need to come to Shasta," I murmur.

"Tell me first. Fucking tell me," he demands.

"She was kidnapped, held by my own fucking VP in Tulelake, in some shitty house. She's been hurt, man," I say as I lift my hand and run it across the back of my neck.

"Hurt," he rasps.

"She didn't want you comin', but brother, you care anything for her, you need to be here."

"Me and a couple boys are leavin' in five," he says before he ends the call.

"Did the right thing," Sniper says from next to me.

"Did I? She didn't want me calling him," I murmur looking up at the sky.

"She don't know what she wants. That was Kentlee, you guys were fighting or you felt like you hated her, you'd want to know if someone hurt her like that," he mumbles, his voice gruff. "And I know Snake. Never met Ginger before, don't know anything about her, but I know him. He's the kinda man that'd want to know."

I lift my chin and then pat Sniper on the back. He's going to be my new VP—he just doesn't know it yet. My brother-in-law, the most solid man I know. I can't deny that I'm glad we found out what was happening, who was buying women—and, odds are, the reason our particular women were being targeted.

"Fuck," I breathe.

"No shit," he chuckles before he turns around. We watch a bunch of cars coming through the gates.

"The Calvary's arrived," he grins.

"They'll help these women," I murmur. Mary-Anne, Sniper's sister, is the first to pull into the parking lot.

"Shit yeah, they will," he grunts.

Cleo

I moan. I hurt. I roll to the side and realize that I'm in a bed. Opening my eyes, I expect to see that rank asshole, or maybe Drifter, but I don't. It's Paxton. He's sitting in a chair by the bed, his head hanging down. He's shirtless with a bandage on his arm. I look around the room and let out a sigh of relief to find that I'm in his room at the clubhouse. I've never been so happy to see this room in my entire life.

"Paxton," I whisper, reaching out to touch him.

As soon as my fingers graze his forearm, he jumps and his stormy blue eyes meet mine. They sweep over me and then land on my eyes. He drinks me in for a moment before he stands and walks over to the side of the bed. I watch silently as he sinks down next to me.

"How you feelin', sweetheart?" he asks as his fingers gently touch my throat.

"Throat's sore," I rasp.

"It's gonna be for a while," he nods. "The rest of you?"

"They didn't hurt me," I say with a small smile. "You got to me before anything happened."

"Fuck, all of this shit is my fault," he rumbles.

I reach up and cup his cheek with my palm, feeling his scruff as I focus on his eyes.

"You don't control the world, Paxton. I'm okay. The other girls may not be, but I am," I say, giving him another small smile.

"Yeah, fuckin' barely. You get kidnapped, shot, then kidnapped and touched. This shit is not okay, and all of it is because of me. You can't talk me out of feelin' that," he announces.

"I love you. Do you love me?" I ask, ignoring his self-pity-fest.

"More than anything, sweetheart," he rasps.

"Then that's all I care about," I say hoarsely. "I'm alive, I'm breathing, and I'm not hurt. You're here, right in front of me, safe and breathing. We have a whole beautiful life ahead of us."

"Fucking hell, I do not deserve you," he chuckles before he places his lips against my palm. He then lowers his head and presses another kiss to my lips.

"Why do you have a bandage on your arm?" I ask, pulling away from him slightly.

"Got shot," he shrugs.

My eyes widen as I gasp before I sit straight up.

"Paxton, oh my god, are you okay?" I ask my voice raspy. My fingers gently touching his bandage.

"I'm fine, sweetheart. Flesh wound. Doc just gave me a couple stitches and some antibiotic. Be good as new in just a few days. Nothin' like what you went through," he murmurs.

"Please tell me this is all over," I beg.

"We don't know exactly what Drifter was doin' or what his reasoning was, so I don't know. I hope to fuck it is, though," he sighs.

"His dad was an Aryan. He said he was playing both sides of the fence," I say, remembering the information that Drifter so sweetly imparted on me before he ripped my shirt off and grabbed my boob.

"I gotta tell Fury and MadDog," he announces, standing up.

He stops, turning back to me, his eyes going soft as he looks at me.

"You'll be okay if I leave for a few?"

"Is Ginger okay?" I ask as my answer.

"I'll send her in if you wanna see for yourself," he grins as he continues to walk out of the door.

"That'd be nice," I sigh.

I'm wearing another one of Paxton's t-shirts, and instead of just panties, I've also got a pair of sweatpants on. I wait and jump slightly when the door opens and Ginger walks through. She looks a million times better than the last time I saw her. Her face is cleaned off from the grime and dirt that had been there. Her blonde hair is even lighter, now that it's clean, and she looks much like me in a pair of men's sweats and oversized t-shirt.

"Cleo," she whispers as she walks up to me. Sitting down on the bed in front of me, she crosses her legs.

"We were found," I grin.

"We were," she nods. She's not smiling, though, and it makes me curious.

"What is it?" I ask.

"I know someone called my Old Man. He'll be here," she whispers. "The other girl's men have been filing in all day long."

"You don't want him here?" I ask in confusion.

"I don't want him to think that he has to take care of me because his name is inked on my neck," she states.

"How long have you been together?" I blurt, though I

don't know why.

"Before I was taken, we'd been off and on for six months. Before that, we had been together for six months straight," she explains. "I'm broken now," she whispers. "We fought a lot, and we're both stubborn, and now this," she shakes her head as she wipes a tear from her eye.

"You're not broken. You didn't ask for the things that happened to you. Paxton and I fight a lot; but we also love each other a lot, and the love I have for him outweighs everything else," I say.

"I love him so much. Prescott is everything. But I'm flawed, now, in a way that it can never be undone," she whispers.

"How so? Because some men, who you didn't give permission to, violated you?" I ask.

She looks down in her lap and twists her fingers together. I shake my head and reach over to grab her hands.

"You love him? Really love him?" I ask, giving her hands a squeeze.

"I do," she rasps.

"Then you let him take the lead," I offer with a sad smile. "Let him tell you what he can handle and what he can't. I think that he'll surprise you," I whisper, my throat hurting more with each word I speak.

"Thank you," she says before she throws her arms around me in a hug.

"For what?" I laugh, hugging her back.

"For being absolutely awesome," she says as she sits back, giving me a huge grin.

"Ginger," I smile back, wiping a tear from my eye.

Taking a closer look at her I realize that she's younger

than me. This poor girl and the hells she'd been through.

"Seriously."

We spend the next fifteen minutes chatting about nothing, and it feels good. I can see that she doesn't want to talk about any heavy stuff anymore, and I give her that. The woman has been through enough, and I have a feeling, once Snake walks through the clubhouse doors, her stress level is going to go through the roof.

chapter thirty-one

Torch

The men fill the room, standing room only. A mix of Idaho and Cali brothers surround me, and we're all melancholy. One of our own hurt the women of the Devils. Not just girlfriends, not just whores, but Old Ladies. He hurt them in a way that wouldn't be acceptable for any of our women, girlfriends and whores alike—but for Old Ladies? I shake my head in disgust.

"All right, I have an update," MadDog announces as he slams down his gavel, his voice booming throughout the room.

We all settle and wait for him to continue.

"Called Oliver. Fuck, those Russian's really got a great tech guy," he says, shaking his head with a grin tipping his lips. "Anyway, Drifter's real name was Joshua Thompson.

He's a third-generation white supremacist. He infiltrated the club when he was eighteen, and it was his job to be eyes and ears for his family, especially when I accepted a contract with the fuckers. When shit went down, and when Kentlee was kidnapped, only a small portion of their crew was killed. He chose to stay, played the part of devoted VP to the Devil's, and continued to feed information to the Aryans. He would feed them information on Old Ladies. Most of the time, women that either were separated from their Old Men, so they wouldn't be looked for awfully hard, with the assumption they had just run off."

I close my eyes at his words. Disgusted by this man I called a brother for my entire fucking life. A man I thought was my fucking family. Disgusted with my fucking self too, for leaving Cleo the way I did, for leaving her open to be a goddamn target the way I did.

"*The Cartel* was easy to get in on it. The Aryan's paid them to get the girls, and they happily took and sold the women. Since they fuckin' love that shit anyway. Anytime they had a girl that didn't fit the Aryan's need, they'd put them up to sell to someone else. I don't know if we'll ever find out exactly how many women were taken," MadDog murmurs.

"Fuck, how many times does this shit gotta happen?" I ask, my face twisting in anger. "Where are all the pregnant women?"

"Pregnant?" Fury asks in confusion.

"The one's we found, they said every time a woman got pregnant, they never saw her again. They're somewhere," I state.

"*Fuck*," MadDog hisses.

"Yeah, *fuck*. How do we find them?" I ask.

I don't know why it's so fucking important to me, but maybe it's just because Cleo could have been one of them. We don't know how long this has been going on. Probably years. How many women could that be? Dozens, hundreds?

"We need a meeting, a charter wide meeting, all of the presidents. Set that up for me?" MadDog asks, turning to Fury.

"Yeah, Pops," he nods.

"I'll call the Russian's, see if their man can find anything else on those racist fucks. Maybe he can find their hidey hole," he grumbles.

"You know they're livin' off the grid in bunkers," I grunt.

"Probably, but they're gonna fuck up again. We'll find them when they do, and kill every single fucking one of them," he booms, his angry voice bouncing off of the walls.

Church ends, and everybody disperses, the room feeling heavy with the weight of our new knowledge. I have no desire to drink, or to do anything but hold my woman. She's breathin', alive and safe.

I march back to my room. Cleo's curled in a ball, and I strip off my clothes before I crawl in behind her, wrapping my arms around her perfect, curvy, soft body.

I don't fall asleep. How can I sleep? I'll probably never sleep again. My wife was taken, touched by another man, and almost raped. I move my hand from around her waist to rest just above her tit, feeling her heart pound beneath my palm. She's alive, she's breathing, she's unhurt, but that doesn't mean that I will ever rest easy again.

My phone buzzes from my jeans pocket on the floor, and I reach down, quietly answering it without moving around too much.

"Is she okay?" Lisandro asks.

I'd called him when everything went down, then sent a text when I got her, then called him again once the doc checked her out.

"She's sleepin' now," I murmur.

"When can we see her?" he asks.

I can't help my lips from tipping in a smile at his question. He's asking me, not demanding, and I like that. I tell him to come down anytime. She'll probably be sleeping for a while, but they can text me when they're almost here and I'll wake her up. He thanks me and I end the call.

Lisandro and Theo are so important to Cleo that I can't imagine them not being part of her life anymore. They're part of her, they love her, and they're her family. With her comes them, and I'm grateful for that. My woman should have the love of good people, and they're good men. No, they're great fuckin' men.

Cleo rolls over in my arms as soon as I turn back to face her. I watch as her eyes flutter open and a smile appears on her lips.

"Why're you awake?" I ask as I trail my fingers up her back, beneath the shirt of mine she's wearing.

"Missed your weight against me. Woke me up," she shrugs.

"You doin' okay?" I ask as my eyes take her in.

"I am. It was scary, but I'm okay," she whispers.

"Good. Think you could handle me bein' inside you?" I ask as I lower my head and press my lips to hers once. I then move my mouth to her neck and lick her soft skin.

"Yeah," she breathes as she trembles lightly in my arms.

I move my hand down to her waist, then her hip, before

I dip beneath the sweats she's wearing and push them down over her ass. My fingers gently caress her skin before I cup her pussy with my palm, squeezing gently as my lips continue to kiss her neck, my tongue tasting her every so often.

"Pax," she hums.

"Thought I would never touch you again, sweetheart," I murmur as I slide two fingers inside of her warm pussy.

She moans as she widens her legs and falls onto her back. I roll with her, covering half of her body with mine as I continue to fuck her with my fingers, enjoying the little whimpering sounds she's starting to make as her hips move beneath my touch.

"Paxton," she moans as her hand wraps around the side of my neck. Her hips thrust up, and she grinds her clit against my palm.

"Fuck, Cleo. Come all over my hand," I groan against her neck, feeling her pussy flutter around my fingers.

It doesn't take her long; her hips start to jerk, and then she throws back her head as her pussy squeezes my fingers. She cries out as her release consumes her. I let her completely control the moment, until her body relaxes and she looks up at me, her face flush, and a smile playing on her lips.

I pull her sweats the rest of the way off, along with her panties, then I push my boxer briefs down before I settle between her legs and guide my cock to push against her center. I slowly sink inside of her, pushing her shirt over her tits, making sure my gaze is focused on hers as I bury myself inside of her.

"I love you," she whispers.

Once I'm fully seated inside of her, I shudder. She's so goddamn tight, so warm, and all mine. My eyes scan down her bruised throat and I tamp down the anger that begins to build at the fact that a man hurt her, my wife.

"Move, please," she whines.

"No," I grind through clenched teeth.

"Paxton."

"Thought I'd never have this again, for the third time. Let me feel you for a bit, Clee," I rumble.

Cleo

His words almost undo me. I hold it together, but just barely, as he starts to move inside of me. His strokes are long, slow, and purposeful. He wants me to feel every single inch of him as he feels every piece of me.

My body starts to heat as I climb toward my second release. Paxton's eyes focus on mine, and one of his hands plays with my nipple. The other hand rests next to my head to keep the majority of his weight off of me. Keeping my grasp around his neck, I roll my hips so that our strokes meet, lifting my legs around his waist.

"You're never allowed out of my sight again," he murmurs. I laugh softly, but he's serious as he continues to gently thrust inside of me.

"Paxton," I whisper.

"Never, Cleo. Fuckin' almost lost you, *again*. Promise me."

He's serious, *completely* serious as he takes me in, waiting for my response while his body owns me, the way that it always has and always will. I think about the crazy as shit things that have happened over the past couple of months, and I can't say if the roles were reversed that I wouldn't feel the same. Maybe in a couple months he'll feel better and I can go back to work for Lisandro, but for now, I need to give him peace of mind.

"Okay," I say on a moan.

He doesn't say anything. His hand leaves my breast and wraps around the back of my knee, lifting and spreading me even wider as he starts to fuck me, hard and rough. I throw my head back on a long moan, loving the way he crashes into me with each thrust of his hips.

It doesn't take long before I'm sweating. Then, without warning, I come. Like a freight train, it completely takes over me, and I start to shake beneath him. After a few hard thrusts, he groans before he collapses on me and buries his face in my neck.

"Never leavin' me again, sweetheart," he murmurs against my sweat soaked skin.

"Okay, Pax," I whisper, my fingers tracing his back, gently.

"Mmmm," he hums. "Feel's good."

We fall asleep wrapped in each other's arms, but not for long. A few hours later, the phone rings and Paxton groans before he rolls off of me to answer it. Then his eyes move to me and he grins as he hangs up.

"Get dressed, sweetheart," he murmurs.

"Why?" I groan, unable to open my eyes.

"Because two men are feeling particularly excited to give you a hug and check you out," he chuckles.

"Lis and Theo?" I ask, sitting straight up.

"Yeah, hop up. You have enough time for a quick shower and to throw some shit on. I think you still got somethin' in a drawer," he shrugs as he stands.

I watch him pull his jeans up over his glorious naked ass, and I shiver before I pull his shirt over me and walk over to his dresser to look around for some clothes. I find a pair of shorts I left here, but nothing else. I take them, along with a tank of his, and a towel to the showers.

I shower quickly, and throw my clothes on, tying a knot in the oversized black tank, wishing that I at least had a bra. One glance in the mirror, and I can clearly see my nipple rings on proud display through the tank. I have no other choice, though.

I avoid the one thing I hate looking at every time I glance in the mirror, my scar, and let out an exhale. I hurry to the bar, barefoot, my hair in a messy knot on top of my head, but my only focus is seeing Lis and Theo.

Once I'm in the bar area, I see a bunch of brothers, a whole lot of women, and Paxton, who is standing, facing me with a beer dangling from his fingertips. His brows rise when his eyes fall to my breasts and then he looks back up at me. I watch as a lazy grin appears on his lips. I walk over to him, waiting for what, I'm not sure. I can't really read him.

"No bra," he whispers, lifting his thumb to glide over my nipple bar.

"I don't have one here," I whisper.

"Sexy," he murmurs before he dips his head and I feel his breath against my ear.

"You aren't angry?" I breathe as his lips touch my neck.

"*For what?*"

"Well, it's pretty obvious I'm showing more that I normally would," I say, backing up slightly as I look into his eyes. I watch his lazy grin appear again, and then he bites his bottom lip before he speaks.

"Sweetheart, what the fuck do I care if another man looks at my gorgeous wife? Nobody touches without permission, but your tits are fantastic—be a shame to keep them under lock and key all the time," he chuckles.

"*Paxton Hill*," I gasp.

"Don't give a fuck if someone looks, not while you're on my arm with my ring on your finger," he grins.

"I thought you'd be all jealous," I mutter, looking down at my bare feet.

"Want me to be?" he asks, arching a brow. "Want me to kill any man that looks in your direction? For you, sweetheart, I'd fuckin' do it."

"No," I laugh, shaking my head.

"No reason to be jealous. You're sleepin' in my bed, you're comin' on my cock, you're mine," he shrugs before he lifts his beer bottle to his lips and takes a pull.

"This is all true," I agree.

"Cleo! Oh, my god," Lisandro's loud voice screeches from the front door.

I peak around Paxton's body and see he's standing there, looking so disheveled I hardly recognize him.

"Go give him a hug, baby," Paxton mutters.

I look up to him, smile, and then take off toward Lisandro. He opens his arms to accept me, and I don't stop until I've crashed into his body, my legs around his waist and my arms around his neck.

"I was so worried," he whispers, wrapping his arms around me.

"I'm okay," I say as I slide down his body and give him a grin.

"You're bruised," Theo growls.

"The only marks on me, so I'm good. I'm breathing, I'm with my family. God is good," I grin. Both Theo and Lis shake their heads.

"God *is* good," Mary-Anne chimes in from next to us. She's sitting at a pub table, her hand resting on her baby belly, and a smile playing on her lips.

"Well, yes, thank goodness you weren't really hurt," Lis says with ruffled feathers.

"Yes, thank goodness," I giggle.

"*Clee*," he hisses. I look at him in confusion, then realize he's focused on my breasts.

"Pierced. Diamonds," I state.

"You little freak. I love it," he chuckles as he wraps his arm around my shoulders and pulls me into his side. "Everything's good then?" he whispers.

"He doesn't want me to leave his sight for, like, ever," I mutter.

"Everything's good," he grins. "You do that. For a while, at least."

"I was thinking the same thing," I grin.

"I need a fuckin' beer," Theo groans before he walks past us and up to the bar.

"I may have been completely freaked out, and probably drove him to the brink of looney," Lis announces with a shrug and a smile.

"You better make it up to him," I say.

"Planning on it—." He opens his mouth, but I hold my hand up, not wishing to hear exactly *how* he's going to make anything up to Theo.

"Don't wanna know," I mumble.

"I kinda want to know," Mary-Anne grins as MadDog

wraps his arm around her waist and lays a possessive hand on her belly.

"Sweetness," he grunts.

"What? Maybe it'll give me an education and ideas," she says as her eyes dance with mischievousness.

"I like her," Lis announces as he turns his head to look at me.

We all laugh and, thankfully, Lisandro doesn't tell me whatever it is he's going to do to make up his freak-out at Theo. Lis doesn't hide much and I already know way more than I should about his sex life pre-Theo and post-Theo.

We spend the next few hours chatting, drinking, and one by one, the women who were saved come and join us. The whores are nowhere to be seen, and it makes me wonder if they were warned to stay away.

There's a pizza run when people start getting hungry. There's no drama, no naked women, no screwing and nothing crazy. It's just people, friends, and family, hanging out and relaxing after a stressful as shit day.

Paxton stays either in my line of sight or at my side the entire evening, and it makes me feel comforted and good. Almost as if he's wrapping a warm blanket straight from the dryer around me.

"Never thought I'd see you this happy. I'd hoped, but honest, I never thought it would happen. Then all that shit started piling up, you getting shot and kidnapped, and this whole rough club business—I thought there was no way you'd stay with him, and that you'd smile the way you're smiling now."

"Theo," I whisper.

"I can't wait for the rest of your life to play out," Theo murmurs as he slips his arm around my shoulders and hugs me to his side.

"How do you think it will?" I ask, arching a brow.

"I think it's going to be wild and crazy, but I think it's going to be full of so much love and laughter, too. I think that after your years of being shut down and shut off that it's going to fill you up with emotion, every fucking second of it."

"You're making me cry," I breathe as I wipe the tears from my eyes.

"Can't wait to see what tomorrow brings for you, Cleo," he murmurs.

"Sweetheart?" Paxton says as he walks up to us, his brow furrowed in worry.

"I'm okay," I grin with trembling lips.

"Yeah. Ready for bed?" he asks.

I nod but don't walk away immediately. I wrap my arms around Theo and give him a hug, then I make my way to a very drunk Lisandro and give him a hug as well. I grip my hand around Paxton's, and I let him lead me up to bed. Theo is right, I've never been so happy in all of my life.

Kidnapping, shooting, none of it matters. I have Paxton at my side, always looking out for me. I couldn't make it if he weren't, and I wasn't living when he wasn't. I was a shell, barely surviving. But now? I feel everything, and what I feel for him is everything, too.

"I love you, sweetheart," he whispers as he pulls me close to his side once we're undressed and beneath the sheets.

"I never stopped loving you, Paxton," I confess.

"Fucking hell," he murmurs, rolling on top of me.

I giggle as he kisses me, his tongue soft and wet, but insistent, sliding inside of my mouth. I don't resist him at all, opening up for him the way I always have. This man—he has always been it for me, and I've always been his. Neither of us were really ready when we met all those years ago, still trying to find our footing in life.

It's true, he hurt me when he left; but he thought he was saving me from a lifetime of pain. No matter what, we lost years of being together—but in doing that, I gained independence and he found a family and a home. He worked through his demons, and I believe, although he's rough around the edges, he's a better man for it.

The love of my life.

Paxton Hill.

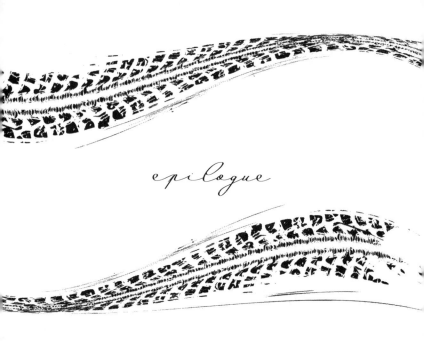

epilogue

SIX-MONTHS LATER

Cleo

"Happy Birthday to you," Lisandro belts out, a little excitedly.

I don't know what else I'm going to wish for, but I bend over the cake slightly and close my eyes, blowing out my candle as I make my last and final wish.

It has been a tough six-months for the club and its members, but it's nice to see all of them here today, celebrating my birthday with me. I watch as Serina, the ex-clubwhore, slides up against Grease and wraps her arms around his large stomach. He's definitely not the kind of man I would curl up next to, but they both look really, *really* happy. In fact, she's sporting her fresh Grease brand on her upper chest, and proudly.

"What'd you wish for, sweetheart?" Paxton asks, his hand sliding around my back and waist as I stand up.

"It was really hard, because I have everything I could have ever wanted." I smile looking up at him.

Mary-Anne takes the cake and starts to cut pieces, being the organized *take-charge-mom*, and I don't mind one bit. I never could cut a cake proportionately anyway. Paxton's hands slide down and cup my ass, squeezing it gently before he smooths down my lilac colored sundress.

"Nothing?" he asks, lifting a brow.

I shake my head as I smile. I literally have everything I want. He doesn't realize it yet, that he's given me the best gift I could imagine.

I'm six-weeks pregnant with his baby.

When I say that it's been a tough six-months, it's not just because of things that happened with the club—that including Soar continuing to stay in prison, officially, for the next three years—but also the fact that Paxton and I had miscarried.

I didn't know it at the time, but I was pregnant when I had been taken by the Aryan's. I miscarried a few weeks later. We'll never really know if the mistreatment I'd suffered from them had anything to do with our loss, but of course we always speculated.

Now, I feel good. At six-weeks, I've already had an ultrasound, and I've seen the baby's little heart beating. I even have a picture to show Pax. I know he's going to be so excited, once he gets past being scared, which will be amplified because of the loss we've already experienced.

"How about something like this?" he asks as he brings up a small jewelry box and opens it for me.

I gasp when I see what's inside. There, twinkling back at

me, are *LeVian* Morganite drop earrings in a *strawberry* gold setting with *vanilla* diamonds surrounding the large teardrop peach stone. They complement my ring—not matching it precisely, but still complementing it nonetheless.

"They're absolutely gorgeous," I whisper.

I know that Lisandro has had a hand in this, not only because the box is from his store, but because he's standing behind Paxton with a shit-eating grin on his face. I throw my arms around Paxton and press my lips against his, opening my mouth when I feel his tongue slide against my lips. I want so badly to tell him about the pregnancy, but I don't. It needs to be something special just between us.

"Okay, a toast," Ginger calls out.

Ginger stayed here, seeking a quiet life, but she's had anything but since Paxton and the rest of the Devils rescued her. Snake didn't take her being kidnapped and abused too well, like any man wouldn't. He confessed his love, apologized for his stubbornness, and expected everything to go back the way it was.

Ginger stood up to him and stood her ground. She'd been hurt for months, and she needed time. Begrudgingly, and with the force of Sniper, MadDog, and Fury, he left. That doesn't mean that he's left her alone. He's called every single day since he left her here in Shasta. Not only has he called, but he's also sent a box of her favorite chocolates every single week. She's teetering on the edge, and I think she's about ready to fall back into him.

"To Cleo," she continues. "The kindest, sweetest, most beautiful woman I have ever had the pleasure of knowing. Your sweetness drips out and touches every person you meet. You are truly a woman that I aspire to be like. Happy

Birthday," she whispers as she wipes a tear from her eye.

Everybody shouts their agreement and then takes a drink from their glass. A baby's cry interrupts us, and I look over to see Mary-Anne has brought her baby out from MadDog's office, where he has a crib set up. He's so hands on.

It's actually really surprising, considering his age. I, for one, thought that he'd make Mary do all of the work, but he doesn't. Every time I'm around, he's got the sweet little girl wrapped in his arms or cuddled against his big chest. It's seriously swoon worthy.

Torch

I watch my woman. I'm sure she doesn't even realize the way she's looking at MadDog and Mary-Anne's baby girl, Riley. I can see the pure want in her eyes. I wish I could give that to her right now. When we lost our own baby, I thought she'd get pregnant again immediately, but here we are five-months later, and nothin'. I know I'm being impatient, but it's hard not to be when you watch the woman you love yearn for something.

"You ready to head home, sweetheart?" I ask a few hours later.

"Uh, yeah," she says, scrunching her nose up as she turns to me.

I look past her and chuckle. I don't judge my brothers and their relationships. Serina is marked, she's Grease's Old Lady, but that doesn't mean that she's only *with* Grease.

In fact, the reason Cleo's nose is all scrunched is because Serina is bent over, one of the guys is fuckin' her ass as she blows her Old Man. It ain't my deal, but it works for them, so who am I to judge?

"You know they always put on a good show," I chuckle as I wrap my arm around her shoulders and lead her outside.

It's a warm night, and we're on the bike. We're only a few minutes from home, but it's long enough we can feel the wind on our faces and the freedom singing past us in the air.

"You know," she says, looking up to me. "They really do," she smiles.

"Let's get home, start our own private show," I grunt.

"Okay," she breathes as she follows behind me.

"Oh, shit," she curses as she slams down on my cock and grinds her clit against my pelvis.

I bite my bottom lip, wanting nothing more than to come deep inside of her. Sliding my hands up her sides, I pinch her piercings and tug, harder than I should, but *goddamn*. Cleo moans and leans back, wrapping her hands around my thighs as she starts to really grind and roll her hips.

Fuck.

I'm going to die.

Moving one of my hands, I press my thumb against her clit and start to stroke her. If I don't speed this up, I'll be the one coming first, and I can't let that happen on her birthday—or *ever*.

"Pax," she breathes as she pushes against my thumb.

"Come, sweetheart," I grind out.

Her legs start to tremble and then her pussy clamps down around me. I breathe out a sign of relief as she cries out. I wrap my hands around her waist and thrust up inside of her a few times before I follow her over the edge in my own climax.

"*Oh, my god*," she whimpers as she falls forward, her chest pressing into mine with each breath she tries to catch.

"Happy Birthday, sweetheart," I murmur against her hair.

"It *is* a happy birthday," she announces as she lifts her head. My eyes catch the new earrings I bought her in the moonlight, and I grin, assuming that's what she's referencing. "I'm pregnant, Paxton."

It takes a second for her words to register, and then I sit up and flip her onto her back as I loom over her. There's a sly grin on her lips, and brightness shining in her eyes.

"Say it again," I demand.

"I'm pregnant, Paxton," she whispers.

"Fuckin' shit," I gasp before my lips crash against hers in a hard kiss.

Then I lift in a complete panic.

"Are you okay? Do you need to go to the hospital? What do you need?" I worry.

"I went to the doctor, everything is good. They're going to keep a really close eye on me, but everything looks awesome right now. It's still really, *really* early," she whispers. I can see the worry etched in her features, even though she's trying to hide it.

"I'm so happy. Worried, but happy," I whisper as I lower my head so that our foreheads are touching.

"Me too," she admits.

"I fuckin' love you, sweetheart," I rasp.

"I love you so, so much, Paxton. Thank you for the best birthday I could ever imagine."

ROUGH & SHAKEN
A SHORT STORY

PART ONE

Ginger

My phone rings. I don't even have to look at the caller ID to know who it is. It's him. *Snake.* Prescott. The man I've loved since I saw him from across the crappy bar almost two years ago.

I moved to a sleepy little Canadian town when I turned twenty-five. It wasn't because I'd wanted to. It was because my uncle, a grumpy assed old man, had become ill and needed help with his bar. He didn't have kids; he didn't have *anyone.* He'd served in *Vietnam*, and as soon as he came back to the US, he packed his shit and went to Canada.

A lot of people assumed he'd been a draft dodger, but he wasn't. He served his country and did it with pride, but it fucked him up, so he left. My mama didn't blame him even a little.

So, when he got sick and couldn't run his bar, she packed my bags and told me to get to Canada and help him out. Didn't matter that she hadn't seen him in decades, family was family and family helped family.

I'd always been a kind of lost soul. Nothing called to me after high school. I fooled around at community college, but never found anything that interested me. At twenty-five, I'd been working aimlessly at a waitressing job. Mama said I was the only one who could go, because I was the one most like uncle Cash.

My first night there, uncle Cash'd frowned when I showed, but he didn't push me away. Instead, he pretended as if he'd known me my whole life, and he started showing me how to run his business, coughing every so often and holding his stomach. He had cancer, pancreatic; there was no beating it.

On my third night, a Friday night, my eyes widened in surprise when a wild group of men came inside around midnight. They were outfitted with leather vests, holey jeans, tight t-shirts, beards, muscles, chains, and boots. I'd never seen so many sexy men in a group in my entire life.

One stood out to me, though, as if he was a beacon. He was almost the tallest, but not quite. He *was* the most muscular, and I swear, his beard made me drool a bit. He was beyond the word sexy. I didn't know what word fit him. Maybe it hadn't been invented yet.

I sucked in a breath and made my way over to their table. I didn't want to, I didn't feel steady enough, but uncle Cash said I couldn't hide behind the bar and wait for customers to come to me. He said I needed to get out and push the booze. So, that's what I did.

The stranger eyed me up and down, then the rest was history. He took me home that first night, and every night after. I had his name tattooed on my body, *my neck*, by the three-month mark, and by six months we were fighting. The back and forth was exciting, stressful, and heartbreaking.

I was about to surrender, give him the control he wanted over us, our main reason for fighting. I was trying to be in charge, but Snake was a man, a leader, a president of a motorcycle club; no woman could be in control of him—*ever*.

Then I was kidnapped. Held for months by the scariest,

cruelest men I had ever encountered in my entire life. It's hard not to think about, the countless numbers of hands that have been on my body, pawing at me, then violating me.

I try not to think about it, to pretend that it didn't happen, but every time I close my eyes, its right there slapping me in the face—the cold hard realty that it was indeed my life for a time.

Now, six months after my rescue, I don't feel worthy of Snake. I was damaged, and I'm not good enough for him. But he won't leave me the hell alone. *Why won't he just leave me alone?*

"Hello," I say bitchily into the phone.

"Hey, peaches," he murmurs, his voice deep, husky and too damn sexy for his own good.

"Prescott," I whisper, using his given name instead of his road name.

"How you doin' today?" he asks.

It's the same question he asks me every day.

"Better," I answer.

It's the same answer I give him every day.

"Miss you," he mutters.

I close my eyes, pinching them closed so tight that I see stars in my vision. I usually don't answer him when he says this, but today, I do.

"You shouldn't, but I miss you, too," I admit as I open my eyes. Tears start to fall down my cheeks.

"You ready to come home to me yet?" he asks.

"No," I whisper.

"Bar's doin' good. Brothers are runnin' it, turnin' profit," he says, changing the subject.

Uncle Cash passed away three months after my arrival.

He left me the bar in his will, as well as his house. The house was wrecked. Snake and his brothers helped me fix it up, then Snake moved in. I kicked his ass out, but he still came over when we'd be on again, at least to sleep with me.

"I'm glad," I say, bringing my knees up and resting my chin on them.

"You need anything?" he asks.

"No," I say.

He's set up an account for me and deposits money into it, claiming it's my income from the bar, but I know better. I know *him* better. I don't mind, though. I'm keeping a tally, and I'll pay him back once I get back to Canada, back to my life—which I should probably do, sooner rather than later. It's been six-months. It's been long enough.

Snake

I end the call and turn to my computer. I don't even have to fill out my information, or Ginger's, anymore. I've sent her so many boxes of chocolate that both of our addresses and my credit card number is saved into the system. Chocolate covered pecans straight from South Georgia. I know they're her favorite, and from her home state, my little Georgia Peach.

"You get your woman handled?" Free, my Vice President, asks as he walks into my office.

"Fuck, no," I grunt, closing my eyes after I press confirm on the chocolate order.

"It's been six-months. She stays away much longer, thinkin' she'll get some fucked up shit in her head and it'll be hard as nails to get her stubborn ass back here," he advises.

"Yeah. I'm leavin' tomorrow," I admit.

"Yeah?"

"Think you can hold the fort down for a week?" I ask.

"A week?" he chuckles.

"It's gonna take a day for me to get there, a day to talk her back into my bed, two full days of fuckin' her to talk her into coming back with me, a half a day for her to talk herself out of coming back, another half a day to talk her into coming. Then two days to drive her ass back here," I say, counting the days on my fingers.

"Got her all figured out, do you?" he asks with a big smile on his face.

"Fuck yeah, I do. Love that woman. Know everything there is to know about her," I shrug.

"You sure about that?" he asks as his eyes darken, most likely thinking about the time she spent held hostage by those sick fuck racists.

"Whatever I don't know, she'll tell me," I murmur.

"Don't count on it," Free announces as he stands up and walks out.

I watch after him, cursing to myself. I forgot about his woman. A woman he loved back when we were younger—a fuck've a lot younger. A woman who was brutally raped and then ended up taking her own life. I remember her, pretty little thing. She had been hurt, but she refused to talk about it. The weight was too much for her to bear, and she swallowed a bunch of pills one night when Free was on a run.

It was years ago, but he's never really gotten over it, never recovered from losing his first love the way he did. I don't want that for Ginger. She's got too much good in her life to leave it behind. I'm going to not only bring her back here, but bring her back to life.

She'll never hurt again. It'll be my mission to make her smile at least once a day. *Fuck*. I'm turning into a giant fuckin' pussy.

I go to my room. Looking around, it doesn't feel like my home anymore. Ginger's house, the place I helped her re-model, that's *home*. I make a decision; one she'll probably be pissed about, but I don't care.

I pack all my shit, carry it down to my pickup truck, and ask a prospect to drive it to her place, following behind him on my bike. I'm moving home, brining my woman back, and marrying her as soon as fuckin' possible.

This shit ends now.

Once I've moved all my shit into her house, not that I had a bunch, I decide to go to bed, wanting to leave before the sun rises tomorrow. Laying in her bed, my head on her pillow, I inhale and close my eyes in defeat. She's been gone so long that I can't smell her scent on her pillows anymore. I should have swallowed my pride when she disappeared. I should have known she wouldn't have walked away from her uncle's bar like that—abandoning it.

I should have known.

I should have looked for her.

I'm swimming in a pool of guilt over her kidnapping, over her abuse. It's my fault. One of the men from my club, a man who was supposed to be my brother—a man who ended up being nothing but a piece of shit traitor—he hurt her, my sweet Georgia Peach. He fuckin' *hurt* her.

I close my eyes and force myself to get at least a couple hours of sleep before I climb on my bike and haul ass to bring my woman home. She's been gone long enough.

Ginger

I curl up in a chair and sip my coffee, watching the birds fly from tree to tree from my front porch. It's my morning routine and the calmest part of the day, the sun shining down on me, the warmth of my coffee filling me from the inside out. I feel older than my almost twenty-seven years, but I also feel smarter than the woman I was just two years ago.

That is—until I hear the sound of a familiar motorcycle buzzing down my street.

I stand and walk over to the porch banister, setting my coffee cup down before it slips out of my fingers. I watch as none other than Prescott—*Snake*—Gordon pulls up in front of my house. His head turns, and though I can't see his eyes behind his helmet and sunglasses, I know that they are aimed right at me. I can almost feel them searing my skin, seeing through the little short and tank set I'm wearing.

I wrap my arms around my stomach, a stupid move to try and protect myself, but I'm frozen as he lifts his leg, swinging it off of his bike. He then takes his helmet off and sets it on his handle bar before he begins to march up my walkway.

I'm staying in a house the club owns. It's a little, two-bedroom, one bath home that they rent out when someone needs help. It just so happened to be empty, so they let me move in for a while.

"We gotta talk," he says, running his hand through his long hair.

I'm surprised to see that it no longer just brushes the tops of his shoulders, but hangs below them now.

His dark green eyes settle on me, and I swear my breath is

completely stolen. I hadn't forgotten how handsome he is; at least I didn't think that I had. I press my lips together, afraid that if I don't, I'll say something really stupid.

He wraps his fingers around my bicep and slides them down to my wrist, gently tugging me until my feet start to move as he pulls me into the house.

Once we're inside, he turns and slams the door closed before he flips the lock shut. Then he faces me. I'm holding my breath, afraid—terrified to say or do anything.

I whimper when his warm hand wraps around the side of my neck. His forehead lowers and presses against mine as his green eyes close and his breath fans my face. I force myself to breathe as well.

"I missed you, peaches," he whispers before he inhales deeply.

Tears stream down my face as his hands wrap around my waist and his fingers dig into my flesh firmly.

"You should go," I whisper.

I feel his body jerk, but he doesn't move. I lift my eyes and look up to see that he's smiling down at me.

"Not goin' anywhere, peaches," he murmurs.

"We can't be anything anymore. You need to go," I say a little firmer. His smile just widens.

"Not leaving you. I love you," he says.

"It doesn't matter. You need to *go*," I practically yell.

"Not happening," he says, shaking his head and smiling like I'm crazy.

"*Prescott!*"

"Shut up, Ginger," he growls.

I scream as he picks me up by my waist and carries me to my bedroom, accidently turning into the empty guest room before he finds my bed and drops me onto my ass.

I bounce once before he falls to his knees, his waist and chest between my thighs and his face directly across from mine. His hands cup my cheeks, pain clearly etched on his face for me to see.

"I'm so fuckin' sorry you were hurt, baby," he whispers, the agony in his voice too much for me to bear.

"Pres," I whimper.

His gaze stays connected to mine, and he wipes the tears from beneath my eyes with his thumbs, not saying a word. Then he moves closer, his lips brushing mine sweetly, his warm lips rough from his ride. His hands move from my face, sweeping over my neck before they travel to my sides. He lifts the hem of my shirt just slightly. His fingertips skim my waist and then gently glide up my back while his lips tease mine.

"I'm so sorry, baby. So fuckin' sorry. I'll never forgive myself for what happened to you. My sweet Georgia Peach," he rasps.

I don't know how to respond to his words, so I don't. Instead, I kiss him back, tasting his lips with my tongue. He applies pressure to my back, pulling me closer to him while he slides his tongue along mine, and then takes over the kiss.

I whimper again, but for no reason other than my want for him. I want him, too—every inch of him. It's as if my entire body has gone up in flames. I wrap my hand around his biceps and pull myself closer to him, wanting to feel that chest that I know is warm and strong against me.

"Fuck, I missed you," he rasps as his lips travel down my jawline, then my neck.

"You need to leave," I weakly demand.

"Never," he murmurs against my skin.

His tongue snakes out to taste my collar bone before his mouth moves to the tattoo I still have on my neck. *Snake* is scrolled in cursive across my skin. It's pretty and delicate, but it's still on my neck. I'll never be able to cover it, unless I wear turtlenecks for life. He wanted it visible always, and I gave him what he wanted. He picked the place and the design.

"Missed my name on your neck. Missed seeing it every day, kissing it—*fuck,* peaches, I just missed *you,*" he rasps, his voice deep and husky.

"I'm no good to you now," I state.

Snake

I sit up, my eyes narrowed on her, and my lips pressed together. She's panting, her face flushed, and I can tell she wants more from me. Her big, brown eyes stare at me, but beyond her pain, I see what she thinks she is hiding inside of her—dirty, wrong, *no good*. It's all bullshit. She's perfect.

"Why is that?" I ask.

I know her answer, I just want her to speak the words; want her to hear how fuckin' stupid they sound after they pass her lips.

"I'm dirty," she whispers.

"Because of what they did to you?"

"Yeah, and how many of them there were," she says with a nod.

I shake my head. *Goddamn.* My sweet girl. She's been so fucking hurt, destroyed by vile men.

"Peaches," I moan, the pain in her eyes slicing straight through me. She's not better. Fucking shit, she's still stuck

357

back there, and it's up to me to bring her home. "You're fucking perfect. Nothing about you is dirty. They're the fucking scumbags; and if they weren't dead, I would hunt them down and torture them one-by-one. I'd let you watch, too, if that's what you wanted."

"Prescott," she gasps, looking halfway horrified, but halfway excited at the thought of watching them suffer. My woman. *So* goddamn strong.

"They're still looking for more. We find 'em, you can watch," I murmur as my head dips and my lips press against hers again.

I don't let her push me away; not that she's even trying as I lift her shirt over her head. She's braless, and I almost whimper at the sight of her luscious tits, tits I thought I'd never see again—let alone touch, suck, and kiss.

My mouth travels down to her hard nipple, gently sucking it in my mouth and licking it with my tongue. She arches toward me, urging me on, and I take her signal, going soft, gentle, and slow.

I'm not going to rush her at all, and I'm not fucking her hard. At least not this first time. She moans as my hands move down to her little shorts. I tug at them and she lifts up so that I can pull them off of her sexy legs.

"Pres," she breathes.

I look up at her, and she's looking down at me. Her eyelids at half-mast, her face flushed, and her chest panting. Wrapping my hands around the backs of her knees, I lift her legs and watch as she falls to her back. Then I spread her thighs before my mouth is on her. When her taste floods my tongue, I can't help the groan.

Fuck.

She tastes better than I remembered.

Ginger's hips roll as her hands fist my long hair, pulling me closer. I don't deny the feeling of victory as she lets out a deep moan of her own, her thighs trembling. I flick her clit with my tongue before sucking on it, and then I fuck her pussy. I want nothing more than to make her come *hard*.

I focus back on her clit as her hips roll and jerk, her legs shaking next to my head. When I slide two fingers inside of her tight, wet heat, she gasps before her body starts to tremble almost violently. She lets out a scream, her cum coating my fingers. I wait until her body relaxes before I sit back and slide my fingers out of her.

"Prescott," she whispers as her head lolls to the side.

I crawl up her body, my fingers painting her parted lips with her release. With wide eyes, she watches as I slide them into my mouth and lick her taste from them; then I dip my head and kiss the rest of her taste from her lips.

"How many women have there been since I left?" she asks. I look down at her in surprise.

"Ginger," I warn.

"I shouldn't care, but I do," she whispers. Her eyes are wild, looking everywhere but at me.

"I haven't touched another woman since I got that phone call from Fury," I admit, watching that news sink in.

I'm not tellin' her shit about the two months she was gone. I thought she'd just walked away from me.

"Really?" she breathes.

"What kind of man do you think I am?" I ask, standing up, anger filling me to the point where I feel like I might explode, which is the last thing I want to do, toward her.

"I just, six-months is a long time," she whispers.

"Yeah, it is. But I'm a man, baby. I don't need to fuck someone every time my dick gets hard. My woman'd been hurt—fucking brutalized. You've been my main focus for six fucking months. You know how hard it was not to come down here and cart you off? Bring you back home? Getting updates from MadDog? Instead of taking care of you myself?" I practically yell, my body vibrating with anger.

"Prescott," she murmurs.

"Killed me every fucking day to wake up and go about my day knowing you were hurting, and there was nothing I could do to make you feel better, to hold you while you cried, to make you feel like the beautiful woman you are."

Without another word, I watch as she stands, completely naked, and wraps her arms around me. She buries her face in my chest while her body starts to shake with sobs. I feel her tears soaking my shirt, but I could give a fuck. My woman wants to cry in my arms, she can fucking cry.

I reach down and grab the blanket that's on the end of her bed and wrap it around her naked body before I walk us over to the top of the bed. It only takes a couple seconds of adjusting before my back is against the headboard and she's curled into my side, still crying. I run my hands soothingly up and down her back, letting her get all her shit out.

"I'm sorry that I refused to go back with you," she hiccups.

I tug on a piece of her long blonde hair and she looks up to me. Her face is splotchy and puffy, and yet she's never looked more beautiful.

"You needed time to heal. I'm not angry. I'm glad that you took that, baby. It's time to come home now, though," I say.

"Home?"

"Yeah, peaches, *home*," I grunt, giving her a smile.

"What does home look like?" she asks, staring at me while she worries her lip with her teeth.

I almost laugh, but I don't. I run my fingertip along the side of her face and down her jawline to her mouth. Tracing her full lips, I smile.

"You, my Georgia Peach. Home looks just like you," I murmur.

"Me?" she exhales with wide eyes.

"Yeah, baby. *You*. It's you lying in my bed, exhausted from taking my dick. It's the lazy satisfied smile you aim at me when you think I'm not looking at you. It's you pressing up to me and curling into my side anytime we're anywhere near each other. It's *us* building a life that is gonna last forever," I explain.

"Prescott," she whispers.

"Ready for you to come home to me, peaches," I murmur. "You ready to come home?"

"I think so," she sighs.

"Thank fuck. I missed the shit outta you," I grin.

PART TWO

Ginger

Prescott's fingers dig into my hips as he wrenches me back, his pelvis thrusting forward at the same time. My neck arches and I let out a long moan. I'm so close, I'm about to explode. When I do, it's going to be magnificent.

"C'mon, peaches," he growls behind me as his fingers dig into my skin even harder.

"Pres," I whimper as my body begins to shake and I come. It's long, it's hard, and it's magnificent—just as I thought it'd be.

Prescott doesn't let me revel in my glory. One of his hands leaves my hip and fists in the back of my hair before he wrenches my body up, my back colliding with his chest. Then he thrusts up inside of me, and doesn't stop until he emits his own long moan, and I feel his cock twitch as he fills me with his release.

"Love you, peaches," he murmurs against my neck.

His tongue traces my tattoo, like he's done every single time we've been together since I came back to him three months ago. I lift my hand and wrap it around the back of his neck, my fingers twisting in his soft hair.

The hand on my hip travels up my side. He slides it across my breasts as he cups one in his hand and just holds me. He's done this a lot since my return as well, holding me, kissing me, loving me so tenderly that he brings tears to my eyes, almost daily.

"I love you, so much," I whisper, tightening my fingers in his hair.

He hums before he disengages from my body. I turn around to face him and wrap my arms around him. He steps closer to the side of the bed and runs his fingertips up and down my spine. We haven't really fought once since I've been back; maybe it's because I've completely surrendered to him, or maybe it's because he's so sweet and gentle it's ridiculous. But whatever the reason, I don't care. I've never been so damn happy before.

"You sure you really want to do this?" he asks, his eyes showing his worry, hiding nothing.

"Yeah," I nod.

"Wouldn't make you any less of a woman. Wouldn't make me think anything less of you at all if you didn't want to do this, peaches," he murmurs as his finger traces my lips.

"I need to," I whisper.

"At any second you can't deal, you walk out. I don't want those demons haunting your eyes again. Took a long fuckin' time for me to eradicate them." I can't help but smile at his words.

I think about him *eradicating* my demons. It's been fun. Lots and lots of great sex, cuddles, and talking. I've felt like a teenager in the midst of puppy love for months.

Although, as a teenager, I didn't go to badass biker club parties on the arm of the badass president. I also didn't run a successful bar. Nope, this is way better than teenager puppy love.

I don't know what it is, but I don't ever want it to end.

"Why are you smilin'?" he asks.

"Because eradicating demons was fun."

"You're fuckin' insane," he chuckles as he pulls me even closer, his nose running alongside mine.

"When does this go down?" I ask, biting my lip.

"Now. Get dressed," he murmurs. His lips touch mine before he takes a step back.

I watch as he walks over to his pile of clothes lying on the floor and he starts to dress. It's early evening, and there are four men waiting for us, probably scared to death, as they should be.

"Dress warm," he grunts.

I walk over to the dresser and grab a new pair of panties, socks, a bra and my thin, silk, long sleeve undershirt. Then I walk over to a pile of jeans that I folded just this morning and pull my favorite ones off of the top—a pair of jean leggings. I slip them on and find a thick sweater that's folded as well. It's light blue.

Once I have my clothes on, I walk over to where my boots are sitting against the wall, and I solemnly pull them on, lacing them all the way up my calves, letting their warmth envelop my toes, feet, and legs.

"Can you wear your hair up?" Prescott asks as he slides his jacket on.

"Why?" I ask, furrowing my brows.

"Want those pieces of shit to see my mark," he growls.

I close my eyes then open them, a smile slowly playing on my lips. I don't wear my hair up; instead, I gather it to the opposite side of my tattoo and I braid it down my shoulder. Prescott grins and traces his road name with his index finger.

"Gorgeous," he rumbles.

"Let's go," I suggest.

"I feel like fuckin' you again," he chuckles.

"Can we fuck after?"

I watch as he throws his head back in laughter and wraps his hand around the back of my neck, giving it a gentle squeeze before he presses his lips to my nose in a kiss. Then tells me, *yeah*.

We walk out of the house together, his arm slung around my shoulders, my arm wrapped tightly around his middle. I'm trying not to show fear, but I'm scared shitless. I don't know exactly what's going to happen when I see these men again, but I guess I'm going to find out in just a few minutes.

Snake

With my hand wrapped around Ginger's, I gently tug her through the cold air and into the slightly warmer warehouse. MadDog has a man, a tech wizard, and he hacked and searched and found four more of the Aryan Brotherhood. They've yet to find any of the pregnant women, or any women at all, which is disheartening. But maybe these four pussies will yield some useful information by the time we're finished with them.

I know when Ginger has seen them. They're all lined up, their feet bound as well as their arms, and they're dangling from the hooks we have hanging from the ceiling.

"Prescott," she whimpers.

I look down at her. I'd wondered if this would do more harm than good, but I decided, as did she, that she needed to face her abusers. Now, I'm not so sure, based off of the fear that I see clearly in her eyes as she gazes upon them.

"These men hurt you, baby?" I ask, keeping my voice low.

"Yeah," she says through trembling lips.

"You want first go at 'em?"

I watch as her eyes move to each man, then back up to me. I see a decision has been made, but I can't tell what it is. Then she rises to her toes, places a kiss on the corner of my mouth, and speaks.

"They're worthless. Get whatever information you can out of them, then finish them," she says with a shrug.

"My strong little Georgia Peach," I murmur as my hand slides around her waist, pressing against her lower back.

"I'll see you at home later?"

"Yeah, baby, you will," I grin before my lips brush against hers. "Free, take my woman home, yeah?"

"Sure thing. C'mon Ging," Free says as he walks up to us.

"I love you, Pres," she murmurs.

"Love you more than I've loved anything else in my whole fuckin' life, peaches," I grin. I release her and take a step back.

Free holds out his hand, and I watch as she slips her smaller one inside. Together, they walk out of the warehouse. I like that she didn't want to stay, that she didn't feel the need to shed blood. Maybe she does; maybe she's leaving it all for me—I don't give a fuck. I'm just happy that those demons didn't reappear in her eyes at the sight of these four pieces of shit standing before me.

"Ready to sequel like piggies, boys?" I ask.

None of them respond, but their fear is so apparent, I can fuckin' taste it.

"Let's have some fun, boys," I say to my brothers as we approach the four dead men hanging.

I strip my clothes, keeping them separate from my cut and boots. I have to burn them in the morning, but I'm too fuckin' tired to worry about it right now.

I shower and wash the blood from my hands and face before I turn off the water and grab a towel. Once I'm fairly dry, I make my way to the bed, our bed. I pull back the sheets and crawl between them, wrapping my arm around Ginger's middle and sliding my thigh between hers.

"You're back," she whispers as my lips touch her shoulder.

"Yeah, I'm back," I admit.

"It's handled?" she asks, her body stock still.

"Yeah, baby, it's all handled," I mutter.

She turns around in my arms, and I wait for the demons, deciding that they must have entered her eyes while I was gone. I'm pleasantly surprised that, through the moonlit room, I see absolutely no trace of them.

"I wonder how many more there are out there?"

"Wish I knew, peaches," I murmur as my nose slides alongside hers.

"Thank you," she whispers before her lips brush mine.

"For what?" I ask, pulling away from her so that I can look into her face.

"For being you. For being my rock during all of this."

"Fuck that rock bullshit," I spit as I pull us both up to a sitting position. Her eyes widen and her mouth drops in surprise.

"Pres," she gasps.

"I'm not your fuckin' rock, peaches. You are your own fuckin' strength. You don't need me. You have me to support you in any way that I can, but baby, you don't *need* me. You're so fuckin' strong, so strong."

367

"Pres," she says as her lips tremble and tears fill her eyes. "So strong, Ginger."

Ginger

Prescott's whispered words of my strength undo me. He sees me as this ultra-strong woman when I feel anything but. I feel weak, and just tonight, I couldn't hurt those men who brutalized me. Yes, they hurt me, and yes, I wanted to hurt them, but something inside of me couldn't do it. Maybe it's exactly *what* is inside of me that is the sole reason I couldn't do it. I can't keep it to myself a second longer, so I tell him.

"I'm pregnant," I whisper.

"You're…" his voice trails off as his eyes widen.

"Do you want a boy or a girl?" I ask with a grin.

"Pregnant," he breathes. I watch as his face slowly breaks out into a huge smile.

I wait for his real reaction. Right now, the news is settling. Then he lifts his head, his smile still wide, and he practically tackles me to my back. One of his hands wraps around the inside of my knee and he spreads me wide.

"Move those panties to the side or I'm ripping them off," he demands, his voice deep and husky.

I do as he requests, and his cock presses against my center. I quickly move my hand out of the way before he slams completely inside of me. I gasp when his hands grab mine and press then above my head. He intertwines our fingers and starts to slowly thrust in and out of me.

"Prescott," I whisper. Our eyes connect, and I watch as he sticks his tongue out and slides it along his bottom lip.

"Pregnant with my baby," he rasps as he continues to fuck me, his long and lazy strokes making sure I feel every inch of him inside of me.

"I am," I nod.

"Peaches," he moans as his hips roll and his pelvis grinds against my clit.

We don't speak. Our eyes stay connected, as do our hands and our bodies. He slides inside of me, over and over again, slow and steady, with long, languid strokes, in no hurry at all whatsoever.

"Pres," I whimper once I feel my heart start to race as I climb closer toward my release.

"Come," he demands on a groan.

He speeds up and I start to pant, climbing closer toward my release. Then, without any warning, I cry out with my climax as my body shakes. He grunts and then his hips start jerking wildly as he fucks me a little harder and a little faster before he arches his back and lets out a cry of his own, coming inside of me.

I shiver when his hands release mine, but slide down my arms as he lowers his face. His lips touch my neck, his tongue gliding against my inked skin. He continues to gently thrust in and out of me as we both catch our breaths.

"Marry me, peaches," he rasps.

"What?" I ask in surprise.

"Marry me. Marry your Old Man," he murmurs.

My hands fly to the back of his neck, my fingers twisting in his hair and I search his face.

"You're serious, "I breathe.

"Fuck yes, I am."

"Yes, yes I'll marry you," I cry out as I giggle.

The movement causes me to lose him from my body. He looks at me in awe for a split second before his head dips and his lips press against mine in a hard, bruising kiss.

"Later today?" he asks.

"Today?" I practically choke.

"Yeah, peaches, today."

I nod, before I smile. He settles behind me, pulling my back against his chest as his tongue traces my neck, like he does every night before he lifts a hand to my breast and squeezes it, telling me to go to sleep.

I lie awake, unable to fall asleep quickly.

I can't wipe the smile from my lips.

I'm pregnant, Prescott and I are getting married, and I'm finally content—completely happy.

Snake

I hold onto her, knowing she's not asleep. It takes her far too long to sleep, but her body finally relaxes and her breathing evens out. I don't sleep, though. I lie awake and look at her tattoo, my name on her neck, my baby inside of her, and to-morrow my ring on her finger.

Everything that I have ever wanted is finally come to a reality.

This woman owns every piece of me, from the inside out. I've never been more proud of a human being, as I am of this woman in my arms. She's stronger than the biggest badass I know. She's everything. And soon she'll be my wife; then she'll be the mother of my children; and with any luck, that strength will transfer on to them.

Almost a year ago, I thought I'd lost her. Nine months ago, I thought she was lost to me. Three months ago, I dragged her ass back here, and I've not regretted one second I've spent with her—not one single fuckin' second.

I can't wait for the future.

I can't wait for what insane shit she's going to bring into my life.

I can't wait for how much love she's going to bring to me.

I can't fuckin' *wait*.

ROUGH & RICH
NOTORIOUS DEVILS MC NOVEL #6

prologue

Imogen

I call his cell phone. *Again.* He sends my call straight to voicemail, and I glare as his voice barks out orders to leave him a message. He calls himself *Soar*, and all of his little buddies call him that, too. I've even got it tattooed on the front of my hip, some misguided act of love and encouragement.

God, I'm such a fucking idiot.

Soar.

How stupid.

His name isn't Soar. It's Sloane Huntington, III. I doubt any of his *brothers* know that, though. Just like none of them know that my name isn't Genny, it's Imogen. We're frauds, the two of us. I'm not some badass biker bitch. I'm Imogen Carolina Stewart-Huntington, the wife of Sloane Huntington III.

We're both from well-to-do upper class families. Not just upper class—no, more like elite. Our parents are trust fund babies, as are we. Neither of us have had to work a day in our lives. We could both spend to our heart's content and still have plenty of money to give our children.

I met Sloane when we were in high school. We went to a

private school, where we were famous for our parent's titles, our hand-me-down last names, and our breeding lineage.

Sloane was a bad boy. He was beautiful in every way a boy could be beautiful to a fifteen-year-old. His blonde hair was never out of place, yet he looked as if he couldn't care about it. His leather jackets were expensive, yet looked like he beat the shit out of them—his jeans were the same.

We were married the day after I turned eighteen. He was twenty-one. He'd been running around with the club by then. Nothing much, just during the week in Shasta, a couple hours from San Francisco. He always reserved his weekends to spend with me. I loved it. I felt so special, considering I was in high school and he was older than me. I thought I was really something. He even took me to all of my formal dances after he left school.

Then we got married.

That's when things started to change.

I didn't know what being a *Notorious Devil* meant.

I didn't know about the women, the booze, the drugs, and the constant parties.

I didn't know about being left at home alone for days while my husband slept with other women.

"Sloane, where the hell are you?" I snap once his greeting is finished. "I'm not taking this shit anymore. I'm done."

I always say that, too.

That I'm done.

Then he comes home and sweet-talks me back. *Every time.* I hate myself a little more each and every time I stay with him instead of leaving and going back home to my parents. They were pissed when I married Sloane. They didn't understand why I wouldn't go after someone else, anyone else.

Now, fourteen years later, I see exactly why they were so angry. Sloane hasn't grown up. He hasn't changed. He hasn't taken on the responsibility of his father's company, and he's still running around getting high, fucking whores. He has zero ambition in life. At this rate, his little brother will be running his father's company and everything will completely bypass him

I hear something in the next room and I know it's Cleo. She's been staying with me for a few days while her man and Sloane have been gone on a run. I feel like a bitch for ignoring her, but I'm so angry that I'm not good company anyway.

The phone rings in my hand but it's not Sloane on the other end, it's MadDog, his president.

"Need you to come down to the clubhouse, darlin'," he murmurs into the phone.

MadDog—now he's a member of the club that I can respect, and one of the only ones. He has ambition, he's in charge, and he doesn't take shit from anyone. He's also fiercely loyal to his woman, Mary-Anne. God, they're so cute and perfect; they make me sick and bitter.

"What's wrong?" I ask, my heart racing inside of my chest.

"Just come on down here. Bring Cleo, too," he says and then ends the call.

"Cleo, we're being summoned to the clubhouse," I call as I walk out of my bedroom and into the doorway of my guestroom where Cleo has been staying. Her head jerks and she looks at me, giving me a sad smile and a nod.

We take separate cars, probably because she thinks I'm a bitch. I am, though. Or at least I am *now*. I wasn't always. When I was young, I was fun, always down for a good time, and always smiling.

Sloane used to call me his *Sunshine*.

He hasn't called me that in at least ten years.

I walk into the clubhouse and MadDog tells me, with regret swimming in his eyes, that Sloane's been arrested.

"What did he have?" I ask.

"I'm sorry, babe, I don't know. I only know they hooked him up and carted his ass off," Torch says, keeping his voice soft and gentle, like I'm some kind of wounded animal.

I nod, understanding filling me. He's gone. I'm done. The entire room watches me like I'm a freak show, waiting for me to go insane. I look around until my eyes catch MadDog's.

"I'm leaving. I'm not coming back. I'm going home to my family, and I'm sorry, but I'm divorcing his ass," I announce.

"Now, Genny. We don't even know if the charges will stick," MadDog rumbles.

"No, fuck that. He doesn't give a fuck about me. He cares about the club and the drugs and the whores. I'm not on that list anywhere. So, he can have it all. He doesn't have to worry about me anymore," I announce as I tamp down my emotions. I'm on the verge of tears, so I take a step toward the front door.

"Babe, you know that's not true," Colleen says.

"Do I?" I ask, arching a brow. "I know he doesn't come home for days, sometimes even weeks. I know he'd rather fuck those whores then come home to me. I know that what I want—it doesn't *fucking* matter."

"What do you want?" Colleen asks.

I shake my head. No way am I telling this room full of people what I want out of my husband. No way am I telling them that I want him to come home at night, to hold me, to whisper to me that he loves me. No way am I telling them that

I want him to slide inside of me bare, make love to me, and fill me with a baby.

I'm thirty-two years old.

I want a family.

I can't let my own husband have sex with me without a condom because I literally do not know where his dick has been. No way am I telling them that I don't want to lie awake at night, crying because my husband doesn't want me. The only man I have ever been with doesn't want anything to do with me. The man I love with everything that I am can't stand to look at me.

"Everything," I whisper, giving them that and nothing else.

"That's too much," Colleen whispers back.

"Then fuck *Him*," I growl before I turn and walk out the door.

"Genny," Mary-Anne calls out, chasing after me.

"What?" I ask, whirling around and giving her a dirty look. I don't mean to be a bitch, but its basically just my personality anymore.

"Don't leave. The club will help you out. We're your family," she says. I know that she's been really sweet, helpful, and kind, but she doesn't know shit. I let out a humorless laugh and shake my head.

"I don't need the club's help," I snort.

"Don't leave like this," she whispers.

"I envy you. Having a man like MadDog who obviously loves the hell out of you and would do anything to keep from hurting you, it's amazing really. I want to hate you, but you're too damn sweet," I chuckle. "I'm glad you have a man like MadDog, but please, don't put Soar in the same category."

I open my car door and slide inside, start the engine, and drive to my parent's house. I leave everything in Shasta. Not wanting one single memory to come with me. Sloane's fancy ass muscle car is in the garage of our house, as is everything else of ours. He can throw my stuff away, or give it to one of his whores. I don't give a shit anymore.

Sloane Huntington is nothing but the past.

Soar

"I'm sorry, man," MadDog says as he sits across from me.

It's visiting day. I'm stuck in fucking prison for three years on a drug charge. It's my own fault. I knew how much was too much to have on me, but I did it anyway. I was high and cocky. Now that I'm in forced sobriety, I can see a bit clearer.

I fucked up.

Big time.

"Why? Because I'm in here? Brother, I did this shit to my-self," I chuckle as I lean back in my chair.

"No, Genny," he says. I sit up a bit straighter.

"She okay?" I ask.

I haven't heard from her, but that doesn't surprise me. My woman, my wife, she's a bit temperamental, high strung, and high fucking maintenance, among other things. I've known her since she was a pretty little fifteen-year-old and I snatched her up quick. I saw the way the other thoroughbreds in school were eyeing her. No way would she be with them. My blonde-haired sunshine needed wild freedom.

I just didn't know that we'd eventually be semi-miserable

together. Love her, but the woman grates on my goddamn nerves sometimes. So I hide out until she's over whatever snit she gets into, then I sweet-talk her down, and it's all good again for a while.

It's a cycle.

"Don't know. The day Torch came back and said you'd been hauled away, she said she was getting shot of you and she left. We've been keeping eyes on your place, but she hasn't come back, not even for her shit. We've had to up our security on the Old Ladies, shit is in limbo."

I close my eyes for a beat. She wouldn't need her shit, She has enough money to buy herself a new outfit every day for the rest of her life, and never repeat it. I know where she's gone. She's gone back to Frisco, back to her parents, back to *society*.

Fuck.

"Don't worry about her," I say with a shrug.

"Soar…"

"Seriously, Pres. She's got so much fuckin' security where she's at, she's safer than the fucking president," I mutter.

"You sure?"

"Yeah, Prez, I'm sure."

MadDog leaves a few minutes later, and I'm taken back to my cell. I pull off the photograph that's taped up on my wall next to my bed and I look at it. It's a picture of Genny. Imogen. She's about twenty-one in it. She's smiling, but it doesn't reach her eyes.

That's my fault.

She hasn't been happy since the day she walked in on me fuckin' a whore while I was high off my ass. It's not that I want to hurt her, but *fuck*, nothing I ever do has made her happy. I bought her a house, and it's about a quarter of the sized house she grew up in. It's not fancy and perfect, but honest to fuck, I don't give a shit about that material stuff, so I didn't think she would either.

Then, she wanted me to come home every night. I have shit to do at the club. I couldn't come home every night. Then, she started holding out on me as a form of *punishment*. We'd been married for two years when she started that shit.

That was when I started fucking clubwhores.

I hadn't been with another woman in over five years. But I stooped, I fucked the bitch out of spite and anger. I didn't get caught, so I kept doing it, it was just another high for me to chase after. Then when she caught me, she threatened to leave, I sweet-talked her and she stayed. Then, *that* was a high.

Fuck, I'm always chasing the next high.

Always.

Now, she's gone and I'm stuck here. No sweet-talking her back home anytime soon, at least not for the next three years.

Fuck.

also by
HAYLEY FAIMAN

MEN OF BASEBALL SERIES—

Pitching for Amalie
Catching Maggie
Forced Play for Libby
Sweet Spot for Victoria

RUSSIAN BRATVA SERIES—

Owned by the Badman
Seducing the Badman
Dancing for the Badman
Living for the Badman
Tempting the Badman
Protected by the Badman
Forever my Badman (Summer 2017)
Betrothed to the Badman (2017)
Chosen by the Badman (2018)
Healing the Badman (2018)

Notorious Devils MC—

Rough & Rowdy

Rough & Raw

Rough & Rugged

Rough & Ruthless

Rough & Ready (June 2017)

Rough & Rich (2017)

Rough & Real (2018)

Standalone Titles

Royally Relinquished: A Modern Day Fairy Tale

Encroachment (December 2017)

Follow me on social media to stay current on the happenings in my little book world.

Website: hayleyfaiman.com

Facebook: www.facebook.com/authorhayleyfaiman

Goodreads: www.goodreads.com/author/show/10735805. Hayley_Faiman

Signup for my Newsletter: hayleyfaiman.us13.list-manage. com/subscribe?u=d0e156a6e8d82f22e819d1065&id=4d4aefa

about the author

As an only child, Hayley Faiman had to entertain herself somehow. She started writing stories at the age of six and never really stopped.

Born in California, she met her now husband at the age of sixteen and married him at the age of twenty in 2004. After all of these years together, he's still the love of her life.

Hayley's husband joined the military and they lived in Oregon, where he was stationed with the US Coast Guard. They moved back to California in 2006, where they had two little boys. Recently, the four of them moved out to the Hill Country of Texas, where they adopted a new family member, a chocolate lab named Optimus Prime.

Most of Hayley's days are spent taking care of her two boys, going to the baseball fields for practice, or helping them with homework. Her evenings are spent with her husband and her nights—those are spent creating alpha book boyfriends.

acknowledgments

I want to thank all of my fans, everyone to took a chance on *Rough & Rowdy* and then decided to continue on with this series! There is so much more coming your way so sit back and hold on, these men of the Notorious Devils are not through with you yet!

I always say a special thank you to my husband, my best friend, and the man who supports me in every single one of my dreams. He's the man who has owned my heart for the past seventeen years. *Thank you babes.*

My mom, she's always supported wholeheartedly everything I have ever decided to take a leap of faith on, including my writing. She's the kindest, most loving, and most supportive mom in the world. Thank you *Banana Boots.*

Rosalyn my editor, my bestie, my confidant. All the words have been said, they'll be said repeatedly, I'll never tire of saying them. God brought us together for a reason, in a time where we truly needed each other's guidance and friendship. I can't wait for all the things that we've been planning to come to fruition!

My sister from another mister, Nisha. Thank you for being my friend and always having my ear and always making a bitch laugh.

Celia, my oldest friend, from the git-n-go until today, thank you for being such an awesome friend. Thanks for the laughs, the cupcakes, the brownies, the cruises in the Mustang, and all of the years together.

Cass, my BOO, thank you for being such a great friend! Thank you for always being there no matter the distance!

Cassy Roop, thank you so much for always making these covers so hot and sexy!

Crystal Snyder thank you for loving my book men, for Beta reading for me, and being such a beautiful person inside and out!

Stacey Blake. Sending my manuscript to you is never "scary" because I know that you'll always make it absolutely gorgeous! Thank you for being so fantastic!

Enticing Journey—Ena and Amanda—I always know that my PR work is safe with you, that you'll represent my book and me in a way that only you can—THE BEST WAY! I truly appreciate all of the hard work you ladies put into everything!

A special thanks to all the Blogger babes that have taken a chance on me…
Thank you from the bottom of my heart.

Made in the USA
San Bernardino, CA
29 April 2017